## PASTIME

"Gripping . . . Vintage hard-core Spenser. One of the Boston P.I.'s
most personal, resonant cases."—*Kirkus Reviews*

Ten years ago, Spenser rescued young Paul Giacomin from a father's
rage. Now on the brink of manhood, Paul wants answers to his past—
and about his mother's sudden disappearance. Spenser is the only person
he can turn to. To find the answers, Spenser must search his own past in
a startling game of memory, desire, and danger.

## DOUBLE DEUCE

"Mr. Parker at his best . . . tense . . . compelling . . .
suspenseful . . . darkly poetic."—*The New York Times Book Review*

Hawk wants his longtime pal, Spenser, to wage war on a Boston street
gang after a drive-by shooting. Meanwhile, Susan wants her longtime
lover, Spenser, to turn their relationship into something a little more
serious. Spenser's completely out of his element—but he's going to give
both his best shot.

## PAPER DOLL

"Parker at the top of his game."—*The Boston Globe*

Olivia Nelson was the perfect wife, the perfect friend, and the perfect
mother. Now someone has made her the perfect victim—bludgeoned to
death with a hammer on the streets of Beacon Hill. A random act of
urban violence? Not exactly. Now Spenser's searching for a motive and
a murderer—and finding more secrets than he counted on.

*continued . . .*

D0191444

# A Triple Shot
# of Spenser

# ROBERT B. PARKER

**B**

BERKLEY BOOKS, NEW YORK

**THE BERKLEY PUBLISHING GROUP**
**Published by the Penguin Group**
**Penguin Group (USA) Inc.**
**375 Hudson Street, New York, New York 10014, USA**
Penguin Group (Canada), 90 Eglinton Avenue East, Suite 700, Toronto, Ontario M4P 2Y3, Canada
(a division of Pearson Penguin Canada Inc.)
Penguin Books Ltd., 80 Strand, London WC2R 0RL, England
Penguin Group Ireland, 25 St. Stephen's Green, Dublin 2, Ireland (a division of Penguin Books Ltd.)
Penguin Group (Australia), 250 Camberwell Road, Camberwell, Victoria 3124, Australia
(a division of Pearson Australia Group Pty. Ltd.)
Penguin Books India Pvt. Ltd., 11 Community Centre, Panchsheel Park, New Delhi—110 017, India
Penguin Group (NZ), Cnr. Airborne and Rosedale Roads, Albany, Auckland 1310, New Zealand
(a division of Pearson New Zealand Ltd.)
Penguin Books (South Africa) (Pty.) Ltd., 24 Sturdee Avenue, Rosebank, Johannesburg 2196,
South Africa

Penguin Books Ltd., Registered Offices: 80 Strand, London WC2R 0RL, England

This is a work of fiction. Names, characters, places, and incidents either are the product of the author's imagination or are used fictitiously, and any resemblance to actual persons, living or dead, business establishments, events, or locales is entirely coincidental.

Copyright © 2005 by Robert B. Parker.
*Pastime* copyright © 1991 by Robert B. Parker.
*Double Deuce* copyright © 1992 by Robert B. Parker.
*Paper Doll* copyright © 1993 by Robert B. Parker.
Cover design by Judith Lagerman.
Cover illustration by Pyrographx.
Text design by Kristin del Rosario.

PRINTING HISTORY
Berkley trade paperback edition / November 2005

Library of Congress Cataloging-in-Publication Data

Parker, Robert B., 1932–
    A triple shot of Spenser / Robert B. Parker.— Berkley trade pbk. ed.
        p. cm.
    His first three novels in one volume.
    Contents: Pastime — Double deuce — Paper doll.
    ISBN 978-0-425-20671-3
    1. Spenser (Fictitious character)—Fiction. 2. Private investigators—Massachusetts—Boston—
Fiction. 3. Detective and mystery stories, American. 4. Boston (Mass.)—Fiction. I. Title.

PS3566.A686A6 2005
813'.54—dc22

                                                                                2005048256

PRINTED IN THE UNITED STATES OF AMERICA

10

# CONTENTS

# Pastime

*For my wife and sons—*
sine qua non

# Chapter 1

The dog was a pointer, a solid chocolate German Shorthair, three years old and smallish for her breed. She sat bolt upright on the couch in Susan Silverman's office and stared at me with her head vigilantly erect in case I might be a partridge.

"Shouldn't she be lying on the couch?" I said.

"She's not in analysis," Susan said.

"She belonged to your ex-husband."

"Yes," Susan said. "Good point."

The dog's eyes shifted from Susan to me as we spoke. The eyes were hazel and, because she was nervous, they showed a lot of white. Her short brown coat was sleek, like a seal's, and her oversized paws looked exaggerated, like a cartoon dog.

"What's her name?" I said.

Susan wrinkled her nose. "Vigilant Virgin."

"And she's not in analysis?"

"I believe they have to have long silly names like that because of the American Kennel Club," Susan said. "She's a hunting dog."

"I know," I said. "I had one like her when I was a kid."

"Like her?"

"Yeah. Same breed, same color, which is not usual. Mine was bigger though."

"Don't listen," Susan said to the dog. "You're perfectly big enough."

The dog canted her head at Susan, and raised her ears slightly.

"What are we going to do with her?" Susan said.

"We? My ex-husband didn't give her to me," I said.

"Well, he gave her to me, and what's mine is yours."

"Not if I have to walk around calling her Vigilant Virgin," I said.

"What was your dog's name?" Susan said.

"Pearl."

"Well, let's call her Pearl."

"And Boink Brain isn't going to want her back?" I said.

"He's not so bad," Susan said.

"Anyone who let you get away is a boink brain," I said.

"Well," Susan said, "perhaps you're right . . . anyway. He's been transferred to London, and you can't even bring a dog in there without a six-month quarantine."

"So she's yours for good," I said.

"Ours."

I nodded. The dog got off the couch quite suddenly, and walked briskly over and put her head on my lap and stood motionless, with her eyes rolled slightly upward looking at me obliquely.

I nodded. "Pearl," I said.

Susan smiled. "Beautiful Jewish-American girls don't grow up with hunting dogs," she said. "If they have dogs at all they are very small dogs with a little bow."

"Sure thing, little lady. This looks to me like man's work."

"I think so," Susan said.

I patted Pearl's head.

"You could have told him no," I said.

"He had nowhere else to place her," Susan said. "And she's a lovely dog."

Pearl sighed. It seemed a sigh of contentment though dogs are often mysterious and sometimes do things I don't understand. Which is true also of people.

"Do we have joint custody?" I said. "I get her on weekends?"

"I think she can stay here," Susan said. "I have a yard. But certainly she could come to your place for sleepovers."

"Bring her jammies and her records? We could make brownies?"

"Something like that," Susan said. "Of course this is the city. We can't let her run loose."

"Which means you'll need to fence your yard."

"I think it's the best thing for us to do," Susan said. "Don't you?"

"No question," I said. "We'll have to work our ass off, of course."

"Beautiful Jewish-American girls do not 'work their ass off,' they bring iced tea in a pretty pitcher to the large goy they've charmed into doing it."

"When do we get to that?"

"The charm?"

"Yeah."

"Well, you remember once you suggested something and I said I'd never done it because I was too embarrassed."

"Certainly. It's one of the two or three times you've ever blushed."

Susan smiled and nodded.

"Today?" I said.

She smiled more widely and nodded again. If a serpent had come by with an apple at that moment she'd have eaten it.

"Spenser's my name," I said. "Fences are my game."

"Do you require a charm down payment?" Susan said.

"Well," I said, "some small gesture of earnest intent might be appropriate."

"Not in front of the baby," Susan said.

Pearl was on the couch again, perfectly still, gazing at us as if she were smarter than we were, but patient.

"Of course not," I said. "What kind of fence would you like?"

"Let's go look at some, she can ride along with us and wait in the car."

"What could be better?" I said.

"You'll find out," Susan said and smiled that smile.

# Chapter 2

Susan had selected a picket fence made of spaced 1-inch dowels in a staggered pattern. I was listening to the ball game and drilling holes in the stringers to accommodate the dowels when a voice said, "Hi, Ozzie. Where's Harriet?"

It was Paul Giacomin, wearing jeans and high-top sneakers and a black T-shirt that said on it *American Dance Festival, 1989,* in white letters. I had taken him in hand when he was a fifteen-year-old kid caught in his parents' divorce feud with no interests but television and no prospects but more of the same. He was twenty-five now, an inch taller than I was, and almost as graceful.

"Making iced tea in a pretty pitcher," I said. "What are you doing here?"

"I tried your apartment first, and then followed my instincts."

"Trained by a master," I said.

Paul came over and shook my hand and patted me on the shoulder. Susan came out of the house and told him how glad she was to see him and gave him a hug and kissed him. Her range of demonstrable emotion is maybe a little wider than mine.

"Wait until you see what we have," Susan said.

She was wearing a glossy black leotard-esque exercise outfit and white sneakers and a bright blue headband and she looked a lot like Hedy Lamarr would have looked if Hedy worked out. She ran back to the house and opened the back door and Pearl came surging out, jumped the three steps off the back porch and, with her ears back, and her mouth open, dashed around the backyard in a slowly imploding circle until she finally ran into me, bounced off, and jammed her head into Paul's groin.

"Jesus Christ," Paul said. Pearl jumped up with her forepaws on his chest, dropped back down, turned in a tight circle as if she were chasing her tail, and jumped up again trying to lap Paul's face before she dropped back down and streaked around the yard again. As she came by the second time, Susan got a hold on her collar and managed to force her to a barely contained stop.

"She gets over her shyness," Paul said, "she might be cute."

"Regal," I said.

"Regal."

"This is Pearl," Susan said. "I inherited her from my ex-husband because he's transferred to London, and her daddy is building her a fence."

"This is embarrassing," Paul said.

"Let's go get a beer," I said, "and you can see how regal she is inside."

It took Pearl maybe fifteen minutes to calm down, climb up into the white satin armchair in Susan's living room, turn around three times, and lie with her head on her back legs in a tight ball and watch us drink beer.

"I recall," Paul said to Susan, "that you used to kick me off that chair. It was for looking at, not sitting in, you said."

"Well, she likes it," Susan said.

Paul nodded. "Oh," he said.

"You going to stay awhile?" I said.

"Maybe," he said. "I left my stuff at your place."

I nodded. There was more. I'd known him since he was a fragmented little kid. I waited.

"How's Paige?" Susan said.

"Fine."

"Have you set a date yet?"

"Sort of."

"How does one sort of set a date?" Susan said.

"You discuss next April with each other, but you don't tell anyone else. It allows for a certain amount of ambivalence."

Susan nodded.

"Want a sandwich or something?" she said.

"What have you got?"

"There's some whole wheat bread," Susan said. "And some lettuce . . ."

Paul waited.

"Oregano," I said. "I think I saw some dried oregano in the refrigerator."

"In the refrigerator?" Paul said.

"Keeps it nice and fresh," Susan said.

"That's it?" Paul said. "A lettuce and oregano sandwich on whole wheat?"

"Low in calories," Susan said, "and nearly fat free."

"Maybe we could go out and get something later," Paul said.

I went to the kitchen and got two more beers and a diet Coke, no ice, for Susan.

"Makes me question myself sometimes," I said when I brought the drinks. "Being the love object of a woman who likes warm diet Coke."

Susan smiled at me.

Paul said, "My mother's missing."

I nodded. "Tell me about it."

"We've been getting along a little better. She's a little easier mother for a twenty-five-year-old man than for a fifteen-year-old boy," Paul said. "And I used to call her maybe every other week and we'd talk, and maybe two three times a year we'd see each other when she was in New York. She even came to a couple of my performances."

On the armchair, Pearl sat up suddenly as if someone had spoken to her and gazed off silently toward the bookcase on the far wall. Her head in profile was perfectly motionless and her face was very serious.

"One thing made her easier was she had a boyfriend, has a boyfriend, I guess. When she's got a boyfriend, she's pretty good. Kind of fun, and interested in me, and not, you know, desperate."

Pearl put her head slowly back down, this time on her front paws, which hung off the front of the armchair. She gazed soberly at the dust motes that drifted in the shaft of sunlight that came through Susan's back window.

"Anyway," Paul said, "I've called her three or four times and got no answer, even though I left messages on her machine. And so I came up and went by her place in Lexington before I went to your place. There's no one there."

Paul drank some beer from the bottle, held it by the neck, and gazed for a moment at the label.

"It's got that look, you know, that says it's empty."

"You have a key?" I said.

"No. I think she didn't want me walking in on her when she had a date. She was always a little embarrassed with me about dating."

"Want me to take a look?"

"Yes."

"Want to go with me?"

"Yes. I want more than that. I want you and me to find her."

"She's probably just off on a little trip with somebody," I said.

"Probably," he said, and I knew he didn't mean it.

"Your father?" Susan said.

Paul shook his head. "I haven't heard from him in maybe six years. I haven't a clue where he is. Once the tuition money stopped . . ." Paul shrugged.

"Okay," I said. "We'll find her."

"I have to know she's all right," Paul said.

"Sure," I said.

"Funny," Paul said. "Ten years ago you found me for her."

The dog uncurled from the chair and hopped down and stretched and came over and got up beside me where I was sitting on the couch and began to lick my face industriously. Her tongue was rough, which was probably useful for stripping meat from bones in the Pleistocene era, but served in the late 20th century as a kind of sloppy dermabrasion.

"It'll be even easier this time," I said with my face clenched. "We'll have a trained hunter to help us."

# Chapter 3

Paul had gone off to the American Rep Theater to watch a performance artist smear herself with chocolate. Susan and I, feeling a little middle class and uptown, went for drinks to the Ritz bar. It had begun to rain when we got there and I got several raindrop spots on my maroon silk tie while I stashed the car with the doorman. Even with the raindrops, I looked Ritz-worthy with my black cashmere blazer and my gray slacks. I had wanted to complete the look by wearing the cowboy boots that had been hand-made for me in L.A. by Willie the Cobbler. But Susan reminded me that I tended to fall off them if I had more than one drink, so I settled for black cordovan loafers.

As we cut through the lobby toward the bar, Callahan, the houseman, nodded at me pleasantly. I shot him with my forefinger and he looked at Susan and whistled silently.

"The house dick just whistled at you," I said.

"At the Ritz?" Susan said.

"Shocking but true," I said.

"Which one is he?" Susan said.

"Big guy with a red nose and gray hair. Looks fatter than he is."

"He looks very discerning," Susan said.

We got a table by the window in the bar, where we could look out through the rain at the Public Gardens. Susan ordered a champagne cocktail. I had scotch and soda.

"No beer?" Susan said.

"Celebration," I said. "I'm here with you and Paul's home. Makes me feel celebratory."

"When did scotch become the drink of celebration?" Susan leaned her chin on her folded hands and rested her gaze on me. The experience was, as it always was, tangible. The weight of her serious intelligence in counterpoint to her playful spoiled princess was culminative.

"Sometimes it's champagne," I said. "Sometimes it's scotch."

The bar was dark. The rain slid down the big window, and the early evening light filtering through it was silvery and slight. Susan picked a cashew from the small bowl of mixed nuts on the table, and bit off maybe a third of it and chewed it carefully.

"I was seventeen," I said, "the first time I had anything but beer. We were bird hunting in Maine, my father and I, and a pointer, Pearl the first. We were looking for pheasant in an old apple orchard that hadn't been farmed in maybe fifty years. You had to go through bad cover to reach it, brambles, and small alder that was clumped together and tangled. My father was maybe thirty yards off to the right, and the dog was ahead, ranging, the way they do, and coming back with her tongue out and her tail erect, and looking at me, and then swinging back out in another arc."

"Did you train her to do that?" Susan said.

"No," I said. "It's in the genes, I guess. They'll range like that and come back; and they'll point birds instinctively, but you've got to teach them to hold the point. Otherwise they'll stalk in on the bird and flush it too soon, and it'll fly when you're out of range. Or, if they're really good, they'll kill the bird."

Susan ate another third of her cashew, and sipped some champagne cocktail. The light through the rain was getting grayer. The silver edge was thinning as the evening came down on us.

"All of a sudden I heard her bark—half hysterical bark, half growl—and she came loping back, stopping every few yards and turning and making her barking snarling sound that had some fear in it, and then she reached me and leaned in hard on my leg and stood like they do, with her front legs stiff and her tail down and her ears sort of flattened back, and growled. And the hair was stiff along her spine. And I remember thinking, 'Jesus, this must be the pheasant that ate Chicago.' We had just come out of the cover and into the orchard and I looked and there was a bear."

"A grizzly?" Susan said. Her eyes were fixed on me and they seemed bottomless and captivated, like a kid listening to ghost stories.

"No, they don't have grizzly bears in Maine. It was a black bear, he'd been feeding on the fallen apples that some of the trees were still producing. They must have been close to rotten, and they must have been fermenting in his stomach, because he was drunk."

"Drunk?"

"Yeah, bears do that sometimes. Usually it happens close to a town, because that's where there are apple orchards, and the forest ranger types dart them and haul them off to some other place in the woods to sober up. But no one had tranquilized this one. He was loose, upright, drunk, and swaying a little. I don't know how big he was. Maybe a hundred and fifty pounds or so. Maybe more. They can get bigger. Standing on his hind legs he looked a lot bigger than I was."

"What did you do?"

"Well, the dog was going crazy now, growling and making a kind of high whining noise, and the bear was reared up and grunting. They sound more like pigs than anything else. I had a shotgun full of birdshot, sevens, I think, and it might have annoyed the bear. It sure as hell wouldn't have stopped him. But I didn't have anything else and I was pretty sure if I ran it would chase me, and they can run about forty miles an hour, so it was going to catch me. So I just stood there with the shotgun leveled. It was a pump. I had one round in the chamber and three more in the magazine, and I prayed that if he charged and if I got him in the face it would make him turn. The dog was in a frenzy, dashing out a few feet and barking and snarling and then running back to lean against my leg. The bear reared up, swaying, and I can still remember how rank the bear smelled and the way everything moved so slowly. And then my father was beside me. He didn't make any noise coming. Afterwards he said he heard the dog and knew it was something, probably a bear, from the way the dog sounded. He had a shotgun too, but he also was carrying a big old .45 hogleg, a six-shooter he'd had ever since he was a kid in Laramie. And he stood beside the dog, next to me, and took that shooter's stance that I always can remember him using, and cocked the .45 and we waited. The bear dropped to all fours, and snorted and grunted and dipped its head and turned around and left. I can see us like a painting on a calendar, my father with the .45 and the dog between us, snarling, and yipping, and me with the shotgun that, if he'd charged, the bear would have picked his teeth with."

It was dark now outside the Ritz bar, and the rain coiling down the windowpane looked black. Susan had finished her cashew and was leaning back in her chair, holding her drink in both hands, watching me.

"The dog was no good for birds the rest of the day, and neither were we, I suppose. We went back to the lodge we were staying at and put Pearl in our room, and fed her, and then my father and I went down to the bar and my father ordered two double scotch whiskies. The bartender looked at me and looked at my father and didn't say anything and brought the whiskey. He put both of them in front of my father and my father pushed one of them over in front of me.

" 'Ran into a bear in the woods today,' my father said without much inflection. He still had the Western sound in his voice. 'Kid stood his ground.'

"The bartender was a lean, dark guy, with a big nose. He looked at me and nodded and moved on down the bar, and my father and I drank the scotch."

"And he never said anything to you," Susan said.

I shook my head.

" 'That brown liquor,' " Susan said, " 'which not women, not boys and children, but only hunters drank.' "

"Faulkner," I said.

Susan smiled. "You're very literate for a man who has to buy extra-long ties."

"I had acted like a man, in his view, so he treated me like a man, in his view."

" 'Not women, not boys and children,' " Susan said.

"Sounds ageist and sexist to me," I said.

"Maybe we can have his Nobel prize posthumously revoked," Susan said.

# Chapter 4

Paul and I were driving out Route 2 toward Lexington to break into Paul's mother's house. It was the first day that had felt like fall this year. And it was still raining, a lighter rain than last night, but steady so that the streets glistened and the cars had their lights on even though it was well after sunrise.

Pearl was sitting in the backseat looking steadily out the window on the passenger side, mostly motionless except when she turned her head to look out the other window. She had wanted very much to come and neither Paul nor I could quite think of a reason sufficient to leave her staring after us with that look.

A school bus passed us going the other way and I felt the pang I always felt in early fall, the remembered pang of school. So many days like this I remembered in the brick elementary school, the lights on inside, the day wet and shiny outside, cars moving past the school with their wipers going, and the smell of steam pipes and disinfectant and limitation and tedium, while outside the adult world moved freely about.

"How was it last night?" I said. I was drinking a cup of coffee as I drove, something I prided myself on doing with the cover off and never a drop spilled. Paul drank his out of a hole he'd torn in the cover. A boy still, with things to learn.

"She's good," Paul said, "very interesting. Essentially it's just a one-woman show, like, ah, whosis, Lily Tomlin, except a lot more angry and foul-mouthed."

"I never heard of her," I said.

"I know her from New York," Paul said. "She's just a regular down-town performer, like me, trying to find performance space someplace in the East Village, except that she was lucky enough to be denied an NEA grant. Now she's making big money. And playing high-visibility theaters. And getting written up in *Time*."

"Have you thought of applying?"

"The tricky part is to make a grant application good enough to get approved by the peer review panel, and still exotic enough to be officially rejected."

"Maybe I should take Susan," I said.

Paul laughed. "She might like it," he said. "You'd hate it."

We pulled off into Lexington. The traffic was at a crawl, stuck behind a school bus that stopped every few blocks and took on children.

"Do you know your mother's new boyfriend?" I said.

Paul shook his head. "Never met him. His name is Rich something or other."

"What's he do?"

"My mother says he's a consultant."

"Self-employed?"

Paul shook his head. "I don't know. She seemed a little vague about what he did. She never wants to talk much about any of her boyfriends. Like I said, she's always embarrassed about them."

We went through the middle of Lexington, past the Battle Green, with the minuteman statue at the near end of it and the restored colonial buildings across the street. Paul was staring around at the town as if it were a Martian landscape.

"Every Patriots' Day there was a big parade in town," Paul said. "It was always exciting. Every April 19, I'd wake up excited, and my mother and father and I would come down and get a good spot and watch for the parade, and afterwards we'd go home and there'd be nothing to do and I'd feel let down, and the next day would be school."

I turned into Emerson Road.

"Parade was usually good, though," Paul said.

Patty Giacomin's house was as I remembered it, set back a bit from the road, among trees. The trees were probably fuller than they had been ten years ago when I'd come out here before. But they looked the same and so did the dense spread of pachysandra that did service as lawn around her house.

The house itself was angular, and shingled; modern looking without violating either the site or the colonial town in which it stood.

I parked next to a Honda Prelude in the driveway. We rolled the windows half down and left Pearl in the car. I went and opened the trunk and took out a gym bag with tools in it. As we walked toward the house I automatically felt the hood of the Prelude. It was cold.

There was no answer when we rang the bell. The house had that stillness that Paul had mentioned. In the interests of not looking like a jerk, I tried the doorknob. It was locked.

"I already did that," Paul said.

"It's a Dick Tracy crime stopper," I said. "Always try the door before jimmying it."

"Great working with a pro," Paul said.

There was no sign of flies on the inside of the windows, which was encouraging. I looked at the door. There was a keyhole in the handle. No other lock, so it was probably a spring lock, though it didn't have to be. It could be a combination spring and deadbolt, but at least there was no separate keyhole, which there would be most certainly for a deadbolt. There was a strip of molding down along the lock side of the door to prevent someone from slipping a flat blade like a putty knife in there and springing the lock. I looked at the molding closely. The house was stained rather than painted, which made it easier to see the line where the molding butted up to the doorjamb. While I was examining it, I took a deep inhale. I smelled nothing dead, which was even more encouraging.

"Okay," I said. "I'll open this thing unless you have a better thought."

Paul shook his head. His face looked tight. I took a flat chisel from the bag, and a hammer, and gently loosened the molding along the door strip. No point trashing the house.

"I'll get this off intact," I said. "We can put it back on when we get through."

Paul nodded. I pried the molding away, a little at a time, all along its length, and then got a flat bar under it at the nail holes and pried it carefully loose so that it came off nails still sticking through it. I handed it to Paul and he leaned it against a tree. I put the flat bar and the chisel and the hammer away and got out a putty knife with an inch-and-a-half blade and slid it into the door crack at the latch and felt for the lock tongue. I found it and pressed and felt the tongue give and the blade of the putty knife push in. I held the putty knife in place with my right hand, and with the flat of my left, pushed the door open. There was no smell.

"We're not going to find anything bad," I said to Paul. "Promise."

"That's good," he said. His voice was a little hoarse.

We were in a small entry hall, with a polished flagstone floor, then up a couple of steps to the living room, the kitchen to the right, a view of the woods straight ahead through the big picture window across the back. Off the kitchen, constituting a short L to the living room, was a dining area where once Patty Giacomin had served me dinner and propositioned me. It hadn't been me, really, just the need to validate herself with a man, and there I was. I had declined, but I remembered it well. I always thought about the ones I'd missed, and speculated about how they'd have been, even though wisdom and experience would suggest that they'd have been much like the ones I hadn't missed. The thing was, though, that I always thought about the ones I hadn't missed too.

The house was still and close, and neat. We walked around, checked the bedrooms. Patty's big, pink, puffy bed was made, her bathroom was orderly, though it didn't look like it had been put in order by someone who was leaving. Around the mirror were postcards with amusing pictures.

"I sent her those," Paul said, "from wherever I was performing. She kept them."

The other bedroom, where Paul had slept, was perfectly neat, with a high school picture of Paul still in its cardboard frame set up on the dresser. The picture had been taken the year he'd graduated from prep school, three years after I'd met him, and already the aimlessness had disappeared from his face. He was still very young there, but it was a face that knew more than most eighteen-year-old faces knew.

Paul looked at the picture. "Three years of therapy," he said.

"And more to come," I said.

"For sure," he said.

There was a neat green corduroy spread over the single bed, with a plaid blanket folded neatly at the foot. There was a student desk with a reading lamp on it and a green blotter that matched the spread.

We went back downstairs. On the coffee table in the living room was a green imitation leather scrapbook. I picked it up and opened it. Carefully pasted in were clippings: reviews of Paul's dance concerts, listings from the newspaper of performances to come. There were ticket stubs and program covers and the program pages listing Paul's name, or Paige's or both. There were pictures of Paul, often with Paige, sometimes with other dancers, taken in places domestic and foreign, where they had danced. I handed the album to him without comment and he took it and looked at it and sat down slowly on the couch and leafed slowly through it.

"I used to think," he said, "that because she was so needy of my father, and after she lost him, so needy for other men, that she didn't care about me." He turned the pages in the album slowly, as he talked. He'd seen them already. He wasn't looking at them. It was merely something the hands did. "Sort of an *either-or* situation. *Me* or *them*. It took me a long time to see that it was both. That she cared about me too."

"As best she could," I said.

"Her best wasn't enough," Paul said.

"No. It's why we separated you."

"And we were right," Paul said.

"Yeah."

Paul closed the album and put it back on the coffee table.

"If she'd gotten some help, maybe if she would have seen somebody . . ."

I shrugged.

"You don't think so."

"No," I said. "I don't think she's smart enough. I don't think she's got enough will."

Paul nodded slowly. He looked down at the scrapbook on the coffee table.

"She is what she is," he said.

# Chapter 5

Paul went out to the car and brought Pearl in. She raced around the house with her nose to the ground for about fifteen minutes before she was able to slow down and follow me around while I searched the house.

The refrigerator was on, but nearly empty, and there was nothing perishable in it. There was no fruit in the bowl on the table. The strainer was out of the drain in the kitchen sink. There was no suitcase to be found in the house, which meant either that she had packed it and taken it with her or that she didn't have one. Paul didn't know if she had one, and he couldn't tell if any of her clothes were missing. There were very few cosmetics in the bathroom. There were eleven messages on her answering machine, three from Paul. I copied down the names and phone numbers that had been left. Mostly they were first names only, and Paul didn't know who they were. But the phone numbers could lead to something. I couldn't find an address book.

"Did she have one?" I said.

"Yes. I know she did. She carried it around with her and she was always afraid of losing it."

"She work?"

"Yes. She sold real estate. Worked for a company called *Chez Vous*."

"Cute."

"Hey," Paul said. "We're in the suburbs. *Cute* is important out here."

"You New York kids are so jaded," I said. "Do you know where she met Rich?"

"No."

"Probably a dating bar called *Entre Nous*," I said.

"Or *Cherchez la Femme*," Paul said.

"That betrays a preconception about dating bars," I said.

"I suppose it does," Paul said. "How about what you've found here? You have any conclusions to reach?"

"Everything here says that she left of her own accord," I said. "There's no mail piled up, which means she stopped it at the post office. There's no suitcase. Most people have one, which suggests that she took it. There's a dearth of cosmetics, which suggests that she packed them. The house is neat, but not like no one's ever coming back. There are no perishables in the refrigerator, which suggests that she was planning to be gone for a while."

"Without telling me?"

"We agree that's she's not Mother Courage," I said.

"True."

"You want me to find where she went?"

"I feel like kind of a jerk," Paul said. "I wouldn't want the police involved."

"But you'd still like to know where she is," I said.

Paul nodded. "I think she'd have called, or written me a postcard, something."

"Sure," I said.

"Of course I want to think that," Paul said. "I don't want to think she went off and didn't think about me."

"Well, let's find out," I said.

"What will you do?"

"First we'll track down Rich. There must be people know his last name. If he's also not around we'll have a reasonable presumption."

"And then what?"

"We'll ask everyone we can find who knows either of them if they know where Patty and Rich are."

"And if no one knows?"

"We check airlines, trains, local travel agencies, that stuff. We see if Rich's car is missing. If it is we run a trace on his license number. If it's not missing we check the car rental agencies."

"And if none of that works?"

"Some of it will work," I said. "You keep asking enough questions and checking enough options, something will come up, and that will lead to something, and that will lead to something else. We'll be getting information in ways, and from people, that we don't even know about now."

"You can't be sure of that," Paul said.

"I've done this for a long time, Paul. It's a high probability. If you want to find someone, you can find them. Even if they don't want to be found."

Paul nodded. "And you're good at this," he said.

"Few better," I said.

"Few?"

"Actually, none," I said. "I was trying for humble."

"And failing," Paul said.

# Chapter 6

It was a nearly perfect September day. Temperature around 72, sky blue, foliage not yet turned. There was still sweet corn at the farm stands, and native tomatoes, and the air moved gently among the yet green leaves of the old trees that still stood just off the main drag undaunted by exhaust fumes or ancestral voices prophesying war. Paul was in my office with the list of callers from his mother's answering machine. I was back out in Lexington at the post office in the center of town, where a woman clerk with her pinkish hair teased high told me that Patty Giacomin had put an indefinite hold-for-pickup on her mail. There was no forwarding address.

I went to *Chez Vous,* which was located next to an ice cream parlor behind a bookstore in a small shopping center on Massachusetts Avenue. Four desks, four swivel chairs, four phones, four side chairs, and a sofa with maplewood arms and a small floral print covering. The wall was decorated with flattering photos of the property available, and the floor was covered with a big braided rug in mostly blues and reds. Two of the desks were empty, a woman with blue-black hair and large green-rimmed glasses sat at one of the remaining desks speaking on the phone. She was speaking about a house that the office was listing and she was being enthusiastic. The other desk was occupied by a very slender blonde woman wearing a lot of clothes. Her white skirt reached her ankles, nearly covering her black-laced high-heeled boots. Over the skirt she wore a longish ivory-colored tunic and a black leather belt with a huge buckle and a small crocheted beige sleeveless sweater, and a beige scarf at her neck, and ivory earrings that were carved in the shape of Japanese dolls, and rings on all her fingers, and a white bow in her hair.

"Hi, I'm Nancy," she said. "Can I help?"

I took a card out of my shirt pocket and gave it to her. It had my name on it, and my address and phone number and the word Investigator. Nothing else. Susan had said that a Tommy gun, with a fifty-round drum, spewing flame from the muzzle, was undignified.

"I'm representing Paul Giacomin, whose mother works here."

Nancy was still eyeballing the card. "Does this mean, like a *Private* Investigator?"

I smiled winningly and nodded.

"Like a Private Eye?"

"The stuff that dreams are made of, sweetheart," I said.

The woman with the blue-black hair hung up the phone.

"Hey, PJ," Nancy said. "This is a Private Eye."

"Like on television?" PJ said. Where Nancy was flat, PJ was curved. Where Nancy was overdressed, PJ wore a sleeveless crimson blouse and gray slacks which fitted very smoothly over her sumptuous thighs. She had bare ankles and high-heeled red shoes. Around her left ankle was a gold chain.

"Just like television," I said. "Car chases, shootouts, beautiful broads . . ."

"Which is where we come in," PJ said. She had on pale lipstick and small gold earrings. There were small laugh wrinkles around her eyes, and she looked altogether like more fun than was probably legal in Lexington.

"My point exactly," I said. "I'm trying to locate Patty Giacomin."

"For her son?" Nancy said.

"Yes. She's apparently gone, and he doesn't know where and he wants to."

"I don't blame him," PJ said.

"You know where she is?"

Both women shook their heads. "She hasn't been in for about ten days," PJ said.

"A week ago last Monday," Nancy said.

"Is that usual?"

"No. I mean, it's not like she's on salary. She doesn't come in, she doesn't get listings, she doesn't sell anything, she doesn't get commission," PJ said. "But usually she was in here three, four days a week—she was sort of part-time."

"Who runs the place?"

"I do," PJ said.

"Are you *Chez* or *Vous?*"

PJ grinned. "Is that awful, or what? No. My name's P. J. Garfield. PJ stands for Patty Jean. But with Patty Giacomin working here, it was easier to use PJ, saved confusion. I bought the place from the previous owner when she retired. *Chez Vous* was her idea. I didn't want to change the name."

"Either of you know Patty's boyfriend?" I said.

"Rich?" Nancy said.

"Rich what?"

Nancy looked at PJ. She shrugged.

"Rich . . ." PJ said. "Rich . . . she brought him to the Christmas party last year. An absolute hunk. Rich . . . Broderick, I think, something like that. Rich Broderick? Bachrach? Beaumont?"

"Beaumont," Nancy said.

"You sure?"

"Oh." She put her hand to her mouth. "No, God no, I'm not sure. I don't want anyone to get in trouble."

"How nice," I said. "Do we know where Rich lives?"

"Somewhere on the water," Nancy said. She looked at PJ.

PJ shrugged. "Could be. I frankly paid very little attention to him. He's not Patty's first boyfriend. And most of them are not, ah *mensches*."

"What can you remember?" I said.

"Me?" Nancy said.

"Either of you. What did he look like? What did he do for a living? What did he talk about? Did he like baseball, or horse racing, or sailboats? Was he married, separated, single, divorced? Did he have children? Did he have any physical handicap, any odd mannerisms, did he have an accent? Did he mention parents, brothers, sisters? Did he like dogs?"

PJ answered. "He was as tall as you, probably not as"—she searched for the word—"thick. Dark hair worn longish, good haircut"—her eyes crinkled—"great buns."

"So we have that in common too," I said. Nancy looked at her desk.

"His clothes were expensive," PJ said. "And they fit him well. He's probably a good off-the-rack size."

"What size?"

"What size are you?" PJ said.

"Fifty," I said, "fifty-two, depends."

"He'd probably be a forty-four, maybe. He's more, ah, willowy."

"How grand for him," I said.

"I like husky men, myself," PJ said.

"Phew!"

"He didn't have an accent," Nancy said.

"You mean he talked like everyone else around here?"

"No. I mean he had no accent at all," Nancy said. "Like a radio announcer. He didn't sound like he was from here. He didn't sound like he was from the South, or from anywhere."

Nancy was maybe a little keener than she seemed.

"Good-looking guy?" I said.

Nancy nodded very vigorously. PJ noticed it and grinned.

"He was pretty as hell," she said. "Straight nose, dimple in his chin, kind of pouty lips, smooth-shaven, though you could see that his beard is dark. Kind of man that wears cologne, silk shorts."

Nancy got a little touch of pink on her cheekbones.

"Okay," I said. "The consensus is that his name is Rich Beaumont, or thereabouts, that he's six feet one, maybe a hundred eighty-five pounds, dark longish hair, well styled, good clothes, handsome, and particularly attractive to slender blonde women."

"What do you mean?" Nancy said.

"A wild guess," I said. "He speaks in an accentless way, and lives near the water."

"Hell," PJ said. "We knew more than we thought we did."

"Masterful questioning," I said, "brings it out. You have any thoughts at all about where Patty Giacomin might be?"

"No. Really," Nancy said, "I can't imagine."

"You find the boyfriend," PJ said, "you'll probably find her. Patty doesn't do much without a man. Usually not that good a man."

"Thank you," I said. "The kid's worried. If you hear anything, please call me."

"Certainly," Nancy said.

PJ grinned so that her eyes crinkled a little.

"You had lunch?" she said.

"Can't," I said. "I got a dog in the car."

"An actual dog or is that an unkind euphemism?"

"An actual dog, named Pearl. Can euphemisms be unkind?"

"I don't know. There's always dinner? Or are you married?"

"Well, I have a friend."

"Don't they all," PJ said. "Too bad. We'd have had fun."

"Yeah," I said. "We would have in fact."

I went out of *Chez Vous*, and went back to the car.

# Chapter 7

When I got to my car, Pearl was curled tightly in the driver's seat. She sprang up when I opened the door and insinuated herself between the bucket front seats into the back. When I got in she lapped the side of my face vigorously.

"I thought you were Susan's dog," I said.

She made no response.

Back in my office she guzzled down some water from a bowl placed for that purpose by Paul.

"Did you know that they drink by curling their tongue backwards?" I said. "Under?"

"How exciting," Paul said. "Thank you for sharing that with me."

"How'd you do on the phone?"

"Not very well," he said. "No one knew where she was. Some of the calls were from real estate customers who don't know anything about her. One woman said she was my mother's best friend. I figure she's worth a visit."

"She know anything?"

"She was late for aerobics, she said. But I could call later."

"Better to visit," I said. "Where is she?"

"Lives in Concord. She gave me the address."

"Okay. I'll run out and have a talk with her," I said.

"I'll go with you."

"No need to."

"Yes," Paul said. "There is a need to."

"Okay."

"You took care of everything when I was fifteen," he said. "I'm not fifteen now. I need to do part of this."

"Sure," I said. Paul's presence would make it harder. People would be less frank about Patty in front of her son. But he wasn't fifteen anymore and it was his mother. Pearl had gotten herself up onto the narrow client's chair and was curled precariously, mouthing the yellow tennis ball she'd tracked down on a walk in Cambridge. Her eyes followed every movement I made. I got her leash and snapped it on and took her to the car and drove her and Paul to Concord.

Most of the way up Route 2 she had her head on my left shoulder, her nose out the open window, sampling the wind.

"It is not entirely clear," I said to Paul, "why I am bringing this hound with me everywhere I go."

"Cathexis," Paul said.

"I knew you'd know."

"What did they say about my mother?" he said.

"The people at *Chez Vous?*"

"*Oui.*"

"They had no real idea where she might be."

"I know, you told me that. But what did they say?"

"They said she worked, usually, three or four days a week, on commission. That she had brought Rich to a Christmas party last year and that he was very good-looking."

"That all?"

"They didn't exactly say, but made it quite clear that they thought that your mother's choices of men were often ill-advised."

"Many men?"

"They suggested that she needed to be with a man, and that if we found Rich we'd find her."

"Did they talk about her need to be with men?"

"Not a lot. They seemed to record it as a fact of your mother's nature that she wasn't likely to go very far, very often, without the company of a man."

"That could get you in trouble," Paul said.

I nodded. We left Route 2, onto 2A, which was the old Revolutionary War road, where the embattled farmers sniped at the redcoats from behind the fieldstone walls. We passed historic houses—the Wayside, the Alcott House—all the way into Concord center.

Not all of the historical places in Massachusetts look the way you'd like them to. But Concord does. It has overarching trees, spacious colonial homes, a green, a clean little downtown made mostly of red brick, a rambling white clapboard inn that looks as if stagecoaches should still be stopping there. There are the historic sights, the academy, the river where one can rent a canoe and spend a day of transcendental paddling, as Susan and I had occasionally done, pausing to picnic one day almost beneath the rude bridge that arched the flood.

The address we wanted was a recycled jelly factory in downtown Concord. They'd sandblasted the brick and cleaned up the clock tower and gutted the interior and built blond-wood-with-white-walls condominium apartments inside. Out back was a big parking lot. A hopeful sales office was still open on the first floor of the building.

The woman's name was Caitlin Moore. She answered the bell in a pink spandex leotard, white sneakers, and a pink sweatband. She was built like the cheerleaders of my youth, chunky, bouncy, not very tall. Her extremely blonde hair was caught into a ponytail. She had on green eye shadow and false eyelashes and whitish lip gloss, which made her look a little spectral.

"Hi," she said, friendly. "I'm Caitlin. You must be Paul, who I talked with on the phone."

Paul said he was, and introduced me.

"You're a detective?"

"Yes."

"Could I see something?"

"Sure." I gave her my license, she looked at it for a moment, then went to a bleached oak table and got a pair of half-glasses and put them on and came back looking further at my license. "Well," she said. "A hard man is good to find."

She smiled. I smiled. Paul smiled.

"Come on in," Caitlin said. "Want some coffee? All I got is instant, but I can microwave it in no time."

Paul and I declined. Caitlin led us into her sitting room, her prominent little butt waggling ahead of us as we followed her. With its bleached woodwork and stark white walls and ceiling, and anodized combination windows, the room was standard condo modern. It appeared to have been furnished by Betsy Ross. There was an old maple standup desk, an antique pine harvest table, a pine thumbback rocker, a coffee table made from a cobbler's bench. It went with the room the way Liberace goes with *Faust*.

"I love early American," she said as we sat down. Paul and me on the sofa. Caitlin on the thumbback rocker, where she crossed both legs under her. "When I got divorced I made the bastard give me all the furniture."

"Great," I said.

"You're my mother's best friend?" Paul said.

"Oh, absolutely," Caitlin said. "Patty and I are like twins. She's always talking about you."

"What does she say?"

"She talks about how successful you are. You're in the movies, I think?"

"I'm a dancer in New York," Paul said. "I was on-screen for a minute and twenty-six seconds in a film about American Dance that played on PBS."

"Yuh, I knew it was something like that. Anyway, we been really close ever since we were in aerobics together at Sweats Plus. Something about us, you know, we just hit it off. Both been divorced and all. I don't have any kids, but, well, we knew something about pain, and recovery."

"Know her current boyfriend?" I said.

"I introduced them."

"Tell us a little about him," Paul said.

"He's a real doll. Friend of my brother's. I knew Patty was looking to go out, and I knew Rich was single. So I . . ." Caitlin spread her hands and shrugged. "They really connected, you know, right from the start. It was something. You worried about her? Maybe she and Rich just went off, they were crazy like that, I don't mean anything bad about your mom, Paul, she was just ready for fun anytime. I bet they just went off somewhere for a while on the spur."

"They have a place they usually go?" I said.

"Oh, they'd go anywhere. I don't know. Miami, Atlantic City, Club Med. You name it."

"What's Rich's last name?" Paul said.

"Beaumont. Rich Beaumont." She pronounced it with the stress on the last syllable.

"Where's he live?" I said.

"Over in Revere someplace, I think. On the water. I think he's got a condo on the beach."

"Got an address?"

"No, not really. I don't think I ever knew it exactly."

"Phone number?"

Caitlin smiled and spread her hands. "I'd always meet him through my brother."

"Can we talk with your brother?" Paul said.

"Marty? I don't know what Marty can tell you."

"How's your brother know Rich?"

"I don't know, they play handball together. Double-date. I think they did some business sometime."

"What's Rich's business?"

"Consultant."

"You know what he consults in?"

"No, just some kind of consulting business."

"What's your brother do?"

"Marty's a paving contractor. Hot top, you know, that stuff."

"And his last name?" I said.

"Martinelli."

"Martin Martinelli?" I said.

"Yeah. My mother was a lunatic. How about Caitlin Martinelli? My old lady was nuts."

"What was it like being my mother's friend?" Paul said.

"Huh?"

"What's she like?"

"You're her kid," Caitlin said. "You should know—better than anybody."

"I should but I don't. What does she care about?"

The question was too hard for Caitlin. She frowned. "What did she care about?"

"Yeah."

Caitlin lifted her shoulders. "Ah . . ." Caitlin waved her hands vaguely.

"She, ah. She liked aerobics. You know she cared about her body, and how she looked. And she knew a lot about makeup."

Paul nodded.

Caitlin had a thread to follow out of her confusion. She tumbled on. "And fun," Caitlin said. "Patty loved to have fun."

Paul nodded again.

"Who were her other close friends?" I said.

"I don't really know her other friends. . . . She had a friend named Sonny, was a traffic reporter, you know, from a helicopter."

"Man or woman?" I said.

"Woman."

"She have a last name?"

"Oh, sure. I mean, doesn't everybody? I don't know it, though. Just Sonny."

"Know the station she reported for?"

Caitlin shook her head.

"We'd like to talk with your brother," I said. "Could you give us an address?"

Caitlin looked flustered. "Gee, I don't know. Marty won't be too thrilled. Marty's a very private guy. Very successful businessman, very private."

"I know his name," I said. "I know his business. I can find him. Will he like me finding him, asking around about him?"

"God, no. Listen. I'll give you his work address. That way you won't be bothering him at home."

"Sure," I said.

She gave me an address on the Revere Beach Parkway in Everett.

"Did she ever talk about my father?" Paul said.

"Her ex? What's-his-name, Mel? Sure did. She called him a cheap sonovabitch every chance she could. Excuse me, I know he's your dad and all."

"That's okay," Paul said. "I can hear whatever there is to hear. I *need* to hear it."

"Well, don't worry about her. I'm sure she's off someplace with Rich having a ball. Your mother is a fun lady!"

"You don't think she might go someplace without Rich?" Paul said.

Caitlin looked startled. "No," she said. "Of course not. What fun is it alone?"

# Chapter 8

Susan said, "When Pearl sleeps with you does she get under the covers?"

We were sitting at the same table in the Ritz bar. On a Wednesday with the baseball season dwindling, and the kids grimly back in school. It was raining again. The Ritz bar is a good place to spend a rainy weekday afternoon.

"Of course," I said. "Don't you?"

"I'm not sure all dogs do that," Susan said.

"We shouldn't generalize," I said.

Susan nodded. "True," she said.

I was drinking Sam Adams. Susan had a glass of Riesling which would last her the day. The bar was nearly empty. It wasn't the old Ritz bar. It had been refurbished by new owners into something that looked like an English hunting club, or the last twenty-five hotel bars you'd been in. But you could still have a table by the window, looking out at Arlington Street and the Public Gardens.

"What do you think about Paul?" I said. "It's not just that he wants to locate his mother. He wants to find out about her."

"He's thinking about getting married," Susan said.

"Yeah?"

"For a kid like Paul whose parents' marriage was a failure, whose own life has made him careful, and introspective, the idea of marriage carries with it heavy baggage."

"His mother really is missing," I said.

"His mother has always been missing."

"Mine too," I said.

Susan took a gram of Riesling and swallowed it carefully and put the glass back down. She looked out at the wet street for a moment.

"How long have we been together?" she said.

"If you date *together* from the time I first got your clothes off," I said, "sixteen years."

"Aren't you the romantic fool," Susan said.

"How do you date it?" I said.

Susan thought a minute. Outside, chic Back Bay women were picking their way past the rain puddles on their high heels, bending in under the little black umbrellas they all had, most of them holding skirts down by pressing their left hand and forearm across their thighs as the wind pushed at them.

"I'd say it begins with the time you first got my clothes off."

"September," I said. "Nineteen seventy-four. After Labor Day. It's almost an anniversary now that I think of it. You had on red undies with big black polka dots and a little black bow on the side."

"Selected with great care," Susan said. "I planned that you'd get my clothes off."

Outside on Arlington Street, the taxis all had their lights on in the rain and the overcast. The yellow headlights mixed with the neon and the traffic lights to make glistening streaks on the wet pavement—red, green, and yellow mostly. Two young Boston cops strolled past, heading toward Park Square, their slickers gleaming in the rain, the plastic covers on their hats looking oddly out of keeping.

"In all that time," Susan said, "you have spoken maybe for five minutes, total, about your past."

"My past?"

"Yes, your past."

"What is this, an old Bette Davis movie?"

"No," Susan said. "I know you as I am sure no one in the world knows you. But I only know you since we undressed that first time in September 1974. I don't to this day know how you got to be what you are. I don't know about other women, about family, about what you were like as a little boy, peeking out at the adult world, trying to grow up, getting scarred in the process."

"Heavens," I said.

Susan smiled. Dampened the tip of her tongue with her wine. I drank the rest of my Sam Adams. The waiter noticed and raised an inquiring eyebrow. I nodded and he hustled over a fresh bottle on a silver tray.

"It's a rainy day," Susan said. "We have nothing to do but look at the rain and watch the people go by on whatever street that is out there."

"You've lived here since the Johnstown flood," I said. "That's Arlington Street, runs from Beacon Street in the north to Tremont Street in the South End."

Susan smiled the smile she always smiled when you knew she hadn't the slightest interest in what you were saying, and she knew it, and she knew you knew it.

"Of course," she said.

The only other people in the bar were two women at a table, with Bonwit's shopping bags piled on the two empty chairs; and a guy at the bar, reading the *Wall Street Journal* and sipping what looked like a Gibson, up. The women were drinking white wine. Both of them smoked. Susan settled her gaze on me and waited.

"Well, we had a dog named Pearl," I said.

"I know that," Susan said. "And I know that you were born in Laramie, Wyoming, and that your mother died while she carried you and you were born by caesarean section and your father and your two uncles, who were your mother's brothers, raised you."

"Me and Macbeth," I said.

"Not of woman born," Susan said. "But that's all I know."

"And all ye need to know," I said.

"Many people would welcome the chance to sit in a quiet bar on a rainy afternoon and talk about themselves to an attentive listener," Susan said. "Many people pay one hundred and fifty dollars an hour to come and sit in a quiet office and talk to me about themselves."

"Do they know you used to wear polka dot panties with a bow?" I said.

"Most of them don't."

I drank some beer. I looked out the window at the wet, wind-driven cityscape. *The small rain down can rain.*

"My father was a carpenter," I said, "in business with his wife's two brothers. They were very young when I was born. My uncles were seventeen and eighteen. My father was twenty."

"My God," Susan said. "Children raising children."

"I suppose so," I said. "But this was the depression, remember, and people grew up early those years. Everyone worked as soon as he could, especially in a place like Laramie."

"Your father never remarried."

"No."

"And your uncles lived with you?"

"Yeah, until they got married. They both married late. I was in my teens."

"So you grew up in an all-male household."

I nodded.

"My uncles dated a lot, so did my father. There were always girlfriends around. But they didn't have anything to do with the family. The family was us."

"Three men and a boy," Susan said.

"Maybe four boys," I said.

"All unified by a connection to one woman."

"Yeah."

"Who was dead," Susan said.

I nodded.

"They were all fighters," I said. "My father used to pick up spare money boxing, around the state, at smokers, fairs, stuff like that. And my uncles did the same thing. Heavyweight, all three of them. One uncle fought for a while at light heavy until he filled out."

"And they taught you."

"Yeah. I could box as far back as I can remember."

"What were they like?" Susan said.

"They were like each other," I said. "Other than that it's hard to summarize. They were fairly wild, tough men. But one thing was clear. We were family, the four of us, and in that family I was the treasure."

"They loved you."

"They loved me without reservation," I said. "No conditions. Nothing about their love depended on my grades or my behavior. They expected me to learn how to act by observing them. And God save anyone who didn't treat me properly."

"Like what?" Susan said. I could see how she'd gotten to be such a good shrink. Her interest was luminous. She listened with her whole self. Her eyes picked up every movement of my hands, every gesture of my soul.

"I went to the store once," I said, "and on the way back, past a saloon, a couple of drunks gave me a hard time. I was probably sort of mouthy."

"Hard to believe," Susan murmured.

"Anyway—I was maybe around ten—the bottle of milk I was carrying got broken. I went home and told my uncle Bob, who was the only one there. One of them was always home. I never had a babysitter. And he grinned and said we'd take care of it, and later that afternoon, we all went down to the place. It was called the Blind Pig Saloon, and my father and my uncles cleaned it out. It was like one of those old John Wayne movies, where bodies would come flying out through the front window. I didn't know if the culprits were even in there when we arrived. Didn't matter. By the time the cops came the place was empty except for me, and everything in there was broken."

"Where were you," Susan said, "while all this was happening?"

"Mostly behind the bar, watching, like the kid in *Shane*. Even had the dog with me."

We were quiet. Susan twirled the stem of her nearly full wineglass. There was the imprint of her lipstick on the rim. I thought about what it might be like going through life with everything having a faint raspberry flavor.

"Parents' day at school was an event," I said. "They'd always come. The three of them. All six feet or more. All around two hundred pounds and hard as the handle on a pickax, and they'd sit in the back row, at the little desks, with their arms folded and not say a word. But they always came."

Across Arlington Street, past the wrought-iron fence that rimmed the Public Gardens, beyond the initial stand of big trees, I could see the weeping willows that stood around the lagoon where the swan boats drifted in pleasant weather. Through the rain the willows had a misty green blur about them, softened by the weather, almost lacy.

"When I was ten or twelve," I said, "we moved east. I think my father and my uncles thought it was a better place for a kid to grow up."

"Boston?" Susan said.

"Yeah. The Athens of America. My father read a lot. My uncles didn't, except to me. Every night one of them would read to me after dinner while the other two cleaned up."

"What did they read?"

"To me? Uncle Remus, Winnie-the-Pooh, Joseph Altscheler, John R. Tunis, stuff like that."

"And what did your father read, to himself?" Susan said.

"He had no formal education, so he had no master plan," I said. "He read whatever came along: Shakespeare, Kenneth Roberts, Faulkner, C. S. Forester, Dos Passos, Rex Stout. Actually I think he was reading Marquand when he decided to move us to Boston. Or Oliver Wendell Holmes, or Henry Adams, somebody like that."

"Because he thought it would be good for you?"

"Yeah. He believed all that Hub of the Universe stuff."

"So you all came."

"Oh yeah, the four of us and Pearl."

"And what about love? Was there someone before me?"

"There were a lot of women before you."

"No. I mean, did you ever love anyone before me?"

"Just once," I said.

"Was she as pretty, sexy, and smart as I am?" Susan said.

"Would you believe, prettier, sexier, and smarter."

"No," Susan said.

"How about younger?" I said.

"Younger is possible."

# Chapter 9

R & B Hot Top and Paving was behind a ragged shopping center off the Revere Beach Parkway in Everett. A red sign with yellow letters that appeared to have been hand painted on a piece of 4 × 8 plywood was nailed to a utility pole out front. There were a couple of asphalt-stained dump trucks parked on the hot-top turnaround, and, next to the Quonset hut that served as an office, a power roller was parked on a trailer. The hot-top apron was maybe four inches thick and gleamed the way new hot top does, but no one had bothered to retain it and it was crumbly and scattered along the edges.

In the backseat Pearl growled in an entirely uncute way, and the hair along her spine went up. A black and tan pit bull terrier appeared in the door of the Quonset with his head down and stared out at the car.

"Pearl appears to want a piece of that pit bull," Paul said.

"That's because she's in here," I said. Paul and I got out of the car carefully so Pearl would stay put. She was stiff-legged in the backseat, growling a low serious growl. The pit bull gazed at us, his yellow eyes unblinking.

"Nice doggie," Paul murmured.

"I'm not sure that's going to work," I said.

We walked toward the door. A squat man appeared in it wearing a gold tank top and blue workout pants with red trim. He had dark curly hair, worn longish, over his ears, and there was a lot of dark hair on his chest and arms. As we got close I could see that he was wearing a small gold loop in his left ear. There were two gold chains around his neck, a gold bracelet on his right wrist, a gold Rolex watch on his left one. On his feet he wore woven leather sandals.

The pit bull growled briefly. The man bent over slightly and took hold of the loose end of the dog's choke collar.

"He won't bother you unless I tell him," the man said.

"Good to know," I said.

"We're looking for Marty Martinelli," Paul said.

"What for?" the man said. The pit bull was motionless, his expressionless yellow eyes staring at us. There was a barely audible rumble in his throat. The man had a forefinger hooked less firmly than I would have liked through the ring on the choke collar. On the back of his wrist, in blue script, was tattooed the name *Marty*.

"We need to ask him a couple of questions about some people," Paul said.

"I do hot top, you know. I put a nice driveway in your yard, put a nice sealer on it. Charge you a fair price. That's what I do. I don't go around answering questions about nobody. Gets you in trouble."

"Sure," Paul said. "I understand that, but I'm looking for my mother, and your sister said you might know something."

"My sister?"

"Caitlin," Paul said. "She said you might be able to help us."

The pit bull kept up his very low rumbling growl.

"What makes you think I got a sister named Caitlin?"

"Well," Paul said, "you've got *Marty* tattooed on your left wrist. I took a sort of guess based on that."

"Smart guy," Marty said.

"Smart enough not to tattoo his name on his arm if he doesn't want people to know it," I said.

"Lot of guys named Marty," he said.

Paul didn't say anything. Neither did I. The dog kept growling. Marty looked at me.

"You a cop?"

"Sort of," I said.

"What the hell is sort of a cop?"

"Private detective," I said.

Marty shook his head. "Caitlin," he said. "The queen of the yuppies. What the fuck kind of name is that for an Italian broad, Caitlin?"

Paul started to speak. I shook my head. We waited.

"I don't know nothing about nobody's mother," Marty said.

"Patty Giacomin," Paul said.

"That your old lady?"

"Yes."

"Hey, that's a good paisano name."

Paul nodded. "Her boyfriend is Rich Beaumont."

Marty grinned. "Hey," he said. "Richie."

"You know him?"

"Sure. Richie's my main man."

"We think he and my mother have gone off together," Paul said, "and we're trying to find them."

"Hey, if she went off with Richie, she's having a good time. Why not leave them be?"

"We just want to know that she's okay," Paul said.

"She's with Richie, kid, she's okay. Hell, she probably . . ."

"Probably what?"

"Nothing. I forgot for a minute she's your mother, you know?"

"You know where they might be?" I said.

Marty shrugged. To do so, he had to let go of the dog. I shrugged my left shoulder slightly to feel the pleasant weight of the Browning under my arm. The dog maintained the steady sound. Maybe he was bored. Maybe he was humming to himself.

"Hell, no."

"You know where Beaumont lives?"

"Sure. Lives on the beach in Revere. One of them new condos."

"Address?"

"Richie won't like it, me giving you his address."

"We won't like it if you don't," I said.

"You getting tough with me, buddy, you like to wrestle with Buster here?"

"Buster's overmatched," I said, "unless he's carrying."

"What's that dog you got, a Doberman?"

I grinned. "Not quite," I said. "What's Rich Beaumont's address?"

Marty hesitated.

"You got all the proper licenses here?" I said. "I don't see any on that hound, for instance. You got the proper permits for everything? Asphalt storage? Vehicle's been inspected lately? That Quonset built to code?"

"Hey," Marty said. "Hey. What the fuck?"

"It'll save us a little time if you give us the address," Paul said. "We can find it anyway. Just take a little longer. You save us some time, we'd be very grateful. We won't tell him where we got it."

Marty looked down at the dog, looked at me, and looked back at Paul. "Sure," he said. "You seem like a nice kid." He gave Paul an address on Revere Beach Boulevard. Then he looked at me. "You catch more flies with honey," he said, "than you do with vinegar. You know?"

"I've heard that," I said. "I've not found it to be true."

# Chapter 10

Rich Beaumont wasn't home. He had a condominium on the top floor of a twelve-story concrete building full of condominia that faced the Atlantic, across Revere Beach. From his living room you could probably see the oil tankers easing into Chelsea Creek. Rich wasn't the only one that wasn't home. Still and clean and smelling strongly of recently cured concrete, the place echoed with emptiness.

"They must have built this place as the condo boom was peaking," Paul said.

"Or slightly after," I said.

Pearl skittered down the empty corridor ahead of us, her claws sliding on the new vinyl. At the elevator she pressed her nose at the crack where the closed doors met and snuffled loudly.

"I thought she only pointed birds," Paul said.

The elevator arrived, the doors opened, and we got in. When we got to the lobby there were two guys in it. One of them was a stocky guy with a high black pompadour. He had on a black, thigh-length leather coat and black pegged pants. His black boots were badly worn at the heels and had sharp toes. The other guy was a slugger. Maybe three hundred pounds, his chin sunk into the folds of fat around his neck. Pearl went directly to them, her tail wagging, her ears pricked, her tongue lolling happily. The slugger backed up involuntarily.

"Watch it," he said to the guy with the hairdo. "That's a Doberman, it'll take your hand off."

The guy with the pompadour barely glanced at him. He put one hand down absently and scratched Pearl behind the ear.

"You the guys looking for Richie Beaumont?" he said.

I looked at Paul. "Now you say, 'Who wants to know?'"

"Who wants to know?" Paul said.

"Good," I said. "Now you." I pointed at Pompadour.

"What are you, a comedian?" he said.

"Breaking the kid in," I said. "I'd appreciate if you answered right. Say, *I want to know.*"

The fat slugger was looking nervously at Pearl. She turned her head toward him and he flinched a little, and put his hand inside his *Members Only* windbreaker.

"Listen, asshole. Vinnie Morris is outside and he wants to talk with you. Now."

"We can do this easy or hard," Sluggo said.

"Careful I don't sic my Doberman on you," I said.

"It ain't a fucking Doberman," Pompadour said, "it's a fucking pointer. Tiny don't know shit from dogs."

"Among other things," I said. "We'll talk with Vinnie."

I put Pearl's leash on and we went out through the wide glass doors and down the empty capacious steps. The light had the brightness of nearby ocean in it, and there was traffic moving on the boulevard. In the turnaround in front of the near empty condominium complex a white Lincoln Town Car was parked. When we reached it, the rear window went down, and there was Vinnie. He still had the thick black mustache, but his hair was shorter now. He still dressed like a *GQ* cover boy.

"What the hell is that on the end of the leash?" he said. "You finally get married?"

"That's Pearl," I said. "This is Paul Giacomin. Vinnie Morris. You still with Joe, Vinnie?"

"You been trying to find Richie Beaumont," Vinnie said.

"Actually we've been trying to find Patty Giacomin," I said. "Beaumont is her boyfriend."

"Why you want her?"

"She's my mother," Paul said.

Vinnie nodded. "She sort of took off on you, huh? And didn't tell you where she was going."

"Yes," Paul said. "Or not. I don't know where she is."

"And you're looking for Richie because he's her boyfriend and you figure he'll know?"

Paul nodded.

"You know Richie Beaumont?" Vinnie said.

"No."

Vinnie nodded again and sucked on his upper lip a little.

"And if you knew where he was you wouldn't be here looking for him."

Neither Paul nor I said anything. Vinnie nodded again, to himself. At the end of the nod he jerked his head at the two soldiers. The guy with the pompadour started around the car toward the driver's side. The slugger made a circle around Pearl as he got in his side.

"I'll bet you never had a puppy as a kid," I said to him.

"Tiny never was a kid," Vinnie said. "You gonna be in your office today?"

"Could be," I said. "Any special time?"

Vinnie looked at his watch. "This afternoon, around four."

"I'll be there," I said.

Vinnie reached his hand out the rear window toward Pearl, who promptly licked it. Vinnie looked at her a moment and shook his head. He took the show handkerchief out of the breast pocket of his dark suit and wiped his hands. The car started up and pulled away, and as it went the tinted rear window eased silently up.

"You care to comment on any of this?" Paul said.

"The two enlisted men don't count. Vinnie Morris is Joe Broz's executive officer. Joe Broz is a crook."

"A crook."

"A major league, nationally known, well-connected crook," I said.

"Well, isn't this getting worse and worse," Paul said.

"Maybe," I said.

"Why are they interested in my mother?"

"I think they're interested in her for the same reason we're interested in Beaumont."

"They're looking for him."

I nodded.

"Why did he want you to be in your office later?"

"He wants to talk with me after he's talked with Joe."

"Mind if I am there?" Paul said.

I shrugged. "I hate an astute kid," I said.

"I shouldn't be there."

"No."

"Because he's got stuff to say about my mother he doesn't want me to hear."

"Probably."

"We should have insisted he say what he had to say."

"Vinnie's hard to insist," I said.

I could see the chill of realization dart through him. I knew the feeling.

"Jesus," he said. "What is she into?"

"Maybe nothing," I said. "Maybe just a boyfriend who will turn out to be sleazy."

"It would be consistent," Paul said.

Pearl had discovered a gum wrapper and was busy sniffing it from all possible perspectives.

"Can we go back to your office and call him now?"

"No," I said.

"But I want to know. I don't want to wait."

"This is a business, like most businesses it has its own rules. We let him call me at the office around four."

"That doesn't make any sense," Paul said. "Why do we have to sweat all afternoon out for some goddamned rules of the game?"

"Look," I said. "Vinnie and I have a kind of working relation, despite the fact that we are, you might say, sworn enemies. Vinnie will do what he says he will do, and so will I. He knows it, and I know it, and we can function that way. It is in our best interest to keep it that way."

"This sucks," Paul said.

Pearl picked up the gum wrapper and chewed it experimentally, and found it without savor and spit it out.

"It often does," I said.

# Chapter 11

At four o'clock the fall sun was glinting off the maroon scaffolding of the new building across Berkeley Street. I used to be able to sit in my office and watch the art director in a large ad agency work at her board. But Linda Thomas was gone, and so was the building, and a new skyscraper was going in, which would help to funnel the wind off the river and increase its velocity as it whistled past Police Headquarters two blocks south. I was watching the ironworkers on the scaffolding and thinking about Linda Thomas when Vinnie Morris came in exactly on time, without knocking.

He'd changed his clothes. This morning it had been a black suit with a pale blue chalk stripe. Now it was an olive brown Harris Tweed jacket, with a tattersall shirt and a rust-colored knit tie, with a wide knot. His slacks were charcoal. His kiltie loafers were mahogany cordovan. His wool socks were rust. I knew he was carrying, but his clothes were so well tailored that I couldn't tell where.

"You got the piece in the small of your back?" I said. "So it won't break the line of your jacket?"

"Yeah."

"It will take you an extra second to get it. Vanity will kill you sometime, Vinnie."

"Hasn't so far," Vinnie said. "The kid hire you?"

"No," I said. "It's personal."

"You and the kid or you and the old lady?"

"The kid. He's like family. The old lady doesn't matter to me except as she matters to the kid."

Vinnie was silent. I waited.

"I talked this over with Joe," Vinnie said. I waited some more. Vinnie didn't need prompting.

Vinnie shook his head and almost smiled. "He can't fucking stand you," he said.

"A tribute," I said, "to years of effort."

"But he left it up to me what I tell you, what I don't."

Vinnie was gazing past my shoulder out over Berkeley Street; there was a slice of sky you could see from that angle, to the right of the new building, and up, before the buildings closed you off across the street.

"We got an interest in Richie Beaumont."

I nodded.

A look of nearly concealed distaste showed at the corners of his mouth for a moment. "He's a friend of Joe's kid."

"Joe deserves Gerry," I said.

"I ain't here to talk about it," Vinnie said. "Gerry brought Rich in and gave him some responsibility."

"And . . . ?"

"And it didn't work out."

"And Rich dropped out of sight," I said.

"Yeah."

"Maybe with some property that Joe feels is not rightfully his."

"Yeah."

"And then you heard I was looking for him."

Vinnie was nodding slowly.

"Martinelli called you."

"Somebody called somebody, don't matter who."

"And you thought I might know something useful. So you collected the two galoots and went to meet me at the condo."

"Okay," Vinnie said. "You got everything we know. Now what do you know?"

"I got nowhere near what you know," I said. "What did Beaumont take that belongs to you? Money? Something he can use for blackmail? What were he and Gerry involved in? It had to be bad. Anything Gerry's involved in would make a buzzard puke."

"You figure Richie took off with this Giacomin broad?" Vinnie said.

"Don't know," I said. "She's not around. Thought it was logical to see if she was with her boyfriend."

"He's not around," Vinnie said.

"Un huh," I said. My repartee grew more elegant with every passing year.

"You got a thought where he might be?"

"Un uh," I said.

Vinnie sat back a little and looked at me. He had one knee crossed over the other and he tossed his foot for a moment while he looked.

"You used to be a mouthy bastard," he said finally.

"Brevity is the soul of wit," I said.

"Why's the kid want to find her?" Vinnie said.

I shrugged. "She's not around."

"So what?" Vinnie said. "My old lady's not around either. I ain't looking for her."

"He cares about her," I said.

"There's one difference right there," Vinnie said. "She got something he wants?"

"His past," I said.

Vinnie looked at me some more, and tossed his foot some more.

"His past," Vinnie said.

I nodded.

"What the fuck is that supposed to mean?"

"Kid's about to get married," I said. "She was pretty much a bitch all his childhood and he wants to know her as something other than that before he moves too far on into adulthood."

"You shoulda been a college professor," Vinnie said.

"You say that because you don't know any college professors," I said.

Vinnie shrugged. "Anyway, that may all be true, whatever the fuck it means, but it don't help my case. Or, far as I can see, yours."

"True," I said. "But you asked me."

"Yeah," Vinnie said. "Sure. The point is you're looking and we're looking and I want to be sure we aren't trampling on each other's feet, you know?"

He took a package of Juicy Fruit gum from his coat pocket and offered me some. I shook my head, and he selected a stick, and peeled it open, and folded it into his mouth.

"Me and Joe don't give a fuck about her," he said. "We want him."

"I don't give a fuck about him," I said. "I want her."

Vinnie smiled widely. "Perfect," he said and chewed his gum slowly.

"How about Gerry?" I said.

This time there was no hint of expression in Vinnie's face. "Hey, he's Joe's kid."

"Joe's a creep," I said, "but compared to his kid he's Abraham Lincoln."

Vinnie turned his hands palms up.

"Is Gerry going to get in the way?" I said.

"Joe told him to stay out of this."

"You think he will?"

Again Vinnie's face was without expression. His voice was entirely neutral.

"No."

"Like I said. What about Gerry?"

"Okay," Vinnie said. "We won't fuck around with this either. I been with Joe a long time. You don't like him. That's okay. He don't like you. But Joe says he'll do something, he will. He says he won't, he won't."

"That's true for you, Vinnie. It's not true for Joe."

"We won't argue. I know Joe a long time. But we both know Gerry and we know he's a fucking ignoramus."

"But he's mean and you can't trust him," I said.

"Exactly," Vinnie said. "And Joe loves him. Joe don't see him for the fucking weasel that he is."

"So you're going to have trouble with Gerry too."

"Nothing I can't handle."

"Tricky though," I said.

"Yeah," Vinnie said.

"You want to tell me what kind of mess Gerry is in with Richie Beaumont?"

"No."

The light was beginning to fade outside, and the traffic sounds drifting up from Boylston Street increased as people started going home. The iron-workers had already left the site where Linda Thomas had worked once, across the street, and the maroon skeleton stood empty. Bare ruined choirs where late the sweet birds sang.

"I have no interest in Richie Beaumont," I said. "But I have a lot of interest in Patty Giacomin. I would not want anything bad to happen to her."

"I got no need to hurt the old lady," Vinnie said.

"You let me know if you find her?"

"You let me know if you find him?"

I grinned. "Maybe."

"Yeah," Vinnie said. "Me too."

We were silent some more, listening to the traffic.

"I don't want trouble with you, Spenser."

"Who would," I said.

"You're probably half as good as you think you are," Vinnie said. "But that's pretty good. And you got resources."

"Hawk," I said.

"You and he can be a large pain in the fungones."

"Nice of you to say so, Vinnie. Hawk will be flattered."

"So let's think about helping each other out, maybe, to the extent we can."

"Sure," I said.

"Good," Vinnie said. Then he stood up and headed for the door. At the door he paused, and then turned slowly back.

"Hawk with you in this?" he said.

"Not so far," I said.

"Gerry's got a lot at stake here," Vinnie said. He looked down, and without looking up said, "Kid's a back-shooter."

"He has to be," I said. "Thanks."

Vinnie was still looking at the floor. He nodded.

"Yeah," he said. And went out.

# Chapter 12

Susan insisted on cooking dinner for Paul and me. When she put her mind to it she could cook, but she had a lot of trouble putting her mind to it, and most of the time she had it delivered from The Harvest Express.

"Helmut hears you're doing your own cooking," I said, "he'll have a heart attack. You represent his profit margin."

"I won't abandon him," Susan said. She had every pot she owned, including two she had just bought for the occasion, out on the counter. Pearl was underfoot sampling the residue in a pan already used. Susan gave us each a Catamount Golden Lager to drink and then went back to her preparation.

"Couscous," she said. "With chicken and vegetables."

"Sounds great," Paul said.

Susan cleared a space among the pans and put some chicken breasts down on the marble counter and began to cut them into cubes. Pearl stood on her hind legs, with her front paws on the counter, and pointed the raw chicken from a distance of three inches.

"Doesn't that tend to beat hell out of the knife blade?" Paul said.

Susan looked at him as if he'd espoused pedophilia.

"No," Paul said quickly. "No, of course it doesn't."

I sipped my beer. Susan continued to hack up the chicken. She had her lower lip caught in her teeth, as she always did when she was concentrating. I liked to watch her.

Paul watched me watching her.

"Is Susan the first woman you ever loved?" he said.

"Yes."

"What about this hussy you mentioned the other day in the Ritz bar?" asked Susan.

"She was a girl," I said.

"And you?" Susan said.

"I was sixteen," I said. "And she sat in front of me in French class."

"Sixteen?" Paul said. "You had a childhood?"

Pearl managed to get a scrap of raw chicken. She got down quickly and trotted to the living room where she put it on the rug and rolled on it.

"I can hardly remember her face now," I said. "But she had long hair the color of thyme honey, and she combed it straight back and it was quite long and very smooth. Her name was Dale Carter, and I used to write her little notes of poetry and slip them to her. And she'd read them and smile and I knew she was flattered."

"Poetry?" Susan said.

Pearl returned from the living room licking her muzzle.

"Yeah. Stuff I'd read and would adjust to fit her. *Dale, thy beauty is to me like those Nicean barks of yore . . .* that kind of thing."

Paul and Susan looked at each other. Pearl continued to point the chicken.

"Well," Susan said, "you were sixteen."

"Barely," I said.

"So," she said, "did it develop?"

"We became friends," I said. "We would talk all the time between classes and we would eat lunch together and sit on the high school steps after school, and I just couldn't get enough of her. I just wanted to look at her and hear her voice."

Paul was sitting quietly, watching me. There was no amusement in his face.

"She was slender," I said. "Medium height, from a well-off and intellectual family in the Back Bay. Very, ah, Brahmin. And there was something about her way of carrying herself. She seemed to walk very lightly. She seemed to be very, very interested in what you said, and she would listen with her lips just a little apart and breathe softly through her mouth while she listened."

Susan wet her lower lip and opened her mouth and leaned forward and panted at me.

"A little more subtly than that," I said. "And she would sort of cock her head a little to the side when she talked and look right at me."

Susan tossed her chicken into a bowl and poured some honey over it, and sprinkled on some spices. Pearl's eyes had never left the chicken. When it went in the bowl her eyes didn't leave the bowl.

"Did you go out?" Susan said.

"Not really," I said. "They used to have sort of a canteen dance every afternoon after school in the basement of the Legion hall across the street. Some sort of keep-the-kids-off-the-street campaign which lasted about six months. And we used to go over there sometimes and dance. I never danced very well."

"I'll say," Susan murmured.

"But with her I was Arthur Murray. She seemed to operate a little off the ground, as if her feet were floating; and her hand on my shoulder was very light and yet she felt every movement of the music and seemed to know exactly where I was going before I went. And she always wore perfume. And good clothes. I don't even remember what they were like, but I knew they were good."

"Longish skirt," Susan said. "Thick white socks halfway up the calf, penny loafers, cashmere sweater, maybe a little white collar like Dorothy Collins on *The Hit Parade*."

"Yeah," I said. "That's exactly right."

"Of course it is. It's what I wore. It's what we all wore, those of us who wore 'good clothes.'"

Paul's attention, I noticed peripherally, had intensified. Pearl had moved out of the kitchen, encouraged by a gentle shove from Susan, and now sat on the floor beside my stool, her shoulder leaning in against my leg, her eyes still fixed on the bowl where the chicken was marinating.

"Sure," I said. "Anyway we'd dance sometimes, and dance close, but no kissing, or protestations of affection, except cloaked as badinage. I never took her out in the sense of going to her house, picking her up, taking her to the movies, to a dance, that stuff. We never had a meal together except in the school cafeteria."

"Why didn't you take her out, kiss her, take her to dinner?"

"Shy."

"Shy?" Susan said. "You?"

"When I was a kid," I said. "I was shy with girls."

"And now you're not."

"No," I said, "now I'm not."

Susan was struggling with the seal on a box of prepackaged couscous.

Pearl was leaning more heavily against my leg, her neck stretched as far as she could stretch it, to rest her head on my thigh.

"Well, weren't you weird," Susan said.

"It's great talking to a professional psychotherapist," I said. "They are so sensitive, so aware of human motivation, so careful to avoid stereotypic labeling."

"Yes, weirdo," Susan said. "We take pride in that. What happened to her?"

Paul reached over to pat Pearl's head. Pearl misread it as a food offer and snuffled at his open palm, and finding no food, settled for lapping Paul's hand. Susan got the box of couscous open and dumped it in another bowl and added some water.

"She told me one day that a close friend of mine had asked her to the junior class dance, and should she accept."

"And of course you told her yes, she should accept," Susan said. "Because that was the honorable thing to do."

"I said yes, that she should accept."

"Now that you are sophisticated and no longer shy with girls, I assume you understand that she was asking you if you were going to ask her to the dance, and was telling you that if you were, she would turn your friend down and go with you."

"I now understand that," I said. "But consider if I had been different.

What if I had not panted after the sweet sorrow of renunciation? What if I'd gone to the dance with her, and we'd become lovers and married and lived happily ever after? What would have become of you?"

"I don't know," Susan said. "I guess I'd have wandered the world tragically, wearing my polka dot panties, looking for Mister Right, never knowing that Mister Right had married his high school sweetheart."

Paul put his hands over his ears.

"Polka dot panties?" he said.

Susan smiled. She transferred the refreshed couscous from the bowl to a cook pot. Neither Paul nor I asked her why she had not refreshed it in the cook pot in the first place. She put the cook pot on the stove and put a lid on it and turned the flame on low.

I rested my hand on Pearl's head. "I think," I said, "that even had Dale and I gone to the dance and lived happily ever after, we wouldn't have lived happily ever after. Any more than you were able to stay with your first husband."

"Because we'd have been looking for each other?"

I nodded.

"That's what you think, isn't it?" Susan said. She was no longer teasing me.

"Yes," I said. "That's what I think. I think your marriage broke up because you weren't married to me. I think neither one of us could be happy with anyone else because we would always be looking for each other, without even knowing it, without knowing who each other was or even knowing there was an each other."

"Do you think that's true of love in general?"

"No," I said. "I only believe that about us."

"Isn't that kind of exclusionary?" Paul said.

"Yes," I said. "Embarrassingly so."

The room was silent now, not the light and airy silence of contentment, but the weighty silence of intensity.

Paul was choosing his words very carefully. It took him a little time.

"But you're not saying I couldn't feel that way?"

"No," I said. "I'm not."

Paul nodded. I could see him thinking some more.

"Do you feel that way?" I said.

"I don't know," he said. "And I feel like I ought to, because you do."

"No need to be like me," I said.

"Who else, then?" he said. "Who would I be like? My father? Who did I learn to be me from?"

"You're right," I said. "I was glib. But you know as well as I do that you can't spend your life feeling as I do, and thinking what I think. You don't now."

"The way you love her makes me feel inadequate," Paul said. "I don't think I can love anyone like that."

Susan was chopping fresh mint on the marble countertop.

"One love at a time," she said.

"Which means what?" Paul said. "My mother?"

Susan smiled her Freudian smile. "We shrinks always imply more than we say."

"There's nothing necessarily bizarre in wanting to find my mother."

"Of course not, and when you do it will help clarify things, maybe."

"Maybe," Paul said.

I sipped a little more of my Catamount Gold and thought about Dale Carter, whom I hadn't seen in so long. It wasn't the first time I'd thought about her. I looked at Susan. She smiled at me, a wholly non-Freudian smile.

"We'd have found each other," she said.

"In fact," I said, "we did it twice."

# Chapter 13

Hawk, wearing white satin sweatpants and no shirt, was hanging upside down in gravity boots in the Harbor Health Club, doing sit-ups. He curled his body up parallel with the floor and eased it back vertical without any apparent effort. The abdominus rictus tightened and relaxed under his shiny black skin. He had his hands clasped loosely behind his head, and the skin over his biceps seemed too tight.

Around him men and women in bright spandex were working out with varying success. All of them and two of the three trainers that Henry Cimoli employed were glancing covertly at Hawk. His upper body and his shaved head were shiny with sweat. But his breath was easy and there was no other indication that what he was doing might be hard.

I said, "You stuck on that apparatus, boy?"

Hawk grinned upside down and did another sit-up.

"Damn," he said. "Can't seem to reach my feet."

He put out his hand upside down and I gave him an understated low five.

"When you get through struggling with that thing," I said, "I'll buy you breakfast."

"Sure," Hawk said.

We worked out for maybe an hour and a half, and took a little steam afterwards. Then, showered and dressed and fragrant with the cheap after-shave that Henry put out in the men's locker room, we strolled out across Atlantic Avenue toward Quincy Market. It was still early in the day, only 9:30, and the autumn sun was mild as it slanted down at us, only a few degrees up over the harbor, and made our shadows long and angular ahead of us.

"Market's nice this time of day," Hawk said.

"Yeah," I said. "Hasn't turned into a five-acre dating bar yet."

"Get a chance to meet a lot of interesting people from Des Moines," Hawk said. "After lunch."

"And some dandy teenagers in from the subs," I said.

We sat at the counter in the nearly quiet central market building. I had some blueberry pancakes. Hawk had four scrambled eggs and toast. We each ordered coffee.

"I thought you quit coffee," Hawk said.

"I changed my mind," I said.

"Couldn't do it, huh?"

"Decided not to," I said and put a spoonful of sugar in and stirred and drank some carefully. Life began again. Behind us along the central aisle the food stalls prepared for the day. One would never starve to death in Quincy Market. Behind us was a shop selling roast goose sandwiches. To our right was an oyster bar. A few tourists strolled through early, wearing cameras, and new Red Sox hats made of plastic mesh that fit badly. Mixed in was an occasional secretary on coffee break, and now and then, resplendently garbed, and moving with great alacrity, were young brokers from the financial district picking up a special blend coffee for the big meeting.

"You have any information on what Gerry Broz is doing these days?" I said.

"No," Hawk said. "You?"

"No, but it involves a guy named Rich Beaumont, who is Patty Giacomin's current squeeze."

"Anything Gerry involved in is not a good thing."

"This is true," I said. "She's missing. Paul wants to find her."

"How 'bout Beaumont?"

"Missing too," I said.

"Un huh."

"Exactly," I said. "You tribal types are so wise."

"We close to nature," Hawk said. The counterman came by and refilled our coffee cups. I managed to stay calm.

"You talk to Vinnie?" Hawk said.

"He talked to me. Wants to be sure we don't get in each other's way."

"He tell you what Gerry doing?"

"No."

"Vinnie can't stand him any more than you or me."

"I know," I said. "But he's Joe's kid."

Hawk drank some coffee. Like everything else he did, it seemed easier for him. The coffee was not too hot. He seemed to drink it the way it had been drawn up, perfectly, without any effort. I'd seen him kill people the same way.

"Joe's damn near as bad as the kid," Hawk said. "Vinnie's what keeps the outfit together."

"Vinnie'd be better off without him," I said.

"Vinnie don't think so," Hawk said.

"I know."

"He been with Joe a long time. Since he been a kid."

"Yeah."

A woman with too much blonde hair went past us wearing stretch jeans and very high heels that caused her hips to sway when she walked. Hawk and I watched her all the way down the length of the market until she turned aside in the rotunda and we lost her.

"Stretch fabric is a good thing," I said.

"We going to talk with Gerry?" Hawk said.

"I thought we might," I said.

Hawk nodded and pushed the last of his scrambled eggs onto his fork with the last of his toast. He put the eggs very delicately into his mouth and followed with the toast. He chewed carefully and swallowed and picked up his cup and drank some coffee. He put the cup down, picked up his napkin, and patted his lips.

"Don't sound like you got anybody else to talk to," he said.

"Nope."

"Paul worried about her?"

"Yes."

He nodded. "Want me to see if I can arrange it?" he said.

I drank more of my second cup. "Soon as I finish my coffee," I said.

# Chapter 14

Paul and I went back to see Martinelli. He wasn't there and the shop was closed. We went back to see his sister Caitlin. She wasn't there. And she wasn't there the next day when we called, nor that evening, nor the next morning. And neither was Martinelli. We went back to the real estate women at *Chez Vous*. They had nothing to add. They didn't know anyone else who would have anything to add. They seemed to know less than when I'd spoken to them first. We talked with three other people we'd tracked down through the answering machine. They didn't know who Rich Beaumont was. They didn't know where Patty might be. At least two sort of hinted that they also didn't care. We called every travel agent in the Yellow Pages and every major airline without success. There was no business listing for Rich Beaumont in the Yellow Pages. The Secretary of State's office had no listing of any company with that name in its title. Nobody at either North or South Station could help us. Nobody at either bus terminal could help us. I got Beaumont's registration number, make, and model from the Registry. There was no car that fit the plate or description parked in the garage of the Revere Beach condo or anywhere around. None had been towed by either Boston or MDC police.

"It looks like they disappeared on purpose," Paul said.

We were walking Pearl along the river, past the lagoon, west of the Hatch Shell. Some ducks were cruising the lagoon, and when Pearl spotted them she got lower and longer and sucked in her stomach and froze in a quivering point. Paul and I stopped and let her point for a moment.

"Yeah, but it doesn't have to mean that. They could simply have gotten in his car and driven off in full innocence. We'd have come up with same zero."

Pearl edged a step closer to the ducks. Her complete self was invested in them. I picked up a small rock and tossed it at them. They rose from the water and swept out toward the river. I said, "Bang," and Pearl broke the point and glanced at me for a moment and then forgot about it and proceeded on, her nose close to the ground, tracking the elusive candy wrapper.

"What about the fact that we can't find either of the two people who had anything useful to tell us?" Paul said.

"Not encouraging," I said.

"Do you think anything happened to them?"

"Probably not," I said. "Probably they were told to go away for a while and they did."

"Joe Broz?"

I shrugged.

"The son, whatsisname?"

"Gerry," I said. "No way to know yet."

"So now what do we do?" Paul said. "A tearful plea on the noon news?"

"Let's hold off a little on that," I said. "Let's go out to Lexington and collect your mother's mail."

"Can you do that?"

"You can," I said. "Just tell them your mother wanted you to pick it up for her. If some postal clerk is really zealous you can prove you're her son."

We finished Pearl's walk, in which she pointed a flock of pigeons, and tracked down the wrapper to a Zagnut Bar, and went back to my place and loaded her into the car and headed out to Lexington.

The postal clerk was the same woman with the teased pink hair that I'd talked with before, though she didn't seem to remember me.

"You talk to your mother's friend?" she said when Paul presented himself.

"No," he said.

"Oh. I figured when we couldn't give him the mail he got hold of you."

"No, my mother didn't mention it," Paul said.

"I hate regulations too," the clerk said. "But they're there. You can't just hand the mail out to anyone who asks."

"Sure," Paul said. "It's a good rule."

"Yeah." She shrugged. "Well, some people get pretty mean about it, but I don't make the rules, you know?"

"I know, you did the right thing."

"But since you're her son, no problem."

Paul nodded encouragingly.

"We should tell him we've got the mail," I said to Paul.

He nodded. I looked at the clerk.

"You wouldn't know who he was, would you?"

"Gee, I have no idea," she said. "Sort of a short guy, lot of hair, combed up in front, like Elvis. Only he's real dark, like a dago or a Frenchman."

I looked at Paul. "Sounds like Uncle Nick," I said.

"Yeah, Nicky's really excitable."

"Well, I don't care if he's your uncle or not. He was mean as hell. He had some ID, he should have shown it to me."

"He's not really my uncle," Paul said. "Just an old friend of my mother's. We call him Uncle Nick."

"Well, he's a mean one," the clerk said.

There were four or five people forming in line behind us at the single window. One of them said something about "social hour" to his line mate. The clerk ignored them.

"We don't get paid enough to take abuse, you know what I'm saying."

"I hear you," Paul said with a straight face.

Behind us the line was shuffling and clearing its various throats. Paul glanced at his watch.

"Wow," he said. "It's late. I didn't realize. We better stop wasting this lady's time."

"Hey," the clerk said. "No problem. We're here every day, serving the public. You're not wasting my time."

Someone in the line said something about "*my* time."

"Well, thanks," Paul said. "I really appreciate it. We better just grab the mail and get rolling." He looked at his watch again and shook his head, *Where does the time go?* The clerk nodded understandingly and strolled slowly back of the partition and was gone maybe two minutes and returned with a bundle of mail held together by large rubber bands. She handed it to Paul. He smiled. I smiled. The clerk smiled. The rest of the line shuffled a little more and shifted its feet. We took the mail and left.

Pearl was sitting in the driver's seat, as she always was when left alone. She insinuated herself into the backseat the minute she saw us coming, and was in perfect position to lap me behind the ear when I got in the car.

"Brilliant," I said to Paul. "Brilliantly charming, and no hint of eagerness. Masterful."

"I am, after all, a performer," Paul said. "I assume the guy that came asking was that short one we saw in Revere, the one with the huge fat pal, the ones with Vinnie Morris."

"I assume," I said. "Means Vinnie is getting nowhere too."

Paul had the mail in his lap. He handed it to me.

"I don't feel right reading her mail," he said. "What if there's letters there with stuff in them I don't want to see?"

"Love letters?"

"Yeah, explicit stuff. You know? *'I'm still thinking about when I bleeped your bleep.'* You want to read stuff like that about your mother?"

"Remember," I said, "I never had one."

"Yes, I forget that sometimes."

We were quiet for a while.

"Mothers are never only mothers," I said.

"I know," Paul said. "Christ, do I know. I've had ten years of psychotherapy. I know shit like that better than I want to. I still don't want to read about my mother boinking some jerk."

I nodded.

"I don't know why I should worry about *reading* it," Paul said. "She's probably been *doing* it since puberty."

I nodded again. I always thought people had the right to boink who they wanted, even a jerk, if they needed to. But that probably wasn't really Paul's issue and shutting up never seemed to do much harm.

"I'll read the mail," I said.

Most of it could be dispensed with unread: catalogues, magazines, direct mail advertising. Paul took the batch and walked across the parking lot and dumped it in a trash barrel. The rest were bills, no boinking. The bills produced nothing much, except finally, the very last entry on her American Express bill, a clothing store in Lenox. I turned to the individual receipts and located it. Tailored Lady, Lenox, Massachusetts, Lingerie. It was dated after her mail had been put on hold. I handed it to Paul.

"Know anything about this?"

"No," he said. "All I know about Lenox is the Berkshires, Tangle-wood. I don't think I've ever been there."

"That your mother's signature?" I said.

"Looks like her writing. I rarely see her signature. When I got money it was usually a check from my father. But it looks like her writing."

"So," I said. "She was probably in Lenox ten days ago."

"Should we go out there?"

"Yes," I said. "We should. But first Hawk and I want to speak with Gerry Broz."

"About my mother?"

"Yeah."

"Both of you?"

"It's always nice to have backup when you talk with Gerry."

"For god's sake what is she mixed up in when even you need backup to talk to people about her?"

"Doesn't need to be awful," I said. "She probably doesn't even know Gerry."

"Well, it sounds awful and everything we learn about it makes it sound worse."

"We'll find out," I said. "In a while we'll know whatever there is to know."

"I'm getting scared," Paul said. "Scared for her."

"Sure you are," I said. "I would if I were you."

"I don't like being scared."

"Nobody does," I said.

"But everybody is," Paul said.

"At one time or another," I said.

"You?"

"Sure."

"Hawk?"

I paused. "I don't know," I said. "You never can be sure with Hawk."

# Chapter 15

Pearl looked painfully resentful as Susan and I left her. Susan had left the television tuned to CNN.

"She likes to watch Catherine Crier," Susan said.

"Me too."

"More than Diane Sawyer?"

"Well, of course not," I said.

Susan had recently acquired one of those turbo-charged Japanese sports cars, which she drove like a New York cabbie, flooring it between stoplights and talking trash to other motorists. We made the fifteen-minute drive from Susan's place to Icarus Restaurant in about seven minutes. And gave the car to the valet kid and went in.

Icarus is very voguish and demure and the sight of Hawk waiting for us at a table was enough to cheer me for the evening. He looked like a moose at a gazelle convention. He stood when he saw Susan and she kissed him. There was a bottle of Krug in an ice bucket beside the table. When we sat, Hawk took it from the ice, wiped it with the towel, and poured champagne into Susan's glass, then mine.

Susan raised her glass and said, "To us." We clinked and drank. The corners of Susan's eyes were crinkled with amusement.

"I can't tell you," she said, "how out of place you two look in here."

"Not our fault we big," Hawk said.

"Of course not," Susan said. "Have you seen pictures of Pearl?"

"Not yet," Hawk said.

Susan rummaged in her purse. Which was quite tricky, since the purse wasn't much bigger than a postcard. She was wearing a white suit with gold braid and epaulets, and she seemed, as she always did, to occupy the center of the room. Everything else seemed to group around her and be ordered by her, like a jar in Tennessee. When you were with Susan you could remain anonymous. No one would notice you.

Even Hawk was less apparent when he was with Susan.

Tonight he was all in black. Suit, shirt, tie. I was even more daring in a blue blazer, tan slacks, a white oxford button-down shirt, and a maroon tie with tiny white dots in it.

"You the world's oldest preppie," Hawk said to me. "You got on wing-tipped cordovans?"

"Like hell," I said and stuck my foot out so he could check the loafers. "Note the stunning little kiltie, as well as the hint of a tassel."

"Probably got an argyle gun," Hawk said.

"In a chino holster," I said. "With a little belt in the back."

Susan found her folder of pictures of Pearl and put them on the table in front of Hawk. He looked at them silently as Susan provided commentary.

"There she is her first day with us," Susan said. "And there she is with her ball. There she is on the bed with himself."

Hawk looked at me. "A dog?" he said.

I shrugged. "I like dogs," I said.

Hawk nodded. "Sure you do. Known that long as I've known you."

We were silent for a moment, looking at the menu. The waiter appeared. We ordered. The waiter departed.

"How long have you known him?" Susan said to Hawk.

Hawk grinned. "You remember?" he said to me.

"Shouldn't smile like that," I said. "Spoils the monochromatic look."

"Whites of my eyes a problem there too," Hawk said.

"*Do* you remember?" Susan said to me.

"Sure. We were fighting a prelim at the Arena."

"We on the card so early, the ushers still dusting off the seats," Hawk said.

"The Arena? That's not the Garden."

"No, the Boston Arena. These days it's a hockey rink. All cleaned up and presentable. Northeastern University owns it now."

"Did you fight each other in this preliminary bout?" Susan said.

"Yeah," I said.

"Well?" Susan said.

"Well what?" I said.

"Hawk?" Susan said.

Hawk looked at her and smiled and raised his eyebrows.

"What?" he said.

"Who won?" Susan said.

"I did," we both said simultaneously.

Susan stared at us for a moment and then smiled. "Of course you did," she said.

"Mostly white fighters in Boston in those days," Hawk said.

"Hawk was the great black hope," I said.

"Night me and Spenser fought, lotta people didn't like a black fighter on the card."

The first course arrived. The waiter put it down and then refreshed our champagne glasses.

"After, ah, one of us won the fight," Hawk said, "I got cleaned up and dressed and I'm coming out of the Arena and I run into a group of young white guys. They drunk. Lot of people go to the fights at the Arena are drunk. And one of them spoke loudly, and unkindly of . . . I believe the phrase was *jigaboos*. At which I took some offense."

"How many were there?" Susan said.

"Enough so they brave," Hawk said. "Six, maybe, eight. Anyway, ah expressed my resentment to the guy who had called me a jigaboo, and it caused him to spit out some of his front teeth. And so his friends jump in. Normally me against eight drunks is probably about even. But I'm a little winded from fighting your friend, and winning—"

"Losing," I said.

"And I'm beginning to give a little ground when Spenser comes out and sees the fight and jumps in on my side and their side calls him a nigger lover and Spenser throw him through a window."

"Open?" Susan said.

"No."

Susan winced.

"Who won?" Susan said. I knew she knew the answer, but she was kind enough to feed it to us.

"We did," Hawk and I said simultaneously.

Susan laughed. "I knew you would," she said. "Did you ever fight each other again?"

"No," I said.

The appetizers went away and the entree came, pork tenderloin with sour cherry sauce, and polenta. I was so pleased with it that I never even noticed what Hawk and Susan were eating.

"But you stayed in touch," Susan said.

"In a manner of speaking, Lollypop," Hawk said.

"We'd go shopping together," I said. "Take in some matinees, have a sundae at Bailey's, after."

"I feel that I am being made sport of," Susan said, "by a pair of sexist oinkers."

"You got that right," Hawk said.

"How did you stay in touch, Porkies?"

"Our work tended to bring us in contact," Hawk said. "First when we fighting, we'd be on the same card sometime, changing in the same back room in some gym."

"And later?" Susan said.

"Our professional lives continued to intersect," I said. "Still do."

"We both involved in the matter of, ah, crime," Hawk said.

"From varying perspectives," I said.

"You are each other's best friend," Susan said. "In some genuine sense you love each other. But you never show it, never speak of it. One would never know."

"You know," Hawk said.

"Only because I know you so well."

"We know," Hawk said.

"And nobody else much matters," Susan said.

Hawk smiled and didn't say anything. Susan looked at him then at me.

"Peas in a pod," she said.


# Chapter 16

I left Pearl with Susan in the morning when Hawk picked me up in his forest green Jaguar sedan.

"She can't go with you?" Susan said.

"Hawk hates dog drool on the leather seats," I said.

"You don't care about that," Susan said. "And neither does Hawk. You think it might be dangerous going to see Gerry Broz and you don't want her to get hurt, or you to get hurt and her to be left alone." Susan was wearing a kimono with vertical black and white stripes, and she hadn't put her makeup on yet. Her face was shiny and vulnerable in its morning innocence.

"Gerry's a weird dude," I said.

She nodded and held up her face and I kissed her, and patted Pearl and went on to Hawk.

"Gonna come by someday, see a tricycle on the porch," Hawk said as he slid the Jag away from the curb in front of Susan's house.

"Maybe Paul will have a kid," I said.

"Get you one of those bumper stickers say ASK ME ABOUT MY GRAND-CHILD," Hawk said.

"There's a Dunkin' Donuts in Union Square, Somerville," I said. "You could get me coffee instead."

Which we did, and drank it as we drove on 93 and 128 to Beverly. We were meeting Gerry in an Italian restaurant called Rocco's Grotto on Rantoul Street. The front of Rocco's was done in fake fieldstone. A big neon sign in the window advertised PIZZA, PASTA, & MORE. There was a bicycle repair shop next door and across the street a billiard parlor. Hawk and I got out of the car and went to the front door. There was a stock sign in the window that said CLOSED on it. I tried the door. It opened and we went in. There were booths down the left-hand wall, a bar down the right, and tables in the space between. Most of the tables had chairs upside down on them. Past the end of the bar was a swinging door to the kitchen, with a pass-through window to the left of it. Beyond that was a short corridor to the rest rooms. Behind the bar was a guy with straggly blond hair and a skinny neck. He was brewing coffee. He looked up when we came in.

"You here for Gerry?" he said.

I said yes.

He jerked his head toward a booth.

"He'll be along," he said.

He had probably been a thin guy once, but as time passed he had gotten sort of plump until the only remnant of his former self was his thin neck.

Hawk ignored the head gesture toward a booth and took the barstool nearest the kitchen. He moved it away from the kitchen door and sat on it, leaning against the back wall. I sat at the other end, near the door. No sense bunching up. The guy with the skinny neck shrugged and looked at his coffeemaker. The water had nearly stopped dripping through the filter. He leaned his hips against the inside of the bar and crossed his arms and studied it as it dripped more and more occasionally. Finally it stopped altogether. The round glass pot was full.

The guy with the skinny neck got a round bar tray from under the bar and put a coffee mug on it, a small cardboard carton of heavy cream, and a bowl filled with paper packets of Equal. He put a teaspoon on the tray beside the coffee mug. Then he put the tray up on the bar top and went into the kitchen. He came back in maybe two minutes with a plate of Italian pastries. I saw raisin cake, biscotti, hazelnut cake, and cannoli. He put the plate on the tray and then he leaned back against the bar again and folded his arms again, and looked at nothing.

Which was what I was looking at.

Then the door opened and a big guy came in wearing a tan Ultrasuede thigh-length coat. He had very big hands, and even though everything seemed to fit him fine, his hands were so big that it made him look like his sleeves were too short.

He looked first at Hawk in the back, and then at me. And then moved on into the restaurant leaving the door ajar and leaned on the wall near Hawk.

Gerry Broz came in next, and after him two more bodyguards. One wore a tan corduroy sport coat over a dark brown sport shirt. The sport coat had brown leather elbow patches but fit him so badly that I could see the bulge on his right hip where he wore a gun. The other bodyguard wore a dark blue three-piece suit. He had on a blue-and-red figured tie with a very wide knot, and a trench coat worn like a cape over his shoulders. As he came through the front door, he reached back with his left hand and pulled it shut. Then he produced a double-barreled shotgun with the barrels sawed off and the stock modified, and held that, muzzle down, in his right hand.

"That it for backup?" I said to Gerry. "Nobody on the roof?"

"Hey, asshole, you asked for this meet," Gerry said.

"One of your many good qualities, Gerry," I said. "You are a master of the clever riposte."

The tall guy with the two big hands said from the back, "Why don't you just shut your fucking mouth."

"Barbarians," I said to Hawk. "We have fallen among barbarians." I looked at the guy behind the bar. "And this seemed like such a nice place too," I said.

He ignored me. He picked up the tray he'd prepared and went over to the booth along the left wall, near the door, where Gerry had slid in by himself. It was getting harder and harder for Gerry to slide into booths. Every time I saw him he seemed to have gained another ten. He wasn't a big guy, and he obviously didn't work out, so that every pound he packed on looked like twice that and very flabby. Moreover his wardrobe hadn't caught up to his poundage, so that everything seemed tight and you had the sense that he was very uncomfortable.

The bartender poured him some coffee, and left the pot. Gerry poured some heavy cream in, added four packets of Equal, and stirred slowly while he ate a biscotto. His hair was cut long in the back and short on top, where it was spiked. He had a camel's hair topcoat on, which he wore open with the belt hanging loose. He wasn't too much older than Paul and already there were small red veins showing on his cheeks. He swallowed the last of his first biscotto, and drank some coffee, and put the mug down.

"Okay, asshole," he said. "Hawk told Lucky you wanted to ask me something." He nodded his head toward the guy with the sawed-off so I should know which one was Lucky.

"What are you and Rich Beaumont doing?" I said.

Nobody said anything. Gerry gazed at me without expression for a long time. The bartender cleared his throat once, softly, turning his head away and covering his mouth as if he were in church.

Finally Gerry said, "Who?"

"Rich Beaumont," I said. "You and he are involved in some kind of scam which has gone sour and now you and everybody else is looking for Rich. I want to know what the scam was."

Gerry looked at me stonily some more. It was supposed to make the marrow congeal in my bones. Then he ate a cannoli, drank some more coffee, looked around the room with what passed in Gerry's life for a big grin.

"Any you guys know Rich Beaumont?" He made a point of mispronouncing it, putting the emphasis on the first syllable.

"You, Lucky?"

The guy with the shotgun shook his head.

"Maishe?"

Maishe was the guy with the oversized hands. "Never heard of him," he said.

"Rock?"

The bartender shook his head.

"Anthony?"

"Never heard of no Rich Beaumont." The guy in the corduroy coat mispronounced Beaumont just as his boss had.

"You got any other questions, asshole?"

"Yeah," I said. "How many more times you think you can screw up like this before your father won't let you play anymore?"

The silence in the restaurant gathered like a fog. Gerry's face got red. His breath rasped. He leaned suddenly forward over the table. An elbow knocked over his mug and coffee puddled on the tabletop.

"You cocksucker," he said. "You can't talk that way to me."

"Why not?" I said. "You think these four guys are enough?"

"Nobody, nobody . . ." He seemed to run out of air and stopped and took in a deep breath.

"Lucky," he said.

The guy with the shotgun half turned toward me and suddenly there was a gun in Hawk's hand. No one had seen any movement, but there it was. Everyone froze for a moment on the big .44, with the long barrel and the hammer thumbed back.

"Gerry goes first," Hawk said.

The focus turned back to me. I had managed to get the Browning out and cocked. Lucky had the shotgun leveled at me. Maishe had a hand under his coat and Anthony stood motionless with his hand half raised toward a shoulder holster. Behind the bar Rocco's hands were out of sight. I kept the gun on Lucky. Nobody moved. It was very close quarters and if the balloon went up it was going to be a mess. I could hear Gerry's breath laboring in and out. The kitchen door swung open and Vinnie Morris walked into the dining room.

"What the fuck?" he said.

Nobody moved. Vinnie walked over to Lucky and casually put a hand on the shotgun and pushed the barrels down. Then he turned toward the booth where Gerry was sitting.

"What the fuck, Gerry?" he said. He gestured with one hand toward Maishe, and with the other toward Anthony. They let their hands drop. I put the Browning back under my arm. Hawk's gun disappeared.

"What are you doing here?" Gerry said finally.

"Joe asked me to hang around, keep an eye on things."

"He knew about this meeting?"

"Sure."

Gerry looked at the guy behind the bar.

"Rocco?" he said.

Rocco shrugged. "Joe's bar," he said.

"You fucking snitch," Gerry said.

"I work for Joe," Rocco said. "No need to give me a batch of shit about it."

"I'll give you any batch of shit I want to, you squealing cocksucker."

"Vinnie?" Rocco said.

Vinnie nodded. To Gerry he said, "Shhh."

"So my father knew. So what?" Gerry said. "What the fuck he have to send you for? He thinks I can't handle this?"

"He don't want you getting hurt," Vinnie said. "He says, Vinnie, go down, stay out of the way. Just keep an eye on things. Make sure nothing goes bad."

"Hurt? Hurt, I'm fucking thirty-one, Vinnie. I'm a fucking grown man."

"Joe wanted to be sure," Vinnie said.

Gerry's voice was shaking. "Stay the fuck away from me, Vinnie. You and him both, stay the fuck out of my life, you unnerstand? I don't need you. I was handling this, for crissake. I don't need you fucking wet-nursing me. I can handle it. I can handle any fucking thing. Stay the fuck away from me . . ."

His voice broke. He got up suddenly and pushed past Vinnie and went out the front door. Vinnie watched him go. He shook his head slowly. Then he turned and in a gesture that included all three bodyguards he jerked his head at the door. They went out after Gerry. Rocco stayed behind the bar.

Hawk remained motionless and silent at the back of the room.

Vinnie walked over and sat on a barstool next to me.

"You want some coffee?" he said to me.

"Sure," I said.

"Hawk?"

"Un huh."

"Rocco, give us three coffees," Vinnie said.

Rocco poured and served, bringing a mug back to Hawk, who accepted it silently. When he got through, Vinnie said, "Leave the pot, Rock, and go on out in the kitchen for a while."

Rocco put the coffeepot on the bar where Vinnie could reach it and went through the swinging doors. Vinnie leaned his elbows back on the bar.

"I thought we was going to cooperate on this thing," Vinnie said.

"I don't remember anything about not asking Gerry questions."

"Kid's a loose cannon, Spenser. You know that. Look what almost happened."

"That's why I badgered him," I said. "I know he's excitable, I thought something might pop out."

"Two barrels full of size-four shot were about to pop out in your face," Vinnie said.

"If he got the shot off," I said.

"Sure, sure," Vinnie said. "I know you're good." He nodded toward Hawk. "And I know he's good. But scattering fucking protoplasm around Rocco's isn't going to do anything for any of us."

I shrugged. "I probably wouldn't push him so hard if I had it to do over," I said.

Vinnie nodded. "You got to stay away from Gerry," he said. "Joe insists on it."

"Can't promise anything, Vinnie. Except that I won't harass him for fun."

"I insist too," Vinnie said.

"I know."

"This is about you too, Hawk," Vinnie said.

"I sort of guessed that, Vinnie."

"We still got some room here," Vinnie said. "But not very much. Joe's going to want to talk with you."

"Sure," I said. "How about Monday morning?"

"Come to the office about ten. Joe don't get in as early as he used to."

"Fine," I said and put the coffee cup down on the bar.

"I'll walk out with you," Vinnie said. "You never know about Gerry."

# Chapter 17

Lenox is two hours west from Boston on the Mass Pike. Paul and I rode out in the afternoon with Pearl leaning against the backseat, staring out the side window, alert as always for any sign of the elusive Burger King.

It doesn't take long on the Mass Pike to get away from the city and into what Massachusetts probably looked like in Squanto's day. Subtract a few houses here and there that back up to the turnpike west of Framingham, cancel out an occasional Roy Rogers or food & fuel stops, and the landscape is mostly low hills and woods, punctuated often enough by bodies of water that looked very brisk under the blue autumn sky. The hilliness allowed for some variety to the trip, allowing as it did for mild scenic vistas as the highway crested one low rise and you could see it curving gently up another hill a mile and a half ahead. It wasn't Arcadia, but it wasn't the New Jersey Turnpike either.

"She probably never should have had a kid," Paul said to me near Grafton.

"Ever?" I said.

He shrugged. "Who knows ever?" he said. "But she wasn't ready for one when I was born."

"How old was she?"

"Twenty. She got pregnant when she was nineteen and she married my father to have me. She was going to enter her junior year in college."

"But she didn't," I said. "Because she had to stay home with the baby."

"Yeah. She went down to Furman, my father played football there."

"I know," I said.

"And they lived in—what did they call them then? The on-campus housing?"

"Probably still called them Vets Apartments then," I said.

"Yes," Paul said. "That's right. When I was a little kid I used to think it meant vet as in veterinarian, and I couldn't figure out why they called it that."

In the backseat Pearl made a loud sigh and turned around once and resettled at the opposite window. I put my hand back and she gave it a lick.

"I was always afraid she'd leave me," Paul said. "As long ago as I can remember, I was afraid she'd just run away and leave me and I'd have to go to the home for little wanderers."

"Your father?" I said.

"He barely counts," Paul said. "It's like he wasn't there. My childhood memories are almost empty of him."

"What are they full of?" I said.

There wasn't much travel midday, midweek, going west. I was doing seventy in the right-hand lane on the theory that cops always look for speeders in the passing lane. A trucker going eastbound flashed his head-lights at me and I slowed as I crested the next hill. There was a two-tone blue state police cruiser parked sideways on the median strip with a radar gun. I cruised serenely past him at about fifty-seven.

"Fear," Paul said. "Fear of being left. I was thin and whiny and had colds all the time and I used to cling to my mother like a cold sore. She couldn't stand it. She'd try to get me away from her so she could breathe and of course the more she tried the more I clung."

I nodded. I could hear the therapist's voice in Paul's, and behind the calm exposition of past events, the pain and lingering fear that engendered the pain. I wished Susan had come with us.

"Hard on both of you," I said.

"Sometimes she would actually hide under the bed," Paul said. "But I'd find her. She could run, but she couldn't hide."

"Too bad your father wasn't around," I said. "Be easier if you'd had more than one person bringing you up."

"He couldn't stand either one of us," Paul said. "Maybe at first he could, or did, or thought he ought to. I think my mother and he actually loved each other, whatever the hell that quite means. But they shouldn't have got married. They just . . ." Paul seemed wordless. He shook his head, put his hands up in a gesture of bafflement. "They just shouldn't have gotten married . . ." He stared straight ahead for a moment. Pearl leaned forward and snuffled at the back of his neck, and he put his hand up absently to pat her muzzle. "Or had me," he said.

"But they did," I said.

"But they did."

# Chapter 18

The Tailored Lady was a boutique off Church Street in downtown Lenox. It was in a sort of shopping center, where private houses had been converted to stores in which you could buy turquoise jewelry and Icelandic sweaters. The woman who ran it wore a blue blazer over a green turtleneck sweater.

She was very polite, but she couldn't tell us anything at all.

"I'm sorry," she said, "that I can't be more helpful. I could find my copy of the American Express receipt, but it would merely duplicate what you have."

"You don't remember if she was with anyone?" Paul said.

She smiled and shook her head. Matching the sweater and blazer was a Black Watch plaid skirt. Her blonde hair was caught back and tied with a little Black Watch ribbon.

"There are so many tourists," she said. "It's the start of the foliage season, and"—she smiled as if she were saying something daring—"the fall getaway time. A lot of women come in for lingerie." She paused as if weighing the propriety of what she said. "Usually there are men with them." She glanced demurely down at her Cobbie Cuddlers shoes.

"Where do they usually stay?" I said.

"Oh, there are so many places. It depends on price, I should think. There's a tourist information booth across the way that could probably give you a list."

She was looking straight at me and I realized she was appraising me. I grinned at her. The grin I used before Susan, the one where women slipped their house keys in my coat pocket as soon as I'd used it. I saw something show through for a moment in her face, passing over it the way the shadow of a cloud moves quickly across a field. And I knew that the Talbot's outfit was a disguise. And I saw the assertive body suddenly, inside the disguise. Then the look was gone again. But I knew I'd seen it, and she knew I'd seen it. It was my move. I smiled again, a modulated version of the killer grin, and said, "Thanks very much. Sorry to bother you."

And she said, "You're welcome." She was wearing an ornate wedding band with diamond chips set in it. But I knew that would not have been an issue. As Paul and I turned and went out of the store toward the tourist information center, I looked back once at the now apparent body that seemed so much realer than its inessential camouflage, and took a deep breath. *The price of monogamy.*

Across the way, a plump woman in a flowered purple dress gave us a printed list of area hotels and bed and breakfast accommodations. There were eighty-seven of them.

"Of course we only cover the immediate Lenox area," she said. "People come from all over the Berkshires and eastern New York State to shop. So your friends might very well be staying in Pittsfield or Williamstown or Albany, New York, even Saratoga."

"How encouraging," I said.

We took the listing, got a road map out of the car, and took both to a restaurant specializing in cheesecake. Paul had a chicken salad on light rye. I ordered a turkey on whole wheat with mustard. And another one plain to go. He had a Coke. I abandoned any hint of prudence and had coffee.

Neither of us had cheesecake.

"How we going to do this?" Paul said.

I drank some coffee. Not as much fun as the woman in the preppie disguise would have been. But better than nothing.

"Say your mother's with Beaumont. Which isn't a bad bet, since no one can find him either, and some good people are looking." I took a bite of the turkey sandwich. The menu had advertised fresh turkey. It seemed to be fresh from the turkey roll. It wasn't particularly good, but that was no reason not to eat it. "That being the case, if they are out here, and he gets a hint that someone's looking for him, they'll be gone ten minutes later. If he's in trouble with Broz he has reason to run."

I had another bite, another draught of coffee.

"So we can't just start calling places up," Paul said, "because somebody might tell him."

"Well, maybe if you called and asked for your mother," I said.

"What if he answers?" Paul said.

The waitress came past with coffee and refilled my cup. I rewarded her with a dazzling smile. She didn't notice.

"Say who you are. Ask for your mother."

"And if he hangs up?"

"We hotfoot it over there and try to get them before they leave."

"And if I get her?" Paul said.

"Tell her the deal," I said. "You're worried about her. You want to see her."

"And what if she hides under the bed?"

"I don't know what to do about that," I said.

"Why not get the police to help?"

I shook my head.

"Too delicate," I said. "The Lenox cops may be the ultimate police machine for all I know. But small-town police forces often aren't, and I'm afraid if they start looking for Richie and your mother that they'll spook them for sure." I put a second spoonful of sugar in my coffee. "Besides," I said, "they haven't done anything illegal that we know, but, if the cops get in it, and they have . . ."

"Yes," Paul said. "I understand. We've got to protect my mother in this."

I finished my sandwich, and ate the chips that came with it, and the sour pickle. I drank some coffee. The pickle made the coffee taste metallic.

"What if they are registered under another name?" Paul said.

"That's harder than everyone thinks it is," I said. "Unless you've got a lot of cash so that you needn't use a credit card, and you register someplace that doesn't require an identification. Most places do. Of course Beaumont may have credit cards and ID in another name. He sounds like the kind of guy that might."

"And if he does, and they use another name?"

"Then we won't find them this way," I said. "We'll find them another way."

"Well," Paul said, and his face seemed tight, and colorless, "it's not much of a plan but it's better than any that I've got."

I nodded. The waitress brought the check. I paid. We got up and went out to the car where I gave Pearl the plain turkey sandwich, and when she was through eating it I got some bottled water and a plastic dish out of the trunk and gave her a drink. Then Paul and I walked her on the leash around Lenox for about a half hour until she'd accomplished everything one would hope for, then we got back in the car and began looking for a motel that took dogs.

# Chapter 19

The Motel Thirty in Lee had no objection to Pearl. They also would have had no objection to the Creature from the Black Lagoon—or Madonna. We sat in a room with pink wallpaper on beds that had pink chenille bedspreads. Each of the beds would vibrate for five minutes if you put two quarters in a slot. Pearl circled the room carefully, went into the bathroom, drank noisily from the toilet bowl, came back out, selected one of the beds, hopped up, turned around three times, and lay down on it. Paul started calling.

It took three hours to call everyone on the list. No one had anyone named Rich Beaumont or Patty Giacomin registered. After the last call, Paul hung up the phone very carefully, and got up and walked to the window and looked out at the blacktop parking lot. He was perfectly still. His shoulders were hunched in angular pain, and for a moment I saw the fifteen-year-old kid I'd originally met, deadened with defeat, paralyzed with desperation.

"We'll find her," I said.

Paul nodded, and continued to stare down at the parking lot.

Pearl was quiet on the bed. Her head resting on her forepaws, her eyes on me, moving as I moved. She always watched me.

"When I was small," Paul said, "and my father was at work, and there was just me and her in the house, I remember I used to scheme to get her attention, not just to be nice, but to be responsible. I wanted her to be a mother. I'd be in my room and I'd spill something and I'd think, 'Okay, now she'll have to come in here and do something.'"

"Like an adult," I said.

Paul's back still had a quality of asymmetric tension to it as he spoke.

"Yeah."

"An adult could be trusted," I said.

"Yeah."

"An adult wouldn't leave you."

Without turning, Paul nodded. He put his hands in his pants pockets and leaned his forehead against the windowpane.

"Like she has again," I said.

The light outside the window was getting gray, and I could hear the wind picking up. Pearl looked uneasy, and her eyes followed me in even small movements.

"I been shrunk so much my skin's about to pucker," Paul said. "I know what's happening to me. I know why I feel like I do, and now I need to come to terms with it. But it still hurts just as if I didn't understand it."

"And when we find her?" I said.

The reminiscent shrug again.

"Getting past that takes more than understanding," I said.

"Yeah?" Paul said. "How about heavy drugs?"

"Always an option," I said.

A few drops of rain splattered heavily against the window. Pearl's ears went up and she stared at the window, then glanced quickly toward me. I put my hand on her shoulder and left it there. Outside it had gotten quite dark.

"You mean *will*, don't you?" Paul said.

"Yeah."

"You mean self-control."

"Yeah."

Paul turned slowly away from the window and looked at me seriously. His hands were still in his pockets. Behind him the fat raindrops were spattering more often against the glass, and the wind was rattling the window and skittering leaves across the blacktop in the parking lot among the economy cars and trucks with hunting caps on them.

"Heavy drugs would be easier," he said.

"I know," I said.

Outside, the storm came with a rush, driven by wind and slashed by lightning. It chattered against the window, and when the thunder followed, Pearl sat bolt upright and leaned against me and swallowed hard.

We were quiet inside the cheap motel room listening to the storm in the gathering darkness.

# Chapter 20

Joe was aging. He still carried himself with the theatricality he'd always had, as if there were an audience watching his every move, and he was playing to it. But he had gotten smaller, and his cheekbones had become more prominent, and his hair had thinned, though most of it was still black.

We were sitting in his office thirty-five floors up at the lower end of State Street. Behind Broz, through the rain-blurred picture window that covered that whole wall, I could see the harbor. The rain that had started yesterday in Lenox had followed us back, and had been slanting in on Boston uninterrupted for nearly twenty hours.

Joe was wearing a black suit with a matching vest. His shirt was white with cutaway collar, and he wore a gray-and-white striped tie with a big Windsor knot. Along the left wall was a full bar, complete with brass rail. Leaning against the bar with his elbows resting was Vinnie Morris.

"Usually," Joe was saying, "you are in the way, and it surprises me to this fucking moment that I haven't had someone hack you."

He had a deep phony voice, like the guys that call up and give you a recorded sales pitch on the phone. He spoke as if diction were hard for him and he had to be careful not to speak badly.

"Everyone makes mistakes," I said.

"And every time I talk to you and listen to your smart mouth it surprises me more." He leaned back in his high-backed blue leather chair and clasped his hands behind his head. "This time we might have a common interest."

"I'd hate to think so," I said.

"Spenser," Vinnie Morris said from the bar, "we're trying to work something out. Whyn't you button it up a little bit."

"We could take a different approach," Joe said.

"Like Gerry did," I said.

"Gerry's got a temper," Joe said. "Who worth his salt don't have a temper? Huh? Tell me that. Guy's going to inherit this." Joe made an inclusive motion with his right hand. "Guy's got to have some pepper. Right, Vinnie?"

"Like you, Joe."

"That's right. I always had the fucking pepper. People knew it. Kept them in line. They knew I wouldn't back off. And they know Gerry's a piece of the same work."

Joe had unlaced his hands from behind his head and placed them flat on the desk where he was leaning over them, looking at me hard when he talked—a picture of intensity. But there was nothing there. It was a performance. Broz didn't believe it anymore. Vinnie and I never had.

Joe was silent for a minute, leaning forward over his desk, staring at me. I had the feeling he might have forgotten what he was saying.

"So what do you want to talk about?" I said.

Joe frowned at me.

"You want to say what the problem is with Gerry and Rich Beaumont?" Vinnie said to Joe.

"He wearing a wire?" Joe said.

"No, Joe."

"You checked him before?"

"Like always, Joe. Every body, every time."

"Good," Joe said. "Good."

We were quiet for a moment.

"Richie Beaumont," Vinnie said.

"Yeah. Richie." Joe shifted a little in his chair so I could see his profile against the rain-translucent picture window. "Him and Gerry were associated in a deal we had going."

"What kind of deal?" I said.

Joe raised the fingers of his left hand maybe two inches. "A deal. We have a lot of deals going."

"And Gerry's involved in all of them," I said.

Joe's shoulders shrugged. The movement was minimal, maybe a half an inch.

"He's my son," Joe said.

"So what makes this deal special?" I said.

Joe shrugged again. His shoulders hunched higher this time.

"Nothing special, just another deal we were doing."

I looked at Vinnie. He shook his head. I sat still and waited.

"Gerry's my only kid," Joe said.

I nodded. He was silent. On the window the rain twisted into thick little braids of water in places.

"I'm seventy-one."

I nodded some more.

"Like anybody coming into a business, he needs some room. Some room to make mistakes, unnerstand? Some chance to learn from the mistakes. How we all . . ." Joe made a little vague circle with his right hand. "How we all learned, got to be men. You and me, Spenser, we're men. You know? Vinnie too. We know how men do things. Because we learned. We made our mistakes and we survived them and we . . ." He made the gesture again with his right hand. "We fucking learned is all."

"Gerry made a mistake," I said.

"Sure," Joe said. "Sure he did. Everybody does when they're starting out. You can tell them, and tell them. But it's not the same, they got to do it themselves, and fuck it up. Like we did."

"Sure," I said.

Out across the harbor I could see a DC 10 angling down out of the overcast, slanting in through the rain toward Logan Airport. Joe was looking down at his hands spread on the desktop. Then he looked up at me, and for a moment the staginess was gone. For a moment there seemed to be something like recognition in his face and his eyes were, briefly, the eyes of an old man, tired, with time running down.

"We gotta let Gerry straighten this out himself," he said.

"So he can learn?"

"So he can feel like one of us, Spenser. So he can be a fucking man."

Broz got up suddenly and turned and stared out the picture window at the rain coming down over the harbor. To my left Vinnie was motionless. In the stillness I could hear the sound the rain made as it sluiced down the window, barely two inches from Broz's face.

"I don't care much about what Gerry becomes, Joe. I'm worried about the kid I know."

"The Giacomin kid." Joe didn't turn around.

"Yeah. He wants to find his mother. I told him we'd find her. We figure she's with Beaumont."

"Vinnie says you been with that kid a long time."

"Un huh."

Joe looked out at the rain some more.

"Tell him about the deal, Vinnie," Joe said. "And make me a drink. You want a drink, Spenser?"

"Sure," I said.

Vinnie moved behind the bar.

"What'll it be?" he said.

"Scotch and soda," I said. "Tall glass. Lot of ice."

Vinnie began to assemble the drinks.

"You know the kind of work we do," Vinnie said. "It requires some give and take with the law, you know?"

I said I knew.

"We make some gifts to people in Vice, to people on the OCU, maybe a captain in Command Staff, maybe an intelligence guy out at Ten Ten."

Vinnie had a Campari and soda mixed and brought it around the bar to Broz. Joe took it without turning from the window. He took a swallow and continued to stare at the rain while he held the glass.

"Some of these are standup guys, still do the job, bust the freaks, take out the street punks, but they give us a little edge. They treat us right, we treat them right. Some mutual respect. We got some good cops we do business with."

Vinnie was back behind the bar. He started putting my scotch and soda together while he talked. His voice was quiet in the big formal room.

"Well, Joe has this, whaddya call it, this network in place for a while. He builds it slow, careful, for a long time. Does business with guys we can trust, our kind of people, steady guys, you know? Not flighty, you might say."

He put the glass up on the bar and I stood and walked across the room and took it and went and sat back down. Vinnie started making himself a drink. Joe's back was perfectly still as he stared out the window. If he heard Vinnie talking he didn't show it. He stared at the rain as if he'd never see it again.

"Well, Joe's interested in Gerry learning all of the business, so he puts Gerry in charge of overseeing that part of things, paying out; and Gerry decides it should be changed a little."

Vinnie had a thick lowball glass of bourbon over ice. He took a taste as he walked around the bar, and leaned on it. He nodded his head slightly, approving of the bourbon. He glanced over at Joe's silent motionless back.

"Gerry started buying up cops like they were made in Hong Kong. He's paying off people at school crossings, you know. And he's got this guy Rich Beaumont as his bagman. Pretty soon Gerry's got a payroll, looks like the welfare list, makes us like the third-biggest employer in the state. And he's not choosy. Anybody he can bribe, he bribes. Joe hears about it first because one of our guys hears one of Gerry's guys bragging about it. About how he's got Gerry shoving money up his nose, and the guy's laughing. The guy can't do him any good. He's like in Community Relations and Gerry thinks he's still in Vice, and the guy's laughing at us."

"And talking," I said.

Vinnie looked at the bourbon in his glass for a long moment. He stuck one finger in and moved the ice around a little and took the finger out and sucked off the bourbon, and ran the back of his hand across his lips.

"And talking," Vinnie said. He took another swallow of bourbon. I drank some scotch.

From the window Joe said, "Vinnie," and held his hand out with the empty glass in it. Vinnie walked over and took it and brought it back and made another one.

"So I talked with Joe about it," Vinnie said. "And we decided we'd have to talk with Gerry about it, only by the time we did get to talk with him . . ."

Vinnie walked across the room with the fresh Campari and soda and put it in Joe's hand. Then he returned to the bar and gazed for a moment at Joe's back. He took in some bourbon. Then he looked straight at me.

". . . Beaumont had taken off with a bagful of our money."

"How much?" I said.

Vinnie shook his head. "You don't need to know."

"No," I said, "I don't. But I need to know if it was enough."

"It was enough," Vinnie said. "He was skimming what he paid out and then, lately, he wasn't paying anybody—and mostly it was okay because the people he was supposed to be paying couldn't do us anything anyway."

"More than a million?" I said.

"Don't matter," Vinnie said.

"Matters when I look for him," I said. "Where I look depends on what he can afford."

"Okay, more than a million. He can afford pretty much anything he wants. But that ain't the point. The point is you can't stay in business and let a chipmunk like Richie Beaumont take your money and give you the finger. He can't be allowed to get away with it."

"I understand that," I said. "I got no problem with that."

We were all quiet then, the three of us, sipping our drinks at 11:30 in the morning, while it rained outside.

From the window Joe said, "You gotta stay out of Gerry's way, Spenser. He's got to find Beaumont himself. He's got to get the money back. He's got to put Beaumont down. He don't do that, what is he? What kind of man is he to run this thing we got? What do they think of him? What do I think of him?"

Joe's voice had none of the audition-booth resonance now; it was hoarse. "What the fuck does he think of himself?"

"We got a problem," I said. "I don't say it can't be resolved, but it's a problem."

"We got nothing against the broad," Vinnie said.

"Sure," I said. "But what if she's with him when Gerry finds him, and he puts up a fight and Gerry has to kill him and she sees it? Or what if he's told her all about his deal with Gerry?"

"We guarantee her safety?" Joe said softly.

"You can't," I said.

"You wouldn't take my word on it?" Joe said. "Vinnie's word?"

"I'd take Vinnie's word, but not Gerry's."

"Or mine?"

I shrugged.

"We can't guarantee it, Joe," Vinnie said. His voice was flat, very careful.

Joe nodded slowly.

"You got a suggestion?" he said to me.

"I'll do the best I can, Joe. I don't like you but he's your kid. I find Beaumont, I'll leave him in place and take the woman. I won't hold Beaumont for Gerry, and I won't tell Gerry where he is, but I'll leave him out there for Gerry to hunt."

"You find him you give him to Vinnie," Broz said.

"And Vinnie will put him where Gerry can find him and Gerry will think he won."

Joe shrugged. I looked at Vinnie. Vinnie was staring past us both, looking at the harbor. There was no expression on his face.

"No," I said. "I won't give Beaumont to Vinnie."

Joe sighed slowly.

"There's an option we ain't spoken of yet," he said. He was tired; the *ain't* had crept in past his self-consciousness. "We could whack you."

"Maybe you could whack me," I said. "It's been tried. But where would that get you? It'll attract the attention of people you'd rather not attract. A lot of people know what I'm working on."

"Hawk," Vinnie said.

"For one," I said. "And there'd be a homicide investigation."

"Quirk," Vinnie said, as if he were counting off a list.

"So you trade me for them," I said, "maybe some others."

My drink was gone. I didn't want another one. The room was full of harshness and pain and a bitterness that had been distilled by silence. I wanted to get out of there.

"It's my kid, Spenser," Broz said. He sounded as if his throat were closing.

"I'm in sort of the same position, Joe."

"He's got to get some respect," Broz said.

I didn't say anything. Gerry wasn't going to get respect. He couldn't earn it and Joe couldn't earn it for him. Joe was silent, his hands folded, looking at his thumbs. He seemed to have gone somewhere.

After a while Vinnie Morris said, "Okay, Spenser. That's it. We'll talk to you later."

I stood. Broz didn't look up. I turned and walked toward the door across the big office. Vinnie walked with me.

At the door I said to Vinnie, "If Gerry gets in my way I will walk over him."

"I know," Vinnie said. He looked back at Joe Broz. "But if you do, you know who Joe will send."

I nodded. I turned back and looked at Joe.

"Tough being the boss's son," I said.

Joe didn't answer. Vinnie held the door open. And I went out.

# Chapter 21

Pearl didn't like the rain. She hung back when Susan and I took an after-dinner stroll, even when Susan pulled on her leash. And when we prevailed through superior strength, she kept turning and looking up at me, and pausing to jump up and put her forepaws on my chest and look at me as if to question my sanity.

"I heard that if you step on their back paws when they jump up like that, they learn not to," Susan said.

"Shhh," I said. "She'll hear you."

Susan had a big blue-and-white striped umbrella and she carried it so that it protected her and Pearl from the rain. Pearl didn't quite get it, and kept drifting out from under its protection and getting splattered and turning to look at me. I had on my leather trench coat and the replica Boston Braves hat that Susan had ordered for me through the catalogue from Manny's Baseball Land. It was black with a red visor and a red button. There was a white **B** on it and when I wore it I looked very much like Nanny Fernandez.

"What will you do?" Susan said.

"I'll try to extract Patty Giacomin from the puzzle and leave the rest of it intact."

"And you won't warn Rich?"

"No need to warn him. He knows he's in trouble."

"But you won't try to save him?"

"No."

"Isn't that a little flinty?" Susan said.

"Yes."

"Officially, here in Cambridge," Susan said, "we're supposed to value all life."

"That's the official view here in Cambridge of people who will never have to act on it," I said.

"That is true of most of the official views here in Cambridge," Susan said.

"My business is with Patty—Paul really. Rich Beaumont had to know what he was getting himself into—and besides I seem to feel a little sorry for Joe."

Pearl had wedged herself between my legs and Susan's, managing to stay mostly under her part of Susan's umbrella, and while she didn't seem happy, she was resigned. We turned the corner off Linnaean Street and walked along Mass Avenue toward Harvard Square.

"You are the oddest combination," Susan said.

"Physical beauty matched with deep humility?"

"Aside from that," Susan said. "Except maybe for Hawk, you look at the world with fewer illusions than anyone I have ever known. And yet you are as sentimental as you would be if the world were pretty-pretty."

"Which it isn't," I said.

"You cook a good chicken too," Susan said.

"Takes a tough man," I said, "to make a tender chicken."

"How come you cook so well?"

"It's a gift," I said.

"One not, apparently, bestowed on me."

"You do nice cornflakes," I said.

"Did you always cook?" she said.

Pearl darted out from under the umbrella long enough to snuffle the possible spoor of a fried chicken wing, near a trash barrel, then remembered the rain and ducked back in against my leg.

"Since I was small," I said.

As we passed Changsho Restaurant, Pearl's head went down and her ears pricked and her body elongated. She had found the lair of the chicken wings she'd been tracking earlier.

"Remember," I said, "there were no women. Just my father, my uncles, and me. So all the chores were done by men. There was no woman's work. There were no rules about what was woman's work. In our house all work was man's work. So I made beds and dusted and did laundry, and so did my father, and my uncles. And they took turns cooking."

We were past Changsho, Pearl looked back over her shoulder at it, but she kept pace with us and the protective umbrella. There was enough neon in this part of Mass Avenue so that the wet rain made it look pretty, reflecting the colors and fusing them on the wet pavement.

"I started when I was old enough to come home from school alone. I'd be hungry, so I'd make myself something to eat. First it was leftovers—

stew, baked beans, meat loaf, whatever. And I'd heat them up. Then I graduated to cooking myself a hamburger, or making a club sandwich, and one day I wanted pie and there wasn't any so I made one."

"And the rest is history," Susan said.

A big MBTA bus pulled up at the stop beside us, the water streaming off its yellow flanks, the big wipers sweeping confidently back and forth across the broad windshield.

"Well, not entirely," I said. "The pie was edible, but a little odd. I didn't like to roll out the crust, so I just pressed overlapping scraps of dough into the bottom of the pie plate until I got a bottom crust."

"And the top crust?"

"Same thing."

The pneumatic doors of the bus closed with that soft, firm sound that they make and the bus ground into gear and plowed off through the rain.

"My father came home and had some and said it was pretty good and I should start sharing in the cooking. So I did."

"So all of you cooked?"

"Yeah, but no one was proprietary about it. It wasn't anyone's accomplishment, it was a way to get food in the proper condition to eat."

"Your father sounds as if he were comfortable with his ego," Susan said.

"He never felt the need to compete with me," I said. "He was always very willing for me to grow up."

Pearl had located a discarded morsel of chewing gum on the pavement and was mouthing it vigorously. Apparently she found it unrewarding, because after a minute of ruminative mouthing she opened her jaws and let it drop out.

"There's something she won't eat," Susan said.

"I would have said there wasn't," I said.

We passed the corner of Shepard Street. Across Mass Avenue, on the corner of Wendell Street, the motel had changed names again.

"I got to shop some too," I said, "though mostly for things like milk and sugar. My father and my uncles had a vegetable garden they kept, and they all hunted, so there was lots of game. My father liked to come home after ten, twelve hours of carpentering and work in his garden. My uncles didn't care for the garden much, but they liked the fresh produce and they were too proud to take it without helping, so they'd be out there too. Took up most of the backyard. In the fall we'd put up a lot of it, and we'd smoke some game."

"Did you work in the garden?" Susan said.

"Sure."

"Do you miss it?"

"No," I said. "I always hated gardening."

"So when we retire you don't want to buy a little cottage and tend your roses?"

"While you're inside baking up some cookies," I said, "maybe brewing a pot of tea, or a batch of lemonade that you'd bring me in a pitcher."

"What a dreadful thought," Susan said.

"Yes," I said. "I prefer to think I can be the bouncer in a retirement home."

The Cambridge Common appeared through the shiny down-slanted rain. Pearl elongated a little when she sniffed it. There were always squirrels there, and Pearl had every intention of catching one.

"And you?" I said.

"When I retire?"

"Yeah."

Susan looked at the wet superstructure of the children's swing set for a moment as we crossed toward it.

"I think," she said, "that I shall remain young and beautiful forever."

We reached the Common and Pearl was now in low tension, leaning against the leash, her nose apparently pressed against the grass, sniffing.

"Well," I said, "you've got a hell of a start on it."

"Actually," she said, "I don't suppose either of us will retire. I'll practice therapy, and teach, and write some. You'll chase around rescuing maidens and slaying dragons, annoying all the right people."

"Someday I may not be the toughest kid on the block," I said.

She shook her head. "Someday you may not be the strongest," she said. "I suspect you'll always be the toughest."

"Good point," I said.

# Chapter 22

Paul and I were working out in the Harbor Health Club. Paul was doing pelvic tilt sit-ups. I could do some. But Paul seemed able to do fifty thousand of them and had the annoying habit of pausing to talk during various phases of the sit-up without any visible strain. He was doing it now.

"Maybe," he said, "we were out in Lenox asking the wrong questions of the wrong people."

I was doing concentration curls, with relatively light weight, and many reps. Paul had been slowly weaning me from the heavy weights. *It's the amount of work, not the amount of weight.*

"Almost by definition," I said, trying to sound easy as I curled the dumbbells. "Since what we did produced nothing."

"Well, I mean I know I'm a dancer and you're a detective, but . . ."

"Go ahead," I said. "If you've got a good idea, my ego can stand it— unless it's brilliant."

"It's not brilliant," Paul said. He curled down and up and down again, and began curling up on an angle to involve the lateral obliques. "But if I had more than a million dollars in cash, and I were running away from the kind of people you've described, maybe I wouldn't stay in a hotel."

I finished the thirtieth curl and began to do hammer curls.

"Because you wouldn't be making a temporary departure," I said.

"That's right," Paul said. "You'd know you could never come back."

"So maybe you'd buy a place, or rent a place."

"Yes. I don't know what property costs, but if I had a million dollars . . ."

"More than a million," I said. "Yeah. You'd stay in a hotel if you were on your way somewhere. But if you were going to make it a permanent hideout, you'd want something more."

"Could you buy a place without proving your identity?" Paul said.

I put down the barbells. They were bright chrome. Everything was upscale at the Harbor Health Club except Henry Cimoli, who owned it. Henry hadn't changed much since he'd fought Willie Pep, except that the scar tissue had, with time, thickened around his eyes, so that now he always looked as if he were squinting into the sun.

"You'd have to give a name, but if you were paying cash, I don't think you'd have to prove it."

"So maybe we should go out there and talk to real estate people," Paul said.

"Yes," I said. "We should."

I finished my set of thirty hammers and went back to straight curls, concentrating on keeping my elbow still, using only the bicep.

"It's an excellent idea," I said.

Paul had gone into a hamstring stretch where he sat on the floor with his legs out straight and pressed his forehead against his kneecap.

"You'd have thought of it anyway," he said.

"Of course," I said. "Because I'm a professional detective, and you're just a performer."

"Certainly," Paul said.

We finished our workout, stretched, took some steam, showered, picked up Pearl from the club office where she had been keeping company with Henry, and strolled out into the fresh-washed fall morning feeling loose and strong with all our pores breathing.

In the car I said, "Is there a picture of your mother?"

"Should be, at the house."

"Okay, let's go out there and break in again and get it."

"No need to break and enter," Paul said. "While we were there last time I got a key. She always was losing hers, so she kept a spare one under the porch overhang. I took it when we left."

We went out Storrow Drive toward Route 2. A little past Mass General Hospital I spotted the tail. It was a maroon Chevy, and it was a very amateurish tail job. He kept fighting to stay right behind me, making himself noticeable as he cut in and cut off drivers to stay near my rear bumper. There was even horn blowing.

I said to Paul, "We are being followed by one of the worst followers in Boston."

Paul turned and looked out the back window.

"Maroon Chevy," I said.

"Right behind us?"

"Yeah. Probably someone from Gerry," I said. "Joe would have someone better. If Vinnie Morris did it you wouldn't notice."

"Would you?"

"Yeah."

"What are we going to do?"

"We'll lose them," I said.

We continued out Storrow and onto Soldiers Field Road, past Harvard Stadium and across the Eliot Bridge by Mt. Auburn Hospital. In the athletic field near the stadium a number of Harvard women were playing field hockey. Their bare legs flashed under the short plaid skirts and their ankles were bulky with thick socks. The river as we crossed it was the color of strong tea, and a little choppy. A loon with his neck arched floated near the boat club. Behind us the maroon Chevy stayed close to our exhaust pipe. I could see two people in it. The guy driving was wearing sunglasses. Near the Cambridge-Belmont line, where Fresh Pond Parkway meets Alewife Brook Parkway there is a traffic circle. I went slowly around it with the Chevy behind me.

"Where we going?" Paul said.

"Ever see a dog circle a raccoon or some other animal it's got out in the open?"

"No."

I went all the way around the circle and started around again.

"They keep circling faster and faster until they get behind it," I said.

I held the car in a tight turn and put more pressure on the accelerator. The Chevy tried to stay tight, but he didn't know what was going on and I did. Also I cornered better than he did. He lost some ground. I pushed the car harder, it bucked a little against the sharpness of the turn but I held it in.

"I get it," Paul said.

"Quicker than the guy in the Chevy," I said. He was still chasing us around the circle. On the third loop I was behind him and as he started around again, I peeled off right and floored it out the Ale-wife Brook Parkway, past the shopping center, ran the light at Rindge Avenue by passing three cars on the inside, and headed up Rindge back into Cambridge. By the time I got to Mass Avenue he had lost us. I turned left and headed out toward Lexington through Arlington.

"Wily," Paul said.

"Float like a butterfly," I said. "Sting like a bee."

"Pearl's looking a little queasy," Paul said.

"Being a canine crime stopper," I said, "is not always pretty."

# Chapter 23

We started in Stockbridge, because Paul and I agreed that Stockbridge was where we'd buy a place if we were on the run. And it was easy. We left Pearl in the car with the windows part open diagonally across from the Red Lion Inn, walked across the street to the biggest real estate office on the main street in Stockbridge, and showed the picture of Patty Giacomin to a thick woman in a pair of green slacks and a pink turtleneck.

"Oh, I know her," the woman said. "That's Mrs. Richards. I just sold them a house."

The house she had sold them was about half a mile from town on Overlook Hill. They had purchased the house for cash under the name Mr. and Mrs. Beaumont Richards.

"Beaumont Richards," I said as we drove up the hill. "Who'd ever guess it was him?"

Paul was silent. His face seemed to have lost color, and he swallowed with difficulty. Pearl had her head forward between us, and Paul was absently scratching her ear.

I parked on the gravel at the edge of the roadway in front of the address we'd been given. It was a recently built Cape, with the unlandscaped raw look that newly built houses have. This one looked even rawer because it was isolated, set into the woods, away from any neighbors. The roadway that we parked on continued into the woods. As if, come spring, an optimistic builder would put up some more houses for spec. Running up behind the house were some wheel ruts which appeared to do service as a driveway. The ruts had probably been created by the builders' heavy equipment and would be smoothed out and re-sodded in spring. To the left the hill sloped down toward the town, and you could see the Red Lion Inn, which dominated the minimalist center. Behind the house the woods ran, as best I could tell, all the way to the Hudson River.

"How to do this?" I said.

"I think I should go in," Paul said.

"Yeah, except Beaumont is bound to be very nervous about callers," I said.

"I'm his paramour's son," Paul said. "That's got to count for something."

"He's scared," I said. "That counts for everything in most people, if they're scared enough."

"I have to do this," Paul said. "I can't have you bring me in to see her. I am a grown man. She has to see me that way. She has to accept that . . . that I matter."

He swallowed. He had the look of bottled tension that he'd had when I first met him.

I nodded. "I'll be here," I said.

Paul made an attempt at a smile, gave me a little thumbs-up gesture, and got out of the car. Pearl immediately came into the front seat and sat where Paul had sat.

I watched him walk up the curving flagstone pathway toward number 12. It had a colonial blue door. The siding was clapboard stained a maple tone. There were diamond panes in the windows. There was no lawn yet, but someone had put in a couple of evergreen shrubs on each side of the front door and a quiet breeze gently tossed the tips of their branches. I wished I could do this for him. It cost him so much and would cost me so little. But it would cost him much more if I did it for him. He stopped on the front steps and, after a moment, rang the doorbell.

The door opened and I could see Paul speak, and pause, and then go in. The door closed behind him. I waited. Pearl stiffened and shifted in the seat as a squirrel darted across the gravel road and into the yellowing woods that had yielded only slightly to the house. I rubbed her neck and watched the front door.

"Life is often very hard on kids, Pearl," I said.

Pearl's attention remained fixed on the squirrel.

There was no sound. And no movement beyond that which the breeze caused to stir in the forest. Beaumont had chosen a bad place to hide. It seemed remote but its remoteness increased his danger. He'd have been better off in a city among a million people. Out here you could fire off cannon and no one would hear.

Pearl's head shifted and her body stiffened. The front door opened and Patty Giacomin came down the front walk with a welcoming look on her face. She still looked good, very trim and neat, with her blonde hair and dark eyes. She was dressed in some kind of Lord & Taylor farmgirl outfit, long skirt over big boots, an ivory-colored, oversized, cable-knit sweater, and her hair caught back with a colorful headband.

I rolled the window down on the passenger side halfway so I could speak to her. Pearl, who was standing on all fours now in the front seat, thrust her head through the opening, her tail wagging.

"Well, hello, you beautiful thing," Patty said and put a hand out for Pearl to sniff. "And you, my friend," she said to me. "How can you sit out in the car like a stranger? Come in, meet Rich, see my new house. It's been too long."

I nodded and smiled. "Nice to see you, Patty," I said and got out of the driver's side. Pearl turned toward me and looked disappointed when I closed the door on her. I went around the car and Patty Giacomin gave me her cheek to kiss.

"Come on in," she said again. "And bring this lovely dog. I couldn't bear it if she had to sit out here all alone, while we're all up in the house visiting."

I opened the passenger door and Pearl jumped out and dashed around in front of the house with her nose to the ground until she found a spot where she could squat. Which she did. I stuck her leash in my hip pocket.

Patty took my hand as if we used to be lovers, and led me to the front door. Pearl joined us there, and when Patty opened it, pushed in ahead of us. Paul was in the living room with a guy that looked like a *People* magazine cover boy. The living room was what I expected it would be. Knotty pine paneling, big fieldstone fireplace. Beams, wooden furniture with colonial print upholstery, a braided rug on the floor.

"Rich," Patty said, "I'd like you to meet someone," and gestured me toward him like I was the ambassador from Peru. Rich put out his hand and I took it. He didn't seem very pleased.

"Coffee?" Patty said. "A drink? Paul, do you drink now?"

Paul said, "Yes, I do, but not right now, thanks."

I shook my head. Rich was leaning against the wall near the fireplace with his arms folded. He was probably my height, which made him 6' 1", sort of willowy without being thin. He had thick dark hair which he wore brushed straight back, and longish so that it curled over his ears. He had a mustache that was just as black, and a tuft of black hair showed at the vee of his shirt, which he wore with the top three buttons open. It was a lavender dress shirt. His jeans were stone washed and designer labeled, and his lizard skin cowboy boots were ivory colored and would have been a nice match to Patty's sweater. Except for the mustache his dark face was cleanshaven, with the shadow of a dark beard lurking. His nose was strong and straight. His eyes were dark and moved a lot. If you had told him he was the cat's ass he'd have given you no argument.

"Paul says he was worried about his mom," Patty said and dazzled me with her even smile. "And I want to thank you for looking out for him."·

"I wasn't looking out for him," I said. "He does that himself. I was helping him look for you."

She smiled again just as if I'd told her that her hair was looking lovely.

"As you can see, I'm fine. Rich and I just wanted to"—she waved her arms a little—"elope."

Paul said, "Did you get married?"

Patty smiled even more beguilingly.

"Well, not exactly, if you mean all that foolishness with organ music and somebody saying a bunch of words. But we love each other and wanted to get away and be alone."

I was quiet. My size made Rich uncomfortable. I don't know how I knew that, but I knew it. There was something about how he looked at me and shifted a little on the wall. But it wasn't a total setback for him; he still managed to look contemptuous.

"And you didn't think you needed to tell me?" Paul said. "Where you were, or even that you were going?"

"Shame on you, young man," Patty said. "Using that tone with your mother."

I could see Paul lower his head a little and shake it as if a swarm of gnats were bothering him. I shut up.

"It's the tone that this calls for," Paul said. His voice was tight, but it was clear. "I am your son, your only child, I should know where you are. Not every minute, but if you are making any moves of substance you should tell me. Do you realize what we've been doing to try and find you?"

"Paul, honey, Rich and I needed to get away, not tell anyone, Rich was very clear about that. Weren't you, darling?"

I've never heard anyone call anyone *darling* without sounding like a fool, except Myrna Loy. Patty wasn't close.

"Your mother and I wanted a kind of a honeymoon," Rich said. He had a great voice. He sounded like William B. Williams. "You're a big boy, we figured she could go off for a bit without you."

"So you went away for a bit and bought a house?" Paul said. He wasn't going to flinch.

Rich shrugged. Patty looked a little confused. "Paulie," she said. "Paulie, did you come all the way here to argue with your mother? Do you care if I'm happy?"

Paul shook his head again and plowed ahead.

"For cash?" Paul said. "Under another name?"

"Jeez," Rich said. "You got some nosy kid here, Patty."

Patty's eyes were bigger than was possible. "No," she said. "No, no."

"Does my mother know what you're running away from?" Paul said. There was a rasp in his voice now. I was perfectly still, near him, and a little behind. I looked at Rich Beaumont. But I said nothing. This was Paul's, not mine.

"Hey, kid, you got some kind of bad mouth," Beaumont said. "For crissake lighten up. We went off and didn't tell you. So let's not make a big fucking deal about it."

"Richard!" Patty said and put the back of her hand against her mouth.

"Do you know?" Paul said.

"Paulie, you stop this. I was glad to see you, but now you're spoiling everything."

"Ma," Paul said. He was leaning forward a little as he talked.

"Listen to me," he said. "Do you know who you're with? Do you know why he doesn't want anyone to know where he is? Do you know why he bought the house under another name? And where he got the money?"

They both spoke at once. Rich said, "Hey—"

And Patty said, "Damn you, Paul, I don't want to know! I'm happy, don't you understand that? I'm happy."

Everyone was quiet then for a moment until Paul said, "Yes, but you're not safe."

The silence rolled in as if from a far place and settled in the room. Everyone stood still, not knowing what to say. Except me. I knew what I should say, which was nothing. And I kept saying it.

Finally Patty looked at Rich, and he said, "Kid, you got no business coming in here and talking like that. And you wouldn't get away with it if you didn't have this Yahoo with you."

"That may be," Paul said, "but here he is."

The Yahoo smiled charmingly and said nothing. He was musing over the prospect of stuffing Rich up the chimney flue if the opportunity appeared. From the sofa where she had settled, Pearl yawned largely. Her jaws opened so wide when she yawned that it ended with a squeak which may have been her jaw hinge. I was never quite sure.

"Paul," Patty said. "Please. Don't do this. I've found someone. Rich cares about me. You don't know what being alone is like."

"The hell I don't," Paul said.

From where I stood I could look into the big round gilded Eagle mirror over the fireplace and see my car parked down the slope of the lawn-to-be.

"What did you mean about safe?" Patty said.

"Are you going to tell her?" Paul said to Rich. "Or am I?"

"I am," Beaumont said. "It's not as bad as it sounds, but I was in business with a guy who turned out to have mob connections, and I took some money he says belongs to him."

"And they want it back," Patty said.

Beaumont nodded.

"Well, just give it to them," Patty said.

Beaumont shook his head.

"Why not?" Patty said. "Tell them you're sorry and give them the money."

"And this house?" Beaumont said.

"Yes, certainly, sell it. Tell them you'll make good. You have some money."

"None I haven't stolen," Beaumont said. There was no scornfulness in his voice this time, nor self-regard. It was the voice of someone noticing an ugly thing about himself.

"I don't care. Give it to them. We have each other, we can start over, give them the money back."

Beaumont was silent. Paul looked at me.

"It's not that simple," I said. "They intend to kill him."

Patty put her hand to her mouth again in the same gesture she'd used when Beaumont said *fuck*. Patty's reaction range was limited.

"But if he gives the money back . . ." she said.

Beaumont was looking past her out the sliding doors at the end of the living room, which opened out onto the green and yellow woods. He didn't say anything.

"It's a matter of principle now," I said. "These particular people can't let him get away with it. They have to kill him."

All of us were quiet.

Patty said, "Richard?"

Beaumont nodded.

"He's right," Beaumont said. "It's why we had to come here and hide. It's why I couldn't let you tell anyone at all. Not even your kid."

"Richard," she said, "we better go away then."

"We're all right here," Beaumont said. "No one knows we're here." He looked at us. "Do they?"

"No," I said.

"No one followed you?"

"No."

"You're sure?"

"Yes."

"Richard, we can't stay here," Patty said. "They might find you."

"How'd you find us?" Beaumont said.

"A charge purchase from Lenox," I said.

Beaumont looked at Patty. "I told you cash," he said. "No charges."

"What harm? It was for us, like our honeymoon. Just that one time is all, Richard. I didn't know."

"What harm? For Christ's sake, Patty, they found us." He tossed his chin at Paul and me. "What if it had been Gerry?"

"Who?"

Beaumont made a dismissive wave with his hand.

"Is Gerry the one you took the money from?"

"Yeah."

"Richard, let's go somewhere else."

Beaumont started to shake his head and then stopped and turned his gaze slowly toward Patty.

"Why?" he said.

"It's too close. They might find us."

"What's going on, Patty?" Beaumont said. "Why might they find us?"

Patty had both hands pressed against her mouth now. She shook her head soundlessly.

"Ma," Paul said, "if you know something you have to say, this is—" He didn't finish.

Patty kept shaking her head with her hands pressed against her mouth.

"You told somebody," Beaumont said. "Goddamn you, you told somebody."

With her head still down and her hands still pressed, she was able to squeeze out the word "Caitlin."

"Caitlin Martinelli? You told her?"

She nodded and took her hands away. "I was so excited," she said, "about buying our house . . ." She wanted to say more and she couldn't.

"Who told her brother," I said, "who told Joe."

Beaumont nodded and turned and went out of the room. He came back almost at once wearing one of those fleece-lined cattleman's jackets that you can buy in a catalogue and carrying a blue-and-red Nike gym bag with a shoulder strap.

"I'm out of here," he said. "If you want to come, Patty, come right now. No packing, just come."

As he turned toward her I could see that he had a white-handled automatic stuck in his belt.

Patty looked at Beaumont and then at Paul, and then at her living room with all its fresh-from-the-showroom-floor furniture.

"I . . ." she said and stopped. "I don't . . ."

"Patty, damn you, decide," Beaumont said, moving toward the back door.

In the big mirror over the fireplace I saw a dark blue Buick sedan pull up behind my car on the gravel roadway. Another car, a white Oldsmobile, pulled in right behind it.

"They're here," I said. "Beaumont, take Paul and Patty. Get the hell out of here. Paul, when you get safe, call Hawk."

Eight men got out of the cars. Four from each. One of them had a shotgun. I knelt by the front window and knocked a diamond pane out with the muzzle of the Browning.

Paul looked at me and then at his mother and didn't say a word. He took her arm and dragged her out through the sliders where Beaumont had already gone.

Outside somebody yelled, "Window to the left of the door!"

I thumbed back the hammer and shot the first guy up the walk in the middle of the chest. He went over backwards and fell on his back. The others dashed for cover behind the cars. Carefully I shot out the tires on each car. Two tires per car, so the spare wouldn't help. I'm a good shot, but I'm not Annie Oakley. It took six rounds. But it also served to pin them down since they didn't know I wasn't shooting at them. At the first gunshot Pearl sat straight upright, at the second round she bolted out through the still-open sliders. I opened my mouth to yell and closed it. It wouldn't do any good, a gun-shy dog will run no matter what, and she was probably better off in the woods than she was going to be in here pretty soon.

Everything was quiet for the moment. Beaumont must have kept his car stashed on the rutted track behind the house. I never heard it start up, never saw it leave. For all the outfit outside knew, I was Beaumont, still in the house.

I had six rounds left in the Browning, and no spare clip. I hadn't thought Stockbridge would require it. There were seven bad guys left. One of them was Gerry Broz. If I shot each of them with one bullet, I would still have Gerry to strangle. It didn't seem good odds. From behind the Buick there was movement and then my window shattered and the shotgun boomed. The odds weren't getting better. The shotgun fired again and I moved to another window in time to see two bad guys crouched low, running right, and two more doing the same thing in the opposite direction. They were going to close me in from all sides. Anyone would. I smashed another pane out and nailed one of the low-running bad guys with my eighth round, and rolled back against the wall as the glass billowed out of this window with the boom of the shotgun. Hard upon the shotgun was the chatter of some kind of small-bore automatic weapon. I had five rounds left and was badly outgunned. Pearl had the right idea. I crouched as low as I could and ran for the open patio door, my feet crunching on the scattered shards of window glass. I felt something slap my left leg and then I was through the door and into the woods. I was maybe thirty yards in before the automatic fire stopped behind me. Behind me there was silence again. And then more automatic fire. The gunfire ceased. All I could hear was the sounds of my own breathing, steady but deep, and the sound I made, moving as quietly as I could through the fall foliage, heading west. My left leg was starting to throb and I could feel the warmth where it was bleeding. I stopped and peeled off my jacket. I ripped the sleeves off my sweatshirt, put my jacket back on. I folded one sleeve into a pad and tied it in place over my jeans, using the other sleeve. It was a bulky bandage and unsightly, but it seemed to suppress the bleeding.

Behind me I heard a yell that was nearly screaming. I knew it was Gerry.

"Richie, you're a dead man! You hear me? We're coming, you motherfucker. We got a tracker, asshole, and we're right behind you."

And then I didn't hear anything.

# Chapter 24

As I moved into the woods it got thicker and the going got harder. There was still green on the trees, mixed with yellow, and the combination gave a soft dappled effect to the forest. I didn't feel soft and dappled. And as the afternoon dwindled it got darker. After about a mile I limped up a low swale and settled in behind a rock to take stock. Behind me the woods had thinned into some sort of meadow; maybe a fire, maybe a homestead, long since consumed by the slow fire of decay. Whatever it had been caused by, it made an open space where I could see anyone following me.

I was wearing New Balance running shoes, jeans, a blue sweatshirt, now sleeveless, and a leather jacket. I had five rounds in my gun, my car keys, a wristwatch, and Pearl's leash still stuck in my hip pocket. My leg was very sore and the pain pulsed steadily along it from hip to ankle. There was a Buck knife in my jacket pocket, and two packets of matches wrapped in foil to keep them dry. I always carried the gun, the keys, and the watch. The knife and the matches were for when I went west of the Charles River. The minute I noticed that I had no food, I started getting hungry. The sun was setting. That would be west. I could keep going until dark without getting turned around. I'd have to stop at night. The sun I could figure out. I couldn't read the stars to save my ass, which was not, in this case, a metaphor.

I needed a plan. First I had to figure out if Gerry and his troops really were after me. Or Richie, which is who they thought I was. If they weren't I could simply backtrack to Stockbridge and wait for Pearl. But if they were behind me, between me and Stockbridge, and if any of them knew how to function in the woods, and if they really had a tracker, then I'd need to take the long way home.

The way to find that out was to sit here behind these rocks, while I still had some ammo, and see if they showed up. They'd leave somebody behind to clean up the shooting scene and call Vinnie Morris and get some new tires. Unless someone came by at the wrong time, or somebody had heard the shooting and called the cops, they'd be okay. They had no way to know that Beaumont had bailed out with Patty and Paul, and that, in a while, Hawk was going to be coming out looking for me.

It didn't figure for Gerry and his posse to blunder around in the woods for several days looking for me. Ordinarily I figured to outrun them even if they did. But my leg wasn't going to improve. And Gerry was crazy. I settled in to wait. The late sun was warm enough on my back, but above me and moving slowly westward was a mass of dark clouds. And as the evening crept in from the east with the clouds, I could feel the edge of cold that was going to come with darkness.

They could have a tracker. They could have picked up a couple of shooters in Pittsfield. One of them could be a woodsman. Or Gerry could have made it up because he'd heard the word once on television.

The woods through which I'd edged my way, and the ones which stretched out behind me, were mostly hardwoods, oak and maple, with some birch clumps scattered among them, dark-ringed white trunks that gleamed among the drabber trees like hope in the midst of sorrow. Sprinkled among the hardwoods were evergreens—a lot of white pine, now and then a good-looking fir tree. The forest floor was a tangle of roots, and fallen trees, and creeping vines. Many of the vines were thorny and would not only trip, but clutch. There were chokecherry bushes, many of them with caterpillar tents stretched across the more comfortable crotches near the trunk. In a pinch, I knew you could eat chokecherries, though they were pretty sharp. You could eat acorns too.

The combination of rain clouds and evening fell darkly across the little open space in front of me. In the woods it would be quite dark. There was some wind. I had already zipped my jacket and turned up my collar. It left me out of options for the moment.

To my right I heard movement in the woods. Quietly I eased the hammer back on the Browning. The movement continued, and then Pearl emerged from the woods, her nose against the ground, her head moving from side to side, her tail erect; she came across the meadow walking very fast, and up the swale, and then raised her head and capered around the rock and began to turn tight circles. I tried to hug her but she was too excited. When she stopped the circles, she sniffed me all over at a great rate. When she sniffed the gun she shied away briefly, and I lowered it beside my thigh, out of sight. She sniffed with special attention at my wounded leg, smelling the blood.

"Nice to see you," I said. She sat intensely and looked at me with her tongue out.

"What are we going to do if I have to shoot again?" I said. "You'll bolt and where will you end up?"

She had no answer. Neither did I. But it was bothersome.

# Chapter 25

It was full dark now, no moon, and the rain had begun. Pearl hated the rain and kept looking at me to do something about it. She also had not been fed since morning and was looking at me to do something about that too.

"You're supposed to be a goddamned hunting dog," I said. "Maybe you should go hunt up something to eat."

She had curled in against the rock, behind me, with her head resting on her rear feet. The leather jacket kept my upper body dry, but my legs were soaked, and my hair, and a trickle of rain was worming down my neck inside the jacket. The bandage felt tight against the wound in my thigh. The leg was swelling.

"It doesn't get much better than this, Pearl."

Pearl's eyes moved toward me when I spoke. The rest of her was motionless.

"We're going to have to find something better," I said. "If Gerry's out there. He won't be chasing me in the rain, at night."

I stood, and Pearl immediately uncurled and stood with me, pushing against my good leg. I started down the swale west toward the woods when I smelled something. I stopped, and with the wind coming from the east driving the rain, I breathed in carefully through my nose, my eyes closed, my head a little forward. What I smelled was woodsmoke. They were in the woods, east of me, and they had hunkered down for the night and gotten a fire going. It meant probably that whether he was a tracker or not, they had someone with them who knew his way in the woods. Gerry couldn't have started a fire in the Public Gardens.

"I could slide over there and pick some of them off," I said.

Pearl pricked her ears and wagged her tail. "But if I do you'll bolt again."

I gazed obliquely off toward the area east, where the wind was bringing the smoke from. I was trying to spot the light of the fire. There had been eight. I had dropped two. At least one guy would have had to stay behind to clean things up at Beaumont's. That meant five people probably. It would need a proper fire to service five people. "I could put on your leash," I said. "But that means dragging you through the woods and holding you while I shoot and you're bucking and struggling to run, and then ducking through the woods with you still on the leash and several gunnies chasing me. And I've only got one leg that's really usable." I was staring up, above the treeline, looking for the glow of the fire. And I found it, east and a little south, some distance away. How far was more than I could estimate. Where was Jungle Jim when you really needed him?

With them in the light and me in the dark, and taking time to aim, I could probably pick off two of them before they got under cover. That would improve the odds. Maybe I could tie her here and pick her up on the way back. If I came back. If I could find this place, running, on one and a half legs, in the dark. I looked at the fire glow in the sky east of me, and looked at Pearl, and turned and began to walk west. Pearl came along, staying close in the cold rain.

Working slowly, bumping into bushes and tree limbs, tripping over things on the forest floor, hurting my leg, I moved west, away from Broz. The darkness was nearly impenetrable. We began to go uphill again. I couldn't see it; I could tell by the increased resistance as I walked. Pearl was directly behind me, letting me break trail. I was cold now, and wet, and tired from fighting through the heavy cover.

At the top of the rise I walked into a big tree that had fallen. I worked my way down toward the root ball and found what I had hoped, the uprooting had left a shallow declivity, with the root ball shielding it partially, so that it was relatively dry in there, close to the roots. Pearl and I went in. I scraped away some of the leaf cover until I found leaves that felt dry. I heaped the leaves against the root ball, crumpled a dollar bill from my wallet in among them, piled on some twigs, and carefully lit the bill. It caught and flickered and spread to the leaves. I hovered over it, shielding it from the wind and stray raindrops. When the twigs caught I had enough flame to cast a little light, and I could see more twigs, and bigger ones. Carefully I added them, and bigger sticks, until I had a committed fire. Then I went out into the ring of light that the fire cast and got real firewood in the form of fallen limbs. I piled these under the shelter of the root ball and added some judiciously until I had a big fire. I augmented the shelter of the root ball with evergreen boughs that I cut and laid carefully in a crisscross pattern. Then I got in under and tried to be comfortable.

"They've got their own fire," I said. "They won't smell this one. Or see it." Pearl was in close to the root ball, near the fire. I could see the steam rise from her coat as she began to dry.

"Tomorrow we'll swing north toward the Mass Pike. Route 90 runs all the way from Boston to Seattle, we're bound to hit it."

I was so tired I couldn't hold my head up. I took the Browning out and held it in my right hand, and folded my left hand over it, and put my head back.

"Okay, Pearl," I said. "Stay alert for prowlers."

My eyes fell shut. I opened them once to look at the dog. She was asleep.

"Better hope for no prowlers," I said. The fire glimmered briskly, the rain fell steadily, and the darkness endured. My eyes fell closed again. And stayed closed. And I slept, though all night I was aware that my leg was throbbing.

# Chapter 26

What woke me was the sound of Pearl drinking water from a puddle which had formed at the other end of the root hole. It was daylight. Still raining. I felt very sore. My leg felt swollen and hot. The fire was out. I wasn't dry. And I was hungry. I scooped a little water out of the puddle with my cupped hand and drank. It was muddy tasting with a nose of pine needles. I looked at the sky.

"Sun would be nice," I said. "Be warmer. Be drier. Be able to tell directions a lot easier."

Pearl was sitting looking at me with the expectation of breakfast.

"Well, it's better than sitting in some quarantine pen in England, isn't it?"

The sky was lightest back where east should be. North was along the top of this slope we had climbed up in the night.

"We'll head out," I said. "And we'll keep an eye out for breakfast. Nature never failed the heart that loved her."

Every few yards I would stop and listen. If they found me they'd kill me. The fact that I wasn't Beaumont would mean nothing. Gerry was going to kill somebody, and if it were me it would please him fine. Ahead of me the land sloped down. The leg would slow me down more and more until I got it cleaned out and healing. Which meant I had better get out of the woods pretty quick or have a plan for dealing with them when they caught up with me. I wasn't going to outwalk them.

As the land continued to drop, I could see a gray glint of water through the trees. I was feeling feverish now, and turned my face up toward the rain to cool it. Pearl was a little ahead of me. She seemed to have gotten used to the rain. I don't think she liked it, but it didn't puzzle her anymore, and she had stopped turning and looking at every raindrop that hit her. Suddenly I saw her drop her head low, her belly sucked up, her neck extended, and then she charged, running like pointers do, using more of their front feet than their rear. She swerved sharply right, then back left, and I realized she had an animal in front of her. It was a groundhog. She had it trapped in the open away from its hole. It couldn't outrun her, and near the edge of a pond it turned and crouched. Pearl swung half around it as she came up on the groundhog and grabbed him by the back of the neck. She gave one sharp shake and broke its neck and dropped it and turned it over and began to eat it, ripping open its belly and eating the viscera.

My baby had given way for a moment to something older and more fundamental. She wasn't cute while she ate the groundhog.

Along the edge of the marsh I found some Jerusalem artichokes, and uprooted one, cut off the potato-esque tubers on the roots, peeled and ate it. It was like eating a raw potato, but less tasty. Still it was nourishment, and it beat chasing down a groundhog. I put a couple more of the tubers in my pocket for through-the-day snacking.

The pond looked like a glacial gouge that had slowly filled in over the millennia. Its surface was dappled with rain, and there were weeds, including Jerusalem artichokes, along the margin. I found an area where I could get at the water and knelt and drank some. It had the strong rank taste of vegetation. Carefully I took off the bloody bandage and washed it in the pond. I dropped my jeans. The wound was dark with crusted blood and the flesh around it was puffy and red. I found some kind of moss in among the rocks along the margin of the pond and wet it and mixed it with some mud and put it on the wound like a kind of poultice. Then I wrapped it with the wet sweatshirt sleeves to hold it in place and tied it again and pulled my pants back up, edging the trouser leg carefully over the mess of a bandage.

Pearl finished with the groundhog. I went over and looked at the carcass. It was about half devoured. I picked it up and put it inside my jacket. Pearl would be hungry again, and despite her initial success, I wasn't confident that she could live off the land. She jumped up to sniff where I had stashed the carcass and rested one big paw on my wounded leg. I yelped and she dropped to the ground and backed off a yard and sat down very quickly, looking at me with her ears pricked forward and her head canted.

"Come on," I said, and we moved north again.

I ate some chokecherries, which were quite biting, and I found some acorns which I cracked and chewed and swallowed despite the strong bitterness of the tannin in them. If I had had something to soak them in, and time, I could have leached out the tannin. But I didn't, and if I had, how good are leached acorns anyway? Later on, as we moved through the heavy cover, I gnawed at some more of the Jerusalem artichoke root. Everything I ate tasted like tarantula juice, but I knew I had to eat, and this was the best I could find.

The drizzle was persistent. By noontime I was beginning to feel light-headed, and the pulsing in my leg was Wagnerian. I wasn't going to be able to walk for too much longer. We crossed a stream, and again I washed my wound and washed the bandages and tied them back in place. I paused and stood still, listening. I couldn't hear anything except the sound the rain made in the woods. The ground rose ahead of me and I went up it. Whenever I could I stayed on the high ground, where it was a little easier going than the hollows. I found a big old pine and climbed it clumsily; my left leg was feeling more and more useless. Except for the pain it was largely without feeling, as if the pulsing insulated it from everything else. When I got as high as the tree could support me, I wedged myself into a crotch, with one arm wrapped around the trunk and waited and watched. Below me Pearl sat on the ground, looking up. The half-gnawed groundhog inside my jacket was beginning to ripen. My hair was wet and the water dripped onto my forehead and into my eyes. I was feverish, and hot, except that I was also cold, and the effort of climbing the tree had made me more than light-headed. I was dizzy.

I took in some air, and exhaled, and did that a couple of times, and concentrated on the woods behind me, where Pearl and I had come from. Maybe a mile back was a bare patch, a basalt outcropping of maybe thirty or forty yards. I focused on it. Pearl and I had crossed it maybe forty minutes ago, and if they were behind us they'd cross it too. Not only did my trail lead that way—if they really had somebody who could follow a trail—but anyone would head for it because it was much easier going, if only for a little ways.

The acorns and chokecherries and Jerusalem artichokes rolled unpleasantly around in my stomach. The drizzle had upgraded again to a steady rain. The smell of pitch and pine needle and wetness was very strong as I pressed against the tree. A double Glenfiddich on the rocks would have been helpful. Pearl whined a little, nervously, from the ground under the tree. I said "shhh" automatically, the way people do with dogs, even though dogs generally don't know what "shhh" means. In Pearl's case I was up so high, and shhh'd so weakly, that Pearl probably didn't hear it anyway.

And then I saw them. Mostly I had been hoping I wouldn't and I could concentrate on making it to the Mass Pike before my leg gave way. But they were there, in three groups. In front a big dark guy, with long black hair, wearing a red-and-black mackinaw. He was tracking—his head down, swiveling slowly back and forth.

"Son of a bitch," I said. My voice sounded hoarse and funny.

Behind him were three other men. I recognized Maishe from the restaurant in Beverly, and Anthony. The third guy wasn't anyone I knew. He carried a white sack in his left hand. And behind them, straggling, maybe ten yards back, was Gerry Broz. He was laboring.

The white sack was probably a pillowcase. He'd probably had the brains to grab it and fill it with whatever foodstuffs he could find in Patty Giacomin's kitchen. He was smallish, and wiry looking, from where I was watching. And he looked country, like the tracker. Maishe had an Uzi, and Anthony carried the shotgun. They looked tired and wet, but still functional. Behind them Gerry was so tired he almost staggered. Even at a half mile I could tell he was exhausted. He was a plump, flabby, small-framed kid. All the muscle he had, he hired.

It had taken me about forty minutes to get to where I was from where they were. They were moving faster than I could, but Gerry slowed them down. I had at least a half hour, and I knew I had better make my stand here. I was nearly spent. I edged down the tree, holding my bad leg carefully away from me. When I reached the ground I had to ward Pearl off, to keep her from hurting my leg again.

"Unerring," I said. "You are unerring."

I moved slowly back down off the rise toward the stream. I made a wide circle as I went, being careful to avoid the path I'd taken up. The tracker would follow my path across the stream and up to the ridgeline before he discovered I'd doubled back. It should be enough time. If things worked out. I reached the stream and entered it about twenty yards below the place I'd crossed before. I waded upstream with Pearl on the bank, moving through the brush, glancing at me in puzzlement now and then, but enjoying the cascade of smells that she was encountering among the weeds along the bank. I took the ripening groundhog carcass from inside my jacket and tossed it across the stream to her. It landed five feet in front of her. She stopped. Dropped her head, raised her rear end, and put her front legs straight out in front of her. Then she pounced on it. Picked it up in her jaws, shook it a couple of times, and dashed off into the woods with it. Which is what I was hoping for.

At the point where I'd crossed before, standing in the water, I bent one branch and broke another, so that the tracker shouldn't miss it. Then I moved across to the far bank and pulled loose a small sapling, as if I had grabbed it to climb the bank and it had pulled loose. The water moved rapidly here, the streambed full up with the long rain. I went back to the far side of the stream, the one they'd come from, and edged myself in against the bank, under the low sweep of a black spruce whose roots were half exposed in the stream bank.

I was hip deep in the water, half crouched against the bank. The cold water numbed my leg. The rain granulated the black surface of the stream. There were no rocks here, no snags, so that the fast water moved sleekly without any show of white. Pearl was out of sight, communing with her lunch. I took the Browning out and cocked it and waited.

In twenty minutes they arrived. The tracker first, moving easily through the cover. On his right hip I saw the nose of a holster poke down beneath the skirt of his mackinaw. He paused at the stream, looked both ways and across, saw the broken branch on the other side. His hair was long and black and wet, plastered by the rain against his skull. In profile he had a nose like Dick Tracy, and around the eye a hint of American Indian. I saw him nod to himself once, then step into the stream and walk across. Behind him came the other three: Maishe and Anthony, and the stranger with the sack. I had been right. It was a pillowcase, soaking wet now, and lumpy with canned goods in the bottom. Maishe looked back once, hesitated, then shrugged and went into the stream. The other two went with him. They were all up the other side and thirty yards beyond before Gerry reached the stream. He was a mess. He was still wearing the camel's hair topcoat he'd worn in Beverly. It was belted up now, and the collar was up. But the coat was sodden with rain and probably added twenty pounds to his load. He was limping, and his breath was audible for ten yards, rasping in and out. Even in the cold rain his face was flushed, and he staggered occasionally as he struggled through the thick woods. He paused on the stream bank, gasping. Across the stream, Maishe turned and looked back. Gerry waved him on. Maishe shrugged again and started up toward the ridgeline after the other three. Gerry gasped in a big gulp of air and then edged into the stream. When he was halfway across I came out from under the tree and caught hold of him by the long modish hair at the back of his neck. I yanked him back toward me and jammed the Browning into his ear.

Gerry made a kind of yowling noise, and the people ahead stopped and turned. I held him motionless there in the stream with my gun screwed into his ear. The tracker hit the ground, rolled once. As he rolled I saw a flash of metallic movement. Then he was behind a rock outcropping with his handgun out. It was a big one, with a long barrel.

The other three stood motionless. The wiry guy with the pillowcase frozen in a sort of half crouch. The other two standing upright, looking at Gerry and me in the water. The noise of the stream and the sound of the rain was all there was.

"It ain't Richie," Maishe said finally.

"And proud of it," I said.

Gerry's voice was barely audible as it croaked out of his throat.

"Spenser?"

"Un huh."

Again silence. Pearl appeared on the rising ground opposite and sniffed at the pillowcase that the wiry guy was holding.

Nobody moved.

I said, "Which one of you wants to tell Joe that you were there when his kid got killed in the woods?"

"There's four of us, Spenser," Maishe said.

"How many did you start with?" I said.

No one spoke. Pearl continued to sniff carefully at the pillowcase, bending her neck and moving her feet a little to get a careful smell survey of the contents from every angle. The guy holding the pillowcase didn't look at her. His eyes were fixed on me.

"Where's Richie?" Maishe said.

Close to me I could hear Gerry's breath, wheezing through his throat as if there were very little room for it.

"Listen," I said. "Here's the deal. You four beat it. Gerry and I walk out of here alone, and when we get to the Mass Pike, I let him go."

"That's it?" Maishe said.

I nodded.

"And if we don't?"

"Then I drop Gerry like a stone and take my chances with you."

"How many rounds you got left?" Maishe said.

I didn't say anything.

Maishe looked at Anthony. Anthony had nothing to say.

"You drop Gerry and you got nothing left to bargain with," Maishe said.

I didn't say anything. Pearl had given up on the pillowcase and walked over to sniff at the tracker on the ground behind the granite. He reached back absently and scratched her ear with his free hand. Her tail wagged. Maishe shifted his feet a little. He looked at Gerry.

"What do you want, Gerry?" he said.

I spoke softly to Gerry, my mouth two inches from his left ear, the pressure of the Browning steady in his right one.

"I would like to kill you, Gerry. It would be a good thing for civilization. And it would be fun. I'll keep you alive if it gets me out of here. But you know that if the show starts, your brains will be floating in the water."

"How do I know you'll let me go?" His voice was little more than a hiss.

"Because I said I would."

Gerry was silent. Maishe spoke again.

"What do you want us to do, Gerry?"

"If I knew you'd let me go . . ." Gerry whispered.

I didn't say anything. Pearl left the tracker and moseyed happily down to the stream edge and drank noisily and long. Ripe woodchuck will give you a thirst.

Gerry raised his voice. "Do what he says."

"You want we should leave you?" Maishe said.

Gerry's voice was shrill with the effort of squeezing it out.

"Do what he says. I believe him. He'll let me go later."

What Gerry really believed was that I'd kill him now. We all knew that.

Maishe shrugged. The tracker got to his feet. He still had the big revolver out but he let it slide down at his side. The guy with the pillowcase eased out of his crouch.

"Go back the way you came," I said. "Cross downstream. Keep going. If I see you or even hear you in the woods I will blow his brains out. And then you can explain to Joe how you let that happen, and who was in charge, and how four of you let one guy do it. Joe will be interested."

Nobody moved for a moment. Then Maishe said, "Fuck it," and the four of them began to drift back toward the stream, twenty yards or so down from where Gerry and I stood. I turned slowly as they went, keeping Gerry between us.

The tracker entered the streambed last. As he walked into the water he said to me, "Your dog?"

"Yeah."

"Nice dog."

"Thanks."

"Mass Pike's about three miles." He jerked his head. "Back that way. Stay on the ridgeline."

I nodded again. Then he was out of the stream.

"Maybe we'll see you down the road," he said.

I didn't answer and he was into the woods, and in a minute he was out of sight.

# Chapter 27

Gerry and I were strolling toward the Pike. My leg was hot and stiff and swollen tight against my jeans. I limped badly and my head swam periodically. I didn't mention this to Gerry. He walked three or four feet ahead of me. Struggling with his own limitations, barely aware of anything except the need to get air into his lungs and stay upright. Pearl hustled along in front of us, sometimes swinging far out of sight and then larruping back through the woods to prance in front of us with her tongue out, before she careened off again. She was able to go through the dense woods at nearly top speed. Groundhog must be nourishing.

I was having trouble concentrating. My mind kept moving back over things. I was cold and wet, but my body felt parched, and the pain in my leg pounded up and down my left side. Pearl came back to nuzzle my hand and went off again. I thought about beer. I had come down to New York, a lifetime ago, to fight a guy named Carmen Ramazottie, from Bayonne. We had fought a prelim at St. Nick's and I had put Carmen down with a very nice combination that my Uncle Bob had worked on with me. Bob and I stayed at a dump on the West Side called the Bristol, and the morning after the fight we checked out and took a subway to Brooklyn to see a ball game at Ebbets Field before we got the late bus home.

It was late August in New York. The subway was dense and sweaty and running slow. I had a headache and the right side of my face under the eye was puffy and darkening steadily from the reiterated application of Carmen's pretty good left jab. Coming up into the harsh city sun made my head hurt worse. I had been thirsty since the second round of last night's fight. I knew I was dehydrated and in time I'd catch up, but it didn't make me less thirsty. As we crossed Flatbush Avenue, the tar was soft from the sun, and the ballpark crowd was damp with sweat. Shirts clung. Bra straps chafed. There were a lot of black faces in the crowd, come to see Jackie Robinson play.

Ebbets Field was small and idiosyncratic. It was a short 297 feet to the right-field screen. The base of the scoreboard in right was angular, and Carl Furillo, and Dixie Walker before him, had made an art of playing to odd caroms off it. There were advertising signs on the outfield walls. The fans were close to the field, and after a game they could stream across the outfield and exit through the gate in deep center field.

The Cardinals were in, their gray road uniforms trimmed in red; Stan Musial and Red Schoendienst. We got seats behind first base while there was still batting practice to watch. I was old enough to drink in New York. In Boston I was still underage. We got two big paper cups of Schaefer beer and settled back.

The beer was cold from the tap and fresh. I felt it seep through me the way spring rain invigorates a flower.

In the bottom of the first inning Duke Snider did his little kick step and hit the ball into Bedford Avenue. My Uncle Bob and I toasted him with another beer. My headache was going. The throbbing in my cheek diminished. Stan Musial. Duke Snider. Cold beer in the sunshine. Only yesterday, when the world was young.

"I gotta rest," Gerry said.

My focus swam back onto him. He had slumped to the ground, his back against a birch tree, his legs sprawled before him, his arms limp at his side. I realized I'd lost track of him entirely. I didn't remember walking the last half mile. I didn't remember coming down the side of this gully.

I was lucky it was Gerry. The tracker would have brained me by now with a rock. I leaned against another birch trunk. If I sat down I wasn't sure I could get up.

"Get up," I said. Time was not my friend. I didn't have much of it left.

Gerry's head was sunk on his chest. He shook it silently.

"Okay," I said. "See you around."

My voice sounded like someone else's. Someone trying to sound perky. And failing. Pearl bounded over and jumped up to lap my face. She put one paw on my leg. I didn't scream. I held the tree with my left arm and fended her off with my right. I noticed that I was still holding the gun in my hand, but I'd let the hammer down. I didn't remember doing that. There was some nausea. It passed slowly, like a wave slowly easing back out to sea. When it was gone enough to move, I jerked my head at Pearl and started off.

Gerry said, "Hey."

I kept going.

He labored to his feet, using the tree trunk. He was behind me now. I kept going. The gun in my right hand, hanging straight down, Pearl, ahead of me, nose to the forest floor, looking for groundhogs.

"Wait up," Gerry gasped.

It had become ludicrous. My hostage was chasing me. It was darkening and the drizzle had finally stopped when we reached the last rise and below us saw the traffic on the Pike. I took the leash from my pocket and whistled for Pearl. She dashed up and sat. She always dashed up and sat when she saw the leash. To her it meant a walk. Even when she was on a walk. I hooked the leash onto her collar. And we started down the slope. Pearl strained against the leash and my leg hurt exceptionally as I went downhill on it, bracing against Pearl's tug. To my right Gerry started to run toward the highway and fell and rolled noisily through the brush for maybe thirty feet before he stopped and struggled up and kept moving.

Most of the cars had their headlights on, though it wasn't really dark yet. And they paraded by swiftly and sporadically, a pageant of ordinariness, the people in them rushing to dinner, or a late meeting, unwounded, unfeverish, unarmed, dry, and at worst maybe a little stiff from their long commute.

The chances of flagging a ride were negligible, but sooner or later a state cop would cruise by, and he'd stop. If he saw us. I looped Pearl's leash over my wrist so that if I passed out she wouldn't wander off into the traffic. Gerry was standing limply ten feet down the highway. He wasn't looking at me. His head was down. His eyes may have been closed; I couldn't see.

"Walk away from me," I said. "That way. Keep going until you're out of sight. If I see you again I'll kill you."

Gerry had no words. He simply turned in the direction I'd pointed and began to stumble along the highway, his head down, weaving as he walked, as if he were drunk. Pearl was close to my leg, shying closer every time a car passed, stirring the leaves and dust along the margin of the roadbed.

I couldn't remember now who had won that baseball game. Cardinals or Dodgers? It had probably mattered greatly then; it mattered now not at all. I felt myself begin to dissolve. I frowned. I concentrated on looking up the Pike at the oncoming headlights. It would be harder to spot me if I keeled over. It would be harder to spot me as it got darker. I looked down the road after Gerry Broz. I couldn't see him. The turnpike curved fifty yards ahead and he was around the curve now. I holstered the Browning. Gerry wouldn't have the energy to circle back and jump me. Nor, probably, now that he was alone, the balls. I remembered that once I had seen Jackie Robinson steal home. Pigeon-toed, elbows pumping, under the tag. He was dead now. Been dead a long time. Died a young man. *He lit up the sky,* my Uncle Bob used to say. The headlights blurred in the mist. Except there wasn't any mist. The rain had stopped an hour ago. The first time Robinson had taken the field, Red Barber had said in his soft Southern voice on the radio, *He is very definitely brunette.* One pair of the blurred headlights swept over me. A car swung up onto the shoulder. The door opened and Hawk got out.

"You are very definitely brunette," I said.

Then Hawk blurred too.

I heard myself say, "Take the dog."

And then I didn't hear anything. Or see anything, except darkness visible.

# Chapter 28

Someone said, "Where's the dog?"

Somebody else said, "In the car with a soup bone."

"On the leather seats?" someone said.

"You bled all over them already," someone else said. "Figured it didn't matter anymore."

My eyes opened. Hawk was standing at the foot of the bed, wearing a black leather jacket over a black turtleneck. He leaned forward and rested his forearms on the bed rail and I could see the butt of his gun under his arm where the jacket fell open.

"How come you were out riding around on the Pike in western Mass?" I said. It had been me speaking all along, but I just realized it.

"Paul told me what happened," Hawk said. "I looked at a map, figured you'd get in the woods and loop for the highway. What I woulda done."

"So you been cruising it," I said.

"Un huh. Lee exit to the New York line and back, two tanks of gas."

"Paul's okay?"

"He at your place. So's his momma and her honey."

"My place?"

"You not using it," Hawk said. "Had to stash them someplace."

I shifted in the bed. There was an IV in the back of my left hand, held in place by tape. The tube ran to a drip bottle on a stand. My leg felt sore, but it wasn't throbbing anymore, and it didn't feel distended. I looked around the room. It was private. There was a silent television on a high shelf opposite, and the usual hospital apparatus on the walls, blood pressure gauges, and oxygen outlets, and spigots for purposes unclear to the lay public.

"I'm in a hospital," I said.

"Wow," Hawk said.

"I'm a trained observer," I said. "Where?"

"Pittsfield," Hawk said.

"Susan?"

"I called her," Hawk said. "She on the way, bringing you some clothes."

I was wearing a hospital johnny. I glanced at the night table.

"Wallet's in the nightstand," Hawk said. "Got your gun."

"How am I?"

"You not going to die, you not going to lose the leg, your personality not going to improve."

"So, two out of three," I said.

"Some people say none out of three," Hawk said. "Where's Gerry?"

"Left him on the turnpike," I said. "Walking toward Stockbridge."

"Want to tell me about it?" Hawk said.

I did.

"Been about thirty hours," Hawk said. "Figure Gerry be home by now."

I raised the sheet and looked at my leg. It was bandaged thickly, around the thigh. The part that showed looked a little bruised but not too puffy.

"Cops been around?" I said.

"Yeah. Hospital called them when they saw the gunshot wound. I told them you was out in the woods with the dog while I waiting in Stockbridge. When you didn't come back I went and found you."

"They believe you?"

"No."

"Don't blame them," I said.

A thin-faced, dark-haired nurse came in.

"Awake," she said.

"Yes."

She smiled without thinking about it and took out an electronic thermometer and took my temperature. She read it and nodded to herself and wrote something on her clipboard. She took my pulse, and my blood pressure, and noted those.

"We hungry yet?" she said.

"I am," I said. "How about you?"

Another automatic smile. "I'll have them bring you something."

She located a remote control unit attached to a cord on the bedside table.

"Want to sit up?"

"Sure."

I noticed that during her time in the room she had not looked at Hawk. But she was aware of him. I could see the awareness in her shoulders and the way she held her neck. She showed me the remote.

"We push this to sit up," she said. "And this turns on our television. And if we need a nurse we push this one."

I said, "Are you going to get into bed with me? Or is this *we* stuff just a tease?"

She looked blankly at me for a moment. Then she grinned.

"Let's wait until your leg is better," she said.

"That's what they all say."

"Oh, I doubt that," she said. "My name is Felicia. You want me"—she grinned—"for medical reasons, press the button."

She watched me while I raised the bed into a nearly sitting position. Then she turned to go. At the door she glanced back at Hawk. He smiled at her and she flushed and went out of the room. In maybe a minute she was back and with her came a young guy wearing a brown Sears and Roebuck suit. He was nearly bald, and what little was left he wore cut very short.

"Officer deShayes wants to see you," she said, and whisked her white skirt back out the door without looking again at Hawk.

DeShayes showed me a badge that said Pittsfield Police on it. Then he put the badge away and took out a small spiral notebook with a red cover.

"Feeling okay?" he said.

"On top of the world," I said.

"Good," he said. "Good. Just some routine questions here. We always have to follow up on gunshot wounds, you know."

"Yeah."

He glanced once at Hawk, who had retired to an uncomfortable chair under the television set and appeared to go to sleep. Now that I was sitting up, I could see that his jeans were black and he wore them tucked inside black cowboy boots.

"Friend of yours?" deShayes said.

"Darth Vader," I said.

DeShayes nodded. "So how did you come by this gunshot wound?"

"Self-inflicted," I said. "Accidental."

"Un huh. Could you describe the events which caused you to perpetrate this self-inflicted wound?"

"Sure. I was walking the dog, in the woods, and thought I'd take a little target practice. And accidentally shot myself."

"And where is this dog now?"

"In his car," I said, nodding at Hawk.

"And the gun with which the wound was inflicted?"

"He's got it," I said. Without opening his eyes Hawk produced my gun from inside his jacket and held it out toward deShayes. DeShayes took it and sniffed the barrel and popped out the magazine and cleared the round from the chamber. It flipped onto the bed near my hip. He thumbed the shells out of the magazine, onto the bed beside the first one. He nodded to himself, the way the nurse had after she'd taken my temperature.

"You're from Boston?" deShayes said. He put the empty magazine back in my gun, put the gun on the night table, picked up the five shells, and dropped them into his suitcoat pocket.

"Yes."

"A private detective."

"Yes."

"Licensed to carry this gun?"

"Yes."

"Do you happen to have the license with you?"

"In the wallet, in the drawer," I said.

He reached into the drawer and took out my wallet and handed it to me.

"Take out the gun permit please, and your ID."

I did, and handed them to him. He looked them over carefully and made a couple of notes in his little spiral notebook with his blue Bic pen. Then he handed the stuff back to me.

"Live in Boston?" he said.

"Yes."

"Where you staying out here?"

"Just came out for the day," I said.

"Why?"

"Take the dog in the woods. She loves the woods."

"Two-hour drive to walk the dog?"

"She's a good dog," I said.

He nodded. His face was blank.

"That's a Browning, isn't it?" DeShayes nodded at the black automatic lying on the night table.

"Yes."

"Don't they usually hold thirteen rounds in the clip?"

"Yeah."

"There's only four rounds in your clip and one in the chamber."

"I fired off eight rounds target shooting."

"One of which hit you, according to the surgeon, in the back middle quadrant of your left thigh."

"Embarrassing, isn't it."

"Actually I think it's more than embarrassing, sir. I think it's bullshit," deShayes said.

I didn't say anything. Hawk remained peaceful with his eyes closed. His legs straight out in front of him, crossed at the ankles.

"How'd you get out here?" deShayes said.

"Drove out, separate cars."

"And where is your car now?"

"Where I parked it, I hope. In the parking lot at the Red Lion."

DeShayes made some more notes.

"Stockbridge police found a car registered to you, this morning, parked in front of a house in town. Tires had been shot out, and most of the windows in the house had been shot out. They're still digging bullets out of the plaster."

"Son of a gun," I said. "Somebody must have hot-wired it."

"No sign of that," deShayes said.

"Car thieves are getting very clever these days, aren't they?"

DeShayes didn't comment. He wrote another thing in his little notebook.

"You have anything to add?" he said.

"You know what I know," I said.

"Sure," deShayes said. "They tell me you'll be here awhile. If you decide to leave before I get back to you, give me a call." He handed me a card that read Detective Joseph E. deShayes.

"What's the *E* for?" I said.

"Make sure you check with me before you leave," deShayes said. "Got it?"

"I think so," I said. "He can help me with the hard parts." I nodded at Hawk.

DeShayes stood. He took my five cartridges out of his pocket and put them in an ashtray on the night table.

"Be careful with these," he said.

# Chapter 29

I dined on chicken broth and raspberry Jell-O, which was an improvement on acorns and chokecherries, but only a small one. After I ate I fell asleep and when I woke up Susan was there. She had on black jeans that fitted the form of her leg, and low-heeled boots that came above midcalf, and a white silk blouse which she wore with the top two buttons open. Her black hair was thick and shiny, and her eyes looked extra large and shadowed in the odd hospital lighting.

Hawk was still in his chair. Susan had pulled a straight chair near the bed and sat in it. She was reading a copy of *Metropolitan Home*. Squinting a little, turning the magazine as she read, trying to catch the light. I lay quietly for a little while watching her.

"Hey," I said.

She raised her head from the magazine and smiled at me, and leaned forward and kissed me on the mouth.

"Hey," she said.

I fumbled for the remote and found it and pushed the button and raised myself up in the bed.

"How are you?" Susan said.

"Fit as a fiddle and ready for love. I could jump over the moon up above."

Susan smiled. "How nice," she said, "that your ordeal has not aged you."

I put my hand out and she took it and we were quiet, holding hands.

Felicia came back in. "Well," she said, "I see we're awake again."

"Felicia identifies with me," I said to Susan.

"Dr. Good will be in to see you in a little while."

"Is his first name Feel?" I said.

"No," Felicia said, "I think it's Jeffrey. He's the chief resident."

Felicia took my temperature and my blood pressure and pulse. She had me lean forward while she smoothed the sheets and plumped the pillows. While this was going on a guy in a white coat came in with a stethoscope hanging loosely from his neck.

"Hi," he said. "I'm Jeff Good. I was in the ER when you came in."

I introduced Susan and started to introduce Hawk.

"I met this gentleman when he brought you in," Dr. Good said. "A very strong guy, it would appear. He carried you in like you were a child."

"He's childlike in many ways," Susan said.

Dr. Good smiled without really paying much attention and pulled back the sheet to look at my leg. He touched it lightly here and there, nodding to himself. The place was full of people who nodded to themselves. Everybody knew stuff. Nobody was saying.

"What's the diagnosis?" I said.

"Blood loss and infection, both the result of a single gunshot wound in your left thigh. Exhaustion. We're pumping you full of antibiotics now, and I think we've got the infection under control. We gave you some blood already."

"When can I go home?"

Good shrugged. "Another day, probably, if your fever stays down, and you promise to see someone in Boston, and stay off the thing for a while."

"Sure," I said.

"Got everything you need?"

"I could use something to eat besides chicken broth and Jell-O."

"Is that what they're feeding you?" Good shook his head. He looked at Felicia, who stood worshipfully aside, gazing at him. "Can we get him a real meal?"

"Of course, Doctor. No restrictions?"

"No."

He nodded at me and went out. Felicia hurried after him.

"I'd say your chances with Felicia aren't as good as they looked," I said to Hawk.

Hawk shrugged. "It's 'cause I'm not trying," he said.

"Would you care to tell me how you came to be here in the hospital?" Susan said. "I've had some high points from Hawk, but I'd like the full treatment if you're not too tired."

"Certainly," I said. "It's a compelling story, which I tell elegantly."

Hawk stood up from his chair. He seemed to do this without effort. In fact without movement. One moment he was sitting and then he was standing.

"I've already heard the story," Hawk said. "I think I'll go walk Pearl. Gun's in the drawer. Round in the chamber."

I opened the night-table drawer as he left and saw my gun. Hawk had reloaded it. I left the drawer open.

Susan looked at the gun and at me and didn't say anything.

"We found Patty," I said. "And Rich. And Gerry Broz found us."

"How?"

"Patty told somebody," I said.

"God, she must feel awful."

"Maybe," I said. "I think she's so needy, and so desperate, that she can't feel anything but the need."

Susan nodded. "So what happened?"

I told her. She listened quietly. I always loved it when I had a story to tell her, because her attention was complete and felt like sunlight. Hawk came back just before the end.

"Pearl actually killed and ate a groundhog?" Susan said.

"Showed that soup bone no mercy, either," Hawk said.

"Let's not spread this around Cambridge," I said. "The Vegetarian Sisterhood will picket her."

"And you let Gerry Broz go?" Susan said.

"Had to. I didn't know how long I was going to stay on my feet. If I passed out while he was there, he'd have shot me with my own gun."

"Could have shot him," Hawk said.

I shrugged.

"Could you do that?" Susan said. "Just shoot him like that?"

I shrugged again.

"Gerry could," Hawk said. "Spenser keels over, Gerry shoots him while he's laying there."

"Will he . . ." Susan stopped. "I don't know how to say it. Will he be less dangerous to you because you let him go?"

"Pretty to think so," Hawk said.

Susan looked at me. I shook my head.

"Hawk's right," I said. "Gerry will have to come for me. He can't stand to have been—the way he would think of it—humiliated in front of his people."

"Maybe then you should have shot him," Susan said.

"As a practical matter," I said.

"Yes," Susan said.

"I love you when you're bloodthirsty," I said.

"Don't patronize me," Susan said. "You know I'm not bloodthirsty, but I love you. I can be very practical about you if I must be, very bloodthirsty if you prefer."

"I know," I said. "I take back bloodthirsty. But . . ." I spread my hands. "Before all this happened I talked to Joe."

"Joe Broz?"

"Yeah. Gerry's father. He's worried about the kid. It's his only kid and he's no good and Joe knows it."

"He ought to know it," Susan said. "What chance did his son have being the child of a mobster?"

"Joe doesn't mind that he's a mobster too," I said. "Joe likes that. What kills Joe is that he's such a crapola mobster."

"He feel sorry for Joe," Hawk said.

We were all silent.

Finally Susan said, "Would you have killed him, Hawk?"

"Absolutely," Hawk said.

"He's dangerous still?"

"He gonna come for us," Hawk said.

At which point the ineffable Felicia came in with my supper.

# Chapter 30

"Whatever happened to that Harvard woman you used to date?" Susan said.

"Daisy or Cindy?" Hawk said. "They both from Harvard."

"Well, tell me about both of them," Susan said. "I didn't realize you had this passion for intellectuals."

"I'se here with you, missy."

"True," Susan said. "Which one was Daisy?"

I probed the sliced turkey with my fork. It was densely blanketed with a dark gravy.

"Daisy is the redhead, taught black studies." Hawk's face was without expression. Susan raised her eyebrows.

"Yeah," Hawk said. "This a while ago. Everybody teaching black studies. Red-haired broad with freckles, grew up in Great Neck, Long Island. Only black people she ever saw were from the Long Island Expressway driving through Jamaica."

"I assume her emphasis tended toward the more theoretical aspects of the black experience," Susan said.

I ate some turkey. It was pretty tender, but the gravy was hard to chew.

"She'd read *Invisible Man* six times," Hawk said. "Everything Angela Davis ever wrote. Told me she ashamed of being white. Told me she thought maybe she black in another life."

I tried some mashed potatoes. They were chewy, too.

"An African princess perhaps?" I said. It came out muffled because I was still gnawing on the mashed potatoes.

"Amazing you should guess that," Hawk said.

"Funny, isn't it," I said—and paused and tried to swallow the potato, and succeeded on the second try—"how people almost never seem to have been four-dollar whores in a Cape Town crib in another life."

"Anyway, me and Daisy used to go to The Harvest for dinner," Hawk said.

"The Harvest?" Susan said.

"Un huh," Hawk said.

I put a forkful of lukewarm succotash in my mouth, chewed it aggressively and swallowed it, hoping to tamp down the potatoes a bit.

"My God," Susan said. "The thought of you at The Harvest."

"Un huh," Hawk said.

"People in The Harvest talk about Proust," Susan said. "And Kierkegaard."

"Daisy talk about my elemental earthiness," Hawk said.

"And they talk about whether they have a date for Saturday night," Susan said. "And sometimes they discuss your sign."

"You been going there without me?" I said.

"Certainly. While you're out waltzing through the woods with your faithful dog, I'm at the bar in The Harvest, wearing a beret, reading *Paris-Match*, sipping white wine, and smoking imported cigarettes with my hand turned the wrong way."

"Waiting for Mister Right?" I said.

"Yes. In a seersucker jacket."

"Mister Right don't wear no seersucker jacket," Hawk said.

"Sandals?" Susan said.

Hawk shook his head.

"Chinos and Bass Weejuns?"

"Nope."

"Does he wear his sweater draped over his shoulder like a shawl?"

"Positively not," Hawk said.

"He wears blue blazers with brass buttons," I said. "And has a nose that's encountered adversity."

"And an eighteen-inch neck?" Susan said.

"That's the guy," I said.

"Yes, it is," Susan said.

"Other woman was Cindy Astor," Hawk said. "Taught at the Kennedy School. Only female full professor they had when I was with her. Specialized in Low Country politics. Had a law degree, a master's in English, a

Ph.D. in Dutch history. Used to work for the State Department, spent some time at the American Embassy in Brussels. Smart."

I worked on the turkey with gravy some more. In a little paper cup next to it was some pink applesauce—maybe.

"Smarter than you?" Susan said.

"No."

"And did you and she dine at The Harvest?"

Hawk shook his head.

"Her place mostly. Sometimes we'd go to the Harvard Faculty Club, get some boiled food."

"Were you impressed with the Harvard Faculty Club?" Susan said.

I knew she knew that Hawk was never impressed with anything, and I knew how much she was enjoying the image of Hawk eating haddock and boiled potatoes among the icons of Harvard intellection.

"Man asked me once what I did for a living," Hawk said. His voice sank into a perfect mimic of the upper-class Yankee honk.

" 'What exactly is it you do, sir?' man say to me. I say, 'I'm in security and enforcement, my good man.' And the man say to me 'How fascinating.' And I say, 'More fascinating if you the enforcer than if you the enforcee.' And he look at me sort of strange and say, 'Yes, yes, certainly,' and he hustle off to the bar, order a double Manhattan. Two cherries."

I ate the dessert. It might have been vanilla pudding.

"But you weren't in love with these women?"

"No."

"Think you'll ever fall in love?"

"Probably not," Hawk said.

"You might," Susan said.

"Maybe I can't," Hawk said.

My eyes were heavy and I leaned back against the pillow.

I heard Susan say, "I hadn't thought of that."

And then I was asleep.

# Chapter 31

Pearl was hurrying around my apartment, sniffing everything, including Rich Beaumont and Patty Giacomin, which neither of them liked much.

"Can you get Pearl to settle down?" Paul said.

"I could speak to her, but she'd continue to do what she wants, and I'd look ineffectual. My approach is to endorse everything she does."

Susan said, "Come here, Pearl." And Pearl went over to her, and Susan gave her a kiss on the mouth, and Pearl wagged her tail; and lapped Susan's face, and turned and went back and sniffed at Patty.

"Isn't that cute," I said.

"Never mind about the damn dog," Beaumont said. "We got a problem here and we need to solve it."

He had helped himself to one of my shirts, which was too big for him, and he hadn't shaved. He looked a little seedier than he had in Stockbridge. He glanced once, uneasily, toward Hawk, leaning on the wall near the front hall entry. Hawk smiled at him cheerily.

"I mean, we can't stay here forever," Beaumont said.

"I thought of that too," I said. "What's your plan?"

"I don't know," Beaumont said. "Can you help us out?"

"He already did that," Paul said.

"Yeah," Beaumont said. "Yeah, sure. I know. I mean, shit, you got yourself shot helping us out. It's not like I don't know that and appreciate it."

"We both do," Patty said. She was sitting beside Beaumont on the couch, holding his hand. "We both appreciate it so much."

"I was you I'd go to the cops," I said.

"Cops?"

"Yeah. You must have enough to trade them for protection."

"Christ—the stuff I got is *on* the cops. Who we paid, when, how much. I wouldn't last a day."

"I'll put you in touch with cops you can trust," I said.

"And they'll have me guarded by cops they can trust, and so on. Sure. But what if they're wrong, or what if you're wrong?"

"I'm not wrong."

"It's a big world," Beaumont said. "We got money to go anywhere in it. All you got to do is get us out of this city."

"How about you, Mom?" Paul said.

Patty shook her head and clutched onto Beaumont's hand.

"You want to go anywhere in the world with him?"

Patty glanced around the room; nobody said anything. She pressed her face against Beaumont's shoulder.

"Sure she does," Beaumont said. "She loves me."

"A crook, Mom? A guy that carries a gun and steals money and is a fugitive from the damned mob?"

Patty sat up straight and rested her clenched fists on her thighs. "It's not so easy for a girl to be alone, Paulie."

Paul said, "You don't go off with a goddamned gangster because it's hard to be alone. If you can't be alone, you can't be anybody. Haven't you ever found that out? To be with somebody first you got to be with you."

"Oh, Paulie, all that psychobabble. I never thought you should have gone to that shrink in the first place."

"And where do you get off calling me a gangster, kid?" Beaumont asked.

"You don't like 'gangster'? How about 'thief'? That better?"

"I don't have to take that shit," Beaumont said.

"Please," Patty said. "Please. Paulie, I can't make it alone. When your father left me I thought I'd die. I have to be with somebody. Rich loves me. There's nothing wrong with being loved. Rich would stand on his head for me."

"Jesus Christ, Ma," Paul said. "My father leaving you was the best chance you had. You didn't love him. He was a creep. You had a chance and instead you went to another creep, and then another. Get away from this guy, be alone for a while. I'll help you. Find out who you are. You could have a decent guy someday if you got your goddamned head together."

"Who you calling a creep?" Beaumont said. He leaned forward as if he were going to stand. Leaning on the wall, Hawk cleared his throat. Beaumont looked at him and froze, then sank back on the couch.

Patty pounded both fists on her thighs. "Goddamn you! I found a man who loves me. I won't let him go. Not for you and all your highfa-luting shrink ideas. You don't know what it's like to be abandoned."

Paul was silent for a moment. No one else spoke. Pearl got up from where she had been sitting near Susan and walked over to sniff at Hawk's pants leg.

"Well, not like I mean," Patty said. "I mean, sure, you had a tough time when you were a kid maybe, but we took care of you. You went to good schools. Now, you turned out fine, see that. How bad a mother could I be? Look at you. Got a career, got a girlfriend. I must have done some-thing right."

Pearl seemed to have found out whatever she wanted to find out by sniffing Hawk's pants leg. She turned and came back across the room and sat down next to me and leaned against my leg. Unerringly she leaned against the bad one. I flinched a little and shifted.

"What I got, Ma," Paul said, "is me. And I didn't get that from you. I got that from him." He nodded toward me.

"Oh, God, it makes me tired to listen to you. It's all words. I don't know what they all mean. I know that Rich loves me. If he goes, I'm going with him. You don't know, none of you do, what it's like being a woman."

"Some of us do," Susan said.

"Yes—and you've got a man," Patty said.

"We have each other," Susan said.

"Well, I've got Rich."

"Happy as a fish with a new bicycle," I said softly.

Paul was silent. He stared at his mother; nobody said anything. Beau-mont stirred a little on the couch.

"It's kind of no-class, kid," he said, "to wash the family linen in front of strangers like this, you know?"

Paul paid no attention to him. He was still looking at his mother. She had linked her arm through Beaumont's and was pressing her cheek, defi-antly, this time, against his shoulder. She looked back at him unflinchingly. They held the stare, and as they held it Paul began to nod slowly.

"Okay," he said. "That was my last shot. I've been talking to you for two days. You do what you need to do. You are my mother, and I love you. If you need something from me, you know where I am."

Patty got up. "Oh, Paulie," she said and put her arms around him and pressed her face into his chest. She cried quietly, and he held her tight and

patted her back, but his gaze over her shoulder was deeply silent and focused on something far down a dwindling perspective.

I looked at Beaumont. "No cops?" I said.

"No cops."

"Does it bother you at all that if you take off I'm going to have to deal
with Broz?"

"You could take off too," Beaumont said. "You need some money, I
can pay you for what you did."

I shook my head.

"Then I can't help you," Beaumont said. "I got to take care of my own
ass."

"And hers," I said.

"Of course," Beaumont said.

"I'd have to deal with Gerry anyway," I said. I looked at Hawk.

"Where you want to go?" he said to Beaumont.

Beaumont hesitated and looked at me, and then at Hawk. He decided.

"Montreal," he said.

Hawk nodded. "Get your things," he said.

# Chapter 32

I was in my office on Monday morning, with my office calendar, figuring
out how many days were left until baseball season began. The door opened
and Vinnie Morris came in and stood aside, and Joe Broz came in, followed by Gerry Broz. I opened the second drawer in my desk, near my
right hand where I kept a spare gun.

"Broz and Broz," I said. "Double the fun."

Vinnie started to close the door and Joe shook his head.

"Wait in the car, Vinnie," he said.

"Joe?" Vinnie said.

"In the car, Vinnie. This is family."

"I'm not family, Joe?"

Broz shook his head again.

"No," he said. "Not quite, Vinnie. Not on this."

"I'll be in the corridor," Vinnie said.

Again Broz shook his head.

"No, Vinnie—*in the car.*"

Vinnie hesitated with the door half open, his hand on the knob. He was looking at Joe.

"Go, Vinnie. Do it."

Vinnie nodded and went out without looking at me and shut the door behind him. Gerry started to pull up one of my client chairs.

"No," Broz said. "Don't sit. We ain't here to sit."

"Jesus, you got to tell me everything to do. Stand? Sit? In front of this creep?"

"Spenser ain't no creep," Joe said. "One of your many problems, Gerry. You don't think about who you're dealing with."

"So whaddya going to do, explain him to me?"

Joe stared at me. It was almost as if we were friends, which we weren't. Then he inhaled slowly and turned to look at his son.

"Man gave you a break," Joe said. "He could have dropped you in the woods."

"He knew what would happen to him if he did," Gerry said.

Gerry was a little taller than his father, but softer. He was dressed on the cutting edge with baggy, stone-washed jeans and an oversized black leather jacket with big lapels. Joe wore a dark suit and a gray tweed over-coat with a black velvet collar. Both were hatless.

"What would have happened?" Joe said.

"You'd have had Vinnie pop him."

Joe nodded without saying anything. I waited. At the moment this had to do with Joe and Gerry.

"And what should I do now?" Joe said.

"Since when do you ask me, Pa? You don't ask me shit. You asking me now?"

Joe nodded.

"Okay—we'll have Vinnie pop him, like you shoulda done a long time ago."

Joe was looking only at Gerry. Gerry's eyes shifted back and forth between Joe, and, obliquely, me.

"You think he's got to go, Gerry?"

Gerry shifted, glanced again at me, and away again.

"For crissake, Pa, I already told you. Yeah. He's trouble. He's in the way. We'd have had Beaumont out west if he hadn't been there."

"And you chased him into the woods with four guys besides yourself, and he took you."

"Pa."

"With a fucking bullet in him."

"Pa, for crissake. You gotta do this here, in front of him?"

Gerry's face was flushed. And his voice sounded thick.

"And he got away with it," Joe said. His voice was flat, scraped bare of feeling by the effort of saying it.

"Pa." Gerry's breathing was very short. Each exhalation was audible, as if the air was too thin. "Pa, don't."

Joe nodded vigorously.

"I got to, Gerry," he said. "I thought about this for three, four days now. I haven't thought about anything else. I got to."

The flush left Gerry's face. It became suddenly very pale, and his voice pitched up a notch.

"What? You got to what?"

"One of these days I'm going to die and the thing will be yours. The whole fucking thing."

Gerry was frozen, staring at his father. I could have been in Eugene, Oregon, for all I mattered right then.

"And when you get it you got to be able to take care of it or they'll bite you in two, you unnerstand, like a fucking chum fish, they'll swallow you."

Gerry seemed to lean backwards. He opened his mouth and closed it and opened it again and said, "Vinnie . . ."

"I wish you was like Vinnie," Joe said. "But you don't take care of this thing by having a guy do it for you. Vinnie can't be tough for you."

"You think I need Vinnie? You think Vinnie has to take care of me? Fuck Vinnie. I'm sick of Vinnie. Who's your son anyway, for crissake? Fucking Vinnie? Is he your son? Whyn't you leave the fucking thing to him, he's so great?"

"Because he's not my son," Joe said.

All of us were still. Outside, there was the sound of traffic on Berkeley Street, dimmed by distance and walls. Inside my office the silence swelled.

Finally Gerry spoke. His voice was small and flat. "What do you want me to do?"

"I want you to deal with him," Joe said and tilted his head toward me.

"I been telling you that," Gerry said. "I been saying that Vinnie—"

"No," Joe said. "Not Vinnie. You. You got to deal with Spenser. You run our thing and there will be people worse to deal with than him. You got to be able to do it, not have it done. You think I started out with Vinnie?"

"You had Phil," Gerry said.

"Before Phil, before anybody, there was me. Me. And after me there's got to be you. Not Vinnie, not four guys from Providence. You."

"You want me to take him out," Gerry said. "You're telling me that right in front of him."

"Right in front," Joe said. "So he knows. So there's no back-shooting and sneaking around. You tell him he's gone and then you take him out."

"Right now?" Gerry's voice was barely audible.

"Now you tell him. You take him out when you're ready to."

"Joe," I said.

They both turned and stared at me as if I'd been eavesdropping.

"He can't," I said. "He's not good enough. You'll get him killed."

Joe was looking sort of up at me with his chin lowered. He shook his head as if there was something buzzing in his ears.

"They'll take everything away from him," Joe said.

"He could find other work," I said.

Joe shook his head.

"I don't want to kill him, Joe," I said.

"You motherfucker," Gerry said. His voice cracked a little as it went up. "You won't kill me. I'll fucking kill you, you fuck."

"Talks good too," I said to Joe.

"You heard him," Joe said. "Be looking for him. Not Vinnie, not me, Gerry. You heard him."

"Goddamn it, Joe," I said. "Let him up. He's not good enough."

"You heard him," Joe said and turned on his heel and went out of the room. Gerry and I looked at each other for a silent pause, then Gerry turned on his heel, just like his poppa, and went out. Nobody shut the door.

I sat for a while and looked at the open door and the empty corridor. I looked at the S & W .357 in the open drawer by my right hand. I closed the drawer, got up, and closed the door. Then I went back and sat down and swiveled my chair and looked out the window for a while.

Spenser, rite of passage.

# Chapter 33

Paul and I were drinking beer at the counter in my kitchen. It was late. Pearl was strolling about the apartment with a yellow tennis ball clamped in her jaws. She was working it the way a pitcher chews tobacco.

"So that's her," Paul said. "That's my mom."

"Yes, it is," I said.

"Not exactly June Cleaver."

"Nobody is," I said.

"Not exactly an adult woman," Paul said.

"No," I said.

"Do you know where Hawk took them?"

"No."

"I wonder if I'll ever hear from her."

"Yes," I said. "I think you will."

"Because she'll miss her baby boy?"

I shrugged.

"Because the relationship with Beaumont won't last and she'll need help and she'll call me."

"Yes."

"You think Beaumont loves her?"

"I think he has some kind of feeling for her," I said. "But love is not usually an issue for guys like Beaumont."

"She's crazy about him."

"Maybe."

"Or she needs him, or someone like him."

Pearl came by and nudged my arm. I tried to ignore her. I didn't want to play ball right now. She nudged again and made a low sound.

"Always a loser," Paul said. "From my father on. Always some flashy second-rate jerk. Like she's not good enough for a decent guy and she knows it, or chooses these guys to punish herself for being . . . whatever she is: sexual, irresponsible, a bad wife, a bad mother, a bad girl instead of the boy her father wanted? How the fuck do I know? Sometimes I think I've talked too long with the shrinks."

"Saved your life at one point," I said.

"Sure," Paul said. He drank some beer from the bottle. His elbows were on the counter and he had to dip his neck to get enough tilt to the bottle. Pearl made another low sound and nudged my arm again. I patted her head and she shied away, hoping to lure me into a grab for the ball. I was too smart for her. I drank a little beer instead.

"Well, we found her," Paul said.

"Yes."

"I needed to find her."

"I know."

"I won't have to find her again."

Pearl stood close to my knee and dropped the tennis ball suggestively and looked at me with her head canted to the right. The ball bounced twice and lay still on the floor. I paid no heed.

"She has no control," Paul said. He bounced his clenched fist gently on the counter top. "She has never taken control of her life—*Who are you? I'm the woman in that man's life*—Jesus Christ!"

"She needs to be alone for a while," I said.

"Of course she does," Paul said. "You think she ever will be?"

"Not by choice," I said.

"She doesn't do anything by choice," Paul said.

"You're not like her," I said.

"Christ what a gene pool, though, her and old Mel, the paterfamilias."

"You're not like your father either," I said.

We were quiet. Pearl had picked up the ball again and was mouthing it at me. Paul got off the stool and got two more beers out of the refrigerator and opened them and handed me one.

"Why don't you and Susan get married?" Paul said.

"I'm not sure," I said. "It's probably in the area of *if it's not broke, don't fix it.*"

"You love her."

"Absolutely."

"You're so sure," Paul said.

"Like I know I'm alive," I said.

"I'm not sure everyone is like you," Paul said.

"Probably just as well," I said. "But . . ." I shrugged.

"I don't know. I don't know if I really love Paige."

I nodded.

"You don't know either, do you?" Paul said.

"If you really love Paige? No, I don't."

"No advice?"

"None."

"It helped, you know, finding my mother," Paul said.

"I know."

"Metaphorically, as well as really," he said.

"I know."

Pearl had the ball again and nudged my arm and murmured at me. I made a lightning move for the ball, and she moved her head half an inch and I missed. She growled and wagged her tail. I grabbed again. She moved her head again. If I'd had her reflexes I'd have beaten Joe Walcott . . . and my nose would be straight. On the third try I grabbed her collar and held her while I pried the ball loose. Then I fired it into the living room where it ricocheted around with Pearl in lickety-split pursuit, her claws scrabbling on the hardwood floors. She got it and brought it back and nudged my arm and made a low sound.

"You needed to find your mother, and you did and you got the chance to look straight at her and now you know what she's like," I said. "That's progress."

"The truth will set you free," Paul said. His voice was angry.

"Not necessarily," I said. "But *pretend* sure as hell doesn't do it."

Paul turned and looked at me for a minute and then raised his bottle and drank and put it back down on the countertop and grinned.

"Malt does more than Milton can," he said, "to justify God's ways to man."

Pearl nudged my arm again. I grabbed at the ball. And missed.

# Chapter 34

I was drinking coffee and eating donuts and reading the *Globe* while I sat in my car in the parking lot of the Dunkin' Donuts shop on Market Street in Allston. Pearl was in the backseat, with her head on my right shoulder, and every once in a while I would give her a piece of donut. I had bought with that in mind, so there were enough. I was studying *Calvin and Hobbes* when Vinnie Morris opened the door on the passenger side and got in.

"I been looking for you," he said.

"You been following me," I said.

Vinnie shrugged.

"Usually they don't make me," he said.

"Usually they're not me," I said. "You alone?"

"Yeah."

I didn't double-check him in the rearview mirror. Vinnie would kill you, but he wouldn't lie to you.

"Get some coffee," I said. "We'll talk."

Vinnie nodded and opened the car door.

"If you get donuts, get extra. The dog likes them."

Vinnie looked at me without comment for a moment and closed the car door. By the time he came back, I had finished the comics and folded the paper and put it on the floor in the backseat. He had two cups of coffee and a bag of donuts.

Pearl wagged her tail and nosed at the bag.

"Can you control this fucking hound?" Vinnie said.

"No," I said.

He handed me the bag and I took out a donut and broke it in two and gave Pearl the smaller half. I took a bite of my half and pried the cover off the fresh coffee. It had been a rainy fall, and it was raining again. Market Street was a bright wet black. The traffic was sporadic and slow. And the parking lot at the discount lumberyard across the street was nearly empty except for one guy in an emergency slicker he'd made from a green trash bag, tying a piece of surplus plywood to the roof of a ten-year-old Subaru wagon.

"I been trying to figure this out," Vinnie said.

Pearl was gazing at the cinnamon donut Vinnie was holding. Her head moved as his hand moved.

"Dog's supposed to get a bite," I said.

"Fuck," Vinnie said, and broke off a small piece and fed it to her gingerly. He wiped his hand on his pants leg.

"I been trying to figure out where I stand in this between you and Gerry and Joe," Vinnie said.

"Un huh."

"Joe figures the only way Gerry's ever going to be a man is to face up to something bad—"

"Which is me," I said.

"Which is you," Vinnie said. He trolled the coffee cup a little to stir it, and had a sip. "To face up to you and to win."

"Except he won't win," I said.

"No," Vinnie said. "He won't. He ain't that kind of man."

"More than one kind," I said.

"Maybe, but Joe don't know that."

"Neither does Gerry," I said.

"No, he don't, and it fucks him up worse than you'd think anything could."

"You think he'll try?" I said.

"Yeah."

Vinnie broke off another small bit of donut and fed Pearl.

"Joe want you to help him?" I said.

"No." Vinnie stared out the window down the nearly empty street at the car wash standing idle, looking better in the rain, like everything seemed to. "No. It's family. You saw him send me out when he come to talk with you. Him and Gerry."

"I always kind of figured you were family, Vinnie."

Vinnie shrugged. "Well, I ain't. I been with Joe since I was seventeen. I was a jerk kid, but I was willing, you know? Nobody too tough. No alley too dark. Nobody too special for me to kill. I was always willing. I was never scared."

"Always for Joe," I said.

"I never had nobody else."

"So Gerry will come after me without backup?" I said.

Vinnie shook his head. "Joe'll send him out alone," Vinnie said. "I know Joe. Because he thinks that's the only way the kid can ever be anything but a sleazy little punk. But he knows he's no good, and he don't want something to happen to him. So he'll come too. He'll trail along behind to protect the kid."

"So if he's right, he'll undercut the kid even if I don't kill him."

"Yeah. Joe loves the kid."

"So he'll either get him killed or he'll take away his victory by not letting him do it alone."

"Yeah."

"Kid would be better off if Joe didn't love him."

"Yeah."

We were quiet. The rain sliding down the front windshield made the traffic lights fluid and impressionistic at the intersection.

"The thing is," Vinnie said, "Joe ain't that good anymore."

I nodded and drank some coffee and took another piece of donut and shared it with Pearl.

"He gets involved," Vinnie said, "and you'll clip him too."

"If I have to," I said.

"I thought about taking you out for him," Vinnie said.

"Which is why you've been following me."

"Yeah."

"But if you do that," I said, "Joe will never forgive you. Because you ruined it for his kid."

"Yeah."

"Easier, wasn't it," I said, "when some guy gave Joe trouble all you had to do was go round and drill him."

Vinnie drank a little more coffee, staring at the rain. He took another donut, and automatically gave Pearl a piece, and ate the rest.

"I'm getting out," Vinnie said. "I'm quitting Joe."

I stared at him. I couldn't think of anything to say.

"You do what you gotta do," Vinnie said. "You have to kill them, you have to kill them. I won't come around asking you about it. I'm out of it."

He drank the last of his coffee. He took the final donut out of the bag and looked at it for a moment, then put the whole donut back for Pearl to take. Which she did. Vinnie opened the door and put one foot out onto the ground.

I put out my hand. Vinnie took it. We shook hands. Then he got out and closed the door. He turned the collar up on his raincoat and walked back to his car and got in. I saw the wipers start. The headlights went on. And he drove away. From the backseat Pearl nosed at my ear. Her breath smelled of donuts.

# Chapter 35

With a pronounced limp, I was walking Pearl on a leash in the Public Gardens when Gerry made his try. He came across the footbridge over the Swan Boat Pond with the low morning sun shining on his left, making his shadow splash long and peculiar across the railing toward Beacon Street. He was walking stiffly, and very slowly, and he held his right hand close in against his right thigh. I stopped near the monumental statue of George Washington and took the Browning out from under my arm.

"You're not going to like this," I said to Pearl, "but there's nothing to be done."

I was surprised at the way he came. I had thought he'd try to shoot me in the back. People on their way to work didn't pay much attention to the fact that there were two men with guns approaching each other in the Public Gardens. It wasn't quite that they didn't see the guns. It was that, hurrying toward work on a pretty morning, they didn't really record them.

The flower beds had been banked for the winter, and the swan boats stored up on the dock. But the grass was still green from the rainy autumn, and the trees, without leaves now, still arched elegantly. The leafless twigs looked lacy in the morning light.

Pearl was pointing a pigeon near the base of the statue.

Gerry kept coming, mechanical, almost spectral, somehow less than human, a disjointed, clumsy, fantastic figure in the bright new day; driven by things I could guess at but would never know, he came.

And behind him from a big car double-parked on Charles Street his father came, wearing a big loose overcoat, holding something under it, hurrying with his head ducked a little and his shoulders hunched, the way people do when they are trying not to be noticed.

Pearl's pigeon flew away and Pearl glanced around at me, annoyed that I hadn't responded to her point. She saw, or maybe smelled, the gun and her ears flattened, and her tail went down.

"Hang on, babe," I said. "I don't like this either, but it will be over quick."

I made sure the leash was looped over my left wrist. I held the stem of the leash tightly in my left hand. Joe was maybe thirty yards behind Gerry. Gerry was in range. I should plug Gerry now so I'd have time to deal with Joe. If I let them both get up on me it was going to be harder.

Gerry kept coming. He moved as if his joints hurt and wouldn't bend properly. He was close enough so I could see his face, shrunk tight, the cords visible in his neck, tension bunching his narrow shoulders.

"Gerry," I said.

He shook his head and kept coming. As he came he raised the gun. It was an automatic, foreign maybe, a Beretta or a Sig Sauer. He held the gun straight out in his right hand as he walked, and hunched his head down a little to squint along the barrel.

For the first time people noticed. They scattered soundlessly. No one spoke, or yelled, or screamed, or sighed. They moved. Behind Gerry, Joe rushed slowly forward. If Gerry could do it, he didn't want to spoil it by interfering. If Gerry didn't do it, he wanted to be able to save him. I had other things to think about, but for a moment I knew how awful this must be for both of them.

Then Gerry fired and missed, as somehow he would have to miss. I'm not sure he even saw me over the gunsight, and I turned sideways and brought the Browning up carefully. Lurching as he was, trying to shoot while coming at me, Gerry didn't have much chance of hitting me. I sighted with my left eye, along the barrel of the gun, and let the middle of his chest sit on the small white dot on the front sight. I cocked it with my thumb and took a careful breath, and dropped the sight and shot Gerry in the right knee. He went down as if his legs had been scythed. Behind him his father screamed, *"Gerry, Jesus Christ, Gerry!"* and flung himself forward on top of his son, shielding him with his body. The sawed-off shotgun he'd been holding under his coat clattered onto the hot-top walkway and skittered maybe six feet.

"My leg," Gerry said in amazement. "My leg, Papa—he shot me in the leg."

"Don't shoot him," Joe was saying, quite softly. "Don't shoot him."

I dropped to one knee, still holding the Browning, and put my arm around Pearl. She was shaking and trying to run at the same time she was trying to climb into my lap.

"I had to shoot him, Joe," I said. "I won't shoot him again if I don't have to."

Gerry began to cry. It was shock mostly. It was too soon probably for the pain to start. In the distance I could hear a siren. If Gerry were lucky there'd be an ambulance soon and somebody could give him a shot before it got bad. Joe was crouching on the sidewalk beside Gerry, patting his face and smoothing his hair.

"You're going to be okay," he said. "I hear the ambulance. It's going to be okay. You're not bleeding bad."

"Papa, I'm scared."

"You'll be okay," Joe said. "You're going to be okay."

Pearl was quieter, but she leaned very hard against me as I knelt beside her. At what probably seemed to them a safe distance, people had stopped and were gazing back at us. The sirens were louder.

Joe looked at me. We were both kneeling.

"You could have killed him," Joe said.

I nodded.

"It was a hell of a shot with somebody chopping away at you."

"Hard to shoot while you're walking fast, and scared," I said.

Joe nodded and looked down at Gerry. Gerry was sniffling, trying not to cry, shifting as the shock began to wear off and the first hint of pain began to come.

"He's my only kid," Joe said.

"Kid doesn't belong in this business, Joe," I said.

"I thought he could learn," Joe said. "If he doesn't take it, who does?"

"Get him into something else, Joe. Landscaping, chorus girls, something. If he takes over the business, he won't last a month."

"Vinnie's gone," Joe said.

"I know."

"Vinnie coulda run it."

"I know."

Gerry moaned. "It's starting to hurt, Papa," he said. "It's starting to hurt like a bastard."

Joe, hunched on his knees, bent awkwardly over with the stiffness of age, and pressed his face against Gerry's.

"It's gonna be okay," he said.

"I came for him, Pa," Gerry said. "I wasn't afraid of him."

"I know," Joe said. "I know."

The sirens were right on us now, and the first prowl car came swerving up the walkway and halted beside us. The two cops in it got out with guns drawn but not leveled. Behind them came another one. On Arlington Street, near the entrance to the Public Gardens a big yellow-and-white ambulance parked, its lights flashing as an unmarked police car swung out around it and came in behind the two prowl cars.

"He's not a shooter, Joe," I said.

"He ain't like me," Joe said. "He's like his mother."

"Let him be, Joe. If he comes after me again I might have to kill him. If it's not me, it'll be somebody else. He's not a shooter, Joe. Let him try to be something else. Keep him alive."

"Yes," Joe said and kept his face pressed against Gerry's until the EMTs showed up.

# Chapter 36

The ambulance took Gerry to the hospital. Joe and two detectives went with him. I knew one of the detectives who stayed with me, a guy named J. Clay Lawson, who was once a cop in Las Vegas before he got serious. He let me take Pearl home and then he and I spent the day with Quirk and Belson and a guy from the DA's office in the homicide squad room.

When they were through discussing my failings, albeit temporarily, I went home and had dinner with Susan, which I cooked, even though she'd wanted to, because I needed to do something.

"You're all right," Susan said.

"Yes."

"You want to talk about it?"

"No."

"Okay."

We ate chili and corn bread in front of the fire in my apartment and drank beer with it. Even Susan drank beer with chili, though she didn't drink much.

"Paige called me today," she said. "She said Paul seems—how did she put it?—'remote,' since he came back to New York."

I nodded, staring at the fire.

"Finding his mother made it more complicated, not less. He thought it would make it less."

"You probably can't help him with that," Susan said.

"I know."

Pearl lay in front of the fire, looking back frequently to check the status of chili and corn bread. Susan ate a small forkful of chili and nibbled the edge of a small piece of corn bread. With the chili and corn bread we had some corn relish that Susan and I had made as an experiment last Labor Day.

Outside it had begun to rain again. The sunny morning had been an illusion.

"You told me how you started to cook," Susan said. "You never have said why you like it."

"I like to make things," I said. "I've spent a lot of my time alone, and I have learned to treat myself as if I were a family. I give myself dinner at night. I give myself breakfast in the morning. I like the process of deciding what to eat and putting it together and seeing how it works, and I like to experiment, and I like to eat. There's nothing lonelier than some guy alone in the kitchen eating Chinese food out of the carton."

"But cooking yourself a meal," Susan said, "and sitting down to eat it with the table set, and maybe a fire in the fireplace . . ."

"And a ball game on . . ."

"And a half bottle of wine, perhaps."

I nodded.

Susan smiled, the way she does when her face seems to get brighter.

"You are the most self-sufficient man I have ever known," she said.

"Except maybe Hawk," I said. "Hawk's so self-sufficient he doesn't need to eat."

"Perhaps," Susan said.

"It's like carpentry," I said. "I get pleasure out of making things."

"But not in groups," Susan said.

I thought about that for a moment.

"True," I said.

"You like to read," Susan said. "You like to cook, you like to lift weights, and jog, and do carpentry, and watch ball games. Do you like to go to the ballpark?"

"I like to go to the park sometimes, keep in touch with the roots of the game, I suppose. But mostly I prefer to watch it on television at home."

"Alone?"

"Yes. Unless you develop an interest."

Susan didn't even bother to comment on that possibility.

"See what I mean?" she said.

"Autonomy?" I said.

"Yes. You only like things you can do alone."

"There are exceptions," I said.

"Yes. And I know the one you're thinking of. Me excepted, your interests are single."

"True," I said.

"You couldn't stand being a member of the police force."

"No. I hate being told what to do."

"You certainly do," Susan said.

"I'm cute though."

"You're more than cute," Susan said. "You're probably peerless, there's a kind of purity you maintain. Everything is inner-directed."

"Except the part about you," I said.

"Except that."

"That's a large part."

"I know that. Sometimes I'm sort of startled at the, ah, honor I'm the one you let in."

"Might be something of a burden sometimes, being the only one."

"No," Susan said. "It's never a burden. It is to be taken seriously, but it is never burdensome."

"You are the woman in my life," I said.

"Surely not the first."

"No, not in that sense," I said. "But remember how I grew up."

Susan nodded. "All men."

"Yeah, all men. It seemed right. Even looking back it seems right. It doesn't seem as if anything was missing. I knew women and had girl-friends, and so did my father and my uncles; but home was male."

Susan looked around the apartment. Pearl made a small snuffing sound in front of the fire and lazed over onto her side.

"And that is still the case," Susan said.

"No," I said, "no more. This is where I live. But home is where you are."

Susan smiled at me. "Yes," she said. "We are home."

We put plates down for Pearl, and cleared the table and put the pre-lapped dishes in the dishwasher.

"I need dessert," I said.

"You certainly do," Susan said.

"There's nothing here," I said.

"What would you like?"

"Pie?"

"Where is the closest source?" Susan said.

Which is how we ended up walking close together underneath a multi-colored golf umbrella along Arlington Street and into the Public Gardens where, so lately, I had been with the Broz family.

"Place near the Colonial Theater," I said, "will sell you pie and coffee almost any time of the day or night."

"Mark of an advanced civilization," Susan said.

She had her arm through mine and her head against my shoulder as we walked through the rain, sheltered by the umbrella. She had her cobalt raincoat on, the collar turned up around her black hair. The lining of the raincoat was chartreuse, and where the collar was up and open at the neck it showed in gleaming contrast under the streetlights. We walked past the statue of Washington, facing up the Commonwealth Avenue Mall across Arlington Street. If there were bloodstains on the sidewalk, the rain had washed them away, or masked them with its gleaming reflections. The garden was empty on a rainy night, and still, except for the sound of the rain. There was light from the lampposts. And the ambient city noise made the silence of the garden seem more complete. In the Swan Boat Pond the ducks were huddled under their feathers among the rocks along the shore of the lagoon.

The Common was ahead, across Charles Street, where once the inner harbor had washed against the foot of Beacon Hill, before they dumped in all the landfill and created the Back Bay and pushed the sea back into the harbor and the basin of the Charles River. Once it had really been a back bay, a mix of river water and ocean into which the oldest part of Boston had pushed like the bulge in a balloon.

Across Charles Street, not waiting for the light because there was no traffic, we moved uphill gently, across the Common, angling toward Boylston Street where an all-night diner served things like pie, and coffee in thick white mugs with cream and sugar. The winding walkways that bent through the Common were shiny with rain, and the unleaved trees glistened blackly. Around the lamps there formed a dim halo of mist that softened the light and made it elegant. To our left Beacon Street went up the hill to the State House, its gold dome lit and visible from everywhere, its Bulfinch front pretending that what went on inside were matters of gravity and portent. The wind that had, in the late afternoon, slanted the rain in hard as I left police headquarters, had died with the daylight, and the rain, softer now, came down in near perfect silence.

There were no pigeons about the Common at this hour, no squirrels. There was a fragrant bum sleeping on one of the benches under some tented cardboard which shed most of the rain. And, further along, several others slept, or at least lay still, wrapped in quilts and sleeping bags and newspapers.

"Are you in a pie reverie?" Susan said.

"Cherry," I said. "Blueberry, apricot."

"No apple?"

"Rarely do they make good apple pie," I said. "Usually they don't cook the apples enough, and sometimes, too often, they leave, yuk, some of the core in there. Cherry is my favorite."

"And coffee?"

"Decaf," I said sadly.

"How embarrassing," Susan said.

"Caffeine, like youth," I said, "is wasted on the young."

We passed the ancient burial grounds, the little cemetery near Boylston Street where earnest Calvinists had settled into the ground, relaxed at last.

"Are you planning on pie?" I said.

"No," Susan said. "I think I'll just have a cup of hot water, with lemon, and watch you."

"You walked a mile in the rain to drink hot water?"

"To be with you," she said. "You're better than pie."

And I turned under the umbrella and embraced her with my free arm and pressed my mouth against hers and held her hard against me and smelled her perfume and closed my eyes and kissed her for a long time in the still rain, and even after we stopped kissing, I held on to her and we stood together in the dark under the umbrella, until finally I didn't need to hold on anymore, and it was time to go across the street and have some cherry pie. Which we did.

# Double Deuce

*For Karen Panasevich,*
*who taught me about youth gangs, and about commitment.*
*And for my wife and sons,*
*who have taught me everything else that matters.*

# Prologue

Her name was Devona Jefferson. She was going to be fifteen years old on April 23, and she had a daughter, three months and ten days old, whom she had named Crystal, after a white woman on television. Crystal had the same dark chocolate skin her mother had, and the large eyes. She probably looked like her father too, because some of her didn't look like Devona. But Devona didn't know which one the father was, and she didn't care, because Crystal was all hers anyway, the first thing she'd ever had that was all hers.

She loved carrying Crystal, loved the weight of her, the smell of her hair, the soft spot still in the back of her skull, where the white lady doctor at City had told her the skull hadn't grown together yet. They were together most of the time, because there was no one to leave Crystal with, but Devona didn't mind much. Crystal was a quiet baby, and Devona would carry her around and talk with her, about their life together and what it would be like when Crystal got bigger and how they'd be friends when Crystal grew up, because they'd be only fourteen years apart.

She had Crystal dressed that day in a new snowsuit with a little hood that she'd bought at Filene's with money she'd gotten from a boyfriend named Tallboy who dealt dope and might be Crystal's father. It was white satin with lace at the hood, and she liked the way Crystal's face looked, so black in the middle of the white satin. Devona had on a pink sweatsuit with pink high-cut sneakers that she wore with rainbow shoelaces. It was a warm spring and she wasn't wearing anything over the sweatsuit, even though she had Crystal bundled in her snowsuit.

She was on Hobart Street. It wasn't her turf, but she wasn't down special with one gang, and she might have even duked one of the Hobart Street Fros sometime. She wasn't sure. Still she felt the little tight feeling in her stomach when the van crawled up behind her and followed along as she walked. She always felt a little protected when she had Crystal. People were usually more careful about a baby, and she always felt like she could protect her baby, which made her feel like she could protect herself.

She rounded the corner by Double Deuce with the spring sun warm in her face. The van came around behind her. Somebody spoke to her from the passenger side.

"You Tallboy's slut?"

"I not no one's slut," she said. "I Crystal's momma."

Somebody else in the van said, "Yeah, she's Tallboy's." And something exploded in her head.

She never heard the shots that killed her, and killed Crystal. There were twelve of them, fired as fast as the trigger would pull, from a 9mm semi-automatic pistol through the back side door of the van. Devona fell on top of her baby, but it didn't matter. Three slugs penetrated her body and lodged in the baby's chest, one of them in her heart. Their blood was mixed on the sidewalk outside Twenty-two Hobart Street, when the first cruiser arrived. It wasn't until the wagon came and they moved her to put her on the litter that anyone even knew the baby was there and they had two homicides and not one.

# Chapter 1

Hawk and I were running along the river in April. It was early, before the Spandex-Walkman group was awake. The sunshine was a little thin where it reflected off the water, but it had promise, and the plantings along the Esplanade were beginning to revive.

"Winter's first green is gold," I said to Hawk.

"Sure," he said.

He ran as he did everything, as if he'd been born to do it, designed for the task by a clever and symmetrical god. He was breathing easily, and running effortlessly. The only sign of energy expended was the sweat that brightened his face and shaved head.

"You working on anything?" Hawk said.

"I was thinking about breakfast," I said.

"I might need some support," Hawk said.

"You might?"

"Yeah. Pay's lousy."

"How much?" I said.

"I'm getting nothing."

"I'll take half," I said.

"You ain't worth half," Hawk said. "Besides I got the job and already put in a lot of time on it. Give you a third."

"Cheap bastard," I said.

"Take it or leave it," Hawk said.

"Okay," I said, "you got me over a barrel. I'm in for a third."

Hawk smiled and with his arm at his side turned his hand palm up backhand. I slapped it lightly once.

"Housing project called Double Deuce," Hawk said. "You know it?"

"Twenty-two Hobart Street," I said.

We were running past the lagoon now, on the outer peninsula. There were ducks there, pleased with the spring, paddling vigorously, and regularly sticking their heads underwater, just for the hell of it.

"Ever been in Double Deuce?"

"No."

Hawk nodded and smiled. "Nobody goes in there. Cops don't go in there, even black cops, except in pairs. Only people go in there are the ones that live there, which is mostly women and small children. And the gangs."

"The gangs run it," I said.

"For a little while longer," Hawk said.

"Then who's going to run it?"

"We is."

We went over the footbridge from the lagoon and rejoined the main body of the Esplanade. There were several sea gulls up on the grass, trying to pass for ducks, and failing. It didn't matter there was nobody feeding either of them at this hour.

"You and me?" I said.

"Un huh."

"Which will require us, first, to clean out the gangs."

"Un huh."

"We got any help on this?"

"Sure," Hawk said. "I got you, and you got me."

"Perfect," I said. "Why are we doing this?"

"Fourteen-year-old kid got killed, and her baby, drive-by shooting."

"Gang?" I said.

"Probably. Church group in the neighborhood, women mostly, some kind of minister, couple of deacons. They got together, decided to stand up to the gangs. Neighborhood watch, public vigil, shit like that."

"Bet that brought the Homeboys to their knees," I said.

"There was another drive-by and one of the deacons got kneecapped."

"Which probably cut back on the turnout for the next vigil," I said.

"Sharply," Hawk said. "And they talk to the Housing Police and the Boston Police and . . ." Hawk shrugged. "So the minister he ask around and he come up with my name, and we talk, and he hire me at the afore-mentioned sum, which I'm generously sharing with you 'cause I know you need the work."

"What do they want done?"

"They want the murderer of the kid and her baby brought to, ah, justice. And they want the gangs out of the project."

"You got a plan?" I said.

"Figure you and me go talk with the minister and the church folks, and then we work one out."

The traffic was just starting to accumulate on Storrow Drive and the first of the young female joggers had appeared. Colorful tights stretched smoothly over tight backsides.

"The gangs don't scare us?" I said.

"I a brother," Hawk said.

"Double Deuce doesn't scare you?" I said.

"No more than you," Hawk said.

"Uh oh!" I said.

# Chapter 2

Susan and I were sitting on her back steps, throwing the ball for Pearl, Susan's German Shorthair. This was more complicated than it had to be because Pearl had the part about chasing the ball and picking it up; but she did not have the part about bringing it back and giving it to you. She wanted you to chase her and pry it loose from her jaws. Which was not restful.

"She can be taught," Susan said.

"You think anyone can be taught," I said. "And you think you can do it."

"You have occasionally shaken my confidence," Susan said. "But generally that's true."

She had on nearly knee-high black boots and some sort of designer jeans that fit like nylons, and a windbreaker that looked like denim and was made of silk, which puzzled me. I'd have thought it should be the other way around. Her thick black hair had recently been cut, and was now a relatively short mass of curls around her face. Her eyes remained huge and bottomless. She had a cup of hot water with lemon which she held in both hands and sipped occasionally. I was drinking coffee.

"Got any thoughts on gangs?" I said.

"Gangs?"

"Yeah, youth gangs," I said.

"Very little," Susan said.

Pearl came close and then shied away when Susan reached for the ball.

"You're a shrink," I said. "You're supposed to know about human behavior."

"I can't even figure out this dog," Susan said. "Why do you want to know about gangs?"

"Hawk and I are going to rid a housing project of them."

"How nice," Susan said. "Maybe it could become a subspecialty for you. In addition to leaping tall buildings at a single bound."

"Spenser's the name. Gangs are the game," I said. "You know anything about youth gangs?"

"No," Susan said. "I don't think many people do. There's a lot of literature. Mostly sociology, but my business is essentially with individuals."

"Mine too," I said.

Pearl came to me with the yellow tennis ball chomped in one side of her mouth, and pushed her nose under my forearm, which caused my coffee to slop from the cup onto my thigh. I put the cup down and reached for the ball and she turned her head away.

"Isn't that adorable," Susan said.

I feinted with my right and grabbed at the ball with my left, Pearl moved her head a quarter inch and I missed again.

"I haven't been this outclassed since I fought Joe Walcott," I said.

Susan got up and went into her kitchen and came out with a damp towel and rubbed out the coffee stain in my jeans.

"That was kind of exciting," I said.

"You want to tell me about this gang thing you're involved in?"

"Sure," I said. "If you'll keep rubbing the coffee stain out of my thigh while I do it."

She didn't but I told her anyway.

While I told her Pearl went across the yard and dropped the tennis ball and looked at it and barked at it. A robin settled on the fence near her and she spotted it and went into her point, foot raised, head and tail extended, like a hunting print. Susan nudged me and nodded at her. I picked up a pebble and tossed it at the robin and said "Bang" as it flew up. Pearl looked after it and then back at me.

"Do you really think the 'bang' fooled her?" Susan said.

"If I fired a real gun she'd run like hell," I said.

"Oh, yes," Susan said.

We were quiet. In the *Globe* I had read that coffee wasn't bad for you after all. I was celebrating by drinking some, in the middle of the morning. Susan had made it for me: instant coffee in the microwave with condensed skim milk instead of cream. But it was still coffee and it was still officially not bad for me.

"I don't see how you and Hawk are going to do that," Susan said.

"I don't either, yet."

"I mean the police gang units in major cities can't prevent gangs. How do you two think you can?"

"Well, for one thing it is we two," I said.

"I'll concede that," Susan said.

"Secondly, the cops are coping with many gangs in a whole city. We only have to worry about the gangs' impact on Double Deuce."

"But even if you succeed, and I don't see how you can, won't it just drive them into another neighborhood? Where they will terrorize other people?"

"That's the kind of problem the cops have," I said. "They are supposed to protect all the people. That's not Hawk's problem or mine. We only have to protect the people in Double Deuce."

"But other people deserve it just as much."

"If the best interest of a patient," I said, "conflicts with the best interest of a nonpatient, what do you do?"

Susan smiled. "I am guided always," she said, "by the best interest of my patient. It is the only way I can do my work."

I nodded.

Pearl picked up the tennis ball and went to the corner of the yard near the still barren grape arbor and dug a hole and buried the ball.

"Do you suppose that this is her final statement on chase-the-bally?" I said.

"I think she's just given up trying to train us," Susan said. "And is putting it in storage until someone smarter shows up."

"Which should be soon," I said.

# Chapter 3

Twenty-two Hobart Street is a collection, actually, of six-story brick rectangles, grouped around an asphalt courtyard. Only one of the buildings fronted Hobart Street. The rest fronted the courtyard. Therefore the whole complex had come to be known as Twenty-two Hobart, or Double Deuce. A lot of the windowglass had been replaced by plywood. The urban planners who had built it to rescue the poor from the consequences of their indolence had fashioned it of materials calculated to endure the known propensity of the poor to ungraciously damage the abodes so generously provided them. Everything was brick and cement and cinderblock and asphalt and metal. Except the windows. The place had all the warmth of a cyanide factory. To the bewilderment of the urban planners, the poor didn't like it there much, and after they'd broken most of the windows, everyone who could get out, got out.

Hawk parked his Jag at the curb under a streetlight and we got out.

"Walk in here," Hawk said, "and you could be anywhere. Any city."

"Except some are higher."

"Except for that," Hawk said.

There was absolutely no life in the courtyard. It was lit by the one security spotlight that no one had been able to break yet. It was littered with beer cans and Seven-up bottles and empty jugs of Mogen David wine. There were sandwich wrappers and the incorruptible plastic hamburger cartons that would be here long after the last ding dong of eternity.

The meeting was in what the urban planners had originally no doubt called the rec room, and, in fact, the vestige of a Ping-Pong table was tipped up against the cinderblock wall at the rear of the room. The walls were painted dark green to discourage graffiti, so the graffiti artists had simply opted for Day-Glo spray paints in contrasting colors. The Celotex ceiling had been pulled down, and most of the metal grid on which the ceiling tiles had rested was bent and twisted. In places long sections of it hung down hazardously. There were recessed light cans with no bulbs in amongst the jumble of broken gridwork. The room light came from a couple of clamp-on portable lights at the end of extension cords. In the middle of the room, in an incomplete circle, a dozen unmatched chairs, mostly straight-backed kitchen chairs, had been set up. All but two of the chairs were occupied. All the occupants were black. I was with Hawk. He was black. I was not. And rarely had I noticed it so forcefully.

A fat black man stood as Hawk and I came in. His head was shaved like Hawk's and he had a full beard. He wore a dark three-piece suit and a pastel flowered tie. His white-on-white shirt had a widespread collar, and gold cuff links with diamond chips glinted at his wrists. When he spoke he sounded like Paul Robeson, which pleased him.

"Come," he said. "Sit here."

I already knew who he was. He was the Reverend Orestes Tillis. He knew who I was and didn't seem to like it.

"You Spenser?"

"Yes."

"This is our community action committee," Tillis said to Hawk. He didn't look at me again.

An old man, third from the left, wearing a Celtics warm-up jacket that had ridden up over the bulge of his stomach, said, "What's the face doing here?"

I looked at Hawk.

"That you," he said and smiled his wide happy smile.

"When Hawk mentioned him," Tillis said, "I assumed him to be a brother."

"You the man?" the old guy said.

"No," I said.

"Don't see why we need some high-priced face down here telling us how to live."

"He's with me," Hawk said.

"Too many goddamn fancy pants uptown faces come down here in their goddamn three-piece suits telling us how to live," the old man said. I was wearing jeans and a leather jacket. The rest of the committee made a sort of neutralized supportive sound.

"Gee," I said. "They don't like me either."

"I can't take you anywhere," Hawk said. He turned toward the old guy and said quietly, "He with me."

The old guy said, "So what?"

Hawk gazed at him quietly for a moment and the old guy shifted in his seat and then, slowly, began nodding his head.

"Sure," he said. "Sure enough."

Hawk said, "I come over here to bail your asses out, and Spenser come with me, because I hired him to, and we probably the only two people in America can bail your asses out. So you tell us your situation, and who giving you grief, and then you sort of get back out the way, and we get to bailing."

"I want to be on record, 'fore we start," Tillis said. "I got no truck with the white Satan. I don't want no help from him, and I don't trust no brother who get help from him. White men can't help us solve our troubles. They the source of our troubles."

"Price you paying," Hawk said. "Can't afford to be too choosy."

"I don't like the face," Tillis said.

I was leaning on the wall with my arms folded.

Hawk gazed pleasantly at Tillis for a moment.

"Orestes," he said. "Shut the fuck up."

There was a soft intake of breath in the room. Hawk and Tillis locked eyes for a moment. Then Tillis turned away.

"I'm on the record," he said, and went and sat on a chair in the front row.

"Now," Hawk said, "anybody got an idea who killed this little girl and her baby?"

"Cops know?" I said.

A woman said, "You know, everybody know."

She had long graceful legs and a thick body, and her skin was the color of coffee ice cream.

"It's the Hobarts, or the Silks, or some other bunch of gangbangers that keep changing the name of the gangs so fast I can't keep track. And how we supposed to stand up to them? We a bunch of women and old men and little kids. How we supposed to make some kind of life here when the gangbangers fuck with us whenever they feel like?"

"They don't fuck with me," the old man said.

"Course they do," the woman said. "You old and fat and you can't do nothing about it. That's why you here. They ain't no men here, 'cept a few old fat ones that couldn't run off."

The old man looked at the ground and didn't say anything, but he shook his head stubbornly.

"They got guns," another woman said. She was smallish and wore tight red pants that came to the middle of her calves and she had two small children in her lap. Both children wore only diapers. They sat quietly, squirming a little, but mostly just sitting staring with surprising dullness at nothing very much. "They got machine guns and rifles and I don't know what kinds of guns they all are."

"And they run the project," Hawk said.

"They run everything," the big woman said. "They own the corridors, the stairwells. They'd own the elevators, if the elevators worked, which a course they don't."

"They got parents?" I said.

Nobody looked at me. The woman with the thick body answered the question, but she answered it to Hawk.

"Ain't no difference they got *parents*," she repeated my word with scorn. "Some do. Some don't. Parents can't do nothing about it, if they do got 'em. How come you brought him here? Reverend didn't tell us we'd have to talk to no white people. White people don't know nothing."

"He knows enough," Hawk said. "Name some names."

The group was silent. One of the babies coughed and his mother patted him on the back. The big-bodied woman with the graceful legs shifted in her seat a little bit. The old guy glowered at the floor. Everyone else sat staring hard at nothing.

"That get a little dangerous, naming names?" Hawk said. He looked at the Reverend Tillis.

Tillis was standing with his hands behind his back, gazing solemnly at the group. He shook his head sadly, as if he would have liked to speak up but grave responsibilities prevented him.

"Sure," Hawk said. "Anybody got an idea why the kid and her baby got shot?"

Nobody said anything.

Hawk looked at me. I shrugged.

"Me and Satan gonna be around here most of the time the next few weeks," Hawk said. "Till we get things straightened out. You have any thoughts be sure to tell us. Either one of us. You talk to Spenser, be like talking to me."

Nobody said anything. Everyone stared at us blankly, except Tillis, who looked at me and didn't like what he saw.

# Chapter 4

We came out of the meeting at about 9:30. It was a fine spring night in the ghetto. And around Hawk's car ten young men in black LA Raiders caps were enjoying it.

A big young guy, an obvious body builder, with a scar along his jawline and his hat on backwards, was sitting on the trunk of the car.

As we approached he said, "This you ride, man?"

Hawk took his car keys out of his pocket with his left hand. Without breaking stride he punched the kid full in the face with his right hand. The kid tipped over backwards and fell off the trunk. Hawk put the key in the lock, popped the trunk, and took out a matte finish Smith and Wesson pump-action 12-gauge shotgun. With the car keys still dangling from the little finger of his left hand, he jacked a round up into the chamber.

The kid he had punched was on his hands and knees. He shook his head slowly back and forth, trying to get the chimes to stop. The rest of the gang was frozen in place under the muzzle of the shotgun.

"You Hobarts?" Hawk said.

Nobody spoke. I stood half facing Hawk so I could see behind us. I didn't have my gun out, but my jacket was open. Hawk took a step forward and jammed the muzzle of the shotgun up under the soft tissue area of the chin of a tall kid with close-cropped hair and very black skin.

"You a Hobart?" Hawk said.

The kid tried to nod but the pressure of the gun prevented it. So he said, "Yeah."

"Fine," Hawk said and removed the gun barrel. He held the shotgun easily in front of him with one hand while he put his car keys in his pocket. Then without moving his eyes from the gang he reached over with his left hand and gently closed the trunk lid.

"Name's Hawk," he said. He jerked his head at me. "His name's Spenser."

The kid who'd taken the punch had gotten to his feet and edged to the fringe of the group where he stood, shaky and unfocused, shielded by his friends.

"There some rules you probably didn't know about, 'cause nobody told you. So we come to tell you."

Hawk paused and let his eyes pass along the assembled gang. He looked at each one carefully, making eye contact.

"Satan," he said, "you care to, ah, promulgate the first rule?"

"As I understand it," I said. I was still watching behind us. "The first rule is, don't sit on Hawk's car."

Hawk smiled widely. "Just so," he said. Again the slow scan of tight black faces. "Any questions?"

"Yeah."

The speaker was the size of a tall welterweight. Which gave Hawk and me maybe sixty pounds on him. He had thick hair and light skin. He wore his Raiders cap bill forward, the old-fashioned way. He had on Adidas high cuts, and stone-washed jeans, and a satin Chicago Bulls warm-up jacket. He had very sharp features and a long face and he looked to be maybe twenty.

Hawk said, "What's your name?"

"Major."

"What's your question, Major?" Hawk showed no sign that the shotgun might be heavy to hold with one hand.

"You a white man's nigger?" Major said.

If the question annoyed Hawk he didn't show it. Which meant nothing. He never showed anything, anyway.

"I suppose you could say I'm nobody's nigger," Hawk said. "How about you?"

"How come you brought him with you?" Major said.

"Company," Hawk said. "You run this outfit?"

I knew he did. So did Hawk. There was something in the way he held himself. And he wasn't scared. Not being scared of Hawk is a rare commodity and is generally a bad mistake. But the kid was real. He wasn't scared.

"We all together here, man. You got some problem with that?"

Hawk shook his head. He smiled. Uncle Hawk. In a minute he'd be telling them Br'er Rabbit stories.

"Not yet," he said.

Major grinned back at Hawk.

"Not sure John Porter believe that entirely," he said and jerked his head at the guy that had been sitting on Hawk's trunk.

"He's not dead," Hawk said.

Major nodded.

"Okay, he be bruising your ride, now he ain't. What you want here?"

"We the new Department of Public Safety," Hawk said.

"Which means what?"

"Which means that starting right now, you obey the 11th commandment or we bust your ass."

"You Iron?" Major said.

"We the Iron here," Hawk said.

"What's the 11th commandment?"

"Leave everybody else the fuck alone," Hawk said.

"You and Irish?" Major said.

"Un huh."

"Two guys?"

"Un huh."

Major laughed and turned to the kid next to him and put out his hand for a low five, which he got, and returned vigorously.

"Good luck to you, motherfuckers," he said, and laughed again and jerked his head at the other kids. They dispersed into the project, and the sound of their laughter trailed back out of the darkness.

"Scared hell out of him, didn't we?" I said.

"Call it a draw," Hawk said.

# Chapter 5

"She was hit seven times," Belson said. He was sitting at his desk in the homicide squad room, looking at the detectives' report from the Devona Jefferson homicide. "They fired more than that. We found ten shell casings, and the crime-scene techs found a slug in the Double Deuce courtyard. Casings were Remington—nine-millimeter Luger, center-fires, 115-grain metal case."

"Browning?" I said.

Belson shrugged.

"Most nines fire the same load," he said. "Whoever shot her probably emptied the piece. Most nines carry thirteen to eighteen in the magazine, and some of the casings probably ejected into the vehicle. Some of the slugs went where we couldn't find them. Happens all the time."

Belson was clean-shaven, but at midday there was already a five o'clock shadow darkening his thin face. He was chewing on a small ugly cold cigar.

"Baby took three, through the mother's body. They were both dead before they hit the ground."

"Suspects?" I said.

I was drinking coffee from a Styrofoam cup. Belson had some in the same kind of cup, because I'd brought some for both of us from the Dunkin' Donuts shop on Boylston Street near the Public Library. I had cream and sugar. Belson drank his black.

"Probably she was shot from a van that drove by slowly with the back door open."

"Gang?"

"Probably."

"Hobarts?"

"Probably."

"Got any evidence?"

"None."

"Any theories?"

"Gang people figure it's a punishment shooting," Belson said. "Maybe she had a boyfriend that did something wrong. Probably drug related. Almost always is."

"They got any suspects?"

"Specific ones? No."

"But they think it's the Hobarts."

"Yeah," Belson said. "Double Deuce is their turf. Anything goes down there it's usually them."

"Investigation ongoing?" I said.

"Sure," Belson said. "City unleashes everything on a shine killing in the ghetto. Treat it just like a couple of white kids got killed in the Back Bay. Pull out all the stops."

"Homicide got anybody on it?" I said.

"Full time?" Belson smiled without meaning it, and shook his head. "District boys are keeping the file open, though."

"Good to know," I said.

"Yeah," Belson said. "Now that you're on it, I imagine they'll relax."

"I hope so," I said. "I wouldn't want one of them to start an actual investigation and confuse everything."

Belson grinned.

"You come across anything, Quirk and I would be pleased to hear about it," he said.

"You're on the A list," I said.


# Chapter 6

I was in a cubicle at the Department of Youth Services, talking to a DYS caseworker named Arlene Rodriguez. She was a thin woman with a large chest and straight black hair pulled back tight into a braid in back. Her cheekbones were high and her eyes were black. She wore bright red lipstick. Her blouse was black. Her slacks were gray and tight and tucked into black boots. She wore no jewelry except a wide gold wedding band.

"Major is his real name," she said. She had a big manila folder open on her desk. "It sounds like a street handle but it's not. His given name is Major Johnson. In his first eighteen years he was arrested thirty-eight times. In the twenty-seven months preceding his eighteenth birthday he was arrested twenty times."

"When he turned eighteen he went off the list?" I said.

"He's no longer a juvenile," she said. "After that you'll have to see his probation officer or the youth gang unit at BPD."

"What were the offenses?" I said.

"All thirty-eight of them?"

"Just give me a sense of it," I said.

"Drugs, intent to sell . . . assault . . . assault . . . possession of burglary tools . . . possession of a machine gun . . . assault . . . suspicion of rape . . . suspicion armed robbery . . ." She shrugged. "You get the idea."

"How much time inside?" I said.

She glanced down at the folder on her desk.

"Six months," she said. "Juvenile Facility in Lakeville."

"Period?"

"Period," she said. "Probably the crimes were committed within the, ah, black community."

"Ah what a shame," I said. "Your work has made you cynical."

"Of course it has. Hasn't yours?"

"Certainly," I said. "You got any background on him—family, education, favorite food?"

"His mother's name was Celia Johnson. She bore him in August of 1971 when she was fifteen years and two months old. She was also addicted to PCP."

"Which meant he was, at birth," I said.

"Un huh. She dumped him with her mother, his grandmother, who was herself, at the time, thirty-two years old. Celia had three more babies before she was nineteen, all of them PCP addicted, all of them handed over to Grandma. One of them died by drowning. There was evidence of child abuse, including sodomy. Grandma was sent away for six months on a child-endangerment conviction."

"Six months?" I said.

"And three years' probation," Arlene Rodriguez said.

"Teach her," I said.

"His mother hanged herself about two months later, doesn't say why, though I seem to remember it had something to do with a boyfriend."

"So Major is on his own," I said.

Arlene Rodriguez looked down at her folder again.

"At eleven years and three months of age," she said.

"Anything else?"

"While we had him at Lakeville," she said, "we did some testing. He doesn't read very well, or he didn't then, but one of the testers devised ways to get around that, and around the cultural bias of the standard tests, and when she did, Major proved to be very smart. If IQ scores meant anything, which they don't, Major would have a very high IQ."

We were quiet. Around us there were other cubicles like this one, and other people like Arlene Rodriguez, whose business it was to deal with lives like Major Johnson's. The cubicle partitions were painted a garish assortment of bright reds and yellows and greens, in some bizarre bureaucratic conceit of cheeriness. The windows were thick with grime, and the spring sunshine barely filtered through it to make pallid splashes on the gray metal desktops.

"Any thoughts on how to deal with this kid?" I said.

Arlene Rodriguez shook her head.

"Any way to turn him around?" I said.

"No."

"Any way to save him?"

"No."

I sat for a moment, then I got up and shook her hand.

"Have a nice day," I said.

# Chapter 7

Susan and I were walking Pearl along the Charles River on one of those retractable leashes which gave her the same illusion of freedom we all have, until she surged after a duck and came abruptly to the end of her tether. The evening had begun to gather, the commuter traffic on both sides of the river had reached the peak of its fever, and the low slant of setting sun made the river rosy.

I had the dog on my right arm, and Susan held my left hand.

"I've been thinking," she said.

"One should do that now and then," I said.

"I think it's time we moved in together."

I nodded at Pearl.

"For the sake of the child?" I said.

"Well, I know you're joking, but she's part of what has made me think about it. She's with me, she spends time with you. She's really our dog but she doesn't live with us."

"Sure she does," I said. "She lives with us serially."

"And we live with each other serially. Sometimes at my house, sometimes at yours, sometimes apart."

"The 'apart' is important too," I said.

"Because it makes the 'together' more intense?"

"Maybe," I said. This had the makings of a minefield. I was being very careful.

"Sort of a 'death is the mother of beauty' concept?"

"Might be," I said. We turned onto the Larz Anderson Bridge.

"That's an intellectual conceit and you know it," Susan said. "No one ever espoused that when death was at hand."

"Probably not," I said.

We were near the middle of the bridge. Pearl paused and stood on her hind legs and rested her forepaws on the low wall of the bridge and contemplated the river. I stopped to wait while she did this.

"Do we love each other?" Susan said.

"Yes."

"Are we monogamous?"

"Yes."

"Then why," Susan said, "aren't we domestic?"

"As in live together, share a bedroom, that kind of domestic?"

"Yes," Susan said. "Exactly that kind."

"I recall proposing such a possibility on Cape Cod fifteen years ago," I said.

"You proposed marriage," Susan said.

"Which involved living together," I said. "You declined."

"That was then," Susan said. "This is now."

Pearl dropped down from her contemplation of the river and moved on, snuffing after the possibility of a gum wrapper in the crevice between the sidewalk and the wall.

"Inarguable," I said.

"Besides, I'm not proposing marriage."

"This matters to you," I said.

"I have been alone since my divorce, almost twenty years. I would like to try what so many other people do routinely."

"We aren't the same people we were when I proposed marriage and you turned me down," I said.

"No. Things changed five years ago."

I nodded. We walked off the bridge and turned west along the south side of the river. We were closer to the outbound commuter traffic now, an unbroken stream of cars, pushing hard toward home, full of people who shared living space.

"Trial period?" Susan said.

"And if it doesn't work, for whatever reason, either of us can call it off."

"And we return to living the way we do now," Susan said.

"Which ain't bad," I said.

"No, it's very good, but maybe this way will be better."

We swung down closer to the river so Pearl could scare a duck. Some joggers went by in the other direction. Pearl ignored them, concentrating on the duck.

"Will you move in with me?" Susan said.

We stopped while Pearl crept forward toward the duck. Susan kept hold of my left hand and moved herself in front of me and leaned against me and looked up at me, her eyes very large.

"Sure," I said.

"When?"

"Tomorrow," I said.

Pearl lunged suddenly against the leash, and the duck flew up and away. Pearl shook herself once, as if in celebration of a job well done. Susan leaned her head against my chest and put her arms around me. And we stood quietly for a moment until Pearl noticed and began to work her head in between us.

"Jealousy, thy name is canine," I said.

"Tomorrow?" Susan said.

"Tomorrow," I said.

*Tomorrow . . . and tomorrow . . . and, after that, tomorrow. . . .*
*Yikes!*

# Chapter 8

Hawk and I sat in Hawk's car in the middle of the empty courtyard of Double Deuce. The only thing moving was an empty foam cup, tumbled weakly across the littered blacktop by the soft spring wind. The walls of the project were ornate with curlicued graffiti, the signature of the urban poor.

Kilroy was here.

There was almost no noise. Occasionally a child would wail.

"This is your plan?" I said to Hawk.

"You got a better idea?" Hawk said.

"No."

"Me either."

"So we sit here and await developments," I said.

"Un huh."

We sat. The wind shifted. The foam cup skittered slowly back across the blacktop.

"You got any thought on what developments we might be awaiting?" I said.

"No."

A rat appeared around the corner of one of the buildings and went swiftly to an overturned trash barrel. It plunged its upper body into the litter. Only its tail showed. The tail moved a little, back and forth, slowly. Then the rat backed out of the trash barrel and went away.

"Maybe we can keep the peace by sitting here in the middle of the project. And maybe we can find out who killed the two kids, mother and daughter," I said. "I doubt it, but maybe we can. Then what? We can't sit here twenty-four hours a day, seven days a week, until the social order changes. No matter how much fun we're having."

Hawk nodded. He was slouched in the driver's seat, his eyes half shut, at rest. He was perfectly capable of staying still for hours, and feeling rested, and missing nothing.

"Something will develop," Hawk said.

"Because we're here," I said.

"Un huh."

"They won't be able to tolerate us sitting here," I said.

Hawk grinned.

"We an affront to their dignity," he said.

"So they'll finally have to do something."

"Un huh."

"Which is what we're sitting here waiting for," I said.

"Un huh."

"Sort of like bait," I said.

"Exactly," Hawk said.

"What a dandy plan!"

"You got a better idea?" Hawk said.

"No."

"Me either."

# Chapter 9

When I got home Susan was in bed eating her supper and watching a movie on cable. Pearl was in bed with her watching closely. Susan was wearing one of my white shirts for a nightdress and her black hair had the sort of loose look it had when it had just been washed. I kissed her.

"And the baby," Susan said.

I kissed Pearl.

"There's some supper waiting for you in the refrigerator," she said.

"Good," I said.

"Why don't you get it and bring it up and we'll eat together and you can tell me about your day."

"I can tell you about my day now. Hawk and I sat for thirteen hours in the middle of Twenty-two Hobart Street."

"And?"

"And nothing. We just sat there."

"How boring," Susan said. "Well, get your supper and we can talk."

I took my gun off my belt and put it on the night-table next to my side of the bed. I took a shower. Then I went downstairs to the kitchen and found supper, a large bowl of cold pasta and chicken. I tasted it. There was raw broccoli in it, and raw carrots, and some sort of fat-free salad dressing that tasted like an analgesic balm. Susan admitted it tasted like an analgesic balm, but she said that with a little fat-free yogurt and some lemon juice and a dash of celery seed mixed in, it was good. I had never agreed with this. I put it back in the refrigerator. When I'd moved in I had brought with me a six-pack of Catamount Beer. I opened one.

In Susan's refrigerator was a half-used cellophane bag of shredded cabbage, some carrots, some broccoli, half a red pepper, half a yellow pepper, and half a green pepper, some skimmed milk, most of a loaf of seven-grain bread, and a package containing two boneless skinless chicken breasts. I sliced up both the chicken breasts on an angle, cut up the peppers, sprinkled everything with some fines herbes that I found in the back of Susan's cupboard, and put it in a fry pan on high. It was a pretty fry pan, a mauve color with a design on it, that went perfectly with the pillows on the love seat in the kitchen. As an instrument for sautéeing it was nearly useless. I splashed a little beer in with the chicken and peppers and when it cooked away, I took the pan off the stove and made up a couple of sandwiches on the seven-grain bread. I put the sandwiches on a plate, got another beer, and took my supper upstairs.

"Oh, I left some pasta salad for you," Susan said.

"I sort of felt like a sandwich," I said.

Susan smiled and nodded. I sat on the edge of the bed and balanced the plate on the edge of the night-table. Pearl shifted on the bed and nosed at it. I told her not to and she withdrew nearly a quarter of an inch. I drank some beer and hunched over the plate, keeping my body between Pearl and the sandwich, and ate. It was not a neat sandwich and some of it fell on the night-table. I picked it up and gave it to Pearl.

The movie was some sort of love story between an elegant rich woman from Beverly Hills, who appeared to be 5'10", and a roughneck ironworker from Queens, who appeared to be 5'6". They were as convincing as Dan Quayle.

I finished my sandwich and got under the covers. Pearl got under the covers when I did, and stretched out between me and Susan.

"There appears to be a German Shorthaired Pointer in bed with us," I said.

"That's where she sleeps," Susan said. "You know that."

I took the *Globe* from the floor beside the bed and opened it. The iron-worker and the elegant lady were playing a love scene on the tube. I glanced at it. In the close-ups he was much taller than she was. I went back to the paper. I noted in the TV listings that the Bulls were playing the Pistons on TNT.

"Why did you sit for all that time in the middle of the project?" Susan said.

"Hawk figures that it will make the gang react," I said.

"Isn't that sort of like being the bait in a trap?" Susan said.

"I raised that point," I said.

"And?"

"It is sort of like being bait," I said.

Susan was silent. Her eyes stayed on the movie. I read the paper some more.

"It is what you do," Susan said.

"Yeah."

"But it scares me," Susan said.

"Hell, it scares me too," I said.

# Chapter 10

I was in Martin Quirk's office in Boston Police Headquarters on Boylston. Quirk's office overlooked Stanhope Street, which was much more of an alley than a street.

Quirk was wearing a beige corduroy jacket today, with a tattersall shirt and a maroon knit tie. His dark thick hair was cut very short and his thick hands were nicely manicured. He was sitting at his desk so I couldn't see his pants, but I knew they'd be creased and his shoes would gleam with polish and would match his belt. His desk was empty except for a picture of his wife, children, and dog.

"You are the neatest bastard I ever saw," I said. "Except maybe Hawk."

"So?" Quirk said.

"And the gabbiest."

Quirk didn't say anything. He merely sat, his hands quiet on the bare desk top.

"You called me," I said.

"How you doing on the killing outside Double Deuce?" Quirk said.

"We're hanging around awaiting developments," I said.

"And?"

"Hobarts have noticed us."

"And?"

"And nothing much. Kid named Major Johnson seems to run things."

"They make a run at you yet?"

"Nothing serious," I said.

Quirk nodded.

"Will be," Quirk said. "They buzz the kid and her baby?"

"Probably," I said. "They seem to be the force in Double Deuce."

"You doing any investigating or are you just sitting around scaring the Homies?"

"Mostly sitting," I said.

"Anybody in the project talk with you?"

"Nearly as much as they talk with you," I said.

Quirk nodded.

"Tillis got a line on anything?"

"He thinks I'm the white Satan."

"He thinks whatever will get his face on television," Quirk said. "Just happens to be right this time."

"Be more photo opportunities if the kids were white."

Quirk shrugged.

"You got any problem with us looking into this?" I said.

"No," Quirk said. "I hope you find out who did it and Hawk kills him. What's he doing in this?"

"Hard to say about Hawk," I said.

"We won't bother you," Quirk said. "I want someone to go down for killing the kid and her baby. We got the slugs. We can identify the gun if we find it."

"I know," I said. "Nine millimeter. I'll keep an eye out."

"Not hard to find on Hobart Street," Quirk said. "We can help, we will. Hawk wants to handle it his way, be fine with me."

"Me too," I said.

# Chapter 11

When Hawk picked me up in the morning there was a woman with him. She was stunning and black with a wide mouth and big eyes and her hair cut fashionably short. She wore a light gray suit with a short skirt. Even sitting in the car she was tall, and her thighs were noticeably winsome. I got in the back. Hawk introduced us. The woman's name was Jackie Raines. In her lap she held a briefcase.

"Jackie's going to sit with us today," Hawk said. He put the Jag in gear and we slid away from the curb in front of Susan's place and headed down Linnaean Street.

"Good," I said. "I was getting really sick of you."

"I'm a producer," Jackie said. "For *The Marge Eagen Show.*"

"Television?" I said.

"My God, yes," Jackie said. "It's the most successful local talk show in the country."

"Un huh," I said.

"Not a fan?" Jackie said.

"Mostly I only watch television if there's a ball involved, or maybe horses."

"Well, Marge wants to do a major, week-long, five-part series on the gangs in Boston," Jackie said. "And she spoke to me about it. She thought we'd be best to focus on an event related to one gang, in one locale. We knew of course about the murder and the problems at Double Deuce, so I spoke to Hawk."

"Of course," I said.

"I thought if anyone could help those people it would be Hawk, and I could tag along and get my story. And we could get it on in time for sweeps period."

I smiled.

"That sounds swell," I said. "Have you and Hawk known one another for long?"

"I've known Jackie most of my life," Hawk said.

Jackie put her hand lightly on his thigh.

"I hadn't seen Hawk for years, and then, after my divorce, I ran into him again."

"Gee whiz, Hawkster," I said. "You forgot to mention Jackie when you hired me to solve the murders and save all the poor folks at Double Deuce. How'd you happen to hear about the problems at Double Deuce, Jackie?"

"The local minister, man named Orestes Tillis," Jackie said. "He wants to be a state senator."

"Anyone would," I said. "So Hawk and I are going to clean up Double Deuce and you're going to cover it, and Marge Eagen is going to be able to charge more for commercial time on her show. And Rev Tillis will get elected."

"I know you're being cynical, but I guess, in fact, that's the truth. On the other hand, if you do clean up Double Deuce, it really will be good for the people there. Regardless of Marge Eagen or Orestes Tillis. And who-ever killed that child and her baby . . ."

"Sure," I said.

"He's just mad," Hawk said, "because he likes to think he's a catcher in the rye."

"I'm disappointed that I didn't figure out something was up."

"I don't follow this," Jackie said.

"Hawk seemed to be helping people for no good reason. Hawk doesn't do that."

"Except you," Hawk said.

"Except me," I said. "And Susan, and probably Henry Cimoli."

"Who's Susan?" Jackie said.

"She's with me," I said.

"I thought of money, or getting even, or paying something off. I never thought of you."

"Me?"

"He's doing it for you."

Jackie looked at Hawk. Her hand still rested quietly on his thigh.

"That why you're doing it, Hawk?" she said.

"Sure," Hawk said.

She smiled at him, as good a smile as I'd seen in a while—except for Susan's—and patted his thigh.

"That's very heartwarming," she said.

Hawk smiled back at her and put one hand on top of her hand as it rested on his thigh.

Good heavens!

# Chapter 12

As soon as we pulled into the Double Deuce quadrangle the Reverend Tillis and a woman with short gray-streaked hair came out of the building. Tillis had on a dashiki over his suit today. The woman wore faded pink jeans and a Patriots sweatshirt. Hawk got out of the car as they approached. Neither of them looked at me.

"This is Mrs. Brown," Tillis said. "She has a complaint about the Hobarts."

Hawk smiled at her and nodded his head once.

"Go ahead," Tillis said to her.

"They been messing with my boy," the woman said. "He going to school and they take his books away from him and they take his lunch money. I saved out that lunch money and they took it. And one of them push him down and tell him he better get some protection for himself."

The woman put both hands on her hips as she talked and her face was raised at Hawk as if she were expecting him to challenge her and she was ready to fight back.

"Where's your son?" Hawk said.

She shook her head and looked down.

"Boy's afraid to come," Tillis said.

Hawk nodded.

"Which one pushed him down?"

The woman raised her head defiantly. "My boy won't say."

"You know where I can find them?" Hawk said.

"They hanging on the corner, Hobart and McCrory," she said. "That where they be hassling my boy."

Hawk nodded again. I got out of the car on Hawk's side. Jackie got out the other.

"What you planning on?" Tillis said to Hawk.

"I tell you how to write sermons?" Hawk said.

"I represent these people," Tillis said. "I got a right to ask."

"Sure," Hawk said. "You know Jackie, I guess."

Tillis nodded and put out his hand. "Jackie. Working on that show?"

"Tagging along," she said.

"Figure this is for us?" I said.

"See what we do," Hawk said. "Otherwise no point to it. It ain't exactly the crime of the century."

"Mrs. Brown, I think you and I should allow Hawk to deal with this," Reverend Tillis said, making it sound regretful. Hawk grinned to himself.

There was no one in sight as we walked across the project. Jackie stayed with us. I looked at Hawk. He made no sign. It was warm for April. Nothing moved. The sun shone down. No wind stirred. Jackie took a small tape recorder out of her shoulder bag.

Ahead of us was a loud radio. The sound of it came from a van, parked at the corner. A couple kids were sitting in the van with the doors open. Major leaned against a lamppost. The big kid that Hawk had nailed last time was standing near him. The others were fanned out around. There were eighteen of them. I didn't see any weapons. The music abruptly shut off. The sound of Jackie's heels was suddenly loud on the hot top.

Major smiled at us as we stopped in front of him. I heard Jackie's tape recorder click on.

"What's you got the wiggle for, Fro?" Major said. "She for backup?"

The kids fanned out around him laughed.

"Which one of you hassled the Brown kid?" Hawk said.

"We all brown kids here, Fro," Major said.

Again laughter from the gang.

Hawk waited. Still no sign of weapons. I was betting on the van. It had a pair of doors on the side that open out. One of them was open maybe six inches. It would come from there. I wasn't wearing a jacket. The gun on my hip was apparent. It didn't matter. They all knew I had one, anyway. Hawk's gun was still out of sight under a black silk windbreaker he wore unzipped. That didn't matter either, they knew he had one too.

"What you going to do, Fro, you find the hobo that hassed him?" Major said.

"One way to find out," Hawk said.

Major turned and grinned at the audience. Then he looked at the big kid next to him.

"John Porter, you do that?"

John Porter said "Ya," which was probably half the things John Porter could say. From his small dark eyes no gleam of intelligence shone.

"There be your man, Fro," Major said. "Lass time you mace him, he say you sucker him. He ain't ready, he say."

Hawk grinned. "That right, John Porter?"

The cork was going to pop. There was no way that it wouldn't. Without moving my head I kept a peripheral fix on the van door.

John Porter said, "Ya."

"You ready now, John Porter?" Hawk said.

John Porter obviously was ready now. His knees were flexed, his shoulders hunched up a little. He had his chin tucked in behind his left shoulder. There was some scar tissue around his right eye. There was the scar along his jawline, and his nose looked as if it had thickened. Maybe boxed a little. Probably a lot of fights in prison.

"Care to even things up for the sucker punch?" Hawk said.

"John Porter say he gon whang yo ass, Fro," Major said. "First chance he get."

The laughter still skittered around the edges of everything Major said. But his voice was tauter now than it had been.

"Right, John Porter?" Major said.

John Porter nodded. His eyes reminded me of the eyes of a Cape buffalo I'd seen once in the San Diego Zoo. He kept his stare on Hawk. It was what the gang kids called mad-dogging. Hawk's grin got wider and friendlier.

"Well, John Porter," Hawk said, friendly as a Bible salesman. "You right 'bout that sucker punch. And being as how you a brother and all, I'll let you sucker me. Go on ahead and lay one upside my head, and that way we start out even, should anything, ah, develop."

John Porter looked at Major.

"Go on, John Porter, do what the man say. Put a charge on his head, Homes."

John Porter was giving this some thought, which was clearly hard for him. Was there some sort of trickery here?

"Come on, John Porter," Major said. "Man, you can't fickle on me now. You tol me you going to crate this Thompson first chance. You tol me that, Homes." In everything Major said there was derision.

John Porter put out a decent overhand left at Hawk, which missed. Hawk didn't seem to do anything, but the punch missed his chin by a quarter of an inch. John Porter had done some boxing. He shuffled in behind the left with a right cross, which also missed by a quarter of an inch. John Porter began to lose form. He lunged and Hawk stepped aside and John Porter had to scramble to keep his balance.

"See, the thing is," Hawk said, "you're in over your head, John Porter. You don't know what you are dealing with here."

John Porter rushed at Hawk this time, and Hawk moved effortlessly out of the way. John Porter was starting to puff. He wasn't quite chasing Hawk yet. He had enough ring savvy left to know that you could get your clock cleaned by a Boy Scout if you started chasing him incautiously. But chasing Hawk cautiously wasn't working. John Porter had been trained, probably in some jail-house boxing program, in the way to fight with his fists. And it wasn't working. It had probably nearly always worked. He was 6'2" and probably weighed 240, and all of it muscle. He might not have lost a fight since the fourth grade. Maybe never. But he was losing this one and the guy wasn't even fighting. John Porter didn't get it. He stopped, his hands still up, puffing a little, and squinted at Hawk.

"What you doing?" he said.

Major stepped behind John Porter and kicked him in the butt.

"You fry him, John Porter, and you do it now," Major said.

There was no derision in Major's voice.

"He can't," Hawk said, not unkindly.

John Porter made a sudden sweep at Hawk with his right hand and missed. The side door of the van slid an inch and I jumped at it and rammed it shut with my shoulder on someone's hand, someone yelled in pain, something clattered on the street. I kept my back against the door and came up with the Browning and leveled it sort of inclusively at the group. Hawk had a left handful of John Porter's hair. He held John Porter's head down in front of him, and with his right hand, pressed the muzzle of a Sig Sauer automatic into John Porter's left ear. Jackie had dropped flat to the pavement and was trying with her left hand to smooth her skirt down over her backside, while her right hand pushed the tape recorder as far forward toward the action as she could.

Somewhere on the other side of McCrory Street a couple of birds chirped. Inside the truck someone was grunting with pain. I could feel him struggle to get his arm out of the door. A couple of gang members were frozen in midreach toward inside pockets or under jackets.

"Now this time," Hawk was saying, "we all going to walk away from this."

No one moved. Major stood with no expression on his face, as if he were watching an event that didn't interest him.

"Next time some of you will be gone for good," Hawk said. "Spenser, bring him out of the truck."

I kept my eyes on the gang and slid my back off the door. It swung open and a small quick-looking kid no more than fourteen, in a black Adidas sweatsuit, came out clutching his right wrist against him. In the gutter by the curb, below the open door, was an automatic pistol. I picked it up and stuck it in my belt.

"You all walk away from here, now," Hawk said. No one moved.

"Do what I say," Hawk said. There was no anger in his voice. Hawk pursed his lips as he looked at the gang members standing stolidly in place. Behind him Jackie was on her feet again, her tape recorder still running, some sand clinging to the front of her dress.

Hawk smiled suddenly.

"Sure," he said.

He looked at me.

"They won't leave without him," Hawk said.

I nodded. Hawk released his grip on John Porter's hair and Porter straightened. He walked away from Hawk with his head down.

"You fucked yourself," Major said without any particular emotion. "You dead, motherfucker."

"Not likely," Hawk said.

Major stood silently for a moment, looking at Hawk, then he looked at me.

"Enjoy yourself, slut," he said to Jackie. And his face broke into a wide smile.

Then he turned and nodded at the gang. They followed him, and in a moment they were gone and all there was, was the two birds across the street, chirping.

# Chapter 13

We were back in Hawk's car. Jackie in back this time, Hawk and I in the front seat. Both of us had shotguns.

"Would you like to reprise all of that for me?" Jackie said.

"Kid's playing a game," Hawk said.

"The leader? Major?"

"Un huh."

"Well, could you explain the game?"

Hawk grinned back at her over his shoulder. "Un uh," he said.

"Well, I mean, is it turf?" Jackie said.

"Sure it's turf, but it's more," Hawk said.

"I didn't even understand half what he was saying," Jackie said.

"Gangs have their own talk," Hawk said.

"You didn't understand it either," Jackie said.

"Not all of it. Got the drift though."

"I wonder if he's trying to see how you'll act?" I said to Hawk.

"He's heard of me?" Hawk said. Hawk considered everything genuinely. He had almost no assumptions.

"Maybe," I said. I looked at Jackie. "I don't want to hear any of this on *The Marge Eagen Show*."

"No," Jackie said. "Unless I warn you, it's background only. Okay?"

I nodded.

"Maybe Major has heard of you. Maybe you are a kind of ghetto legend, like Connie Hawkins was on the New York playgrounds, say, for different reasons. . . ."

"Who's Connie Hawkins?" Jackie said.

"Basketball player," Hawk said. He kept his eyes on me. "Yeah?"

"So maybe Major wants to learn," I said.

Hawk nodded slowly and kept nodding.

"Learn how to handle trouble?" Jackie said.

"How a man behaves," Hawk said. He kept nodding. "That's why they haven't just done a drive-by and sprayed us."

"Which is not to say they won't," I said.

"But if he want to learn, he will escalate slow," Hawk said.

"And observe, and if it goes right for him, maybe he can win over his father."

"Father?" Jackie said.

Hawk grinned again. "Spenser got a shrink for a girlfriend," he said. "Sometimes he get a little fancy."

"I try not to use any big words, though. I respect your limitations."

"Limitations?" Hawk said. "I got no limitations. Why you think I'm a ghetto legend?"

"Beats me," I said.

# Chapter 14

"So what's she like?" Susan said.

We were having a supper, which I'd cooked, and sipping some Sonoma Riesling, in the kitchen of what Susan now insisted on calling "our house."

"Well, she's brave as hell," I said. "When the guns came out this morning, she hit the pavement facedown, but she kept her tape recorder going."

Susan moved some of her chicken cutlet about in the wine lemon sauce I had made.

"Smart?"

"I think so," I said. "She asks a lot of questions—but that is, after all, her job."

Susan cut a becomingly modest triangle of chicken, speared it with her fork, raised it to her lips, and bit off half of it. Pearl sat quietly with her head on Susan's thigh, her eyes fixed poignantly on the supper. Susan put the fork down and Pearl took the remaining bite quite delicately.

"There are dogs," I said, "who eat Gaines Meal from a bowl on the floor."

"There are dogs who are not treated properly," Susan said. "Is she attractive?"

"Jackie? Yeah, she's stunning."

"Is she the most stunning woman you know?" Susan said. She put her fork down and picked up her napkin from her lap. She patted her lips with it, put it back, picked up her wineglass, and drank some wine.

"She is not," I said, "as stunning as you are."

"You're sure?"

"No one is as stunning as you are," I said.

She smiled and sipped more of her wine.

"Thank you," she said.

I had cooked some buckwheat noodles to go with the chicken, and some broccoli, and some whole-wheat biscuits. We both attended to that, for a bit, while Pearl inspected every movement.

"Am I as stunning as Hawk?" I said.

Susan gazed at me for a moment without any expression. "Of course not," she said and returned to her food.

I waited. I knew she couldn't hold it. In a moment her shoulders started to shake and finally she giggled audibly. She raised her head, giggling, and I could see the way her eyes tightened at the corners as they always did when she was really pleased.

"You don't meet that many shrinks that giggle," I said.

"Or have reason to," Susan said as her giggling became sporadic. "What's for dessert?"

"I could tear off your clothes and force myself upon you," I said.

"We had that last night," Susan said. "Why can't we have desserts like other people—you know, Jell-O Pudding, maybe some Yankee Doodles?"

"You wouldn't say that if I was as stunning as Hawk," I said.

"True," Susan said. "Do you think he's serious about her?"

"What is Hawk serious about?" I said. "I've never known him before to bring a woman along when we were working."

"Well, is she serious about him?"

"She acts it. She touches him a lot. She looks at him a lot. She listens when he speaks."

"That doesn't mean eternal devotion," Susan said.

"No, some women treat every guy like that," I said. "Early conditioning, I suppose. But Jackie doesn't seem like one of them. I'd say she's interested."

"And he's taking on this gang for her," Susan said.

"Yeah, but that may be less significant than it seems," I said. "Hawk does things sometimes because he feels like doing them. There aren't always reasons, at least reasons that you and I would understand, for what he does."

"I agree that I wouldn't always understand them," Susan said. "I'm not so sure you wouldn't."

I shrugged.

"Whatever," I said. "He may have decided to do this just to see how it would work out."

Susan held her glass up and looked at the last of the sunset glowing through it from her west-facing kitchen windows.

"I would not wish to be in love with Hawk," Susan said.

"You're in love with me," I said.

"That's bad enough," she said.

# Chapter 15

Hawk parked the Jag parallel to Hobart Street in the middle of the project. It was a great April day and we got out of the car and leaned on the side of it away from the street. Jackie and her magic tape recorder were there, listening to the silence of the project.

"How come in books and movies the ghetto is always teeming with life: dogs barking, children crying, women shouting, radios playing, that sort of thing? And I come to a real ghetto, with two actual black people, and I can hear my hair growing?"

"Things are not always what they seem," Hawk said. He was as relaxed as he always was, arms folded on the roof of the car. But I knew he saw everything. He always did.

"Oh," I said.

"This is the first ghetto I've ever been to," Jackie said. "I grew up in

Ho-Ho-Kus, New Jersey. My father is an architect. I thought it would be like that too."

"Mostly in a place like this," Hawk said, "people can't afford dogs and radios. You can afford those, you can afford to get out. Here it's just people got no money and no power, and what kids they got they keep inside to protect them. People here don't want to attract attention. Somebody know you got a radio, they steal it. People want to be invisible. This place belongs to the Hobart Street Gang. They the only ones with radios. The only ones noisy."

"And we've quieted them down," I said.

"For the moment," Hawk said.

Jackie was standing between Hawk and me. She was leaning her shoulder slightly against Hawk's.

"Did you grow up in a place like this, Hawk?"

Hawk smiled.

A faded powder blue Chevy van pulled around the corner of Hobart Street and cruised slowly past us. Its sides were covered with graffiti. Hawk watched it silently as it drove past. It didn't slow and no one paid us any attention. It turned right at McCrory Street and disappeared.

"You think that was a gang car?" Jackie said.

"Some gang," Hawk said.

"Hobart?"

Hawk shrugged.

"So how do you know it's a gang van?" Jackie said.

"Nobody else would have one," Hawk said.

"Because they couldn't afford it?"

Hawk nodded. He was looking at the courtyard.

"Gang would probably take it away from anyone who wasn't a member," I said.

Jackie looked at Hawk.

"Is that right?" she said.

Hawk nodded.

"You can usually trust what he say," Hawk said. "He's not as dumb as most white folks."

"Does this mean we're going steady?" I said to Hawk.

He grinned, his eyes still watching the silent empty place. Cars passed occasionally on Hobart Street, but not very many. The sun was strong for this early in spring, and there were some pleasant white clouds here and there making the sky look bluer than it probably was. To the north I could see the big insurance towers in the Back Bay. The glass Hancock tower gleamed like the promise of Easter; the sun and sky reflected in its bright facing.

"Well, did you?" Jackie said.

"Don't matter," Hawk said.

Jackie looked at me.

"I grew up in Laramie, Wyoming," I said.

"And do you know where he grew up?" Jackie said.

"No."

Jackie took in a long slow breath and let it out. She shook her head slightly.

"God," she said. "Men."

"Can't live with them," I said. "Can't live without them."

Across the empty blacktop courtyard, out from between two buildings, Major Johnson sauntered as if he were walking into a room full of mirrors. He was in the full Adidas today, high-tops, and a black warm-up suit, jacket half zipped over his flat bare chest. He wore his Raiders hat carefully askew, with the bill pointing off toward about 4 A.M. He was alone.

Hawk began to whistle through his teeth, softly to himself, the theme from *High Noon*. Between us, I could feel Jackie stiffen.

"How you all doing today?" Major said when he reached the car. He stood on the opposite side and rested his forearms on the roof as Hawk was doing. He was shorter than Hawk, and the position looked less comfortable.

Hawk had no reaction. He didn't speak. He didn't look at Major. He didn't look away. It was as if there were no Major. Major shifted his gaze to me. He was the first person who'd looked at me since I'd come to Double Deuce.

"How you doing, Irish?"

"How's he know I'm Irish?" I said to Hawk.

"You white," Hawk said.

"You call all white people Irish?" Jackie said. She had placed her tape recorder on the car roof.

"We gon be on TV?" Major said, looking at the tape recorder.

"Maybe," Jackie said. "Right now I'm just doing research."

"Goddamn," Major said. "I sure pretty enough to be on TV."

He turned his head in profile.

"You want to know 'bout my sad life?" he said.

"Anything you'd care to tell me," Jackie said.

"I don't care to tell you nothing, sly," Major said.

"I'm sorry you feel that way," Jackie said.

"I don't know no better, you understand. I is an underprivileged ghetto youth."

"Mostly you are an asshole," Hawk said. He was looking at Major now. His voice had no emotion in it, just the usual pleasant inflection.

"Not a good idea to dis me, Fro," Major said. "You in my crib now."

"Not anymore," Hawk said. "Belongs to me."

"The whole Double Deuce, Fro? You been smoking too much grain. You head is juiced."

Hawk smiled serenely.

"Why you think you and the flap can shut the Deuce down? Five-oh can't do it. Why you think you can?"

"We got nothing else to do," Hawk said.

Major grinned suddenly and patted the roof of the Jaguar.

"Like your ride," he said.

Jackie wasn't a quitter. "Can you tell me anything about being a gang member?" she said.

"Like what you want to know?"

"Well," Jackie said, "you are a member of a gang."

"I down with the Hobarts," he said.

"Why?"

Major looked at Jackie as if she had just questioned him about gravity.

"We all down," he said.

"Who's we?"

Again the look of incredulity. He glanced at Hawk.

"All the Homeboys," he said.

"What does membership in the gang mean?"

Major looked at Hawk again and shook his head.

"I'll see you all again," he said and turned and sauntered off into one of the alleys between the monolithic brick project buildings and disappeared. Hawk watched him until he was out of sight.

"I'm not sure it was fatherly to call him an asshole," I said.

"Honest, though," Hawk said.

"What was that all about?" Jackie said. "You guys are like his mortal enemy. Why would he come talk to you?"

"Ever read about Plains Indians?" Hawk said. "They had something called a coup stick and it was a mark of the greatest bravery to touch an enemy with it. Counting coup they called it. Not killing him, counting coup on him. That's what they'd brag about."

"Was that what Major was doing? Was he counting coup on you?"

Hawk nodded.

"More than that," I said. "To a kid like Major, Hawk is the ultimate guy. The one who's made it. Drives a Jag. Dresses top dollar—I think he looks pretty silly, but Major would be impressed—got a top-of-the-line girlfriend."

"Me? How would he know I was Hawk's girlfriend?"

"All you could be," Hawk said. His eyes were still resting on the alley where Major had disappeared. "In his world there aren't any women who are television producers. There's mothers, grandmothers, sisters, aunts, and girlfriends."

"For crissake—that defines women only in reference to men," Jackie said.

"Ain't that the truth," Hawk said.

# Chapter 16

It was quarter to nine when I came into the house on Linnaean Street in Cambridge. Susan had her office and waiting room on the first floor; and she, and now I, lived upstairs. Pearl capered about and lapped my face when I came in, and Susan came from the kitchen and gave me a peck on the lips.

"Where you been?" she said.

"Double Deuce," I said.

I went past her to the kitchen. There were three bottles of Catamount beer in behind some cartons of low-fat lemon yogurt sweetened with aspartame. I got a bottle of beer out and opened it and drank from the bottle. On the stove, a pot of water was coming to a boil. I put the bottle down and tipped it a little and Pearl slurped a little beer from it.

"You don't like it when I ask where you've been," Susan said.

I shrugged.

"I don't mean it in any censorious way," Susan said.

"I know." I wiped the bottle mouth off with my hand and drank a little more beer. "I have lived all my life, nearly, in circumstances where I went where I would and did what I did and accounted to no one."

"Even as a boy?"

"My father and my uncles, once I was old enough to go out alone, didn't ask where I'd been."

"But two people who live with one another, who share a life . . . It is a reasonable question."

"I know," I said. "Which is why I don't say anything."

"But you do," Susan said. "Your whole body resents the question. The way you hold your head when you answer, the way you roll your shoulders."

"Betrayed," I said, "by my expressive body."

"I'm afraid so," Susan said.

She held her gaze on me. Her huge dark eyes were serious. Her mouth showed the little lines at the corner that showed only when she was angry.

"Suze, I've lived alone all my adult life. Now I'm cohabitating in a large house in Cambridge with a yard and a dog."

"You love that dog," Susan said.

"Of course I do. And I love you. But it is an adjustment."

She kept her gaze on my face another moment and then she smiled and put her hand on my cheek and leaned forward, bending from the waist as she always did, a perfect lady, and kissed me softly, but not hastily, on the mouth.

"I'm having pasta and broccoli for supper," she said. "Would you care for some?"

"No, thank you," I said. "I'll drink a couple of beers and then maybe make a sandwich or something and watch the Celtics game."

"Fine," Susan said.

She cut the tops off the broccoli and threw the stalks away. Then she separated the flowerets and piled them up on her cutting board. I sat on a stool opposite her and watched.

"You could peel those stalks and freeze them," I said. "Be great for making a nice soup when you felt like it."

Susan looked at me as if I had begun speaking in tongues.

"In my entire life," Susan said, "I have never, ever felt like making a nice soup."

Susan put some whole-wheat pasta in the pot, watched while it came back to a boil again, and tossed in her broccoli. It came to a second boil and she reached over and set the timer on her stove. While it cooked she tossed herself a large salad with some shaved carrots and slices of yellow squash and a lot of lettuce.

"Susan," I said, "you're cooking. I'm not sure I've ever seen you cooking."

"We've done a lot of cooking together," Susan said. "Holidays, things like that."

"Yeah. But this is just cooking supper," I said. "It's very odd to see you cooking supper."

"Actually I kind of like cooking for myself," Susan said. "I can have what I want and cook it the way I want to and not be subject to suggestions, or complaints, or derision—even if I throw away broccoli stalks."

"Actually I throw them away too," I said. "After I've peeled them and frozen them and left them in the freezer for a year."

"See," Susan said, "I've eliminated two steps in the process." She stirred her pasta and broccoli around once in the pot with a wooden spoon and got out a pale mauve plastic colander and put it in the sink.

"I have been talking to a woman I know who works with the gangs," she said.

"Oh?"

"She would be willing to talk with you. Not the television woman, just you. And Hawk if he wishes."

"Social worker?" I said.

Susan shook her head.

"No, she's a teacher. And after school she spends her time on the street. It's what she does. It's her life."

"She black?"

"No."

"And the kids tolerate her?"

"They trust her," Susan said. "You want to talk?"

"Sure," I said. "Pays to understand your enemy."

"She does not see them as the enemy," Susan said.

"She's not hired to protect people from them," I said.

"If you want her input," Susan said, "you should probably not stress that aspect."

"Good point," I said.

# Chapter 17

Orestes Tillis was waiting for us when we arrived for work at Double Deuce the next day.

"They set twelve fires last night," he said.

Hawk nodded. Jackie clicked on her recorder.

"They set one in every trash can in the project," Tillis said. He glanced at Jackie's recorder. "And I believe I know why. It is an affront to every African-American that you should have one of the oppressors with you, protecting black people from each other."

Hawk nodded again.

"That's probably it," he said.

"You cannot be taken seriously as long as you appear allied with the oppressor," Tillis said.

"Sure," Hawk said.

"Are you saying that blacks and whites cannot work together?" Jackie said. Unconsciously she held the tape recorder forward. Tillis pointed it like a spaniel with a partridge.

"Could slaves work with slaveholders?" he said. "The white man is still trying to enslave us economically. He tries to destroy us with drugs and guns. Where does all the dope come from here? Do you see heroin labs in the ghetto? Do you see any firearms factories in the ghetto?"

Tillis pointed at me rather dramatically, considering that it was only us and the tape recorder.

"His people are practicing genocide, should we ask them for help?"

"You shut that thing off," Hawk said to Jackie, "and he'll shut up."

She looked startled, but she switched off the tape recorder. Tillis stopped gazing into it and looked at Hawk.

"They will not take you seriously," he said, "if you work with a white man."

Hawk stared at Tillis without expression for probably fifteen seconds. Then he shook his head slowly.

"You got it backwards," he said. "We the only thing they do take seriously. We all they can think about sitting out in the middle of their turf. They set those fires to see what we'd do. They don't care about you. We are an affront to them. They think about us all the time."

"Why don't they just shoot you?" Tillis said.

"Maybe one reason being they can't," Hawk said. "And maybe they kind of interested, see what we do."

"Why?"

"They admire Hawk," Jackie said.

Hawk continued as if neither of them had spoken.

"And they going to keep doing things, a little worse, and a little worse, and finally they going to get into shooting with us and we going to kill some of them."

Tillis' eyes shifted to Jackie and back to Hawk.

"Just like that?" he said.

"Un huh," Hawk said. "Maybe get lucky and one of the ones we kill will be the dude that did Devona and Crystal."

Tillis started to say "who?" and then remembered and caught himself.

"You sound like you are talking about simply shooting them to clean up the problem," he said.

"Un huh."

"I want no part of that," Tillis said. He glanced again at Jackie, who was all the media he had at the moment. "I can't condone murder."

Hawk shrugged.

"What makes you think they won't kill you?" Tillis said.

"Blue-eyed devil here," Hawk said, "going to prevent them."

"And I thought you'd never even noticed my eyes," I said.

# Chapter 18

Erin Macklin came to my office at about 9:30 in the evening. She had thick dark hair cut short and salted with a touch of gray. Her features were even. Her makeup was understated but careful. She wore big horn-rimmed glasses, a string of big pearls, matching pearl earrings, a black suit, and a white blouse with the collar points worn out over the lapels of the suit. Her shoes were black, with medium heels. Dress for success. She looked around my office, located the customer's chair, and sat in it.

"I am here," she said, "because two people I know tell me Susan Silverman is to be trusted, and Susan Silverman says you can be trusted."

"One can't be too careful," I said.

"I also know a woman named Iris Milford who says she knew you nearly twenty years ago, and, at least at that time, you could leap tall buildings at a single bound."

"Iris exaggerates a little," I said becomingly. "When I knew her she was a student. How is she?"

"She has stayed in the community," Erin Macklin said. "She has made a difference."

"She seemed like she might," I said.

"You and another man are attempting to deal with the Hobart Street Raiders," she said.

"Actually," I said, "we *are* dealing with them."

"And Susan told me that you would like to know what I know about the gangs."

"Yes," I said. "But first I'd probably like to know a little about you."

"I was about to say the same thing," Erin Macklin said. "You first."

"I used to be a fighter. I used to be a cop. Now I am a private detective," I said. "I read a lot. I love Susan."

I paused for a moment thinking about it.

"The list," I said, "is probably in reverse order."

"A romantic," she said. "You don't look it."

I nodded.

"The man you are working with?"

"My friend," I said.

"Nothing more?"

"Lots more, but most of it I don't know."

"He's black," she said.

"Yes."

We were quiet while she looked at me. There was no challenge in the look, and the silence seemed to embarrass neither of us.

"I used to be a nun," she said. "Now I am a teacher at the Marcus Garvey Middle School on Cardinal Road. I teach a course titled the History of Contemporary America. When I began we had no books, no paper, no pencils, no chalk for the blackboard, no maps. This made for innovation. I started by telling them stories, and then by getting them to talk about the things that they had to talk about. And when what they said didn't shock me, and I didn't dash for the dean of discipline, they told me more about the things they knew. The course is now a kind of seminar on life for fourteen-year-old black children in the ghetto."

"Any books yet?"

"Yes. I bought them books," she said. "But they won't read them much. Hard to find books that have anything to do with them."

"*The March of Democracy* is not persuasive," I said.

She almost smiled.

"No," she said. "It is not persuasive."

She paused again, without discomfort, and looked at me some more. Her eyes were very calm and her gaze was steady.

"I used to work in day care, and we'd try to test some of the kids when they came in. The test required them, among other things, to draw with crayons. When we gave them to the kids they didn't know what the crayons were. Several tried to eat them."

"The test was constructed for white kids," I said.

"The test was constructed for middle-class kids," she said. "The basal reader family."

"Mom, Dad, Dick, and Jane," I said.

"And Spot," she said. "And the green tree."

"You and God have a lovers' quarrel?" I said.

Again she almost smiled.

"Gracious," she said. "A literate private eye."

"Anything's possible," I said.

"No. I had no quarrel with God. He just began to seem irrelevant. I could find no sign of Him in these kids' lives. And the kids' lives became more important to me than He did."

"The ways of the Lord," I said, "are often dark, but never pleasant."

"Adler?"

"Theodor Reik, I think."

She nodded.

"It also became apparent to me that they needed more than I could give them in class. So I stayed after school for them and then I began going out into the streets for them. Now I'm there after school until I get too sleepy, four or five days a week. I came from there now."

"Dangerous?" I said.

"Yes."

"But you get along."

"Yes."

"Is being white a handicap?"

She did smile. "Kids say I'm beige. Getting beiger."

"Save many?" I said.

"No."

"Worth the try," I said.

"One is worth the try," she said.

"Yes."

"You understand that, don't you?" she said.

"Yes."

She nodded several times, sort of encouragingly. She leaned back a little in her chair, and crossed her legs, and automatically smoothed her skirt over her knees. I liked her legs. I wondered for a moment if there would ever be an occasion, no matter how serious, no matter who the woman, when I would not make a quick evaluation when a woman crossed her legs. I concluded that there would never be such an occasion, and also that it was a fact best kept to myself.

"A while back the state decided to train some women to work with the kids in the ghetto. The training was mainly in self-effacement. Don't wear jewelry, don't bring a purse, don't wear makeup, move gingerly on the street, don't make eye contact. Be as peripheral as possible."

She shook her head sadly.

"If I behaved that way I'd get nowhere. I make eye contact. I say *hi*. Not to do that is to *dis* them. If you *dis* them they retaliate."

"*Dis* as in disrespect," I said.

"Yes. The thing is that, to the people training the women, these kids were a hypothesis. They didn't know them. Everything is like that. It's theory imposed on a situation, rather than facts derived from it. You understand?"

"Sure," I said. "It's deductive, and life is essentially inductive. Happens everywhere."

"But here, with these kids, when it happens it's lethal. They are almost lost anyway. You can't afford the luxury of theory. You have to know."

"And you know," I said.

"Yes," she said. "I know. I'm there every day, alone, on my own, without a theory. I listen, I watch. I work at it. I don't have an agenda. I don't have some vision of what the truth ought to be."

She was alive with the intensity of her commitment.

"Nobody knows," she said. "Nobody knows what those kids know, and until you do, and you're there with them, you can't do anything but try to contain them." She paused and stared past me out the dark window.

"Had one of my kids on probation," she said. "Juvie judge gave him a nine P.M. curfew and he kept missing it. There was a drug dealer, used to work the corner by the kid's house every night. So I got him to keep an eye on the kid, and every night he'd make sure the kid was in by nine."

She smiled. "You got to know," she said.

"And if you do know," I said, "and you are there, how many can you save?"

She took in a long slow breath and let it out through her nose.

"A few," she said.

The overhead light was on, as well as my desk lamp, and the room was quite harsh in the flat light of it. I had the window cracked open behind me, and there was enough traffic on Berkeley and Boylston streets to make a sporadic background noise. But my building was empty except for me, and Erin Macklin, and its silence seemed to overwhelm the occasional traffic.

# Chapter 19

I kept two water glasses in the office. In case someone were overcome with emotion, I could offer them a glass of water, or if they became hysterical I could throw water in their face. I also kept a bottle of Irish whiskey in the office, and Erin Macklin and I were using the water glasses to sip some of the Irish whiskey while we talked.

"A little kid," she said, "goes to the store. He has to cross somebody else's turf. Means he has to sneak. In a car he has to crouch down. The amount of energy they have to expend simply to survive . . ." She paused and looked down into her whiskey. She swirled it slightly in the bottom of the water glass.

"They live in anxiety," she said. "If they wear the wrong color hat; if their leather jacket is desirable, or their sneakers; if they have a gold chain that someone wants; they are in danger. One out of four young men in the inner city dies violently. These kids are in a war. They have combat fatigue."

"And they're mad," I said.

I had shut the overhead light off, and the room was lit like *film noir,* with my desk lamp and the ambient light from the streets casting elongated vertical shadows against the top of my office walls and spilling their long black shapes onto my ceiling. I felt like Charlie Chan.

"Yes," she said. "They are very angry. And the only thing they can do with that anger, pretty much, is to harm each other over trivial matters."

She took in some of her whiskey. She sat still for a moment and let it work.

"Something has to matter," I said.

"Yes," she said. "That's exactly right."

"Are there turf issues?" I said.

"Sure, but a lot of the extreme violence grows out of small issues between individuals. Who *dissed* who. Who looked at my girl, who stepped on my sneaker."

"Something's got to matter."

"You get it, don't you," she said. "I didn't expect you would. I figured you'd be different."

"It has always seemed to me that there's some sort of inverse ratio between social structure and, what . . . honor codes? Maybe a little highfaluting for the issue at hand, but I can't think of better."

"By honor do you mean inner-directed behavior? Because these kids are not inner directed."

"No, I know they're not. I guess I mean that nature hates a vacuum. If there are no things which are important, then things are assigned importance arbitrarily and defended at great risk. Because the risk validates the importance."

Erin Macklin sat back in her chair a little. She was holding her whiskey glass in both hands in her lap. She looked at my face as if she were reading directions.

"You're not just talking about these kids, are you?" she said.

"Any of them got families?" I said. "Besides the gang?"

"Not always, but sometimes," she said.

Outside a siren whooped: fire, ambulance, cops. If you live in any city you hear sirens all the time. And you pay no attention. It's an environmental sound. Like wind and birdsong in the country. Neither of us reacted.

"Often the families are dysfunctional because of dope or booze or pathology. Sometimes they are abusive, the kind you see on television. But sometimes they are Utopian—my kid can do no wrong. My kid is fine. The other ones are bad. It's the myth by which the parent reassures herself, or occasionally himself, that everything is okay. And of course it isn't and the pressure on the kid to be the source, so to speak, of 'okayness' for the family adds to his stress and drives him to the gang. Sometimes the kid is the family caretaker. He's the one putting food on the table—usually from dealing drugs—nobody asks him where he got the money. He's valued for it." She raised her glass with both hands from her lap and drank some more of the whiskey.

"If you're dealing," she said, "you have to be down with the gang where you're dealing."

I stood and went around my desk and poured a little more whiskey into her glass. She made no protest. She had settled back into her chair a little; she seemed in a reverie as she talked about what was obviously her life's work.

"Then there's the other myth. The bad-seed myth. The family that tells the kid he's bad from birth. One of my kids got shot in the chest and was dying of it. I was there, and his mother was there. 'I told him he was no good,' she said to me. 'I told him he'd end up with a bullet in him before he was twenty. And I was right.'"

"What a triumph for her," I said.

The whiskey seemed to have no effect on her, and she drank like one who enjoyed whiskey—not like someone who needed it. She smiled, almost dreamily.

"Had a kid, about fifteen, named Coke. Smart kid, had a lot of imagination, felt a lot of things. He knew the numbers, one in four, and he was sure he was going to be the one. So, because he was certain he'd die young, he set out to impregnate as many girls as he could. Even had a schedule set up, so he could achieve the maximum possible pregnancies before he died."

"There'll be one child left to carry on," I said.

"Unfortunately there are twenty or thirty children left to carry on. All of them with junior high school girls for mothers, and no father."

"Did he die young?"

"Not yet," she said. "But he's not around for those children."

"They were a stay against confusion," I said.

"A continuation, a kind of self," she said, "that would survive him when the world he lived in overwhelmed him."

"And he never identified with the three out of four that don't die violently in youth," I said.

"No. The life's too hard for that kind of optimism."

"Seventy-five percent is good odds in blackjack," I said. "But for dying, it would not seem a source of much comfort."

"Where I work," she said, "there is no source of much comfort."

"Except maybe you," I said.

She smiled a little and sipped a little more whiskey.

"Isn't it pretty to think so," she said.

"Well," I said, "a literate ex-nun."

"Anything's possible," she said.

# Chapter 20

"Are you going to do anything about them setting the fires?" Jackie said.

Hawk shook his head. We were back in the Double Deuce quadrangle looking at nothing.

"Why not?" Jackie said.

"Trivial," Hawk said.

"But it's a challenge, isn't it?"

"Not if we not challenged," Hawk said.

We were quiet. Nothing moved in Double Deuce. The sun was steady. There was no wind and the temperature was in the sixties.

Jackie sighed.

"Are you familiar with the word *enigmatic?*" she said.

"Un huh," Hawk said. He was looking at the empty courtyard just as if there were something to see.

"How about the word *uncommunicative?*"

Hawk grinned and didn't speak.

"Hawk, I'm not just asking to be nosy. I'm a reporter, I'm trying to work."

He nodded and turned his head to look at her. She was in the front seat beside him.

"What would you like to know?" he said.

"Everything," she said. "Including answers to questions I don't know enough to ask."

"That's a lot," Hawk said.

"Between strangers, yes," Jackie said. "Among casual acquaintances, even friends, yes. But I am under the impression that we are more than that."

"Un huh," Hawk said.

I was in the backseat, sitting crosswise with my legs stretched out as much as you can stretch legs out in the backseat of a Jaguar sedan. I had found a way to sit so that my gun didn't dig into my back, and I was at peace.

"Is that impression accurate?" Jackie said.

"Yes," Hawk said.

"Then for Christ sake why don't you, goddamn it, talk?"

"Jackie," Hawk said, "you think there's a plan. You'd have a plan. Probably do. So you ask questions like there was some plan at work. In the kind of work I do, there is no plan. Reason we so good at this work is we know it."

When he said "we" he moved his head slightly in my direction so she'd know who "we" was.

"So how do you decide?" Jackie said. "Like now, how do you decide that you won't respond to the trash fires?"

"Same way I decided that you and I be more than friends," Hawk said. "Seem like the right thing to do."

"I had something to do with deciding that," Jackie said.

"Sure," Hawk said.

"So you have a feeling that it's best to let the trash fires slide?" Jackie said.

Hawk looked at me.

"Jump in anytime you like," he said.

"I was just congratulating myself on not being in on this," I said.

Jackie turned in her seat. Her lipstick was very bright, and she had on a carmine blouse open at the throat. She looked like about twenty-two million dollars. *More than friends,* I thought. *Hawk, you devil.*

"You too?" she said. "What's wrong with you people, don't you talk?"

"Most people are grateful," I said.

"Jesus Christ," she said. "You are just like him, a master of the fucking oblique answer."

Hawk and I were silent for a moment.

"It's not willful," I said. "It's that very often we don't know how to explain what we know. We tend to think from the inside out. We tend to feel our way along. And because of the way we live it is more important usually to know what to do than to know how we know it."

"God—I thought that was the woman's rap," Jackie said. "Creatures of feeling. I thought men were supposed to be reasonable."

"I wouldn't generalize about men and women," I said. "But I don't think Hawk or I are operating on emotional whim. It's just the way we experience things sometimes needs to get translated sort of promptly into a, ah, course of action. So we have tended to bypass the meditative circuit."

"Wow," Hawk said.

I nodded. "I kind of like that myself," I said. "And going back afterwards and filling in feels like kind of a waste of time."

"Because the consequences of your actions will prove if you were right," Jackie said.

"Ya," I said.

Hawk nodded. He smiled happily.

"Is it intuition?" Jackie said.

"No, it's the sort of automatic compilation of data without thinking about it, and comparing it with other data previously recorded," I said. "Most of it sort of volition-less."

"The thing with these kids," Hawk said, "they want to see what I do, or Major does, and he seems to be the one calls the plays, because they want to know who we are and what we're like."

"Because of you," Jackie said.

"Un huh. And if they can get us to chase around after them for a misdemeanor like setting trash fires we going to look like fools. What do we do about it? Do we shoot them? For torching trash barrels? Do we slap them around? How do we know who did it?"

"So you let them get away with it?"

"Sure," Hawk said. "We ignore it. We're above it."

"You know those junior high school principals," I said, "who suspend students for stuff like wearing Bart Simpson T-shirts?"

"Yes," Jackie said. "They make themselves look like jerks."

I nodded. Hawk nodded. Jackie smiled. And she nodded.

"I get it," she said. "Why didn't you say that in the first place?"

Hawk and I were both silent for a moment.

"We didn't know it," Hawk said, "in the first place."

# Chapter 21

Jackie and Hawk and I were savoring some chicken fajita subs that Hawk had bought us on Huntington Ave., when Marge Eagen rolled up in a NewsCenter 3 van with her driver, her secretary, a soundwoman, and a cameraman. Two Housing Authority cops parked their car behind the van. A car from the Boston Housing Authority with three civilians in it parked behind the cops.

"Marge always likes to make a site visit," Jackie said to us. "She's very thorough."

"Inconspicuous too," I said.

The Housing Authority cops got out and looked around. The civilians got out and grouped near the van. The driver got out and opened the van doors. The secretary got out of the back. The cameraman and the sound-woman got out of the front. And then Marge Eagen stepped out into the sunlight. The civilians stood a little straighter. The cops looked at her. One of them said something under his breath to the other one. They both looked like they wanted to laugh, but knew they shouldn't. Marge stopped with one foot on the ground and one foot still in the van. A lot of her leg showed. The cameraman took her picture.

"Good leg," I said to Hawk.

"From here," Hawk said.

"Her legs are very good," Jackie said. "And she wants the world to know it. Don't you ever watch?"

"No," I said.

Hawk shook his head.

"It's the trademark opening shot every day. Low shot, her with a hand mike, sitting on a high stool, key lit, legs crossed. Tight skirt."

The cameraman finished. Marge Eagen finished stepping from the van and strode across toward us. Everyone in Boston knew her. She was a television fixture. Blonde hair, wide mouth, straight nose, and an on-camera persona that resonated with compassion. I had never actually watched her show, but she was legendarily intense and caring and issue-oriented. Jackie got out of the car. Hawk and I didn't.

"Jackie," she said. "How bleak."

Her voice had a soft husky quality that made you think of perfume and silk lingerie. At least it made me think of that, but Susan had once suggested that almost everything did.

"Her voice make you think of perfume and silk lingerie?" I said to Hawk.

He shook his head.

"Money," he said.

"Everything makes you think of that," I said.

"Are these the two centurions?" Marge Eagen said. She bent forward and looked in the car at us. She had on a black silk raincoat open over a low-cut ruffled blouse that looked like a man's tuxedo shirt. While she was bent over looking in at us, I could see that she was also wearing a white bra with lace trim, probably a C cup.

Jackie introduced us.

"Step out," Marge said, "so we can get a picture of you."

"No picture," Hawk said.

"Oh come on, Hawk," Marge said. "We need it for interior promo. This is going to be the biggest series ever done on local."

Hawk shook his head. Marge pretended not to see him. With a big smile she opened the car door.

"In fact I suspect it's going to show up on network. Just the idea circulating has got the network kiddies on the horn already. Don't be shy," she said. "Crawl out of there. Let's get that handsome *punim* on film."

Hawk stepped lazily out of the car. He looked past Marge Eagen to the cameraman.

"If you take a picture of me," he said, "I will take your camera away and hit you with it."

He looked steadily at the cameraman, who was a friendly-looking little guy with receding hair which he concealed by artful combing. He stepped back a full step under the impact of Hawk's stare and glanced quickly at the two Housing cops.

"Oh, stop the nonsense," Marge Eagen was saying. "Don't be—"

Hawk shifted his gaze to her. There was something in his eyes, though his face seemed entirely still. She stopped in midsentence, and while she didn't step back, she seemed somehow to recede a little. Jackie stepped slightly between them as if she weren't aware she was doing it.

"We want pictures of Marge really, Harry. That's the big thing. Against the background of the buildings, looking at them, gazing down an alley. Pointing maybe, while she talks with Mr. Albanese."

Harry nodded and began looking at the light. Marge Eagen sort of snorted and walked away with him. The soundwoman followed.

"Why couldn't you let him take a picture, for God's sake?" Jackie said under her breath.

"Rather not," Hawk said pleasantly.

"That's no reason," Jackie said and turned as the suits from the Housing Authority approached. "Sam Albanese, Jim Doyle," she said and introduced us. "I'm afraid I don't know your name," she said to the third guy.

"John Boc," he said. "Authority Police Force." He didn't offer to shake hands.

"Oh, sure." Jackie was jollier than the hostess at a sock hop. "You're the Chief, of course."

"This isn't the time," Albanese said. "But we don't appreciate a couple of hired thugs trying to do our job for us. It's vigilante-ism."

"Actually," I said, "vigilante-ism would be if the residents banded together to do your job for you. This is more like consulting-ism, I think."

"We the Arthur D. Little," Hawk said, "of hired thugdom."

"Go ahead," Albanese said, "be funny. I've asked our counsel"—he nodded at Mr. Doyle, who was looking at us sternly—"to see if there may not be some violation of statute here."

Jackie clicked her tape recorder on very quietly while Albanese was talking. But he heard it. He was the kind of guy who spent his life listening for the click of tape recorders and the hum of a television camera.

Without breaking stride he said, "I think what Ms. Eagen is doing will be a major television event, and I can tell you here and now that every resource of my office will be at your disposal. Gangs are the scourge of public housing. The few bad kids give a lot of decent hardworking citizens a bad name."

"And drank rapidly a glass of water," I said.

"Excuse me?" Albanese said.

"A literary allusion," I said, "e.e. cummings."

"Don't know him," Albanese said.

I smiled politely.

We all stood without anything to say for a while and watched Marge being filmed. When they were through, she came back over to us. Harry took some film of her with Albanese. The soundwoman followed along behind although no one was talking and as far as I could see there was no sound to record.

Then it was our turn again. Marge was going to charm us. She gave us a very big smile and the full force of her large blue eyes.

"Now," she said, "what are we to do with you gentlemen?"

"We could go bowling," I said. "And maybe a pizza after?"

She shook her head the way a parent does to a willful child.

"We'd like you to be in this piece," she said. "Both of you."

Hawk and I remained calm.

"This series will make a real contribution to the most disadvantaged among us," she said. "I'd like to get your slant on it, two men who have bridged the racial gulf and are teamed up to try and help others bridge it."

Hawk turned his head and looked over his shoulder. Then he looked back at Marge Eagen.

"You reading that off something?" he said.

"You don't believe in what you're doing?" she said.

Up close I could see the small crow's-feet around her eyes. It didn't hurt her appearance. In some ways I thought it helped, made her look like a grown-up.

"I don't believe much," Hawk said, "and one of the things I don't believe is that some broad in a Donna Karan dress gonna do much to liberate the darkies."

"Well," Marge Eagen said, "there's no need to be offensive."

"Hell there ain't," Hawk said.

Marge Eagen said, "Jackie," and jerked her head at the van, did a brisk about-face, and marched away. Everybody except Boc, the Authority Police Chief, hustled after her. Hawk and I watched them silently.

"Don't pay attention to Albanese," Boc said. "We need all the help we can get down here, and if you can keep these fucking maggots quiet, you're not going to get any shit from us."

Hawk nodded. He was still looking after Marge.

"Good to know," he said.

Boc turned and went after the rest of them.

After maybe five minutes Jackie came back from the van. Her face was very tight.

"You asshole," she said to Hawk. "She's yanking me out of here. I don't even know if we're going to do the series."

Hawk nodded. Jackie got her purse out of Hawk's car, put her tape recorder in it, and went back to the van. She got in the van. It started up and pulled away. The Housing Authority car and the police car followed and Hawk and I were alone again in the middle of Double Deuce.

We looked at each other.

"How'd you know it was a Donna Karan dress?" I said.

# Chapter 22

"Did you let her eat that bone on the couch?" Susan said.

It was 9:30 at night. I was reading *Calvin and Hobbes* in the morning edition of the *Globe*.

"Yeah," I said.

"Why didn't you stop her?"

"I didn't notice," I said. "Besides, why shouldn't she eat a bone on the couch?"

"Because she gets bone juice all over my cushions," Susan said. "How could you not notice?"

Answering questions like that had never proven fruitful. So I smiled ruefully and gave my head a beguiling twist and started back to *Calvin and Hobbes*. Then I would move to *Tank McNamara,* and finish with *Doonesbury*. I had my evening all planned out.

"It is not funny," Susan said.

"No," I said, "that was a rueful smile."

"I'm serious," she said. "My stuff means a lot to me."

"I thought it was our stuff," I said.

"You know what I mean. I care about it. You don't."

"I know," I said. "I know that a lot of you goes into design and decor. It is part of your art. And the results are in fact artful. It's just that preventing the dog getting bone juice on your cushions was sort of on the back burner. I was feeling like I could read the paper and relax my vigilance for a bit."

"You were reading the comics," Susan said and walked out of the living room. I looked at Pearl, she did not seem abashed. She was vigorously getting bone juice on the rug.

# Chapter 23

I was in my office evaluating the health hazard of a third cup of coffee, compounded by the possibility of a donut. Outside my window it was overcast with the hard look of rain toward the river. A good day for coffee and donuts.

My office door opened, and there, radiant in a white raincoat and matching hat with a lot of blue polka dot showing at her neck, was Marge Eagen herself, the host of the number-one-rated local show in the country. My heart beat faster.

"Hello," I said.

"I wasn't sure whether to knock or not," Marge Eagen said. She smiled beautifully. "I thought you might have a receptionist."

"I did," I said, "but she returned to her first love, neurosurgery, a while back and I haven't bothered to replace her."

Marge Eagen laughed delightedly.

"I heard you were funny," she said.

"Lot of people say that."

"May I sit down?"

"Of course," I said.

I nodded at the chair. She sat and glanced around my office.

"Great location," she said.

I didn't comment.

"Is it as fascinating as it seems," Marge Eagen said, "being a private detective?"

"Better than working," I said.

"Oh, I'm sure," she said, "that you work pretty damned hard."

"So what can I do for you?" I said.

"My, my," she said. "So businesslike."

She had unbuttoned her shiny white raincoat and let it fall off her shoulders over the back of the chair. She had on a dark blue dress with big white polka dots. When she crossed her legs, she showed me a lot of thigh. I remained calm.

"I really need to know what the problem is," Marge Eagen said.

I nodded encouragingly.

"Just what is the issue with your black friend," Marge said. "We're out there trying to do a story that should help his people, and, frankly, he seems to have a real attitude."

"Hawk?" I said. "An attitude?"

"Oh, come now, don't be coy, Mr. Spenser. What is his problem?"

"Why not consult with him?" I said.

"Well, I don't know where to find him, and in truth I'm more comfortable talking with you."

"Is it because I'm so cuddlesome?" I said.

She smiled the smile that launched a thousand commercials.

"Well, that's certainly part of it," she said.

"And I'm not a surly nigger," I said. "That's probably appealing too."

"There's no need to be coarse," Marge Eagen said. "The stations are really behind this. We believe in the project. We care."

"Hawk probably thinks you are a self-important ninny who is looking for television ratings and using the problems of the ghetto to that end. Hawk probably thinks that your coverage will do no good, and will make people think it's doing good, thus making things, if possible, worse."

Marge Eagen's face got red.

"You arrogant fucking prick," she said.

"Everyone says that," I said.

She stood, and turned, angrily shrugging her coat back on.

"Of course maybe he just doesn't like having his picture taken," I said. "With Hawk you never know."

She didn't answer. Without looking back she stalked out my door and slammed it shut behind her.

No business like show business.

# Chapter 24

It was raining when Major Johnson showed up with what appeared to be the whole Hobart posse. It was a light rain, and sometimes it would stop for a while and then pick up again, and the weather was warm. On the whole it was a nice rainy spring afternoon.

The Hobarts came down the alley from the back end of the project in single file. They all had on Raiders caps and Adidas sneakers. Most of them were in sweatsuits. Major had on a leather jacket with padded shoulders and a lot of zippers. As they came Hawk and I got out of the car to face them. I had the shotgun.

The Hobarts fanned out in a semicircle around us. I didn't see John Porter. I took a look along the rooftops and saw nothing. Major stood inside the half-circle opposite us. He had the same half-amused, half-tense quality I had seen before.

"How you doing," Major said.

Hawk nodded slightly.

"Thought I should introduce you to the crew," Major said.

Hawk waited.

"Figure you suppose to be scrambling with us, you ought to see who you gonna have to hass."

There was still no movement on the roofline. The rain misted down softly, and no one seemed to mind it. The boys stood arrayed.

"This here is Shoe," Major said, "and Honk, Goodyear, Moon-man, Halfway, Hose."

At each name Hawk would shift his eyes onto the person introduced. He made no other sign. Shoe was the kid I'd yanked out of the van. Goodyear looked like he'd been named for the Blimp. Honk was very light. Halfway was very short. Major moved slowly around the semicircle.

"This here is X, and Bobby High."

I kept watching the roof, alternating glances at the street. The rain came a little harder.

". . . and Junior," Major said. "And Ray . . ."

There were maybe twenty kids in all. Major was around twenty. The youngest looked to be twelve or thirteen.

"Where's John Porter?" Hawk said.

Major shrugged. "He ain't here," Major said. "I think maybe he soaking his hose." He grinned. "John Porter heavy on soaking it. Say he need to soak it every day since he got out of rails, you know? Say his slut spend most of her time looking at the ceiling."

"You come to tell me about John Porter's sex life?" Hawk said.

"Come to see you, Fro. Come to intro the Homes. You ever been in rails, Fro?"

Hawk said, "It's raining. You want to stand around in the rain?"

"We used to standing around," Major said. "Stand around a lot. Stand around sell some sub. Stand around pick up some wiggle, stand around throat a little beverage. Maybe trace somebody."

"Trace?" I said.

Major grinned. "You know, line somebody, haul out you nine and . . ." With his thumb and forefinger he mimicked shooting a handgun.

"Ah," I said. "Of course."

"What kind of sub you sell?" Hawk said.

"Grain, glass, classic, Jock, motor, harp, what you need is what we got."

Hawk looked at me. "Grass," he said. "Rock cocaine, regular powdered coke, heroin." He looked at Major. "What's motor? Speed?"

"Un huh."

"And PCP," Hawk finished.

"You think I didn't know that?" I said.

"What do you use?" Hawk said.

"We don't use that shit, man. You think we use that? We see what it does to people, man. We ain't stupid."

"So what do you use?" Hawk said.

"Beverage, Fro. I already tol you that. Some Mogen, some Juke, hot day maybe, some six. You use something?"

"I drink the blood of my enemies," Hawk said and smiled his wide happy smile. His eyes never left Major.

"Whoa," Major said. "That is dope, man!" He turned toward the others. "Is this a fresh dude? Did I tell you he was bad? The blood of the fucking enemies—shit!"

"How many people you lined?" Shoe asked Hawk.

Hawk looked at him as if he hadn't spoken.

"I killed me a Jeek, last month," Shoe said. "Motherfucker tried to stiff me on a buy and I nined him right there." Shoe nodded toward the barren blacktop playground across the street. There were iron swing sets without swings, and a half-moon metal backboard with no hoop. The metal was shiny in the rain, and the blacktop gleamed with false promise.

"Doing much business since we here?" Hawk said.

"Do business when we want to," Major said.

"Who's your truck?" Hawk said.

Major looked at me for a minute and back at Hawk.

"Tony Marcus," he said proudly.

Hawk smiled even more widely.

"Really," he said.

"You know him?" Major said.

"Un huh," Hawk said. "My associate here once punched him in the mouth."

The entire semicircle was silent for a moment. For all their ferocity they were kids. And a man who had punched Tony Marcus, and survived, got their attention.

"You do that?" Major said.

"He annoyed me," I said.

"I don't believe you done that," Major said.

I shrugged.

We were quiet for a while standing in the rain.

"Where the sly?" Major said. "She don't like us no more?"

"Why should she be different?" Hawk said.

"This mean we not going to be on TV?"

Hawk was quiet for a moment. He looked at Major while he was being quiet.

"We need to talk," Hawk said finally.

"What the fuck we doing, man?"

"Now, right now, you're profiling," Hawk said. "And I'm being bored."

"You bored, man, whyn't you put your mother-fucking ass someplace else, then?"

"Why don't you and me sit in the car, out of the rain, and we talk?" Hawk said.

You could tell that Major liked that—he and Hawk as equals, the two commanders conferring while the troops stood in the rain. Besides, it was a Jaguar sedan with leather upholstery.

"No reason to get wet," Major said.

Hawk opened the back door and Major got in. Hawk got in after him. He grinned at me as he got in. I stayed outside the car, with the shotgun, staring at about nineteen hostile gangbangers, in the rain, which was coming harder.

# Chapter 25

We were at the other end of life. Susan and I and Hawk and Jackie were sharing a bottle of Iron Horse champagne and having dinner on the top floor of the Bostonian Hotel. Hawk had on a black silk suit and a white shirt with a pleated front. I was wearing my dark blue suit, which I almost always wore, because it flattered my eyes, and because I didn't have another one. I was sure we didn't look like people who spent their days sitting with guns in the middle of a housing project. And the women we were with didn't look like they'd date such people.

Jackie was wearing a little black dress with pearls. She rested her forearm on the back of Hawk's chair and traced small circles between his shoulder blades with her forefinger.

"You talked with the boy?" she said. "Actually talked?"

"Un huh."

"And are you going to tell me what he said?"

"Background only," Hawk said.

Jackie nodded.

"You notice," I said to Susan, "that the King-fish accent seems to go away when he talks to Jackie?"

Susan smiled, which is something to see.

"Yes," she said, "but I am far too delicate to mention it."

"That is mostly for you honkies," Hawk said in a kind of David Niven accent, "so as not to confound your expectations."

"What did you and Major talk about?" Jackie said.

"Woman is not easily distracted," Hawk said.

"As you have every reason to know," Jackie said.

"I wasn't talking about that," Hawk said.

There was a moment of silence while Jackie smiled at him and Hawk gave her the same kindly look that he gave everyone.

"Major got in the car," Hawk said, "and I said to him, 'We can go two ways. We can talk, and work out an arrangement, or we can pop the cork on this thing.' Major looking mostly at the car while I'm talking. And when I say that, he sort of nod and keep looking at the car. And I say, 'I will kill you if I need to.' And he stop looking at the car and he sort of laugh."

"Really intimidated," I said.

"Yuh. He must know your reputation too, 'cause he say I be dead and the Mickey, which is you, be dead long time ago, except he says no."

"We've had two encounters and come out first both times," I said. "Doesn't that tell him anything?"

"No shooting," Hawk said. "Kids only impressed with shooting. Everybody got a gun. What you and I would punch somebody on the chops for, these kids shoot you."

"Makes you nostalgic for street fighters," I said.

Hawk nodded.

"Mickey?" Susan said.

"Irish," Hawk said, "means white."

"All whites?" Susan said.

"Un huh."

"Would I be Irish?" she said.

"You'd be slut, or sly, or wiggle," Hawk said. "Women's race don't matter."

"Sexism again," Susan said.

"You might be an Irish slut, though," I said.

"Gee," Susan said, "my chance to pass."

"Make you an IAP," I said.

"There's no such thing," Susan said.

Hawk had some champagne. He drank it the way people drink Pepsi-Cola. I had never seen it change him. Actually I had never seen anything change him.

"I ask him why he hasn't given the word already, and he say he trying to give me some respect, 'cause everybody know 'bout me."

"Everybody?" Jackie said.

"He mean everybody on Hobart Street," Hawk said.

"Which to him is everybody," I said.

"Say everybody wondering why I am there with a flap," Hawk said and nodded at me. "They trying to figure that out. And he say, why am I? And I tell him it seem like a good idea at the time. He doesn't like the answer, so he sit a minute and he think about it. And then he say, 'So what you going to do?' And I say they can do what they want to do somewhere else, not my problem. I say they can't do it here, in this project. And he say if they just move someplace else and do it, what's the point of moving them out, and I say the point is, I said I would. And he sit there awhile, and then he say, 'I can dig it.' And he sit awhile longer and he say, 'But I can't let you and the Mickey chase me out, you understand. I can't let you dis me.' And I say, 'You willing to die for that?' And he say, 'What else I got?' "

We were all quiet. The waiter came silently by and poured champagne into our glasses and returned the bottle to the ice bucket. It was a quiet room. The tables were spaced so that everyone had space around them. The conversation was muted. There was thick carpeting on the floors so that the waiters in tuxedos moved as silently as assassins among the patrons, their shirtfronts gleaming in the soft light.

"I can dig it," I said.

# Chapter 26

Belson called me at 6:30 in the morning while I was making coffee.

"Piece you gave us doesn't check out," he said.

"It didn't kill the kid and her baby?"

"No."

"Got a next of kin?" I said.

"No. Only way we ID'd her was that the kid was born at Boston City and they had a footprint."

"Where'd she live?" I said.

"No address."

"Baby's father?"

"Don't know."

"Hot on the trail," I said.

"You bet."

"Well, she had to live somewhere."

"Yeah."

"And there had to be a father."

"Yeah."

"So I guess I'll have to find him."

"Sure," Belson said and hung up the phone.

Susan was at the kitchen counter eating some kind of bran cereal with orange segments on it and drinking hot water with a wedge of lemon. Pearl sat on the floor, watching closely.

"The gun you took from the gang kids?"

"Yeah." I put some cream in my coffee and two sugars. Susan was ready for the day. She had on a gray suit, and her thick black hair gleamed with ogalala nut oil or whatever she had washed it with.

"Full day?" I said.

She put her empty cereal bowl down for Pearl.

"Patients all morning, and then I have my seminar at Tufts," she said.

She stood up. I looked at her. I felt the same feeling I always felt when I looked at her. It was almost a way to monitor my existence. Like a pulse. If I looked at her and didn't feel the feeling, I'd know I had died.

"Be home for supper?" she said.

"Depends," I said. "If I find the guy who killed the kid and her baby, and Hawk and I get Double Deuce stabilized, I may be home by midafternoon."

She leaned forward and kissed me. I patted her on the butt.

"You'll not take it as a gesture of no-confidence should I go ahead and eat without you?" she said.

"You shrinks are a cynical lot," I said.

Susan went downstairs to see patients. Pearl went to the door with her and then came back to supervise my breakfast. I was having a turkey cutlet sandwich on an onion roll with a lot of Heinz 57 sauce on it. I gave Pearl a bite.

"Hell of an improvement over bran and orange segments," I said.

Pear was too loyal to comment but I knew she agreed.

# Chapter 27

I picked Erin Macklin up on Cardinal Road in front of the Garvey School. It was raining as she came down the stairs, and she was wearing a short green slicker over tan slacks. On her feet were low-cut L. L. Bean gum rubber boots with leather tops. She was bareheaded. She looked like somebody's suburban housewife on her way to a Little League hockey game. The fact that she didn't seem to be worried that her hair was getting wet, however, proved that she wasn't somebody's suburban housewife at all.

"Your friend is sitting alone at Double Deuce?" she said when she got in the car.

"He seems calm about it," I said.

"Ah yes," she said, "the ironist."

"You know me that well on such brief notice?" I said.

"Your reputation precedes you," she said. "It is coloring my judgment."

Cardinal Road was once Irish. White Catholic people my age had been born there. The houses were nearly all clapboard three-deckers with flat roofs and bay windows and a piazza across the back at each level. The doors were generally to the left side. There was a small porch, three steps to a walk made of cement, and a tiny yard. Along Cardinal Road the yards were neat and mostly enclosed with a low-clipped barberry hedge. On the minuscule lawns, greening in the spring rain, there were tricycles and big wheels. The houses were painted. In the windows there were curtains. It looked like most of the other blue-collar neighborhoods in Boston. But in this one, every face was black.

"I need more help," I said.

Erin's eyes moved carefully over the cityscape as we drove.

"Tell me what you need," she said.

"A young girl, not quite fifteen, was murdered," I said. "Around Double Deuce. She had her three-month-old baby with her. The baby was killed too."

"Boy or girl?" Erin said.

"Girl. Crystal. You're right. She shouldn't be anonymous."

"Yes," Erin said. "Helps to focus."

"Girl's name was Devona Jefferson," I said.

"I don't know her."

"Nobody seems to, but somebody did. I want to find somebody who knew her."

"Why?"

"Because I want to know who killed her."

"And when you know?" Erin said.

"Depends. If there's evidence we'll give it to the cops."

"If there isn't?"

"We'll see," I said.

"Would you take some sort of action yourself?"

"I might."

"And your friend?"

"He might."

We turned onto Alewife Way. It had the same three-deckers, the same tiny yards. But the yards had no grass, and the rain had made the bare earth muddy. The houses seemed to have sagged more on Alewife, and the front porches had sagged. There was a sway in the piazzas. The houses badly needed painting. Many of the windows were patched with cardboard, and the yards were littered. There were empty bottles of Wild Irish Rose, and the plastic rings that six-packs came in, small brown paper sacks, and fast-food wrappers, some empty wine cooler cartons, and empty cigarette hard-packs with the tops open. People were out in the rain, but they seemed to hate it and walked in sullen slouches, hunching close to walls and standing in the doorway of the variety store with the thick wire mesh over the windows.

At the corner of Colonial Drive was a playground: some blacktop inside a chain-link fence with two metal backboards. One rim had no net, the other had one made of wire mesh.

"Bury one from the corner," I said, "and it won't swish, it'll clang."

"Mesh nets are supposed to last longer. But they don't. The kids use them for weapons."

I nodded. "Gather one end and tape it," I said. "Kids make do, don't they."

"Yes," she said. "They are often quite ingenious. They function barely at all in school, and the standard aptitude tests seem beyond them, and yet they are very intelligent about surviving in fearful conditions. They are often resourceful, they fashion what they need out of what they have. They endure in conditions that would simply suffocate most of the Harvard senior class."

"Probably more than one kind of intelligence," I said.

"Probably," Erin said. "Let's talk to these kids."

There were six of them leaning against the chain-link fence in the rain. One of them had a basketball. All of them wore Adidas high-tops and stone-washed jeans, and purple Lakers jackets. Three of them had white Lakers hats, two wore them backwards. They seemed at ease standing in the rain. The one with the basketball was dribbling it around himself behind his back through his legs in a figure-eight pattern. The others were smoking. Their faces froze into the uniform look of tough indifference when I pulled up. They thought we were cops. When Erin got out they relaxed, though the look flickered on again when they saw me.

"Quintin," she said. "How are you?"

She put her hand out and the boy with the ball tucked it under his left arm and slapped her right palm once, gently.

"Lady Beige," he said. "Looking good."

He didn't look at me.

"He's not a cop," Erin said. "He's with me."

Quintin shrugged. The tough look flickered again. They would never be easy with a big white guy in their yard, and the look, if it wasn't quite tough hostile, wasn't welcoming.

"Girl named Devona Jefferson was killed a little while ago over in front of Double Deuce. She had a baby. Baby's name was Crystal. They killed her too."

Quintin shrugged again.

"Do you know her?"

"What her name?"

"Devona," Erin said. "Devona Jefferson."

"Ain't down with the Silks," Quintin said. "What they shoot her with?"

"A nine millimeter," I said.

"Use a fresh pipe anyway," Quintin said.

"You don't know her?" I said.

"Hell, no," Quintin said. "Anybody know her?"

The other five all said no they didn't know her. Erin said thank you and we got back in the car. We drove around in the rain talking with people for the rest of the day, not finding anything out.

# Chapter 28

It was still raining the next morning when I checked in with Hawk at Double Deuce. There was no sign of life in the project. The rain made Hawk's dark green Jaguar look black as it beaded and slid off the finish. I parked next to him and got out and got in his car. Jackie was sitting in the front seat with him.

"We been renewed?" I said.

She smiled.

"Marge has forgiven you."

"Thank God," I said. "She finds me irresistible?"

"We'd already hyped the thing too much informally. We didn't want some columnist to question why we'd said we were going to do this feature and then backed off."

"Almost like finding you irresistible," Hawk said. "How 'bout the detection?"

"I'm seeing a lot of the ghetto."

Hawk nodded.

"Nobody has confessed," I said.

"Only a matter of time," Hawk said. "Nothing folks in the ghetto want to do more than to find some big honkie and confess to him. Been wanting to myself."

"I don't want to hear it," I said. "It would take too long."

"What are you detecting?" Jackie said.

"Who killed Devona and Crystal Jefferson."

"Really?"

"Un huh."

"Well, I mean I knew that was part of what you, we're, ah, supposed to do. But, I mean what about the police?"

"Police have hung it up," I said.

"And what about here?"

"You and Hawk have that covered," I said.

"And we got Marge Eagen," Hawk said, "for backup."

"Can you move around in the black community?"

"I have a guide," I said.

"And you think you can do what the police have given up on?"

"You bet," I said.

"I don't want to sound either naive or cynical, I don't know which," Jackie said, "but why?"

"Why do I think I can find him?"

"No, why are you willing to try?"

"Somebody ought to," I said.

Jackie stared at me. The rain came down on the car roof in its pleasant way. The sound of rain on a car roof always made me feel comfortable.

"That's it?" Jackie said.

"Yeah."

"Why should somebody *ought to?*"

"Fourteen-year-old kid got murdered, and a three-month-old kid got murdered, and as far as anyone can see they had nothing to do with it. That shouldn't go unremarked."

"I'll be damned," Jackie said.

# Chapter 29

It was nearly noon when Erin and I pulled into a fast-food hamburger place on Lister Way. Three kids were sitting in a gray and black Aerostar van with the doors open and the tape deck blaring. The parking lot was crowded and the restaurant was full of people getting out of the rain. Nobody was over twenty.

"This time let's try you stay in the car," Erin said.

"Okay."

I sat while she got out and went to the van. Again she put out her hand, again the gentle slap. Then she got in the backseat of the van and I couldn't see her. The two kids in front turned to talk with her. The rain made the bright colors of the pseudocolonial restaurant shiny and clean looking. There was a litter of hamburger cartons and paper wrappers and cardboard cups among the cars, and the trash barrel near the front door of the place was overfilled. With Erin out of sight I was the only white face in a sea of black ones. If I weren't so self-assured it would have made me a little uncomfortable. If I had been uncomfortable no one would have noticed. No one paid any attention to me at all.

I shut the motor off. The rain collected on the windshield and made the colors of the restaurant streak into a kind of impressionist blur. *Here's looking at you, Claude Monet.* The restaurant and its parking lot stood alone, the only principle of order in a panorama of urban blight. There were vacant lots on both sides of the place. Each one littered with the detritus of buildings long since dismantled. Across the street was a salvage yard with spiraling coils of razor wire atop a chain-link fence. Even prettified by the rain this was not the garden at Giverny.

Erin got back in the car. "Want a cheeseburger?" she said.

"Too far from medical help," I said.

Erin smiled and closed the car door.

"These kids know Devona Jefferson," she said.

"And?"

"She had a boyfriend named Tallboy."

"In a gang?"

"They're all in gangs," Erin said. "It's how they survive."

"Know which gang?"

"Yes," Erin said. "Tallboy's a member of the Dillard Street Posse."

"Progress," I said.

"More than that," Erin said. "I know him."

# Chapter 30

Tallboy wasn't anywhere we looked for the rest of the day. Erin and I stopped in my office for a drink.

"Some of them are only seven or eight years old," Erin said.

She had half a glass of Irish whiskey which she held in both hands.

"Some of the older gang kids will recruit the wannabes to carry the weapon, or the drugs, even sometimes do the shooting—they're juveniles. If they're caught, the penalty is lighter. And the little ones are thrilled. Peer acceptance, peer approval." She smiled a little and sipped her whiskey. "Upward mobility," she said.

I nodded. Outside the window the rain was still with us, straight down in the windless darkness, making the pleasant hush hush sound it makes.

"The thing is," I said, "is that that's true. The gangs are upward mobility."

"Oh, certainly," Erin said. It was obviously so ordinary a part of what she knew that she hadn't thought that anyone might not know it. "These kids are capitalists. They watch television and they believe it. They have the values they've seen on the tube. They think that the Cosby family is reality, and it is so remote from their reality that they find their own life unbearable. The inequity enrages them. It is not arrogance that causes so many explosions of violence, it's the opposite."

"Would the term 'low self-esteem' be useful?" I said.

"Accurate," Erin said. "But not very useful. None of the things people say on talk shows are very useful. What they see on television is a life entirely different than theirs, and as far as they can see, what makes the difference is money. The way for them to get money is to sell drugs or to steal from people who sell drugs—there isn't anybody else in their world that has money to steal—and since either enterprise is dangerous, the gang offers protection, identity, even a kind of nurturance."

"Everybody needs some," I said.

The whiskey was nearly vaporous when I sipped it, less liquid than a kind of warm miasma in the mouth. It was warm in my office, and dry, and in the quiet light the two of us were comfortable.

"Where do you get yours?" I said.

"Nurturance?" She sipped her whiskey again, bending toward the glass a little as she drank. Then she raised her head and smiled at me. "From the kids, I suppose. I guess the gangs provide me meaning and belonging and emotional sustenance."

"Whatever works," I said.

We were quiet briefly while the rain fell and the whiskey worked. There was no uneasiness in the silence. Either of us would talk when we had something to say. Neither of us felt the need to talk when we didn't.

"Do you know Maslow's hierarchy of needs?" Erin said.

"Don't even know Maslow," I said.

"Maslow's studies indicate that humans have a descending order of fundamental needs: physical fulfillment, food, warmth, that sort of thing; then safety, love, and belonging; and self-esteem. Whoever—or whatever—provides for those needs will command loyalty and love."

"Which the gangs do."

"Yes," Erin said. "They do."

Again we were quiet. Erin finished her whiskey and held her glass out. I poured her another drink. Me too.

"There's even a girls' gang," Erin said. "Really vicious, hostile."

"I will make no remark about the female of the species," I said.

"Ghetto life is sexist in the extreme," Erin said. "Among the gangs, women are second-class citizens. Good for sex and little else. Maybe it has to do with a matriarchal society. Maybe all sexism does—the struggle between son and mother over son's freedom. I have no theories on it—I have no theories on anything. I haven't time."

She drank again and seemed lost for a moment in thoughts I had no access to.

"You were talking about a female gang," I said.

Erin shook her head, half smiling. "The Crockettes. More macho than anyone. One of the girls, name was Whistle, I don't know why, stabbed her mother and put out a contract on her stepfather."

"And then demanded leniency because she was an orphan."

"It is almost like a joke, isn't it?" Erin said. "She paid off the contract with sex. Even in the toughest of female gangs, that's their edge, they pay for what they want by fucking."

Erin's voice was hard. I knew she'd chosen the word carefully.

"So finally, no matter what else they do, they perpetuate their status," I said.

Erin nodded slowly, gazing past me at the dark vertical rain.

"The only thing that can save them, boys or girls, the only thing that works," she said, "is if they can get some sort of positive relationship with an adult. They have no role models, nobody to demonstrate a way of life better than the one they're in . . . or the church. I know it sounds silly but if these kids get religion, they have something. The Muslims have saved a lot."

"Another kind of gang."

"Sure—Muslims, Baptists, the Marine Corps. Anybody, anything that can provide for Maslow's hierarchy, that can show them that they are part of something, that they matter."

She was leaning forward in her chair, the whiskey held in two hands in her lap and forgotten. I raised my glass toward her and gestured and took a drink.

"What I hope for you, Sister Macklin, is that you never lose this . . . but you get something else too."

She smiled at me.

"That would be nice," she said.

# Chapter 31

I got home just after Susan's last patient had departed. Susan was on the phone. Which she was a lot. She knew more people than Ivana Trump, and she talked to all of them, nearly every day, after work. Pearl was eating some dry dog food mixed with water in the kitchen and was profoundly ambivalent whether to greet me or keep eating. She made one fast dash at me and then returned to her supper. But she wagged her tail vigorously as she ate. Good enough. Susan waved at me but stayed on the phone. I didn't mind. I liked listening to her talk on the phone. It was a performance—animated, intimate, compelling, rich with overtones, radiant with interest. I didn't even know to whom she was talking, or about what. I just liked the sound of it, the way I like the sound of music.

I got a pork tenderloin out and brushed it with honey and sprinkled it with rosemary and put it in the oven. While it roasted I mixed up some corn flour biscuits and let them sit while I tossed a salad of white beans and peppers and doused it with some olive oil and cilantro. When the pork was done I took it out and let it rest while I baked the biscuits. I put some boysenberry jam out to have with the biscuits and sat down to eat.

I had already put away a biscuit when Susan hung up the phone and walked across the kitchen and gave me a kiss. She pursed her lips slightly and then nodded.

"Boysenberry," she said.

"Yes," I said.

"We got it last fall at that stand in Belfast, Maine."

"Sensitive palate and good memory," I said.

"And great kisser?"

"Everyone says so," I said. "You want a little supper?"

She smiled and shook her head.

"I'll have something later," she said. "I still have to go to the club."

"Aerobics?"

"Yes. I'm taking a step class and then I'll probably do some weights. You eat much too early for me."

I nodded.

"Any progress today?" Susan said.

"Some," I said. "We got the name of Devona's boyfriend."

"Can you find him?" Susan said.

"He can run," I said. "But he can't hide."

"Isn't that a sports saying of some sort?"

"Yeah. Joe Louis said it about Billy Conn."

"Do you think he had to do with killing her?"

"We find him," I said, "we'll ask."

Susan nodded. She looked at my supper. "That looks good," she said. "Well, I've got to get moving. I still have my revolting workout."

"I know this is silly," I said, "but if you find it revolting, why do you do it?"

"That's silly," Susan said.

"I knew it was when I said it. Well, it's working great, anyway."

"Thank you," she said and hurried off to change.

As I ate my supper with the first round of the playoffs on the tube, I thought about how I had almost never seen Susan when she wasn't in a hurry. I didn't mind it exactly, but I had noticed it less when we lived apart.

# Chapter 32

We were on Hafford Avenue, with the enduring rain coming steadily against the windshield and the wipers barely holding their own.

"I thought posses were Jamaican," I said.

"Language changes very fast here. Now it just means a small gang. There are gangs with five or six kids in them if that's all there are in the neighborhood," Erin said.

We turned onto McCrory Street, a block from Double Deuce, and left onto Dillard Street and pulled up into the apron of an abandoned gas station. The pumps were gone, and the place where they had been torn out of the island looked like an open wound. The station windows had been replaced with plywood; and the plywood, and the walls of the station itself, were covered completely with fluorescent graffiti. The overhead door to the service bay was up and half a dozen kids sat in the bay on recycled furniture and looked at the rain. There was a thunderous rap group on at peak volume, and the kids were passing around a jug of white Concord grape wine.

"The one with the wispy goatee is Tallboy," Erin said.

He was sprawled on a broken chaise lounge: plumpish, and not very tall, wearing a red sweatshirt with the hood up.

"Tallboy?" I said.

"He usually drinks beer in the twenty-four-ounce cans," Erin said. She rolled down the window and called to him.

"Tallboy, I need to talk with you."

"Who you with, Miss Macklin?" Tallboy said.

He hadn't moved but he'd tightened up. All of them had, and they gazed out at me in dark silence from their cave.

"A friend," she said. "I need to talk. Can you come sit in the car?"

Tallboy got up slowly and came even more slowly toward the car. He walked with a kind of wide-legged swagger. He might have been a little drunk. When he was in the back he left the door open.

"What you need, Miss Macklin?"

"You knew Devona Jefferson," she said.

"Yeah?"

"I know you did, Tallboy. She was your girlfriend."

"So?"

"And she was killed."

"Don't know nothing about that," he said. He looked hard at me. "Who you?" he said.

"Guy looking for the people killed your girlfriend."

"You DT?"

"No."

"So what you care who piped Devona?"

"They killed your baby too," I said.

"Hey, man, what you talking shit to me for? You don't even know that my little girl."

I waited. Tallboy glanced back toward the open garage where the jug was.

"She prob'ly was," he said. "She look like me."

He looked back toward the wine again. I reached under the front seat and brought out a bottle of Glenfiddich Single Malt Scotch Whiskey. It's handy to have around, because there are times when it is a better bribe than money.

"Try a little of this," I said.

Tallboy stared at it and then took the bottle and swallowed some.

"Damn," he said, "that is some juke, man. That is some bad beverage."

"You know who killed her?" I said.

His eyes slid away from mine and he took another pull on the Glenfiddich. Then he looked back at me and his eyes were tearing. He was drunker than I thought and the scotch was moving him along.

"Sure you do. But you don't care. You want them to get away with it."

He shifted his gaze to Erin.

"That ain't so, Miss Macklin."

"I know," she said. "I know you don't want them to get away with it." She put her hand over the back of the seat and he took it and she held his hand. The tears were running down his face now. I was quiet. We waited. He drank again.

"Nine my fucking baby," he said. "Motherfuckers."

"Who?" Erin said.

"Motherfucking Hobarts." He was mumbling. I had to listen hard. "Dealing some classic for them and I a little short, I gonna pay them. I just a little short that minute. And motherfuckers nine my little girl."

"You sure?" I said.

"Who else it gonna be?" Tallboy said.

"You know which Hobart?" I said.

He shook his head.

"It ain't over," he said. "We gon take care of business. Can't fuck with us and ride." His head had sunk to his chest. He was talking into the bottle . . . and out of it. "Can't dis a Dillard and ride, man."

I looked at Erin and gestured with my head.

"Thank you, Tallboy," she said. "You know how to call me up, don't you?"

Tallboy nodded.

"If you want to talk about this anymore, you call me," she said.

"Yass, Miss Macklin."

Tallboy lurched out of the car holding the bottle of Glenfiddich. He held it up in one hand and waved it at the rest of the posse.

"Fine," he said and started to say something else, and didn't seem able to and lurched on into the garage, out of the rain.

I slid the car into gear and pulled away.

"He isn't even tough," I said.

"Of course he isn't," Erin said. "He tries, but he's not."

"Tough is the only way to survive in here," I said.

"I know," Erin said. "Some of them are tougher than one would think possible . . . and some of them aren't."

# Chapter 33

Erin and Hawk and I were nibbling at some Irish whiskey in my office. It was dark in the Back Bay. The rain had stopped, but everything was still wet and the streets gleamed blackly when I looked out the window.

"Say the Hobarts did it is saying Major did it," Hawk said.

"If Tallboy's right," I said.

"Tallboy will never testify," Erin said.

"No need," Hawk said.

"Spenser said something like that," Erin said. "I asked him if he might take action of his own. He said he might."

Hawk smiled. He drank some whiskey. And rolled it a little on his tongue and swallowed. Then he stood and went to the sink in the corner and added a little tap water. He stood while he sampled it, nodded to himself, and came back to his chair.

Erin said, "What would you consider appropriate action?"

"We could kill him," Hawk said.

Erin looked at me.

"You?" she said.

"Somebody is going to," I said.

"I don't think you would," she said, "simply execute him yourself."

I let that slide. There was nothing there for me.

She looked back at Hawk.

"You feel no sympathy for these kids, do you," she said.

Hawk looked friendly but puzzled.

"Got nothing to do with sympathy," Hawk said. "Got to do with work. Work I do you kill people sometimes. Major seems as good a person to kill as anybody."

"When you were twenty," Erin said, "you probably weren't so different from Major."

"Am now," Hawk said. He drank another swallow of whiskey.

Erin was holding her whiskey glass in both hands. She stared into it quietly for a moment.

"You got out," she said. "You were no better off than Major, probably, and you got out."

Hawk looked at her pleasantly.

"Now you are a free man," Erin said. "Autonomous, sure of yourself, unashamed, unafraid. Nobody's nigger."

Hawk listened politely. He seemed interested.

"And you've paid a terrible price," she said.

"Worth the cost," Hawk said.

"I know what you're like," she said. "I see young men who, were they stronger, or braver, or smarter, would grow up to be like you. Young men who have put away feelings. Who make a kind of Thoreauvian virtue out of stripping their emotional lives to the necessities."

"Probably seem a good idea at the time," Hawk said.

"Of course it does," Erin said. "It is probably what they must do to live. But what a tragedy, to put aside, in order to live, the things that make it worth anything to live."

"Worse," Hawk said, "if you do that and don't live anyway."

"Yes," Erin said.

We all sat for a while nursing the whiskey, listening to the damp traffic sounds from Berkeley Street, where it crosses Boylston. Erin was still staring down into her glass. When she raised her head, I could see that her eyes were moist.

"It's not just Major that you mourn for," I said.

She shook her head silently.

"If Hawk talked about things like this, which he doesn't, he might say that you misread him. That what you see as the absence of emotion is something rather more like calm."

"Calm?"

I nodded.

"I worse than Major," Hawk said quietly. "And I got better, and I got out, and I got out by myself."

"And that makes you calm?"

"I know I can trust me," Hawk said.

"And you'd kill Major?"

"Don't know if I will, know I could."

"And you wouldn't mind," Erin said. "I can't understand that."
Erin's glance rested on Hawk. She wasn't staring at her whiskey now.
"I can't understand that."
"I know," Hawk said.
"I don't want to understand that," Erin said.
"I know that too," Hawk said.

# Chapter 34

The rain had paused, but it was still overcast, and cold for spring, when Hawk pulled his Jaguar into the quadrangle in front of Double Deuce. He stopped. In front of us, on the wet blacktop where we normally parked, was a body. Hawk let the car idle while we got out and looked. It was Tallboy, lying on his back, his mouth ajar, his eyes staring up at the rainclouds, one leg doubled under the other. No need to feel for a pulse, he was stiff with death. Hawk and I both knew it.

"Know him?" Hawk said.

"Name was Tallboy," I said. "He was Devona Jefferson's boyfriend and maybe the baby's father."

"You just talked to him."

"Yeah."

"So he here for us."

"Yeah."

Hawk nodded. He looked slowly around the project. Nothing moved. He looked back down at Tallboy.

"Don't seem too tall," he said.

"He liked the big beer cans," I said.

Hawk nodded some more, still looking almost absently at the boy's body. His clothes were wet, which meant he'd been left here while it was still raining. There was a dark patch of blood on the front of his sweatshirt, in the middle of his chest.

"Ain't no trash-can fire," Hawk said.

He was surveying the project again.

"He told me he was going to even up for his girlfriend," I said. "He was drunk."

"Probably drunk when he tried," Hawk said, his eyes moving carefully over the silent buildings.

"Figure they're watching from somewhere?" I said.

"They kids," Hawk said. "They got to be watching, see what we do."

I was still looking at Tallboy. I didn't bother looking for the gang. If they were there, Hawk would see them. Tallboy appeared to be maybe sixteen in death's frozen repose. Soft faced, not mean. Kind of kid would probably really rather have stayed home and talked with his mother and his aunts, if he'd had any, and they were sober, and their boyfriends wouldn't slap him around. Might have not gotten killed if I hadn't gone and talked with him and gotten him stirred up about who killed his girlfriend and her baby, that might have been his baby. He probably liked the baby, not like a father; not to change diapers, and earn money, and take care of—that would have been beyond him. But she'd have been fun to hug, and she'd have been cute, and he would probably have liked it when the three of them were alone and they could play together. It had started to rain again, not much, a light drizzle that beaded sparsely on his upturned defenseless face.

Hawk said, "Third building from the right, second floor, three middle windows."

I glanced up slowly, and not toward the windows. I glanced obliquely past them and looked out of the corner of my eye. There was a shade half drawn and some movement behind it.

"What makes you think it's them?" I said.

"Been here every day," Hawk said. "While you and the schoolteacher dashing around the ghetto. Nobody live on that floor."

"Well, maybe some evasive action and come up behind them?" I said.

"Sure," Hawk said. "Little acting too." He gestured suddenly at the vacant lot across the street. I whirled to look where he pointed.

"Now we hustle into the car," Hawk said.

And we did, and pulled out of the quadrangle with Hawk's tires screaming as they spun on the wet pavement. We went around the corner onto McCrory Street and slammed into the alley back of the third building. Hawk popped the trunk and we each grabbed a shotgun. As we moved toward the back door of the building each of us pumped a shell into the chamber at the same moment.

"We could set this to music," I said.

The back entryway had been padlocked, but the hasp had been jimmied loose and it hung, with its still intact padlock attached, limply beside the partly open door. We went in, I to the right, Hawk to the left. We were in a dim cellar. It was full of cardboard boxes which had gotten wet and collapsed, spilling whatever had once been in them onto the floor, where whatever soaked the boxes had, over time, reduced it to an indeterminate mass of mildewing stuff. In the middle of the cellar was a defunct boiler with rust staining the sides of it and adding to the indiscernible detritus on the floor.

We moved past the boiler to the stairs. Hawk, in high-top Reebok pump-ups, moved through the trash beneath the building like a dark ghost, holding the eight-pound shotgun in his right hand as if it were a wand. It was as if he were floating. We went up the two flights of stairs without a sound. In the dim, claustrophobic corridor we paused, Hawk counting the doors until he found what we wanted. He stepped to it and put his ear against it and listened. There was litter nearly ankle deep in places all up and down the corridor—broken glass, fast-food paper and plastic, beer cans, and food scraps that were no longer identifiable. In the silence while Hawk listened I could hear vermin rustle in the trash. I waited. Hawk listened. Then he smiled at me and nodded.

With the shotgun in my right hand I reached over with my left and took hold of the knob and turned it slowly. It gave and the door opened inward and Hawk went in and left. I came in behind him and moved right. There were eight kids in there grouped near the windows, wondering where we were. Beside the window was a large cable spool, standing on end. On top of it lay a Tec-9 automatic which would fire thirty-two rounds if we let it.

One kid spun toward the gun. It was the same small, quick one I'd taken the Browning from in the van. I fired at the cable spool and hit it, chips of plastic flew off the handle of the Tec-9, and a ragged chunk of the wooden top flew up as well. The handgun ricocheted off the wall and bounced on the floor, the clip separated and skittered across the room, some of the shotgun pellets pocked the wall beyond.

Everyone froze.

In the reverberating silence after the gunshot, Hawk's voice was almost piercing.

"Where's Major?" Hawk said quietly.

No one said anything.

"Guess he won't be going down for it," Hawk said.

No one said a word. All eight stood in perfect stillness. Under the gun like that they didn't seem frightful. They seemed like scared kids whose prank had gotten out of hand. They were that, but they were the other thing too, they were kids who would shoot a fourteen-year-old girl and her three-month-old baby. They were kids who would gun down her boyfriend and leave him as a statement. That was the hard part, remembering that they weren't inhuman predators, and that they were. *One must have a mind of winter,* I thought, *to behold the nothing that is not there and the nothing that is.*

"Any of you guys read Wallace Stevens?" I said.

No one spoke. The shotgun felt solid and weighty as I held it. The faint smell of the exploded shell lingered.

"We'll check the slug that killed Tallboy," Hawk said. "And we'll check the Tec-9, and we'll see whose prints are on it."

Hawk let his gaze rest quietly on the kid who'd first made a move for the gun.

"You the shooter, Shoe?"

Hawk was making it up as he went along. It wasn't clear to me that the Tec-9 would fire even a test round anymore, and it probably had more prints on it than a subway door, but Shoe seemed impressed.

"I didn't trace nobody," he said.

"You think you won't go down for it?" Hawk said. "You think maybe you gotta lot of influence downtown, and they won't drop you in a jar as soon as we bring you in? If we feel like bringing you in?"

"I didn't trace Tallboy," Shoe said.

"Don't matter if you did or didn't," Hawk said. "We prove you did and it's one less problem for Double Deuce. Fact we prove you all accessories and we got Double Deuce's problems solved."

"We didn't do nothing." It was a fat kid they called Goodyear. His voice had an asthmatic whisper around the edges of it. "We just looking out the window, see what's happening."

"We got you at the scene of a crime, with the murder weapon," I said. "There's three unsolved murders cleaned up if we can tag you with them. You think we can't?"

"Shoe didn't do it," Goodyear said.

"Yeah, he did," Hawk said.

"No," Shoe said. His voice had outrage in it. The other kids muttered that he really hadn't.

"He didn't," Goodyear said.

"Move out," Hawk said. "We'll call downtown from my car."

Nobody moved. Still holding the shotgun in one hand, Hawk put the muzzle against Shoe's upper lip, right under his nose.

"Going down anyway, Shoe, may as well die here as Walpole."

"They don't burn nobody in this state," Shoe said.

"For killing a three-month-old baby?" Hawk smiled.

"I never done that," Shoe said.

"And her momma."

"No," Shoe said, his head tipped back a little by the pressure of the shotgun muzzle.

"And Tallboy. You be lucky to make it to Walpole."

"No," Shoe said.

"Course it coulda been Major," he said.

"No. Major didn't," Shoe said.

Hawk was silent for a long time while we all stood there and waited. Finally he lowered the shotgun.

"Beat it," he said. They all stood motionless for a moment, then Shoe walked past him and out the open door. One by one they followed. No one spoke. In a moment it was just Hawk and me alone in the dingy room with the damaged remnants of a Tec-9.

# Chapter 35

"Isn't that fascinating," Susan said. "They wouldn't budge."

We were sitting at the counter in the kitchen. I was drinking some Catamount beer, and Susan, to be sociable, was occasionally wetting her bottom lip in a glass of Cabernet Blanc. Pearl sprawled on the floor, her four feet out straight, her eyes nearly closed, occasionally glancing over to make sure no food had made a surreptitious appearance.

"They were scared," I said. "Hawk could scare Mount Rushmore. But they wouldn't give in."

"It's interesting, isn't it. These kids have many of the same virtues and vices that other kids have, misapplied."

"They're applied to what's there," I said.

Susan nodded. "And the consequences may be fatal," she said.

Across the counter, in the small kitchen, there was evidence that Susan had prepared a meal . . . or that the kitchen had been ransacked. Since there was a pot of something simmering on the stove, I assumed the former.

"The thing is," I said, "we all knew Major did the killing. They knew it; we knew it; they knew we knew it; we knew they knew—"

"You admire their loyalty," Susan said.

She was wearing black spandex tights and a leotard top. The outfit revealed nearly everything about her body. I looked at her eyes, and felt as I always did, that I could breathe more deeply when I looked at her, that the air was oxygen rich, and that we would live forever.

"Windows of the soul," I said.

She grinned at me.

"Augmented with just a touch of eyeliner," she said.

"What's in the pot?" I said.

She glanced back at the stove.

"Jesus," she said and jumped up and dashed around the counter. She picked up a big spoon and jostled the pot lid off with it. She looked in and smiled.

"It's okay," she said.

"Maybe Christmas," I said, "I'll buy you a potholder."

"I've got some, but I couldn't find it right away and I was afraid it would burn."

She was trying to balance the pot lid on her big spoon and put it back on the pot. It teetered, she touched it with her left hand to balance it, and burned her hand, and flinched and the lid fell to the floor.

"Fuck," she said.

Pearl had leapt to attention when the lid hit the floor and now was sitting behind the legs of my stool and looking out at Susan with something that might have been disapproval. Susan saw her.

"Everyone's a goddamned critic," she said.

"What is it?" I said neutrally.

"Brunswick stew," Susan said. "There was a recipe in the paper."

She found one potholder under an overturned colander and used it to pick up the pot lid and put it back on the pot.

"One of my favorites," I said.

"I know," Susan said. "It's why I made it."

"I'll like it," I said.

"And if you don't," she said, "lie."

"It is my every intention," I said.

She set the counter in front of us, got me another beer, and ladled two servings of Brunswick stew into our plates. I took a bite. It was pretty good. I had some more.

"Do I detect a dumpling in here?" I said.

"No," Susan said. "I tried to thicken the gravy. What you detect is some flour in a congealed glump."

"What you do," I said, "is mix the flour in a little cold water first, then when the slurry is smooth you stir it into the stew."

"Gee, isn't that smart," Susan said.

I knew she didn't mean it. I decided not to make other helpful suggestions. We ate quietly for a while. The congealed flour lumps had tasted better when I thought they were dumplings. When I finished I got up and walked around Pearl to the stove and got a second helping.

"Oh, for Christ sake don't patronize me," Susan said.

"I'm hungry," I said. "The stew's good. Are we saving it for breakfast?"

"The stew's not good. You're just eating it to make me feel good."

"Not true, but if it were, why would that be so bad?"

"Oh, shit," Susan said, and her eyes began to fill.

I said, "Suze, you never cry."

"It's not working," she said. Her voice was very tight and very shaky. She got up and left the kitchen and went in the bedroom and closed the door.

I stood for a while holding the stew and looking after her. Then I looked at Pearl. She was focused on the plate of stew.

"The thing is," I said to Pearl, "she's right."

And I put the plate down for Pearl to finish.

# Chapter 36

Tony Marcus agreed to meet us at a muffin shop on the arcade in South Station.

"Tony like muffins?" I said.

"Tony likes open public places," Hawk said.

"Makes sense," I said. "Get trapped in a place like Locke-Ober, you could get umbrella'd to death."

South Station was new, almost. They'd jacked up the old façade and slid a new station in behind it. Where once pigeons had flown about in the semidarkness, and winos had slept fragrantly on the benches, there were now muffin shops and lots of light and a model train set. What had once been the dank remnant of the old railroad days was now as slick and cheery as the food circus in a shopping mall.

The muffin shop was there, to the right, past the frozen lo-fat yogurt stand. Tony Marcus was there at a cute little iron filigree table, alone. At the next table was his bodyguard, a stolid black man about the size of Nairobi. The bodyguard's name was Billy. Tony was a middle-sized black guy, a little soft, with a careful moustache. I always thought he looked like Billy Eckstine, but Hawk never saw it. We stopped at the counter. I bought two coffees, gave one to Hawk, and went to Tony's table.

Tony nodded very slightly when we arrived. Billy looked at us as if we were dust motes. Billy's eyes were very small. He looked like a Cape buffalo. I shot at him with a forefinger and thumb.

"Hey, Billy," I said. "Every time I see you you get more winsome."

Billy gazed at me without expression.

Tony said, "You want a muffin?"

Hawk and I both shook our heads.

"Good muffins," Tony said. "Praline chocolate chip are excellent."

Hawk said, "Jesus Christ."

Tony had two on a paper plate in front of him. He picked one up and took a bite out of it, the way you'd eat an apple.

"So what you need?" he said around the mouthful of muffin.

"Gang of kids running drugs out of a housing project at Twenty-two Hobart Street," I said.

Tony nodded and chewed on his muffin.

"Couple people been killed," I said.

Tony shook his head. "Fucking younger generation," he said.

"Going to hell in a handbasket," I said. "Tenants at Double Deuce hired Hawk and me to bring order out of chaos there."

Marcus looked at his bodyguard. "You hear how he talks, Billy? 'Order out of chaos.' Ain't that something?"

"And the most successful local television show in the country is doing a five-part investigative series on the whole deal."

It got Tony's attention.

"What television show?"

"*Marge Eagen, Live,*" I said.

"The blonde broad with the big tits?"

I smiled. Hawk smiled.

"What do you mean, an investigation?" Tony said.

"What's wrong in the ghetto," Hawk said. "Who's selling drugs, how to save kids from the gangs, how to make black folks just like white folks."

Marcus was silent for the time it took him to eat the rest of his second muffin.

When he finished he said, "You in on that?"

"Sorta parallel," I said.

Tony pursed his lips slightly and nodded, and kept nodding, as if he'd forgotten he was doing it. He picked up his coffee cup and discovered it was empty. Billy got him another one. Tony stirred three spoonfuls of sugar carefully into the coffee and laid his spoon down and took a sip. Then he looked at me.

"So?" he said.

"The investigation is centered on the project," I said. "And"—I looked at Billy—"while I don't wish to seem immodest here, Bill, the investigation, so called, will go where we direct it."

Billy continued to conceal his amusement.

"So?" Marcus said.

"Any drugs moving in the ghetto are yours," I said.

Marcus rolled back in his chair and widened his eyes. He spread his hands.

"Me?" he said.

"And if there is a thorough investigation of the drugs trade in and around Double Deuce, then you are going to be more famous than Oliver North."

"Unless?" Tony said.

"Voilà," I said.

Tony said, "Don't fuck around, Spenser. You want something, say what."

"Move the operation," I said.

"Where?"

"Anywhere but Double Deuce."

"Hawk?" Marcus said.

Hawk nodded.

"Say I could do that? Say I could persuade them to go someplace else?"

"Then you would be as famous as John Marsh."

"Who the fuck is John Marsh?" Tony said.

"My point exactly," I said.

Behind us a train came in, an hour and a half late, from Washington, and people straggled wearily through the bright station.

"Okay," Marcus said.

"Good," I said. "One thing, though."

Marcus waited.

"Kid named Major Johnson," I said. "He's going to have to go down."

"Why?"

"Killed three children," I said.

Marcus shrugged.

"Lots more where he came from," Marcus said.

# Chapter 37

Susan and I were eating blueberry pancakes and drinking coffee on Sunday morning. The sun was flooding in through the east window of the kitchen, and Susan looked like the Queen of Sheba in a white silk robe, with her black hair loose around her face.

Susan gave Pearl a forkful of pancake.

"Good for her," Susan said. "Whole wheat, fresh fruit, a nice change of pace from bone meal and soy grits."

"Almost anything would be," I said.

"Are you going to put on a shirt," Susan said, "before Jackie arrives?"

"Keep her from flinging herself on me?" I said.

"Sure," Susan said. "Why is she coming over?"

"She didn't say. Just that she needed to talk and would we be home."

Pearl edged her nose under my elbow and pushed my arm.

"Of course," I said.

I cut a wedge from my pancake stack and fed it to her.

"You think we might be spoiling this dog?" I said.

"Of course," Susan said. "But how else will she learn to eat from the table?"

I looked down at Pearl. She was perfectly concentrated on the pancakes, her gaze shifting as one or the other of us ate.

"A canine American princess," I said.

"Nothing wrong with that," Susan said.

The doorbell rang and Susan got up to answer. I left my pancakes and went to the bedroom and put on a shirt. When I came back Pearl was still sitting gazing at my plate, but the plate was empty and clean. I looked at her. She looked back clear-eyed and guilt free, alert for another opportunity.

"Ah yes," I said, "a hunting dog."

Susan came back with Jackie. I gave her a half hug and a kiss on the cheek. Pearl jumped around. Susan poured Jackie some coffee. Jackie de-clined pancakes. I had a few more.

"I'm sorry to intrude on your Sunday morning," Jackie said. "But I have to talk about Hawk."

I nodded.

"Puzzling, isn't he," Susan said.

Jackie shook her head.

"You know him," she said to me. "You must know him better than anyone."

I smiled encouragingly.

"I think I'm falling in love with him," Jackie said.

Susan and I both smiled encouragingly.

"But I"—she searched for the right way to say it—"I can't . . . he won't . . ."

"You can't get at him," I said.

"Yes."

Jackie was silent contemplating that, as if having found the right phrase for it, she could rethink it in some useful way.

"I mean, what's not to like? He's fun to be with. He's funny. He knows stuff. He's a dandy lover. . . . But I can't seem to get at him."

I ate some more pancake. I'd made them with buckwheat flour, and they were very tasty. Jackie was looking at me. I glanced at Susan. This was her area, and I was hoping she'd step in. She didn't, she was looking at me too.

So was Pearl. But all Pearl wanted was food. Dogs are easy.

"Part of what Hawk is," I said, "is that you can't get at him. Erin Macklin thinks that's the price he paid to get out."

"Out of what?" Jackie said. "Being black? Being black's hard on everybody. I don't shut him out."

Susan remained quiet. She looked like someone watching a good movie.

"Well," I said, "if you're a certain kind of guy—"

"Guy?" Jackie said. "Guy? Is that it? Some fucking arcane guy shit?"

"Jackie," I said, "I didn't come over to your place and say, 'Let me ex-plain Hawk to you.' "

She took a deep inhale and held it for a moment with her lips clamped together, then she let it out through her nose and nodded.

"Of course you didn't," she said. "I'm sorry. I'm just very stressed."

"Being in love with Hawk would be stressful," I said.

"I don't think I'm in love with him yet. But I will be soon, and I want to figure this out before it's too late."

I nodded. Susan watched.

"You were saying?" Jackie said.

"You have a sense of who you are," I said. "And you're determined to keep on being who you are, and maybe the only way you can keep on being who you are is to go inside, to be inaccessible. Especially, I would think, if you're a black man. And more especially if you do the kind of work Hawk does."

"So why do it?"

"Because he knows how," I said. "It's what he's good at."

"And that means he can't love anybody," Jackie said.

"It means you keep a little of yourself to yourself."

"Why?" Jackie said.

"Suze," I said, "you want to offer any interpretation?"

"No."

I looked at Pearl. She appeared to be fantasizing about buckwheat pancakes.

"I don't suppose," I said, "that you'd settle for an eloquent shrug of the shoulders?"

"Not unless you're willing to admit that you've gotten bogged down in your own bullshit and you don't know how to get out," Jackie said.

"It's not bullshit," I said. "But it is something one feels more than something one thinks about, and it's hard to explain to someone who doesn't live Hawk's life."

"Like a woman?"

I shook my head.

"Hawk sometimes kills people. People sometimes try to kill him. Keeping yourself intact while you do that kind of work requires so much resolution that it has to be carefully protected."

"Even from someone who loves him?"

"Especially," I said.

We were all silent.

"This is probably as much of Hawk as I will ever get," she said.

"Probably," I said.

"I don't think it's enough," Jackie said.

"It might be," Susan said, "if you can adjust your expectations."

Jackie looked at Susan and at me.

"You've been lucky," Jackie said. "I guess I'm envious."

Susan looked straight at me and I could feel the connection between us.

"Luck has nothing to do with it," Susan said.

# Chapter 38

Hawk and I were sitting in my office in the late afternoon on a day that made you feel eternal. All the trees on the Common were budded. Early flowers bloomed in the Public Gardens, and the college kids littered the embankment along Storrow Drive, soaking up the rays behind BU.

We'd been asking around after Major for a couple of weeks now. And the more we asked where he was, the more no one knew.

"He'll show up," Hawk said.

"He's maybe killed three people," I said. "Be good if we found him rather than the other way around."

"We'll hear from him," Hawk said. "He's going to have to know."

"Know what you'll do?"

"What I'll do, and what he'll do when I do it," Hawk said.

"You've given him a lot of slack," I said. "I've seen you be quite abrupt with people who were a lot less annoying than Major is."

"Kind of want to see what he'll do too," Hawk said.

"I sort of guessed that you might," I said.

"We'll hear from him," Hawk said.

And we did.

The phone rang just after six, when the sun had pretty well departed, but it was still bright daylight.

"Got a message for Hawk," the voice said. It was Major.

"Sure," I said. "He's here."

I clicked onto speakerphone.

Hawk said, "Go ahead."

"This Hawk?" Major said.

"Un huh."

"You know who this is?"

"Un huh."

"You can't prove I done those people," Major said, "can you?"

"You got something to say, say it."

"Maybe I didn't do them."

"Un huh."

"That all you say?"

Hawk made no response at all.

"You been looking for me," Major said.

"Un huh."

"You can't find me."

"Yet," Hawk said.

"You never find me 'less I want you to."

Again Hawk was silent.

"You find me, you can't do nothing. You got no evidence."

"I know you did it," Hawk said.

"You think I done it."

Hawk was silent.

"So what you do, you find me?"

Hawk didn't say anything.

"What you think you do?"

More silence.

"Can't do shit, man."

"Un huh."

The speaker buzzed softly in the silence. Hawk was leaning his hips against the edge of my desk, arms folded. He looked like he might be waiting for a bus.

"You still there?" Major said.

"Sure."

"Want to meet me?"

"Sure."

"You know the stadium in the Fenway? By Park Drive?" Major said.

"Un huh."

"Be there, five A.M."

"Tomorrow," Hawk said.

Again the scratchy silence lingered on the speakerphone, and then Major hung up. I hit the speakerphone button and broke the connection. Hawk looked over at me and grinned.

"Think he's alone?" I said.

"No. They won't leave him."

"Even when Tony Marcus says to?"

"We crate Major and they'll go," Hawk said. "But they won't leave him there."

"And they will probably bother us while we're trying to crate him," I said.

"Only twenty of them," Hawk said.

"Against you and me?" I said. "I like our odds."

Hawk shrugged.

We were quiet for a while, listening to the traffic sound wisp in through the window.

"We don't know he did it," I said.

"You hear him say he didn't?" Hawk said.

"Haven't heard him say he did," I said. "Exactly."

"How you feel 'bout the Easter bunny?" Hawk said.

"Maybe Major's just profiling," I said. "Makes him feel important, being a suspect."

"We see him tomorrow," Hawk said. "We ask him."

# Chapter 39

Hawk was gone and I sat in my office without turning the lights on and looked at the flossy new building across the street. The whole thing at Double Deuce was rolling faster than it should.

Hawk's scenario—and I knew he believed it—made good enough sense. Tallboy had welshed on a drug deal and Major had shot Tallboy's girlfriend and probably by accident the little girl. Then, when Tallboy had felt obliged to revenge it, he wasn't good enough and Major had snuffed him too. Nothing wrong with that. Things like that happened.

I got up and stood looking out the window with my arms folded. So what was bothering me?

One thing was that I figured that tomorrow would escalate, and Hawk would kill Major. Somebody probably would, sooner or later. But I wasn't sure it should be us.

Another thing was that it didn't seem like Major's style. He was a show-off. If Tallboy was holding out, Major would face him off in front of an audience. And he'd brag about it. Just as he'd bragged that Tony Marcus was his supplier. And if there was a murder or two in any deal where Tony Marcus was part of the mix, why wouldn't you wonder about him?

I stood looking out the window and wondered about Tony for a while. It didn't lead me anywhere. Below me on Berkeley Street a man walked three greyhounds on a tripartite leash. There was some sort of organization in town that arranged adoptions for overaged racing dogs. Maybe I should consider a career change.

We would meet Major in the morning. I knew Hawk well enough to know that he wouldn't waver on that. I didn't know him well enough to know why he wouldn't. There was something about Major. There was something going on between them that didn't include me. He'd go whether I went with him or not, and I couldn't let him go alone.

The guy with the greyhounds turned the corner on Stuart Street and headed toward Copley Square. I watched until they disappeared behind the old Hancock Building.

"Well," I said aloud to no one, "better do something."

And since I couldn't think of anything else to do, I got in my car and drove to Double Deuce.

There was a light showing in the window of the second-floor apartment that Hawk and I had rousted. I went up the dark stairs and along the sad corridor toward the light that showed under the partly sprung door. I felt my whiteness more than I had when I'd come with Hawk. Then we'd been chasing something. Now I was an intruder from a land as alien to these kids as Tasmania.

I took a deep breath and let it out slowly and knocked. The sounds of the room stopped and the light went out. I heard a shuffle of footsteps and then a voice said through the closed door:

"Yo?"

The voice had a soft rasp. It was probably Goodyear.

"Spenser," I said. "Alone."

"What you want?"

"Talk."

" 'Bout what?"

"Saving Major's ass," I said.

"He ain't here."

"You'll do," I said. "I don't have a lot of time."

I could hear some whispering, then the door lock slid back and the door opened and I walked into the dark room.

# Chapter 40

When I got home it was nearly 8:30 and the Braves and the Dodgers were on cable. Susan was in the kitchen. There was a bottle of Krug Rosé Champagne in a crystal ice bucket on the counter and two fluted glasses. Susan was wearing a suit the pale green-gold color of spring foliage. It was an odd color, but it went wonderfully with her dark hair. The suit had a very short skirt too. Pearl was on the couch that occupied most of the far wall in front of the big picture window, where, if you were there at the right time, you could look at the sunset. Now there was only darkness. She cavorted about for a moment to greet me and then went back to her couch.

I looked at the champagne.

"Does this bode well for me?" I said. "Or are you having company?"

"It's to sip while we talk," Susan said. "If you'll open it."

I did and carefully poured two glasses. I gave one to her. She touched its rim to mine and said, "To us."

"I'll drink to that," I said. And we did.

I looked down at her legs, much of which were showing under the short skirt.

"Great wheels," I said.

"Thank you," she said. "I'm afraid I've been a goddamned fool."

"Anything's possible," I said.

We each drank a little more champagne.

"First, to state the obvious, I love you."

"Yes," I said. "I know that."

"Second, and I'm afraid about as obvious, I do better with other people's childhoods than I do with my own."

"Don't we all," I said.

"I was bought up in a well-related suburb by affluent parents. My father went to business, my mother stayed home with the children. My father's consuming passion was business; my mother's was homemaking. I was expected to marry a man who went to business and loved it, to stay home with the children, and make a home."

I didn't say anything. Pearl lay still on the couch, her back legs stretched out, her head on her front paws, motionless except for her eyes, which watched us carefully.

"And I did," Susan said. She drank another swallow of champagne, and put the glass back on the counter and looked into the glass where the bubbles drifted toward the surface.

"Except that the marriage was awful and there were no children, and I got divorced and had to work and met you."

" 'Bye-'bye, Miss American Pie," I said.

Susan smiled.

"Most of the rest you know," she said. "We both know. When I left Sunnybrook Farm I left with a vengeance—the job, then the Ph.D., moving to the city. Part of your charm at first was that you were so unsuburban. You were dangerous, you were your own and not someone else's. And you gave me room."

I poured some more champagne in her glass, carefully, so it wouldn't foam up and overflow.

"But always I was failing. I wasn't keeping house, I wasn't raising children. I wasn't doing it right. It's one of the reasons I left you."

"For a while," I said.

"And it's the reason I wanted you to live with me."

"Not because I am cuter than a bug's ear?"

"That too," Susan said. "But mostly I wanted to pretend to be what I had never been."

"Which is to say, your mother," I said.

Susan smiled again.

"I'll bet you can claim the thickest neck of any Freudian in the country," she said.

"I'm not sure that's a challenge," I said. "Joyce Brothers is probably second."

"And I strong-armed you into moving in, and it hasn't been any fun at all."

"Except maybe last Sunday morning after I let Pearl out," I said.

"Except for that."

We were quiet while we each had some more champagne.

"So what's your plan?" I said.

"I think we should live separately," Susan said. "Don't misunderstand me. I think we should continue to live intimately, and monogamously . . . but not quite so proximate."

"Proximate," I said.

Susan laughed, though only a little.

"Yes," she said, "proximate. I do, after all, have a Ph.D.—from Harvard."

"Nothing to be ashamed of," I said.

"How do you feel about it, living apart again?" Susan said.

"I agree with your analysis and share your conclusion."

"You don't mind?"

"No, I like it."

"It'll be the way it was."

"Maybe better," I said. "You won't be wishing we could live together."

"Where will you go?" Susan said.

"I kept my apartment," I said.

Susan widened her eyes at me.

"Did you really?" she said.

I nodded and drank some more champagne and offered to pour some more in her glass; she shook her head, still looking at me.

"Not quite a ringing endorsement of the original move," she said.

I couldn't think of an answer to that, so I kept quiet. I have rarely regretted keeping quiet. I promised myself to work on it.

"You knew I was a goddamned fool," she said.

"I knew it was important to you. I trusted you to work it out."

She reached out and patted my hand.

"I did not make a mistake in you," she said.

"No," I said, "you didn't."

The doorbell rang.

Susan said, "I wanted a last supper as roommates."

She smiled a wide genuine smile.

"But I've abandoned pretense. It's the Chinese place in Inman Square that delivers."

I raised my champagne glass.

"*À votre santé,*" I said.

Susan went down and brought up the food in a big white paper sack and put it on top of the refrigerator where Pearl couldn't reach it.

"Before we dine," Susan said, "I thought we might wish to screw our brains out."

"Kind of a salute to freedom," I said.

"Exactly," Susan said.

# Chapter 41

The Fenway is part of what Frederick Law Olmsted called the emerald necklace when he designed it in the nineteenth century—an uninterrupted stretch of green space following the Charles River and branching off along the Muddy River to Jamaica Pond, and continuing, with modest interference from the city, to Franklin Park and the Arboretum. It was a democratic green space and it remained pleasant through demographic shifts which moved the necklace in and out of bad neighborhoods. Along the Park Drive section of the Fenway the neighborhood was what the urban planners probably called transitional. There were apartments full of nurses and graduate students along Park Drive, and across the Fenway there was the proud rear end of the Museum of Fine Arts. Simmons College was on a stretch on Fenway, and Northeastern University was a block away and just up the street was Harvard Medical School.

But the Fenway itself was a kind of Riviera for both black and Hispanic gangs taking occasional leave from their duties in the ghetto. And they didn't have to go far. The ghetto spread sullenly beyond the museum and behind the university. The stadium at the southwest end of the Fenway midsection was dense with gang graffiti.

At two minutes to five in the morning, Hawk and I parked up on the grass near the Victory Gardens where Park Drive branches off Boylston Street. We thought it would be wise to walk in from this end and get a look at things as we came. There wasn't much traffic yet, and as we walked into the Fenway the grass was still wet. A hint of vapor hovered over the Muddy River, and two early ducks floated pleasantly out from under the arched fieldstone bridge.

"We figured out exactly what we're doing?" I said.

I had on a blue sweatshirt with the sleeves cut off, and jeans, and white leather New Balance gym shoes. I wore a Browning 9mm pistol in a brown leather holster tipped a little forward on my right hip, and a pair of drop-dead Ray-Ban sunglasses.

"Thinking 'bout making a citizen's arrest," Hawk said. He was wearing Asics Tiger gels, and a black satin-finish Adidas warm-up suit with red trim. The jacket was half zipped, and the butt of something that appeared to be an antitank gun showed under his left arm.

"I don't want to kill him if we don't have to," I said.

"He's in the way," Hawk said. "We don't get him out the way we got problems at Double Deuce. Plus he buzzes three people—and he strolls?"

"If he really buzzed three," I said.

"He did, 'less you find me somebody better."

"I'm working on that," I said.

"Better hurry," Hawk said. "Got about thirty-five seconds 'fore the gate opens."

Ahead of us was the stadium, poured concrete with bleacher seats rising up at either end. A skin baseball diamond was at the near end. Another diamond wedged in against the stadium administrative tower at the far end. The place must have been built in the thirties. It had, on a small scale, that neo-Roman look like the LA Coliseum. The tower was closed. It had always been closed. I had never seen it open.

As we came into the open end of the stadium from the north, I could see maybe twenty black kids in Raiders caps sitting in a single line, not talking, in the top row of the bleachers on the east side of the stadium, the sun half risen behind them. We kept coming, and as we did, Major appeared from behind the tower, walking slowly toward us.

Hawk laughed softly.

"Major been watching those Western movies," Hawk said.

Major was all in black. Shirts, jeans, high-topped sneakers, Raiders cap. As he came toward us I could see the sun glint on the surface of a handgun stuck in his belt.

"Piece in his belt," I said. "In front."

"Un huh."

We were in front of the assembled Hobart Raiders now. We stopped. Major, fifteen yards from us, stopped when we stopped. One point for us; you needed to be pretty good to count on shooting well at forty-five feet with a handgun. Hawk and I were pretty good. Odds were that Major wasn't. Odds were on the other hand that if all the kids in the stands opened up, some of them might hit us. Odds were, though, that not all of them had weapons.

"Life's uncertain," I said to Hawk.

Hawk was looking at Major.

"What we need now," Hawk said. "Deep thinking."

"Talked with Goodyear and Shoe last night," I said.

Hawk's eyes moved calmly between Major and the Raiders in the stands.

"They said that Major didn't kill Devona."

"How 'bout Tallboy?" Hawk said.

"Major killed Tallboy because Tallboy came in on them drunk and waving a gun."

"So," Major said, "Hawk, my man, what's happening?"

"Let's see," Hawk said.

"You come to get me? You and the Mickey?"

"Me," Hawk said.

"So why you bring him?"

"Didn't bring him," Hawk said. "He come on his own."

"Make you look like a fucking Tom," Major said.

"You invited me, boy," Hawk said. "You got something in mind, whyn't you get to it."

"Good move," I said to Hawk. "Placate him."

Hawk grinned.

"What you smiling for?" Major said. "I don't let no one laugh at me."

Major paused and looked at the gang members in the stands. They were all standing now, motionless along the top row of seats. He was playing to them. He looked back at us.

"You know the fucking law, Hawk. Respect. You like made the fucking law, man. Respect. You don't get treated with respect, you see to it."

"Heard maybe you backshot a fourteen-year-old girl," I said. "Hard not to dis you."

"Fuck you, Irish. I didn't shoot no sly. But if I do, what you know about it? You don't know shit. You live in some kind of big white-ass fucking house, and you drive your fancy white-ass car. And you don't know a fucking thing about me. You live where I live, and what you got is respect, and you ain't got that you ain't got shit. Don't matter who you spike or how, you get respect. Hawk know that. Am I right or wrong, Hawk?"

"Never had to backshoot a fourteen-year-old girl," Hawk said.

"You think I shot her, you think what you fucking want. Everybody know you, Hawk. You the man. You the one set the standard. Well I be the man now, you dig? I set the standard. All of them"—he jerked his head toward the gang members—"they looking at me. I want them here, they here. I let someone dis me, he dis them. That mean some sly got to bite the dust." Major shrugged elaborately. "Plenty of them around," he said. "You know why I the man? I have to do one, I'll do one. There some brothers bigger than me, some Homeboys real strong fighters like John Porter. But he ain't the man, and they ain't the man. I the man. You know why? 'Cause I crazy enough. I crazy enough to do anything. And everybody know. Maybe somebody got to die. I willing. I step up. Ain't afraid to die, ain't afraid at all. I die what I be losing?"

Major paused. Hawk waited.

"So you be thinking I lined Tallboy's wiggle, then you wrong. But if I wanted to I would have and I wouldn't give a fuck what you or the flap or anybody thought 'bout it."

Hawk was perfectly still, and perfectly relaxed like he always was in this kind of moment. But he was different. He didn't, I realized all at once, want to kill Major. I knew he would if he had to, but in all the years I'd known him I'd never seen him want or not want. Killing was a practical matter to Hawk.

"You didn't kill her," Hawk said, "who did?"

"Hawk, you and me the same," Major said. "It got to be done we step up. Ain't afraid to be killing, ain't afraid to be dying."

Major was playing to his audience, and, I realized, he was playing most of all to Hawk.

Quietly I said, "How many guns, you think?"

Hawk said, "Besides Major, probably two or three. Kids have them, pass them around. Kid with the raincoat probably has a long gun. One with the jacket probably got one."

"What you talking 'bout?" Major said. "You better be listening to me."

"We arguing which one of us going to fry you," Hawk said.

"You, Hawk." There was something almost like panic in Major's voice. "You and me, Hawk. Not me and some flap-fucking Irish."

I was scanning the crowd in the stands. Hawk was right. Only two of them wore coats that would conceal a gun. Some of them might have it stuck under a shirt or in an ankle holster, but the good odds were to fire at the ones with coats first.

Major raised his voice. "John Porter."

Around the corner of the grandstand came John Porter with Jackie Raines. John Porter had her arm and he held a revolver to her head. Jackie's face was pinched with fear. She walked stiffly, trying not to be compliant, but not strong enough to resist John Porter.

"Got this here fine nigger lady," Major said.

Jackie looked at us. Her eyes were wide.

"Hawk," she said. She said it like a request. Hawk didn't move. His expression didn't change.

"Come around without you," Major said, the laughter lilting in his voice. "Say we all black folks, and I'm trying to get the *low-down* on what it's like for you poor nigger boys in the *ghet-to*. And John Porter he say how come you don't go *low down* on this?"

Major laughed. It was real laughter. It wasn't for effect, but it had a crazy tremolo along its edge. John Porter smiled vacantly, proud to be mentioned by Major.

"So she say I know you gonna meet with Hawk and he won't tell me where. So I say we tell you where, slut. Fact we bring you along with us."

Hawk said to me, "When it starts, you take the stands."

I said, "Um hmm."

Major said, "I tol you, you better be listening to me, Hawk. You want your slut back, you better be paying attention to me."

Hawk looked at Major, full focus, and slowly nodded his head once.

"You want the slut back, you ask me nice, you say please, Mr. Major, and maybe I tell John Porter to let her go."

Hawk's gaze didn't falter. He was waiting. Major didn't know him like I did. Major thought he was hesitant.

"Go ahead, man. Say please, Mr. Major Johnson, sir."

Major was excited. He moved back and forth in a kind of wide-legged strut as he talked. The gun in his belt was a Glock, 9mm, retail price around $550, magazine capacity seventeen rounds. It was enough to make you nostalgic for zip guns.

"Hawk," Jackie said again. "Please."

"Better hurry up, Hawk, better ask me nice and polite, 'fore I put a bullet up her ass."

In the stands a kid in a black satin hip-length warm-up jacket brought an Uzi out from underneath it.

"*No,*" Major screamed. "*Nobody shoots!* This is me and Hawk! Nobody shoots! Hawk! Me and Hawk!"

Hawk reached thoughtfully under his arm and brought out the big Magnum. He turned deliberately sideways toward Major and Jackie.

"Hawk," Jackie screamed. "Don't!"

"You shoot at me, Hawk," Major shouted, "John Porter kill the slut." Major's voice was full of high vibrato.

Hawk brought the gun down onto his target.

"Don't!" Jackie screamed again.

"He'll kill her"—Major was screaming now too—"'less you ask me nice."

I drew my Browning and cocked it as it cleared the holster. Everything seemed to be moving languidly through liquid crystal. Hawk settled the handgun on his target and squeezed off a round and John Porter's face contorted. His gun spun away from him and he flung out both his arms and fell backwards, sprawling on the ground behind Jackie. Jackie was standing with both hands pressed against her open mouth. She looked as if she were trying to scream and couldn't. The kids in the stands were motionless.

Hawk walked slowly toward Major, the big Magnum still in his hand, hanging loosely at his side. When he reached him he looked straight down at Major. And stood, looking at him and not speaking. Then he reached over and took the Glock out of Major's belt and dropped it in his pocket. He looked down at John Porter. John Porter was sitting up now with his left hand pressed against his right shoulder, and some blood slowly showing through his fingers and smearing on the smooth finish of his half-zippered warm-up jacket. There was no pain in his face yet, just surprise, and a kind of numb shock.

"Who iced Devona Jefferson?" Hawk said. He didn't speak very loudly, but his voice seemed too loud in the frightening silence.

I put my gun away and walked over and stood beside Jackie. The first cars of the morning rush hour were beginning to move around the Fenway.

"Who killed her?" Hawk said again.

Major seemed dazed, staring at Hawk as if he'd never seen him before. The ducks had flown, frightened by the gunfire. I put an arm around Jackie's shoulder. No one spoke. No one moved.

Then Major said, "Marcus. Tallboy was skimming on us and Tony say be a good lesson for everybody."

"He didn't do it himself," Hawk said.

"Billy done it," Major said. "Done Tallboy too, and left him in Double Deuce so we'd see and remember."

"I heard you did Tallboy," I said.

"Tol everybody I did," Major said. "But it was Billy."

"Marcus got to take the jump for it," Hawk said.

Major nodded. He seemed transfixed, gazing at Hawk.

"I want you out of Double Deuce," Hawk said.

Major nodded slowly.

"We gonna go," he said. "Tony already say so."

"Tony going to be gone," Hawk said. "I say so."

Everyone lingered.

Hawk said, "I'll see to John Porter."

"We be going," Major said.

Hawk nodded and Major turned and walked away across the field toward the open end. From the stands the long silent row of black kids in Raiders hats went with him, one after the other jumping down off the grandstand and following him in silence.

"He might have killed me," Jackie said.

Hawk was motionless, looking after Major.

"For Christ sake, Hawk," Jackie said. Her voice was still very shaky. "You might have killed me shooting at him."

"No," Hawk said. "I wouldn't have."

Hawk looked down at John Porter for another silent moment. John Porter stared at the ground, waiting for whatever would happen. Then

Hawk put the big Magnum back carefully under his arm and looked again at Major, now nearly across the field, with his gang filing after him.

"Can we use him?" I said to Hawk. "Will he stay?"

Hawk nodded. The sun was well up now, and the ducks had returned and were once again paddling in the Muddy River.

"Kid more like me than a lot of people," Hawk said.

# Chapter 42

Belson and I were sitting at the bar in Grill 23 across the street from police headquarters and two blocks from my office. We were each drinking a martini. I had mine with a twist. Around us were a host of young insurance executives and ad agency creative types wearing expensive clothes and talking frantically about business and exercise. Campari and soda seemed popular.

"One of the Hobart Street Raiders got shot," Belson said.

There were mixed nuts in a cut-glass bowl on the bar. I selected out a few cashews and ate them.

"That so?" I said.

"Dude named John Porter. Somebody dropped him off at City Hospital ER with a slug in his shoulder. John Porter wouldn't say who."

"John Porter?" I said.

"Yeah. You been dealing with the Raiders, haven't you?"

"Small world," I said.

I sipped my drink. It takes awhile acquiring a taste for martinis, but it's worth the effort.

"Raiders have cleared out of the Double Deuce apartments," Belson said. "Packed up and left. Hear from the gang unit that Tony Marcus put out the word."

"Public-spirited," I said.

"Tony? Yeah. Anyway, they're gone."

Belson drank the rest of his martini and ordered another. His were straight-up and made with gin and an olive. Mine was made with Absolut vodka, on the rocks. I ordered one too.

"Just being polite," I said. "Don't want you to feel like a lush."

"Thanks," Belson said. He sorted through the mixed nuts.

"You eating all the cashews?" he said.

"Of course."

"One-way bastard," Belson said.

He found a half cashew and took it, and two Brazil nuts and ate them and sipped from his second martini. His jacket was unbuttoned and I could see the butt of his gun. He wore it in a holster inside his waistband.

"Marty and I were talking," Belson said. "Figure whoever spiked Porter probably did us a favor. Been in and out of jail most of his life. Leg-breaker. Some homicides we could never prove."

We each drank a little. Around us the after-work social scene whirled in a montage of pastel neckties and white pantyhose and perfume and cologne and cocktails, and talk of StairMasters and group therapy and re-cent movies.

"Old for a gangbanger," Belson said. "Nearly thirty."

I nodded. I rummaged unsuccessfully for cashews. They were all gone. I ate three hazelnuts instead.

"Kid seemed kind of proud about being shot," Belson said. "Gang kids put a lot of stock in that."

"They got nothing else to put stock in," I said.

"Probably not," Belson said. "But that's not my problem. I investigate shootings. Even if the shooting is maybe necessary, I'm supposed to inves-tigate it."

"And handsomely paid for the work too," I said.

"Sure."

Belson picked up the martini glass and looked through it along the bar, admiring the refracted colors. Then he took a brief sip and put it down.

"Spenser," Belson said, "Marty and me figure you or Hawk done John Porter. And we probably can't prove it, and if we could, why would we want to?"

"Why indeed," I said.

"But I didn't want you thinking we didn't know."

"I understand that," I said. "And I know that if you thought, say, Joe Broz had done it, that maybe you could prove it, and would."

Belson looked at me silently for a moment, then he drank the rest of his martini in a swallow, put the glass on the bar, and put his right hand out, palm up. I slapped it lightly.

"Tony Marcus killed Devona Jefferson and her baby," I said.

"Himself?"

"He had Billy do it. I got a witness."

I looked around the bar. There were several attractive young executive-class women with assertive blue suits and tight butts. I could ask one to join me for a discussion of Madonna's iconographic impact on mass culture. The very thought made my blood boil.

"Who you got?" Belson said. A new drink sat undisturbed in front of him on the bar.

"Major Johnson," I said.

"Kid runs the Hobart Street Raiders."

"Yeah. He was in the truck when she got hit. He won't say so, but he probably ID'd her for Billy."

"And?" Belson said.

"He'll need immunity."

"I can rig that," Belson said. "Can he tie Tony to it?"

"Heard him give the order," I said. "Whole thing supposed to be an object lesson for the gangs. Tony wanted them to remember who was in charge."

Belson nodded.

"Sort of dangerous being the only eyewitness against Tony Marcus," he said.

"We'll protect him," I said.

"You and Hawk?"

"Yeah."

"Still, it's his word against Tony's. Tony ain't much, but neither is the kid."

"Thought of that," I said.

"You got a plan?"

I smiled.

"Surely you jest," I said.

Belson pushed the undrunk martini away from him and leaned his elbows on the bar.

"Tell me," he said.

I did.

# Chapter 43

International Place nestles in the curve of the High Street off-ramp from the Central Artery, right across the street from the new Rowe's Wharf development on the waterfront. It's about forty stories tall, with a four-story atrium lobby full of marble and glass. In the lobby is a dining space, and at one end of the dining space is a croissant shop. Hawk and I were sitting at one of the little tables in front of the croissant shop, having some coffee and acting just like we belonged there. The glass walls let in the sun and the movement of urban business outside. It was 10:20 in the morning and most of the tables were empty. A roundish young woman at the next table was enjoying black coffee with artificial sweetener, and a chocolate croissant.

"Tony know the spots, don't he?" Hawk said.

He was wearing a teal silk tweed jacket over a black silk T-shirt, with jeans, and black cowboy boots. He leaned back in his chair, his legs straight out, his feet crossed comfortably at the ankles. I had on a blue blazer and sneakers. If there were a *GQ* talent scout in the building, our careers would be made.

"Major's okay?" I said.

"Yeah. I told him Tony's answer when we said Major had to take the fall."

" 'Plenty more where he came from'?"

Hawk grinned. "What Major hate was not so much that Tony would let him take the rap, but that he didn't matter. Major like to think he important."

"Here's his chance," I said.

We each had a little coffee. We examined some of the secretaries on coffee break. There was one with sort of auburn hair whose dress was some kind of spring knit and fit her very well. We examined her with special care.

"You talked with Jackie?" I said.

"Un huh."

"How was that?"

"Jackie don't like shooting," Hawk said.

"Nothing wrong with that," I said.

"Except that I'm a shooter," Hawk said.

The woman with the auburn hair and the knit dress got up and walked out of the dining area. We watched her go.

"She said she couldn't love no shooter," Hawk said.

I nodded.

"I said did she want me to get a paper route?"

"Nice compromise," I said.

Hawk grinned.

"Jackie said that maybe there was a third alternative. She talks like that, *third alternative*. I said I was a little long in the tooth for *third alternatives*."

"Never too late," I said.

Hawk was silent for a moment. His face showed nothing, but his gaze was very heavy on me.

"Yeah, it is," Hawk said. "Too late for me to be something else a long time ago. Anything but what I am is a step down."

"Yes," I said.

"You're smart," Hawk said. "You could do other things."

I shrugged.

"How come you do this?" Hawk said.

"It's what I know how to do," I said. "I'm good at it."

Hawk grinned.

"You want to be good at selling vinyl siding?"

"Rather die," I said.

"Jackie don't quite get that," Hawk said.

A new coffee break shift appeared. Hawk and I were alert to it, but no one compared to the one with the auburn hair.

"Tony's late," Hawk said.

"Surprising," I said, "seeing as there's some kind of sweet glop to be eaten."

A blonde woman in pale gray slacks went up and got a cappuccino and a whole-wheat roll and came back past us. She was wearing a nice perfume.

"So Jackie's gone?" I said.

"Un huh."

"Too bad," I said.

Hawk shrugged.

"You care?" I said.

"Don't plan to," Hawk said.

"She was a nice woman," I said.

"Un huh."

"You love her?" I said.

"You really bored," Hawk said, "or what."

"No, I just figured Susan would ask me, and if I said I hadn't asked she would have shaken her head without saying anything. Now, if she does it, she'll be implying something about you, not me."

Hawk grinned again.

"You believe in love," he said.

"I have reason to."

"Yeah, maybe," Hawk said. "But you have reason to because you believe in it, not the other way around."

"How'd we end up," I said, "talking about me?"

Hawk made a self-deprecating gesture with his hands as if to say, *It was easy.*

"It never seemed a good idea to believe in it," Hawk said. "Always seemed easier to me to stay intact if you didn't."

We were quiet. The coffee was gone. The sun that had slanted in and squared our table had moved on toward the service bar.

"Erin was right," I said.

"About me?" Hawk said.

"Yeah," I said. "You've paid a big price."

"Never said I didn't."

"And sometimes it hurts," I said.

It was as far as I'd ever pushed him.

"Un huh."

It was as far as he'd ever gone.

# Chapter 44

Across the dining area, Tony Marcus came strolling in from the outer lobby. Billy loomed behind him. Tony saw us across the room and they came to the table.

"Get me couple of those chocolate croissant," Marcus said. "Some coffee, three sugars, lotta cream."

Billy went silently to the counter. I'd never heard him speak. Would he order or just point at what he wanted? Marcus sat. He spoke to Hawk. He always spoke to Hawk. Unless he had to, he never spoke to me, or looked at me.

"What do you need now, Hawk?" Tony said.

"Need somebody to take the fall for Devona and Crystal Jefferson," Hawk said. "Told you that before."

"And I gave you the kid, Johnson," Marcus said.

"He didn't do it," Hawk said.

Marcus shrugged. "So what? He probably did something. Bag him for this."

"You did it, Tony."

Marcus shrugged again. "So what?"

"You wanted to remind the gang kids how tough you were. Must be a little tricky doing business with the gang kids, them being kind of crazy and all."

"You got that right," Marcus said.

"So you had Billy ace the kid, Devona."

"Got their attention," Marcus said. "Nobody saw the baby." Another shrug. "Shit happens."

Billy came back with the coffee and croissants, and Marcus bit off half of one and chewed it carefully.

"Billy used a nine," Hawk said.

Billy was standing near his boss, blocking out most of the light on that side of the room. Hawk leaned back a little more in his chair and looked at him.

"I'll bet you didn't get rid of it," Hawk said. "Dump some fourteen-year-old ghetto broad—who's going to notice? I'll bet you still got the piece."

Billy made an almost indiscernible gesture toward his right hip and caught himself. Hawk grinned.

"Bet you carrying it now," Hawk said.

Marcus finished chewing his croissant.

He said, "Cut the bullshit, Hawk. So Billy dusted the kid, so I told him, so the kid thinks he'll testify. So what? That's all bullshit. Even if he gets to talk, nobody is going to believe him, a gangbanger punk? I got twenty people will swear Billy and I were playing cards in Albany, Georgia, when it happened."

"Albany, Georgia?" I said.

"Wherever you like," Marcus said. "So cut the bullshit and tell me what you want."

Hawk grinned at him. Across the room, Quirk and Belson strolled in from the outer lobby and walked toward the table. Marcus didn't notice. There were a couple of other cops that I recognized, in plainclothes, lingering near the entryway. Hawk opened his teal jacket and there was a microphone pinned to the black silk T-shirt.

"Peekaboo," Hawk said.

Marcus stared at the microphone.

"A wire," he said. "You wore a fucking wire on me, you Tom motherfucker."

"Told you somebody had to roll over for those two girls," Hawk said.

Quirk and Belson arrived at the table.

"Say all the legal shit to them, Frank," Quirk said. "Billy—give me the piece you're carrying."

Belson began to recite the formalized litany of arrest like a kid reciting the alphabet. Billy looked at Marcus. Marcus wasn't looking at him. He was still staring at Hawk.

*"Now, Billy."* Quirk's voice had an edge to it.

Billy lunged past him. Quirk seemed to barely notice, as if he were thinking of something else. But he made some sort of efficient compact movement and Billy hit the floor like a foundered walrus. Quirk held

Billy's right arm at an awkward angle with his left hand and reached around and took the Browning off Billy's hip. It was stainless, with a walnut handle.

"Nice piece. Don't you have one like it?"

Without pausing in his recitation, Belson produced a clear plastic bag and held it open and Quirk dropped the gun into it.

"Mine's only got the black finish," I said, "and a black plastic handle. Got a nice white dot on the front sight, though."

Belson finished his recitation and they cuffed Tony Marcus and Billy and hauled them off. Marcus kept staring at Hawk until he was out of sight.

"I think he feels betrayed," I said.

Hawk nodded, looking around the room. Everyone there was staring at us or trying not to.

"You think that the red hair and tight dress will come back in here for lunch?" he said.

# Chapter 45

Susan and I were having supper on Rowe's Wharf, across from International Place in the dining room at the Boston Harbor Hotel. I had an Absolut martini on the rocks, with a twist. Susan had a glass of Riesling, which she probably wouldn't finish.

"Was it the gun?" Susan said.

"Yes," I said.

"Can they convict him with it?" Susan said.

"The gun, the tape, Major's testimony. Sure."

"I'm surprised that Major is willing to testify."

"Hawk says he will."

"Because Hawk told him to?" Susan said.

"Yeah, I imagine so. And, too, it's a chance to be important."

"Interesting, isn't it. He had to know that Hawk could beat him."

"Established the command structure," I said. "I guess any order is better than none."

Susan rested her chin on her upturned palm. The twilight glancing in off the harbor highlighted her huge dark eyes.

"I talked with Jackie," Susan said.

"Too much for her?" I said.

"Yes," Susan said. "She's—overwhelmed, I guess, is the best way to describe it."

"Not just the violence," I said.

"No," Susan said. "She saw Hawk, I suppose, for the first time."

"He saved her life," I said.

"She knows that," Susan said. "But there might have been another way. He shot right past her head to do it without a moment's hesitation."

"It was the best way," I said.

Susan nodded. "Yes, I'm sure it was. Maybe even Jackie is sure it was, but she can't . . . do you see? She can't be with a man who could do that."

"I see," I said. "Could you?"

"I am," Susan said.

I drank some of my martini. I checked the glass. There were at least two swallows left.

"You think we'll see her again?" I said.

With her chin still in her hand, Susan shook her head slowly. The waiter brought menus. We read them. The waiter came back. We ordered. The waiter left. The twilight softened into darkness outside the window, and the harbor water, wavering against the wharf, was very black.

"What do you think?" Susan said. "Is there a future for Major and those other kids?"

"I doubt it," I said.

The waiter returned with food. I mastered the desire for maybe thirteen more martinis, and when Susan and I finished supper and left, I was still sober. It made me proud. We drove back to Cambridge and I parked in the driveway of her place on Linnaean Street.

"You don't think any of them will make it?" Susan said.

"Kids in Double Deuce?" I said. "No, probably not."

"Hawk did," Susan said.

"Sort of," I said.

"That's an awfully grim view," she said.

I shrugged.

"Maybe I'm wrong," I said.

She leaned her head back against the seat cushion.

"Well, as you always say, 'It's never over till it's over.' "

"Yes," I said.

I could see insects little bigger than dust motes swarming in the street-light, an occasional moth among them.

"First night apart," she said.

"Yeah."

She put her hand out and I took it and we were quiet for a while. Then she spoke.

"I have to say something."

"Sure," I said.

"I'm looking forward to being alone."

"Me too," I said.

"God, what a relief."

"I know," I said.

"See you this weekend," she said.

"Yes," I said. "I'll pick Pearl up tomorrow night for a sleepover. Like before."

"Yes."

Susan leaned toward me in the dark and gave me a long, happy kiss.

"I love you," she said and got out of the car. I watched her until she was inside, then pulled out and drove back across the river to my place on Marlborough Street.

The apartment was stuffy and I walked through it opening windows so that the spring night could circulate. Then I went into the kitchen and took some vodka from the freezer and some vermouth from under the sink and made a large martini over ice with a twist. I put it on the bedside table to let the ice work while I showered and toweled off, and turned back the bed, and got in. I propped up the pillows and turned on the television with the remote. The Braves were still in first place, and they were playing the Giants on cable. Fifth inning, Ron Gant hitting. I sipped my martini and watched the ball game and listened to Skip Caray.

Alone.

I could feel myself smiling. Gant spiked a double into the left-field corner. I took another sip and spoke aloud in the dark room.

"Perfect," I said.

# Paper Doll

*For Joan:*
*Music all around me*

# Chapter 1

Loudon Tripp, wearing a seersucker suit and a Harvard tie, sat in my office on a very nice day in September and told me he'd looked into my background and might hire me.

"Oh boy," I said.

"You've had some college," Tripp said. He was maybe fifty, a tall angular man with a red face. He held a typewritten sheet of paper in his hand, reading it through half glasses.

"No harm to it," I said. "I thought I was going to do something else."

"I went to Harvard. You played football in college."

I nodded. He didn't care if I nodded or not. But I liked to.

"You were a prizefighter."

Nod.

"You fought in Korea. Were you an officer?"

"No."

"Too bad. After that you were a policeman."

Nod.

"This presents a small problem; you were dismissed. Could you comment, please, on that."

"I am trustworthy, loyal, and helpful. But I struggle with *obedient*."

Tripp smiled faintly. "I'm not looking for a Boy Scout," he said.

"Next best thing," I said.

"Well," Tripp said, "Lieutenant Quirk said you could be annoying, but you were not undependable."

"He's always admired me," I said.

"Obviously you are independent," Tripp said. "I understand that. I've had my moments. 'He who would be a man must be a nonconformist.'"

I nodded encouragingly.

"Do you know who said that?" Tripp asked.

I nodded again.

Tripp waited a moment.

Finally he said, "Well, who?"

"Emerson."

"Very good," Tripp said.

"Will this be on the final?" I said.

Tripp leaned his head toward me in a gesture of apology.

"Sorry, I guess that seemed pretentious. It's just that I am trying to get a sense of you."

I shrugged.

"They had no way of judging a man," I said, "except as he handled an axe."

Tripp frowned for a moment. And twitched his shoulders as if to get rid of a horsefly.

"So," he paused. "I guess you'll do."

I tried to look pleased.

He stared past me out the window for a moment, and took in a slow breath and let it out.

"Are you familiar," he said, "with Olivia Nelson?"

"The woman who was murdered a couple of months back," I said. "Right in Louisburg Square."

He nodded.

"She used her birth name," he said. "She was my wife."

"I'm sorry," I said.

"Yes."

We were quiet for a moment while we considered the sullen fact.

"The police have exhausted all of their options," Tripp said. "They have concluded it was probably an act of random violence, and the killer, having left no clues, will very likely not be caught until, or if, he strikes again."

"You disagree?" I said.

"I want him hunted down," Tripp said stiffly, "and punished."

"And you want me to do that?"

"Yes . . . Lieutenant Quirk suggested you, when I expressed concern about the official lack of progress."

"So you and I are clear," I said, "I will hunt him down for you. But punishment is not what I do."

"I believe in the system," Tripp said. "If you can find him, I am sure the courts will punish him."

I said, "Un huh."

"You are skeptical of the courts?" Tripp said.

"I'm skeptical of most things," I said. "Is there anyone assigned to the case, now?"

"Yes, a young detective."

"What's his name?"

"Farrell. Detective Farrell. I can't say I'm entirely happy with him."

"Why?"

"Well, he's young. I was hoping for a more senior man."

I nodded. There was more, I could tell.

"And there's something, a little, I don't know. He doesn't seem like a typical police detective."

I waited. Tripp didn't elaborate. Since I figured I'd meet Farrell anyway, I didn't press. I could decide for myself how typical he was.

"Do you have any theories on the murder?" I said.

"None. I can't imagine who would wish to kill Olivia. Perhaps it is a madman."

"Okay," I said. "I'll talk to the cops, first. So at least I'll know what they know."

"You'll take the case, then?"

"Sure," I said.

We talked a little about my fee, and the prospects of a retainer. He had no objections to a retainer. Me either.

"The only thing you need to understand," I said, "is that once I start I go where it takes me. Which may mean I ask you lots of questions. And your friends and relatives lots of questions. People sometimes get restive about me invading their privacy. You have to understand at the start that invading your privacy, and the privacy of people you know, is what you're hiring me to do."

"I understand," Tripp said. "If you go too far, I'll let you know."

"You can let me know," I said. "But it won't change anything. I do what I do. And I keep doing it until I'm finished."

"You will be working for me, Mr. Spenser."

"Yes, and you can pay me, and you can expect that I'll work on your problem and that I won't cheat you and that I won't lie to you. But you can't tell me what to do, and if you're not willing to accept that, we can't do business."

Tripp didn't like it. But he got out his checkbook and put it on the edge of my desk and dug a real fountain pen out of his inside coat pocket.

"When I need surgery," he said, "I don't, I guess, tell the surgeon how to operate."

"Nice analogy," I said.

He nodded, and wrote me out a check in a stately, flowing Palmer-method hand. It was a fine big check. A check you could deposit proudly, which, after Tripp left, I did.

# Chapter 2

"He hit her with a framing hammer," Quirk said. "The kind with the long wooden handle that gives you leverage so you can drive a sixteen-penny nail with two strokes. Hit her at least five times."

Quirk was wearing a gray silk tweed jacket with a faint lavender chalk line, a blue Oxford button-down shirt, and a lavender knit tie. There was a dark blue display handkerchief in his jacket pocket. As he talked, he straightened the stuff on his desk, making sure everything was square and properly spaced. There wasn't much: a phone, a legal-sized lined yellow pad, a translucent Bic pen with a black top, and a big plastic cube with pictures of his wife, his children, and a golden retriever. He was careful to have the cube exactly centered along the back rim of his desk. He wasn't thinking about what he was doing. It was what he did while he thought about something else.

"He left it at the crime scene."

"Or she," I said.

Quirk realigned his pictures an eighth of an inch. His hands were big and thick, the nails manicured. They looked like the hands of a tough surgeon.

"Ah, yes," Quirk said. "Liberation. It could have been a woman. But if it was, it was a strong one. He, or she, must have held the hammer down at the end and taken a full swing, like you would drive a nail. Most of the bones in her head were broken."

"Only the head?"

"Yeah," Quirk said. "That bothered me too. If some fruitcake runs amok with a framing hammer and assaults a random victim, why was his aim so good? Head only. Except where he seems to have missed once and badly bruised her left shoulder."

"Seems more like premeditation," I said. "If you're going to murder somebody with a hammer, you don't waste time hitting them in the body."

"I know," Quirk said. His hands were perfectly still now, one resting on top of the other. "It bothered us too. But things always do in a homicide. You know that. There's always stuff you can't account for, stuff that doesn't fit exactly. Homicide cases aren't neat, even the neat ones."

"You think this is a neat one?"

"In one sense," Quirk said. He looked at the pictures on the plastic cube while he talked. He was not so much weary as calm. He'd seen too much, and it had left him with that cop calm that some of them get—not without feeling, really, but without excitement.

"We have an explanation for it that works. It's not laying around loose—except that we don't have the perpetrator."

"Perpetrator," I said admiringly.

"I been watching a lot of those reality cop shows," Quirk said.

"Her husband wants the guy caught," I said.

"Sure he does," Quirk said. "Me too."

"You can't find a motive," I said.

Quirk shook his head.

"This broad is Mary Poppins, for crissake. Mother of the year, wife of the decade, loyal friend, good citizen, great human being, dedicated teacher, accomplished cook, and probably great in the sack."

"Never is heard a discouraging word," I said.

"None," Quirk said. "Nobody had a reason to kill her."

"Almost nobody," I said.

"The crazed-killer thing still works," Quirk said. "It happens."

"Husband checks out?"

Quirk looked at me as if I'd asked him his sign.

"How long you think I been doing this? Who do we think of first when a wife is killed?"

"Cherchez la hubby," I said.

"Thank you," Quirk said.

"No problems between them?"

"None that he'd mention."

"He doesn't have a girlfriend?"

"Says he doesn't."

"She doesn't have a boyfriend?"

"Says she didn't."

"You able to confirm that, as they say in the papers, independently?"

"Cops aren't independent," Quirk said. "Hot dogs like yourself are independent."

"But you looked into it."

"Far as we could."

"How far is that?"

Quirk shrugged.

"These are powerful people," Quirk said. "They have powerful friends. Everybody I ask says she was a candidate for sainthood. And he is a candidate for sainthood, and the kids are a couple of saintlettes. You push people like this only so far."

"Before what?"

"Before the commissioner calls you."

"And tells you to desist?"

"And tells me that unless I have hard evidence, I should not assume these people are lying."

"And you don't have hard evidence."

"No."

"You think there's something there?"

Quirk shrugged.

"That's why you sent Tripp to me," I said.

"This wasn't a Jamaican whore got smoked in some vacant lot, twenty miles from the Harvard Club," Quirk said. "This is an upper-crust WASP broad got bludgeoned to death at one corner of Louisburg fucking Square for crissake. We got a U.S. Senator calling to follow up on our progress. I got a call from the Boston Archdiocese. Everybody says solve it, or leave it alone."

"Which isn't the way to solve it," I said.

Again Quirk was silent.

"The way to solve it is to muddle around in it and disrupt everybody's lives and doubt everything everybody says and make a general pain in the ass of yourself."

Quirk nodded.

"You can see why I thought of you," he said.

"So if Tripp doesn't want this solved, why did he hire me?"

"I think he wants it solved, but with his assumptions and on his terms," Quirk said. "He thinks he can control you."

"Somebody ought to," I said. "Any money to inherit?"

"A small life insurance policy, probably covered the funeral."

"No mental illness?"

"No."

"Kids?"

"Son, Loudon, Junior, twenty-two, senior at Williams College. Daughter, Meredith, eighteen, freshman at Williams."

"They seem clean?"

"American dream," Quirk said. "Dean's list for both of them. Son's on the wrestling team, and the debating team. Daughter's president of the drama club and a member of the student council, or whatever the fuck they call it at Williams."

"Any history on the kids that doesn't jibe?"

"Son had a few routine teenage scrapes. Nothing that matters. I'll give you the file," Quirk said.

"You still got a guy on it?" I said.

"Yeah, Lee Farrell," Quirk said.

"He's new," I said.

"Yeah, and he's gay."

"Young and gay," I said.

"I got no problem with it, long as he doesn't kiss me. But command staff don't like it much."

"So he gets the low-maintenance stuff."

"Yeah."

"He any good?"

Quirk leaned back in his swivel chair and clasped his hands behind his back. The muscles in his upper arm swelled against the fabric of his jacket.

"He might be," Quirk said. "Hasn't had a hell of a chance to prove it."

"Doesn't get the choice assignments?"

Quirk smiled without meaning anything by it.

"They had to hire him, and they had to promote him. But they don't have to use him."

"I'll want to talk with Farrell."

"Sure," Quirk said. "You and he will hit it right off."

# Chapter 3

Lee Farrell stopped into my office in the late afternoon while I was opening mail, and throwing it away.

"Lieutenant said you would be freelancing the Olivia Nelson case," he said.

He was a medium-sized young guy, with a moustache, a nice tan, and the tight build of a gymnast. He was nearly bald. What hair he had was close-cropped and the moustache was neatly trimmed. He was wearing white Reeboks, and chinos, and a blue chambray shirt under a tan corduroy jacket. As he turned to sit down, the butt of his gun made an angular snag in his jacket. He shrugged his shoulders automatically to get rid of it.

"Yes," I said.

"Lieutenant said I should cooperate."

"How do you feel about that?" I said.

"Figured I could probably get by without you," Farrell said.

"It's alarming how many people think that," I said.

"No good for business," he said.

"I've read the file," I said.

"Lieutenant doesn't usually hand those out," Farrell said.

"Good to know," I said. "You got anything not in the file?"

"If I had it, it would be in there," Farrell said.

"It wouldn't have to be," I said. "It could be unsubstantiated opinion, guesswork, intuition, stuff like that."

"I deal with facts," Farrell said.

It made me smile.

"You think that's funny?" he said.

"Yeah, kind of. Are you familiar with *Dragnet*?"

"No. I don't like people laughing at me."

"Nobody does," I said. "Think of it as a warm smile of appreciation."

"Hey, asshole," Farrell said. "You think you can fuck with me?"

He stood up, his hands loosely in front of him, one above the other. He probably had some color belt, in some kind of Asian hand-fighting.

"Does this mean you're not feeling cooperative?" I said.

"It means I don't take smart shit from anybody. You think maybe I'm not tough enough? You can step up now and try me."

"Good plan," I said. "We beat the hell out of each other, and when the murderer dashes in to break it up, we collar him."

"Aw, hell," Farrell said. He stood for another moment, shifting a little on his feet, then he shrugged and sat down.

"I don't like being stuck on a no-brainer," he said. "They think it's a dead-file case, but they can't ignore it, so they put the junior man on it."

I nodded.

"The case stinks," he said.

I nodded again. Penetratingly.

"Everything's too perfect. No one had a bad word. Everyone liked her. No one could think of a single reason to kill her. No enemies. No lovers. Nothing. We talked with everybody in the family. Everybody at work. Everybody in her address book. Every return address on her mail. We made a list of every person we'd talked with and asked her husband and children if there was anyone they could think of not on it. We did the same at work. We got a few more names and talked with them. We do not have a single suspect out of any of them. We talked with her gyno, her physical trainer . . ." He spread his hands.

"Do you think there's something wrong," I said, "because you're stuck on a no-brainer and don't want to accept it, or is there something wrong?"

"I'm stuck on five no-brainers," Farrell said. "I've got a full caseload of cases that go nowhere."

"My question stands," I said.

Farrell rubbed his hands slowly together, and opened them and studied the palms for a moment.

"I don't know," he said. "I've thought of that too and I don't know."

# Chapter 4

Louisburg Square is in the heart of Beacon Hill, connecting Mt. Vernon and Pinckney Streets. In the center of the square is a little plot of grass with a black iron fence around it and a statue of Christopher Columbus. Around the square and facing it were a series of three-story, brick-front town houses.

The Tripp-Nelson home was one of them. It had a wide raised panel door, which was painted royal blue. In the middle of the door was a big polished brass knocker in the form of a lion holding a big polished brass ring in his mouth.

I had walked up the hill from Charles Street, the way Olivia Nelson had on the night she was killed. I stopped at the lower corner of the square where it connected to Mt. Vernon. There was nothing remarkable about it. There were no bloodstains, now. The police chalkings and the yellow crime-scene tape were gone. Nobody even came and stood and had their picture taken on the spot where the sixteen-ounce framing hammer had exploded against the back of Olivia Nelson's skull. According to the coroner's report she probably never knew it. She probably felt that one explosion—and the rest was silence.

I had her case file with me. There wasn't anywhere to start on this thing, so I thought it might help to be in her house when I read the file of her murder investigation. It wasn't much of an idea, but it was the only one I had. Tripp knew I was coming. I had told him I needed to look around the house. A round-faced brunette maid with pouty lips and a British accent answered my ring. She had on an actual maid suit, black dress, little white apron, little white cap. You don't see many of those anymore.

"My name's Spenser," I said. "Mr. Tripp said you'd be expecting me."

She looked at me blankly, as if I were an inoffensive but unfamiliar insect that had settled on her salad.

"Yes, sir," she said. "You're to have the freedom of the house, sir. May I take your hat, sir?"

I was wearing a replica Brooklyn Dodgers baseball cap, royal blue with a white B and a white button on top. Susan had ordered it for me at the same time she'd gotten me the replica Braves hat, which I wore with my other outfit.

"I'll keep it," I said. "Makes me look like Gene Hermanski."

"Certainly, sir. If you need me you should ring one of these bells."

She showed me a small brass bell with a rosewood handle sitting on the front hall table.

"How charming," I said.

"Yes, sir."

She backed gracefully away from me and turned and disappeared under the staircase, presumably to the servants' area below stairs. She had pretty good legs. Although in Louisburg Square it was probably incorrect to look at the maid's legs at all.

There was a central stairway in the front hall, with mahogany railing curving down to an ornate newel post, white risers, oak treads. To the right was the living room, to the left a study, straight down the hall was a dining room. The kitchen was past the stairs, to the right of the dining room. With the file under my arm, I walked slowly through the house. The living room was in something a shade darker than ivory, with pastel peach drapes spilling onto the floor. The furniture was white satin, with a low coffee table in the same shade of marble. There were rather formal-looking photographs of Tripp, a woman whom I assumed to be his late wife, and two young people who were doubtless their children. There was a fine painting of an English setter on the wall over a beige marble fireplace, and, over the sofa, on the longest wall, a large painting of a dapple gray horse that looked like it might have been done by George Stubbs and selected because the tones worked with the decor.

The house was very silent, and thickly carpeted. The only noise was the gentle rush of the central air-conditioning. I had on the usual open shirt, jeans and sneakers, plus a navy blue windbreaker. It was too warm for the windbreaker, but I needed something to hide my gun; and the Dodger cap didn't go with any of my sport coats.

The study was forest green with books and dark furniture and a green leather couch and chairs. There was a big desk with an Apple word processor on one corner. It was more out of place than I was. It looked sort of unseemly there. No one had thought of a way to disguise it as a Victorian artifact.

The books were impersonal. Mostly college texts, from thirty years ago, a picture book about Frederic Remington, an American Heritage Dictionary, a World Atlas, Ayn Rand, James Michener, Tom Clancy, Barbara Taylor Bradford, Louis L'Amour, Jean Auel, Rod McKuen, three books on how to be your own shrink, and *A History of the Tripps of New England* in leather, with gilt lettering on the spine. I put my murder file on the desk and took the book down and sat on the green leather couch and thumbed through it. It was obviously a commissioned work, privately printed. The Tripps had arrived in the new world in 1703 in the person of Carroll S. Tripp, a ship's carpenter from Surrey, who settled in what later became Belfast, Maine. His grandson moved to Boston and founded the Tripp Mercantile Company in 1758, and they had remained here since. The organizing principle of the book appeared to be that all the Tripps were nicer than Little Bo Peep, including those from the eighteenth century who had founded the family fortune by making a bundle in the rum, molasses, and slave trade business. It told me nothing about the murder of Olivia Nelson, who had kept her birth name.

# Chapter 5

The house was very still. The soft sound of the air conditioner made it seem stiller, and only the sound of a clock ticking somewhere in another room broke the hush.

I put the family history away and opened the case file Quirk had given me. Sitting on the green leather couch in the silent room of her nearly empty home, I read the coroner's description of Olivia Nelson's death. I read the crime-scene report, the pages of interview summaries, the document checks, I plowed through all of it. I learned nothing useful. I didn't expect to. I was simply being methodical, because I didn't know what else to be. Quirk had turned everything he had loose on this one and come up with nothing.

I put the file down and got up and walked through her house. It was richly decorated in appropriate period. Nothing didn't match. At the top of the stairs I turned right toward the master suite. The cops had already noted that the Tripps had separate bedrooms and baths. The bedrooms were connected by a common sitting room. It had a red-striped Victorian fainting couch, and two straight chairs and a leather-topped table with fat legs in front of the window. There was a copy of *Pride and Prejudice*, by Jane Austen, on the table. It seemed brand-new. It was bound in red leather and matched the tabletop. Against the wall opposite the window was a big mahogany armoire with ornate brass hinges. I opened it. It was empty. The room was as cozy as a dental lab. I went through the sitting room to her room. It was clearly hers: canopied queen-size four-poster, antique lace bedspread, heavy gathered drapes with a gold tone, thick ivory rug, on the wall at the foot of the bed a big nineteenth-century still life of some green pears in a blue and white bowl. Her bureau drawers were full of sweaters and blouses and more exotic lingerie than I'd have expected. There was a walk-in closet full of clothes appropriate to an affluent Beacon Hill pillar of the community. She had maybe thirty pairs of shoes. Her jewelry box was full. She had a lot of makeup.

I sat on her bed. It had about seven pillows on it, carefully arranged as she had left them the last time she was here, or maybe the maid had arranged them this morning. I listened to the quiet. It was a cool day outside, in the low seventies, and the air conditioner had cycled off. I was out of earshot of the clock. I heard only the quiet, and the more I listened the more I heard it. Nothing moved. No one whispered the butler did it.

I stood up and walked across the room and through the sitting room and into Loudon Tripp's bedroom. It had been created by the same sensibility as the rest of the house. Hers, I assumed, or her decorator's. Except that it had no canopy, the big four-poster bed was identical to hers, the fluted mahogany bedposts shaped like tall Indian clubs. On the bedside table was a thick paperback copy of Scott Turow's new novel. A television remote lay next to it. There was a still life on the wall, and an identical armoire stood in the same position that it stood in Olivia's room. I opened it. There was a big-screen television set on an upper shelf, connected through a hole in the back to electrical and cable outlets behind the piece. On the lower shelves were magazines: *Sports Illustrated, Forbes, Time,* two back copies of the *New York Times Magazine,* and a current *TV Guide.* The rest of the rooms were unrevealing. The children's rooms were gender appropriate, impersonal, and perfectly coordinated. There were guest rooms on the third floor.

I went back down to the living room and picked up the picture of Olivia Tripp and sat on the satin-covered couch and looked at it. She was blonde and wore her short hair in the sort of loose blonde way that wealthy WASP women affect. Her skin looked healthy, as if she exercised out-of-doors. Her eyes were wide apart. Her nose was straight, and quite narrow with nostrils that flared sort of dramatically. Her mouth was a little thin, though she'd made it look more generous than it was with the judicious use of lip pencil. There was a strand of pearls just above the point where her neck disappeared into airbrushed gossamer. She looked to be in her early forties.

She was forty-three when she died. Not planning to, no time to get ready for it, walking along in her good clothes, maybe a small aftertaste of Oreo cookie in her mouth, maybe thinking about her children, or her husband, or sex, or sleep, or good works, maybe trying to remember the lyrics to a song by Harry Belafonte. And somebody appearing in the shadows, faceless and silent in the quiet summer night, with a long-handled hammer. Like an old stone-age savage, armed.

But that was to come. The face in the expensive portrait showed no hint of that. It looked out at me tranquil and personless, and devoid of meaning.

"What the hell are you looking at?" a voice said, and I looked up, and there were the children.

# Chapter 6

She was cute. Short, trim body, blonde ponytail, big violet eyes, lips that looked slightly swollen. She wore too much makeup, and there was something about her bearing that murmured *don't look at me,* at the same time that the makeup and the clothes were shouting *see me!* She stood slightly behind her brother, her eyes fixed on the coffee table to the right of me.

"My name's Spenser," I said. "I'm a detective."

She was wearing a white tank top and pink short-shorts and thick white socks and white training shoes with pink laces. She had an immaculate tan.

Her brother looked just like her, except he wasn't cute. And he wasn't self-effacing. He wasn't short either, probably 5'11", but he had the thick wrestler's neck and upper body, and it made him look shorter than he was. He had the pouty lips too. His nose was too small for his face. His eyes were set in deep sockets. His blond hair was cut short, except in front where it was longish and combed back. He looked petulant and angry. It might have been me, but I suspected that it was his permanent expression. He wore a rust tank top and white shorts and gray socks and white high-cut basketball shoes. Rust-rimmed sunglasses with dark green lenses hung on a rust-and-white braided cord from around his neck. His tan was immaculate too.

The two of them stood very close together as they looked at me. Ken and Barbie. Except Barbie wouldn't look at me.

"Put the picture down," he said. "Who the hell let you in here?"

"Your father," I said. "He hired me to find who killed your mother."

"Swell," the brother said, "we don't have enough half-arsed cretin cops slopping around. Dad has to hire an extra one."

"You're Meredith," I said to the sister.

She nodded.

"And you're Loudon, Junior," I said.

He didn't say anything.

"Sorry about your mother," I said.

"Great," he said. "Now why don't you just get lost?"

"Why so hostile?" I said.

"Hostile? Me? If I get hostile, brother, you'll goddamn well know about it."

"Chi-ip," Meredith said. Her voice was very soft.

"Your father probably needs to do this," I said.

"Yeah," Chip said. "Well, I don't like you looking at my mother's picture."

His stare was full of arrogance. It came with wealth and position. And it came with being a wrestler. He thought he could toss me on my kiester.

If I kept talking to them he was going to try it, and find he had misjudged. It would probably be a good thing for him to learn. But now was probably not the best time for him to learn it.

I put the picture down carefully on the table and stood.

"I'm afraid I'll have to keep looking into this. I'll try not to be more annoying than I have to be."

Meredith said, in a voice I could barely hear, "You might make everything worse."

"You better keep your hands off my mom's stuff," Chip said.

I smiled graciously, and went past them and out the front door. It wasn't much of a move, but it was better than wrestling with Chip.

# Chapter 7

I met Lee Farrell in a place called Packie's in the South End. He was alone at the bar when I came in. He had a half-drunk draft beer in front of him and an empty shot glass.

I slid onto the bar stool and looked at the shot glass.

"Old Thompson?" I said.

"Four Roses," he said. "You got a problem with that?"

"Nostalgia," I said. "When I was a kid it was a Croft Ale and a shot of Old Thompson."

"Well, now it's not," Farrell said.

"Jesus," I said, "how old were you when you dropped out of charm school?"

The bartender came down and poured another shot into Farrell's glass. He looked at me.

"Draft," I said. He drew one and put it on a napkin in front of me.

Farrell took in about half his whiskey, washed it down with some draft beer. Then he shifted on the bar stool and leaned back a little and stared at me.

"You got a reputation," he said. "Tough guy."

"Richly deserved," I said.

"Smart too," Farrell said.

"But modest," I said.

It was a little past five-thirty in the evening and the bar was lined with people. Made you wonder about the work people did if they had to get drunk when they finished.

"Quirk says you get full cooperation," Farrell said. His speech wasn't slurred, but there was a thickness to his voice. "Says you're pretty good, says you might come up with something, if there's anything to come up with."

I nodded and sipped a little beer.

"Sort of implies that I won't," Farrell said. "Doesn't it? Sort of implies that maybe I'm not so good."

"You got other things to do. I don't."

Farrell emptied his shot glass, and drank the remainder of his beer. He nodded toward the bartender, who refilled him. There was a flush on Farrell's cheeks, and his eyes seemed bright.

"How many people in this room you figure are gay?" he said.

I glanced around the room. It was full of men. I swallowed a little more beer. I looked at Farrell and shrugged.

"Everybody but me," I said.

"Pretty sure you can tell by just looking?"

"It's a gay bar," I said. "I know you're gay. Quirk told me."

"I'm not so sure I like that," Farrell said.

"Why, is it a secret?"

"No, but why is he talking about it?"

"As an explanation of why you might be stuck on a dead-end case."

"I never thought Quirk cared."

"I don't think he does."

"Lotta people do," Farrell said.

"True," I said.

We sat for a while.

"You figure fags got no iron?" Farrell said.

"I assume some do and some don't," I said. "I don't know enough about it to be sure."

We sat some more.

"I'm as good as any cop," Farrell said.

I nodded encouragingly.

"Good as you too," Farrell said.

"Sure," I said.

Farrell drank more whiskey. His speech was still fully formed, but his voice was very thick.

"You believe that?" he said.

"I don't care," I said. "I don't care if you are as good as I am or not. I don't care if you're tough or not, or smart or not. I don't care if you are gay or straight or both or neither. I care about finding out who killed that broad with a framing hammer, and so far you're not helping me worth shit."

Farrell sat for a while staring at me, with the dead-eyed cop that all of them perfect, then he nodded as if to himself. He picked up the whiskey and sipped a little and put the glass down.

"You know," he said, "sometimes if I'm alone, and there's no one around . . ."

He glanced up and down the bar and lowered his voice.

". . . I order a sloe gin fizz," he said.

"A dead giveaway," I said. "Now that we've established that you're queer and you're here, can we talk about the Nelson case?" I said.

"You got the case file," Farrell said.

"Yeah, and I've seen the house, and I've talked to the children."

"Always a good time," Farrell said. The bartender came down and looked at Farrell's drink. Farrell shook his head.

"They're under stress," I said.

"Sure," Farrell said.

"Tripp and his wife had separate rooms," I said.

"Yeah."

"Which doesn't mean they didn't get along," I said.

"True."

"Un huh. What do you think?"

"Hers doesn't look like she spent much time there," Farrell said.

"What's he do?" I said.

"For work?"

"Yeah."

Farrell shrugged. "Runs the family money, I guess. Got an office and a secretary in the DePaul Building downtown. Goes there every day. Reads the paper, makes some calls, goes over to Locke's for lunch."

"Nice orderly life," I said.

"Maybe it was just a random crazy," Farrell said.

"Maybe. But if we assume that, we got no place to go," I said.

"So you assume it's not random. Where does that leave you?"

"Looking for a motive," I said.

"We been over that," Farrell said. "Me, Belson, Quirk, everybody. You going to go over it again?"

"Probably," I said. "And then, probably, I'll try it from the other end."

"Her past?"

"If it's not a random killing, there's something in her life that caused it. You people have been all over the recent events. I'll go over them again because I'm a methodical guy. But I don't expect to find something you missed. On the other hand, you haven't turned out all the pockets of her history. You don't have the budget."

"But you do?"

"Tripp does," I said.

"Until he decides you're just churning his account," Farrell said.

"Until then," I said.

We sat for a while in the crowded bar. It was full of men. Most of them were in suits and ties. Some were holding hands. A tallish guy with a thin face had his arm around a gray-haired man in a blue blazer. No one paid me any mind.

"You married?" Farrell said.

"Not quite," I said.

Farrell looked past me at the bar scene.

"How about you?" I said.

"I'm with somebody," Farrell said.

We were quiet again. People circulated among the tables. I watched them, and nursed my beer.

"You notice nobody comes over," Farrell said.

"They know you're a cop," I said. "They figure I'm from the outside. They don't want to out you in case you're *en closet*."

"On the money," Farrell said.

I waited. Farrell stared at the crowd.

"I come on too strong about things," Farrell said.

"True," I said.

"You understand why."

"Yeah."

Farrell shifted his eyes toward me and nodded several times.

"I'm sorry," he said finally.

"Okay," I said. "But I don't think I want to go steady."

# Chapter 8

Tripp's secretary was named Ann Summers. It said so on a nice brass plate on her nice dark walnut desk. She was probably forty-five, and elegant, with dark auburn hair worn short. Her large round eyes were hazel. And her big round glasses magnified the eyes very effectively. The glasses had green rims. She wore a short gray skirt and a long gray jacket. She was sitting, with her legs crossed, tilted back in a swivel chair, turned toward the door. Her legs were very good.

On her desk was an in-basket, empty, and an out-basket with a letter in it. There was also a phone, a lamp with a green glass shade, two manila file folders, and to one side a hardback copy of a novel by P. D. James.

"Good morning," she said. Her voice was full of polished overtones. She sounded like she really thought it was a good morning, and hoped that I did too.

I told her who I was. She seemed thrilled to meet me.

"Mr. Tripp is at his club," she said. "I'm sure he didn't realize you were coming."

She was wearing taupe hose that fitted her legs perfectly.

"Actually I'd just as soon talk with you," I said.

She lowered her eyes for a moment, and smiled.

"Really?" she said.

I was probably not the first guy to say that to her, nor, in fact, the first guy to mean it. I hooked a red leather side chair over to her desk and sat down. She smiled again. Ready to help.

"You know I'm looking into Mrs. Tripp's murder?"

"Yes," she said. "How terrible for them all."

"Yes," I said. "How's business?"

She shifted slightly in her chair.

"I beg your pardon?" she said.

"How's business here?" I said.

"I . . . I don't see why you ask."

"Don't know what else to ask," I said.

"I've talked with the police," she said. Her big eyes looked puzzled but hopeful. She'd like to help, but how?

"I know," I said. "No point in saying all that again. So we'll talk about other stuff. Like business. How is it, are you busy?"

She frowned. Conflicting emotional states were a breeze for her. A pretty frown, an understated hip wiggle, a slight shift in her eyes. It was beautiful to see.

"It . . . it's not that kind of business."

"What kind?"

"The kind where you can say *how's business?*" she said and smiled so warmly that I almost asked her to dance.

"Are you busy?" I said.

"Well, no, not in a regular business sense."

"What are your hours?"

"Nine to four," she said.

"And Mr. Tripp?"

"Oh, he's usually here when I arrive, and he frequently leaves after I do. I've offered to come earlier and stay longer, but Mr. Tripp says that is not necessary."

"Is he busier than you are?"

"I . . . well, frankly, I don't see why he would be."

"And how busy are you?"

She shrugged and spread her hands. Her nails were beautifully manicured and painted a pale pink.

"There are some phone calls, there are some letters. Sometimes I make
restaurant reservations, sometimes travel arrangements . . ." She paused.
"I read a great deal."

"Good for the mind," I said. "They eat out a lot?"

"Mr. Tripp has lunch with people nearly every day."

"Dinner?"

"I rarely make dinner reservations," she said.

"They travel much?"

She uncrossed her legs, and crossed them the other way. When she had
them recrossed, she smoothed her skirt along the tops of her thighs.

"Mostly I make arrangements for the children, during school vacations."

"They do a lot of that?"

"Oh, yes, they're very well traveled. Vail or Aspen usually, in the winter. Europe sometimes, during summer vacations. And they were always
flying off to visit friends from college."

"Family travel much together?" I said.

"Mr. Tripp and the children would sometimes go places, especially
when the children were small."

"Ms. Nelson?" I said.

"I don't think Ms. Nelson liked to travel," she said.

I sat for a while and chewed on that. Ann Summers sat quietly, pointing her stunning knees at me: alert, compliant, calm, and stunning.

"And Mr. Tripp comes here early, and leaves late, even though there's
not much work to do?"

She nodded.

"What do you think of that?" I said.

She paused for a moment, and bit her lower lip very gently, for a moment. Then she shook her head.

"I am Mr. Tripp's employee. I like to think also that I am his friend. In
either capacity I am entirely loyal to him," she said. "I would not speculate
about his personal life."

"Not even to me," I said, "after what we've meant to each other?"

Ann Summers shook her head slowly.

Her smile was warm. Her teeth were very white and even. Her eyes
were lively, maybe even inviting. There was something about her that whis-

pered inaudibly of silk sheets and lace negligees, some unarticulated hint of passion, motionless beneath the flawless tranquility of her appearance. I sat for a moment and inhaled it, admired it, contemplated the clear, unexpressed certainty that exotic carnal excess was mine for the asking.

We both knew the moment and understood it.

"Monogamy is not an unmixed blessing," I said.

She nodded slightly, and smiled serenely.

"Please feel free," she said, "if you need anything else . . ." She made a little flutter with her hands.

I stood.

"Sure," I said. "Thanks for your help."

I was pleased that my voice didn't rasp.

At the door I looked back at her, still motionless, legs crossed, smiling. The sunlight from the east window behind her caught the red highlights in her hair. Her hands rested motionless on her thighs. The promise of possibility shimmered in the room between us for another long moment. Then I took in a big breath of air and went out and closed the door.

# Chapter 9

I had lunch with Loudon Tripp at the Harvard Club. In Boston there are two, one downtown in a tall building on Federal Street, and the other, more traditional one in the Back Bay on Commonwealth Ave. Despite the fact that Tripp's office was downtown about a block from the Federal Street site, he chose tradition. So did I. Instead of my World Gym tank top, I wore a brown Harris tweed jacket with a faint maroon line in the weave, a blue Oxford button-down, a maroon knit tie, charcoal slacks, and chocolate suede loafers with charcoal trim. There was a herringbone pattern in my dark gray socks. I had a maroon silk handkerchief in my breast pocket, a fresh haircut, and a clean shave. Except maybe that my nose had been broken about six times, you couldn't tell I wasn't wealthy.

Tripp was wearing a banker's gray Brooks Brothers suit with narrow lapels, and three buttons, and trousers ending at least two inches short of his feet. He had on a narrow tie with black and silver stripes, and scuffed brown shoes with wing tips. You knew he was wealthy.

Tripp shook hands democratically.

"Good of you to come," he said, although I had requested the lunch.

The Harvard Club looked the way it was supposed to. High ceilings and carpeted floors and on the walls pictures of gray-haired WASPs in dark suits. We went to the dining room and sat. Tripp ordered a Manhattan. I had a club soda.

"Don't you drink?" Tripp said. He sounded a little suspicious.

"I'm experimenting," I said, "with intake modification."

"Ah," he said.

We looked at menus. The cuisine ran to baked scrod and minute steak. The waiter brought our drinks. Tripp drank half his Manhattan. I savored a sip of club soda. We ordered.

"Now," Tripp said, "how can I help you?"

"If it is not too painful," I said, "tell me about your family."

"It is not too painful," Tripp said. "What do you wish to know?"

"Whatever you wish to tell me. Talk about them a little, your wife, your kids, what they liked to do, how they got along, anything interesting about them. I'm just looking for a place to start."

Tripp smiled courteously.

"Of course," he said.

He gestured at the waiter to bring him a second Manhattan. I declined a second club soda. I still had plenty left of the first one. Club sodas seemed to last longer than vodka martinis on the rocks with a twist.

"We were," Tripp said, "just about an ideal family. We were committed to one another, loved one another, cared about one another completely."

I nodded. The waiter brought the second Manhattan. Tripp drained the remainder of the first one and handed the glass to the waiter. The waiter completed the exchange and moved away. Tripp stared at the new Manhattan without drinking any.

"The thing was," he said, "not only were Olivia and I husband and wife, we were pals. We enjoyed each other. We enjoyed our children."

He paused, still staring at the untouched drink in front of him. He shuddered briefly. "To have so good a thing shattered so terribly . . ."

I waited. He picked up the Manhattan and took a small sip and re-placed it. I ignored my club soda.

"I know it sounds, probably, too good to be true, nostalgia or something, but, by golly, it was good. There'll never be anyone like her."

He broke off and we sat quietly. In the silence the waiter brought our lunch. I had opted for a chicken sandwich. Tripp had scrod. The food was every bit as good as it was at the Harvard Faculty Club where I had eaten a couple of years ago.

There weren't many women in the dining room. At a table next to the wall two men in suits were ordering more drinks. One of them was a U.S. Senator, still pink from the steam room, whose drink, when it arrived, appeared to be a tall dark scotch and soda. At the table next to me were three guys dressed by the same costumer. All wore dark blue suits with a thin chalk stripe, white shirts with discreetly rolled button-down collars, red ties. The ties varied—one red with tiny white dots, one a darker red with blue stripes, one blue paisley on a red background. He who would be a man must be a nonconformist. One of them was holding forth. He was large without being muscular, and his neck spilled out a little over his collar.

"So there's Buffy," he was saying, "bare ass in the middle of the fucking tennis court, and . . ."

"I suppose it seems idealized to you," Tripp said. "I imagine people tend to talk that way after a great loss."

"I just listen," I said.

"And make no judgments?"

"Open-shuttered and passive," I said. "Not thinking, merely recording."

"Always?"

"At least until all the precincts are heard from," I said.

"I would find that difficult, I guess," Tripp said.

I chewed on my chicken sandwich. The chicken had traveled some distance from the coop. The slices in my sandwich were perfectly round and wafer thin. But the bread was white, and the pale lettuce was limp.

I finished chewing and said, "What I do requires a certain amount of distance, sort of a willful suspension, I suppose."

"A what?"

I shook my head. "Literary allusion," I said. "I was just showing off."

"Olivia was a great one for that. She was always quoting somebody."

"She taught literature, did she not?"

"Yes, and theater, at Shawmut College. Her students loved her."

302     ROBERT B. PARKER

I nodded. I was trying to pick up the conversation at the next table. They were discussing what Buffy had tattooed on her buttocks.

"She was a marvelous teacher," Tripp said. He was eating his scrod at a pace that would take us into the dinner hour. If he and Susan had an eating race you couldn't get a winner.

The Senator had finished one dark scotch and soda, and had another, partly drunk, in his left hand. He was table-hopping. At the table next to us he paused long enough to hear the end of Buffy's adventure, and laughed and said something in an undertone to the storyteller. The whole table laughed excessively. It was clannish laughter, the laughter of insiders, us-boys. It was almost certainly laughter about the aptly named Buffy. Men never laughed quite that way about anything but women in a sexual context. And it was sycophantic laughter, tinged with gratitude that a man of the Senator's prominence had shared with them not only a salacious remark but a salacious view of life.

"Old enough to bleed," the Senator said, "old enough to butcher."

The table was again frantic with grateful hilarity as the Senator turned toward us. The pinkness in his face had given way to a darker red. A tribute perhaps to the dark scotch and soda. He was nearly bald but had combined his hair in the bald man's swoop up from behind one ear, arranged over the baldness, and lacquered in place with hair spray. A smallish man, he looked in good shape. His three-piece blue suit fit him well, and his vest didn't gap—no mean achievement in a politician. When he turned toward us, his expression was grave. He put a hand on Tripp's shoulder.

"Loudon," he said. "How you holding up?"

Tripp looked up at the Senator and nodded.

"As well as one could expect, Senator, thanks."

The Senator looked at me, but Tripp didn't introduce us.

"I'm Bob Stratton," the Senator said, and put out his hand. I said my name and returned his handshake. If he really saw me at all, it was peripherally. In his public self he probably saw everything peripherally. His focus was him.

"Any progress yet in finding the son of a bitch?"

Tripp shook his head.

"Not really," he said. "Spenser here is working on it for me."

"You're a police officer?" the Senator said.

"Private," I said.

"Really?" he said. "Well, you need any doors open, you call my office."

"Sure," I said.

"You have a card?" the Senator said. "I want to alert my people in case you need help."

I gave him a card. He looked at it for a moment, and nodded to himself, and put the card in his shirt pocket. And put his hand back on Tripp's shoulder.

"You hang tough, Loudon. Call me anytime."

Tripp smiled wanly.

"Thanks, Senator."

The Senator squeezed Tripp's shoulder and moved off toward another table, slurping a drink of dark scotch and soda as he went.

"Fine man," Tripp said. "Fine Senator, fine man."

"*E pluribus unum,*" I said.

# Chapter 10

I never saw Susan without feeling a small but discernible thrill. The thrill was mixed with a feeling of gratitude that she was with me, and a feeling of pride that she was with me, and a feeling of arrogance that she was fortunate to be with me. But mostly it was just a quick pulse along the ganglia which, if it were audible, would sound a little like *woof.*

She was as simply dressed tonight as she ever got. Form-fitting jeans, low black boots with silver trim, a lavender silk blouse partly buttoned over some sort of tight black undershirt. She had on jade earrings nowhere near as big as duck pins, and her thick black hair was short and impeccably in place.

"You look like the cat's ass tonight," I said.

"Everything you say is so lyrical," Susan said. She had a glass of Iron Horse champagne, and had already drunk nearly a quarter of it, in barely twenty minutes. "What's for eats?"

"Buffalo tenderloin," I said, "marinated in red wine and garlic, fiddle head ferns, corn pudding, and red potatoes cooked with bay leaf."

"Again?" Susan said.

Pearl the wonder dog was in the kitchen with me, alert to every aspect of the buffalo tenderloin. I sliced off an edge and gave it to her.

Susan came and sat on a stool on the living room side of the counter. She drank another milligram of her champagne. She took the bottle out of the glass ice bucket on the counter and leaned forward and filled my glass.

"Paul telephoned today," she said. "He said he'd tried to get you but you were out."

"I know," I said. "There's a message on my machine."

"He says the wedding is off."

I nodded.

"Did you know?"

"He'd been talking as if it wouldn't happen," I said.

"He had a difficult childhood," Susan said.

"Yeah."

"You disappointed?"

I nodded.

"You know how great I look in a tux," I said.

"Besides that."

"People shouldn't get married unless they are both sure they want to," I said.

"Of course not," Susan said.

"Would have been fun, though," I said.

"Yes."

There was a fire in the living room fireplace. The smell of it always enriched the apartment, though less than Susan did. Outside the living room windows opposite the counter, the darkness had settled firmly into place.

I took a small glass tray out of the refrigerator and put it on the counter.

"Woo woo," Susan said. "Red caviar."

"Salmon roe," I said. "With toast and some crème fraîche."

"Crème fraîche," Susan said, and smiled, and shook her head. I came around from the kitchen and sat on the other stool, beside her. We each ate some caviar.

"You're working on that murder on Beacon Hill," she said.

"Yeah. Quirk sent the husband to me."

"Because?"

"The husband wasn't satisfied with the police work on the case. Quirk had gone as far as he could."

"Was Quirk satisfied with the police work on the case?" Susan said.

"Quirk doesn't say a hell of a lot."

"He isn't satisfied, is he?" Susan said.

"The official explanation," I said, "is that Olivia Nelson was the victim of a random act of violence, doubtless by a deranged person. There is no evidence to suggest anything else."

"And Quirk?"

"He doesn't like it," I said.

"And you?"

"I don't like it," I said.

"Why?"

One of the many things about Susan that I admired was that she never made conversation. When she asked a question she was interested in the answer. Her curiosity was always genuine, and always engendering. When you got through talking with her you usually knew more about the subject than when you started. Even if it was your own subject.

"She was beaten to death with a framing hammer. She had one bruise on her shoulder where she probably flinched up." I demonstrated with my own shoulder. "And all the rest of the damage was to her head. That seems awfully careful for a deranged killer."

"Derangement can be methodical," Susan said.

I nodded and drank some champagne. I put some salmon caviar on a triangle of toast and spooned a little crème fraîche on top. I held it toward Susan, who leaned forward and bit off the point. I ate the rest.

"And," I said, "despite what people think, there aren't that many homicidal maniacs roaming the streets. It's never the best guess."

"True," Susan said. "But it is possible."

"But it's not a useful hypothesis, because it offers no useful way to proceed. The cops have already screened anybody with a record on this kind of thing. Beyond that all you can do is wait, and hope to catch him next time. Or the time after that."

The fire softened the room as we talked. Fire was the heart of the house, Frank Lloyd Wright had said. And if he didn't know, who would.

"But," Susan said after she thought about it, "if you assume that it's not a madman . . ."

"Madperson," I said.

Susan put a hand to her forehead.

"What could I have been thinking?" she said. "If you assume it is not a madperson, then you can begin to do what you know how to do. Look for motive, that sort of thing."

"Yes," I said.

Susan still had half a glass of champagne, but she added a splash from the bottle to reinvigorate it. While she did that I got up and added two logs to the fire.

"Still there's something else," Susan said.

"Just because you're a shrink," I said, "you think you know everything."

"I think I know you," she said, "and it has nothing to do with my profession."

"Good point," I said.

I drank some champagne and ate salmon roe, and thought how to phrase it. Susan was quiet.

"It's that there's an, I don't know, an official version of everything. But the objective data doesn't quite match it. I don't mean it contradicts it, but . . ." I spread my hands.

"For instance," Susan said.

"Well, the home. It's lovely and without character. It's like a display, except for his bedroom; it's as personless as a chain hotel."

"His bedroom?"

"Yeah. That's another thing. They have separate bedrooms separated by a sitting room. His shows signs of use—television set, some books on the bedside table, *TV Guide*. But hers . . ." I shook my head. "The kids' rooms are like hers. Officially designated children's rooms, and appropriately decorated. But no sense that anyone ever smoked a joint in there or read skin magazines with a flashlight under the covers."

"What else?"

"He goes to the office every day early, stays late. There's nothing to do. His secretary, who is, by the way, a knockout, is catching up on her reading."

"This is subtle," Susan said.

"Yeah, it is, though it's not quite as subtle when you're experiencing it. He talks about his children without any sense that now and then they might, or might have sometime, driven him up the wall. They're perfect. She was perfect. His love was all-encompassing. His devotion is unflagging."

"And there's a legal limit on the snow here," Susan said.

I nodded. "Yeah."

"That Camelotian hindsight is not unusual in grief," Susan said.

"I know," I said. "I've seen some grief myself."

"It's a form of denial."

"I know. What I'm trying to get hold of is how long the denial has been going on."

"Yes," Susan said.

"And what's being denied," I said.

Susan nodded. The fire hissed as some sap boiled out of the sawn end of one of the logs. The salmon caviar was gone. The champagne was getting low.

"So what are you going to do?" Susan said.

"Start from the other end."

"You mean look into her past?"

"Yeah. Where she was born. Where she went to school, that stuff. Maybe something will turn up."

"Wouldn't the police have done that?" Susan said.

"On a celebrity case like this, with an uncertain victim, maybe," I said. "But this victim is a well-known pillar of the community. Her life's an open book. They haven't the money or the reason to chase her back to her childhood."

"So why will you do it?" Susan said.

"I don't know what else to do," I said. "You want to eat?"

Susan drank some of her champagne and looked at me over the rim of her glass.

"How attractive was Tripp's secretary, exactly?" Susan said.

"Quite," I said.

Susan smiled.

"How nice," she said. "Perhaps after we've eaten buffalo tenderloin and sipped a dessert wine on the couch and watched the fire settle, you'll want to think about which of us is, or is not, going to ball you in the bedroom until sunrise."

"You're far more attractive than she is, Buffalo gal," I said.

"Oh, good," she said.

We were quiet as I put the meat on the grill and put the corn pudding in the oven.

"Sunrise?" I said.

"The hyperbole of jealous passion," Susan said.

# Chapter 11

I sat with Lee Farrell in the near empty squad room at Homicide. Quirk's office was at the far end of the room. The glass door had *Commander* stenciled on it in black letters. Quirk wasn't there. There was only one cop in the squad room, a heavy bald guy with a red face and a big belly, who had a phone shrugged up against his ear and his feet up on the desk. A cigarette with a long ash hung from his mouth and waggled a little as he talked. Ash occasionally fluttered off the end and flaked onto his shirt-front. He paid it no mind. He had his gun jammed inside his belt in front, and it was obviously digging into him while he sat. Two or three times he shifted to try and ease it, and finally he took it out and put it on his desk. It was a Glock.

"Everybody got Glocks now?" I said.

"Yeah," Farrell said. "Department's trying to stay even with the drug dealers."

"Succeeding?"

Farrell laughed. "Kids got Glocks," he said. "Fucking drug dealers have close air support."

The fat cop continued to talk. He was animated, waving his right hand about as he talked. When the cigarette burned down, he spat it out, stuck another one in his mouth and lit it with one hand.

"The background stuff on Olivia says she was born in Alton, South Carolina, in 1948," I said.

"Yeah."

"Father and mother deceased, no siblings."

"Yeah."

"BA, Duke, 1969; MA, Boston University, 1982."

Farrell nodded. While I talked he unwrapped a stick of gum and shoved it in his mouth. He didn't offer me any.

"Taught Freshman English classes part-time at Shawmut College, gave an Art Appreciation course at Boston Adult Ed in Low Country Realism."

"Whatever that is," Farrell said.

"Vermeer," I said, "Rembrandt, those guys."

"Sure," Farrell said. He chewed his gum gently.

"Worked on the last couple of Stratton campaigns, volunteered on the United Fund, and a bunch of other charities."

"Okay," Farrell said, "so you can read a report."

"And that's it?"

"You got the report," Farrell said.

"Anybody go down to Alton?"

Farrell stared at me.

"You heard about the state of the economy around here?" he said. "I gotta work extra detail to fucking buy ammunition. They're not going to send anybody to Alton, South Carolina, for crissake."

"Just asking," I said.

"I made some phone calls," Farrell said. "They've got a birth certificate on her. The Carolina Academy for Girls has her attendance records. Duke and BU both have her transcripts."

"Perfect," I said.

"You going to go down?" Farrell said.

"Probably," I said. "I'm getting nowhere up here."

"Join the group," Farrell said. "Incidentally, we got an inquiry on you from Senator Stratton's office."

"If nominated I will not run," I said. "If elected I will not serve."

Farrell ignored me.

"Came into the commissioner's office, and they bucked it on down to me."

"Because he mentioned the Nelson case?"

"Yeah. Commissioner's office never heard of you."

"Their loss," I said. "What did they want to know?"

"General background, my impressions of your competence, that stuff."

"Who did you talk to?"

"Guy named Morrissey, said he was the Senator's aide."

"What did you tell them?"

"Said you were cute as a bug's ear," Farrell said.

"You guys," I said, "are obsessed with sex."

"Why should we be different?"

# Chapter 12

I flew to Atlanta the next morning, took a train from the gate to the terminal, got my suitcase off the carousel, picked up a rental car, and headed southeast on Route 20 toward Alton. Most of the trip was through Georgia, Alton being just across the line in the western part of South Carolina, not too far from Augusta. I got there about two-thirty in the afternoon with the sun shining heavy and solid through the trees that sagged over the main road.

It was a busy downtown, maybe two blocks wide and six blocks long. The first building on the left was a three-story white clapboard hotel with a green sign that said *Alton Arms* in gold lettering. Across the street was a Rexall drugstore and lunch counter. Beside it was a men's clothing store. The mannequins in the window were very country-club in blue crested blazers and plaid vests. There were a couple of downscale restaurants redolent of Frialator, a store that sold yarn, and a big Faulknerian courthouse made out of stone. The cars parked nose in to the curb, the way they do in towns, and never do in cities.

I parked, nose to curb, in front of the Alton Arms, and walked around a Bluetick hound sleeping on the hot cement walkway in the sun. His tongue lolled out a little, and his skin twitched as if he were dreaming that he was a wild dog on the East African plains, shrugging off a tsetse fly.

The lobby was air-conditioned, and opened into the dining room, up one step and separated by an oak railing. At one end of the room was a fireplace sufficient to roast a moose, to the left of the entrance was a reception desk, and behind it was a pleasant, efficient-looking woman with silvery hair and a young face.

Her looks were deceptive. She was as efficient as a Russian farm collective, although probably more pleasant. It was twenty minutes to register, and ten more to find a room key. By the time she found it I had folded my arms on the counter and put my head down on them.

She was not amused.

"Please, sir," she said. "I'm doing my best."

"Isn't that discouraging," I said.

When I finally got to my room, I unpacked. I put my razor and toothbrush on the bathroom counter, put my clean shirt on the bureau, and put the Browning 9mm on my belt, back of my hipbone, where the drape of my jacket would hide it in the hollow of my back. Nice thing about an automatic. Being flat, it didn't compromise any fashion statement that you might be making.

I had considered risking Alton, South Carolina, without a gun. But one of Spenser's best crime-buster tips is, never go unarmed on a murder case. So I'd packed it under my shirt, and clean socks, and checked the bag through. I'd probably need it checking out.

I got walking directions to the Carolina Academy from a polite black guy wearing a green porter's uniform, and lounging around the front porch of the hotel. The Bluetick hound was still there, motionless in the sun, but he had turned over on the other side, so I knew he was alive.

Carolina Academy was a cluster of three white frame houses set in a lot of lawn and flower beds, on the other side of Main Street, behind the commercial block that comprised the Alton downtown.

The headmistress was a tall, angular, white-haired woman with a strong nose and small mouth. She wore a long white gauzy dress with a bright blue sash. Her shoes were bright blue also.

"I'm Dr. Pauline MacCallum," she said. She was trying, I think, for crisp and efficient, but her South Carolina drawl masked the effect. She gave me a crisp, efficient handshake and gestured toward the straight-back chair with arms in front of her desk.

"My name is Spenser," I said and gave her one of my cards. "I'm trying to develop a little background on a former student, Olivia Nelson, who would have been a student here during the late fifties—early sixties—I should think."

The small nameplate on the desk said *Pauline MacCallum, Ed.D.* The office was oval shaped, with a big bay window that looked out on the tennis courts beyond a bed of patient lucies. On the walls were pictures of white-gowned graduating classes.

"We provide for K through 12," Dr. MacCallum said. "What year did Miss Nelson start?"

"Don't know," I said. "She was born in 1948, and she graduated from college in 1969."

"So," Dr. MacCallum said, "if she came for the full matriculation, she would have started in 1953, and graduated in 1966."

She got up and went to a bookcase to the left of her desk, and scanned the blue leather-bound yearbooks that filled the case. On the tennis courts there was a group of young women in white tennis dresses being instructed. The coach had a good tan and strong legs, and even from here I could see the muscles in her forearms. Each of the young women took a turn returning a gentle serve. Most of them swiped at the ball eagerly, but limply, as if the racket were too heavy. Rarely did the ball get back across the net.

"I hope that's not your tennis team," I said.

"Miss Pollard is a fine tennis coach," Dr. MacCallum said. "But this is a physical education class. All our girls are required to take physical education three hours a week."

She took the 1966 Carolina Academy Yearbook out from the case and opened it and thumbed through the pictures of graduating seniors.

"Yes," she said. "Here she is, Olivia Nelson. I remember her now that I see the picture. Fine girl. Very nice family."

She walked around her desk and offered me the yearbook. I took it and looked at the picture.

There she was, same narrow nose with the dramatic nostrils, same thin mouth, shaped with lipstick even then. Eighteen years old, in profile, with her hair in a long bob, wearing a high-necked white blouse. There was no hint of Vietnam or dope or all-power-to-the-people in her face. It was not the face of someone who'd listened to Jimi Hendrix, nor smoked dope, nor dated guys who chanted, "Hell no, we won't go." I nodded my head slowly, looking at it.

The chatter beneath her picture said that her hobby was horses, her favorite place was Canterbury Farms, and her ambition was to be the first girl to ride a Derby winner.

"What's Canterbury Farms?" I said.

"It's a racing stable, here in Alton," Dr. MacCallum said. "Mr. Nelson, Olivia's father, was very prominent in racing circles, I believe."

"What can you tell me about her?" I said.

"Why do you wish to know?"

"She was the victim of an unsolved murder," I said. "In Boston."

"But you're not with the police?"

"No, I'm employed by her husband."

She thought about that for a bit. Outside the girls continued to fail at tennis, though Miss Pollard seemed undaunted.

"I can't recall a great deal about her," Dr. MacCallum said. "She was from a prosperous and influential family here in Alton, but, in truth, most of our girls are from families like that. She was a satisfactory student, I think. Her transcript will tell us—I'll arrange for you to get a copy—but I don't remember anything special about her."

She paused for a moment and looked out at the tennis, and smiled.

"Of course, the irony is that I remember the worst students best," she said. "They are the ones I spend the most time with."

"You were headmistress then?" I said.

"In 1966? No, I was the head of the modern languages department," she said. "I do not recall having Olivia Nelson in class."

"Is there anything you can think of about Olivia Nelson which would shed any light on her death?" I said.

Dr. MacCallum sat quietly for a moment gazing past me, outside. Outside the girls in their white dresses were eagerly hitting tennis balls into the net.

"No," she said slowly. "I know of nothing. But understand, I don't have a clear and compelling memory of her. I could put you in touch with our Alumni Secretary, when she comes back from vacation."

I accepted the offer, and got a name and phone number. We talked a little longer, but there was nothing there. I stood, we shook hands, and I left. As I walked down the curving walk I could hear the futile bonk of the tennis rackets.

"You and me, Miss Pollard."

# Chapter 13

Outside the Carolina Academy I paused at the curb to let a dark blue Buick sedan cruise past me, then I crossed the street and went up the low hill past the Alton Free Library toward the Alton Arms.

The white-haired desk clerk with the young face looked at me curiously as I came in through the lobby, and then looked quickly away as I glanced at her, and was suddenly very busy arranging something on a shelf below the counter. I glanced around the lobby. There was no one else in it. I went past the elevator and walked up the stairs and went in my room.

It had been tossed. Not carefully either. The bedspread hung down longer than it had before. The pillows were disordered. The drawers were partly opened. The window shades were exactly even, which they hadn't been earlier. I checked my suitcase. Nothing was missing. There wasn't much to be missing. I looked out the window. There was a dark blue Buick parked across the street.

I thought about the Buick for a while, and about my room being searched, and about how the desk clerk had eyed me when I came in. I looked at the door. It hadn't been forced. I thought about that. Then I went back down to the lobby and said to the desk clerk, "Has anyone been in my room?"

She jumped. It wasn't much, maybe a two-inch vertical leap, but it was a jump.

"No, sir, of course not."

"What's my room number?" I said.

She turned alertly to her computer screen.

"If you'll give me your name, sir, I'll be happy to check for you."

"If you don't know my name or room number," I said, "how do you know that no one's been in there?"

"I, well, no one goes in guests' rooms, sir."

"My watch is missing," I said. "I left it on the bureau and it's gone."

"Oh, my," she said. "Well, he wouldn't . . ."

I waited. She didn't know what to say. I had time. I didn't mind the silence. From the bar down a hallway from the dining room, I could hear a man laughing. I waited.

"I'm sure he wouldn't have stolen your watch, sir."

"Who?"

"Officer Swinny."

"A cop?"

"Yes, sir. That's the only reason I let him into your room. He's a policeman. He said it was an important police matter."

"Alton Police?"

"Yes, sir. He's a detective with the Sheriff's Department."

"You know him?"

"Yes, sir. He was in high school with my brother."

"He drive a dark blue Buick sedan?" I said.

"I don't know, sir. I didn't see him until he came in the lobby. He said it was official police business. Sedale might know about his car."

"Sedale the black guy in the green uniform?"

"Yes, sir. Officer Swinny said I wasn't to tell you. He said it was official business."

"Sure," I said. Then I smiled and looked deliberately at my watch. It was 3:10. She showed no sign that it registered.

I went out onto the wide veranda. Sedale was sweeping off the steps.

I said, "Excuse me, Sedale. You know Officer Swinny of the Alton Police?"

Sedale smiled a little.

"She can't keep a secret for shit, can she," he said.

"Not for shit," I said. "You know what kind of car Swinny drives?"

"Came here he was driving a Ford Ranger pickup. Red one with a black plastic bed liner."

"Happen to know who owns the blue Buick parked across the street?"

Sedale looked over at the Buick and then back at me and shook his head.

"Can't say I do," he said.

"You know Swinny was in my room," I said.

"Sure," Sedale said. "I let him in."

"How come?"

"She told me to."

"You stay with him?"

Sedale shook his head again.

"Just let him in. Don't hang around cops no more than I need to."

"You know when he left?"

"Sure. Left about twenty minutes ago. 'Bout ten minutes 'fore you come back."

I looked at the Buick again. It had no telltale whip antenna. But there was a small cellular phone antenna on the back window. The windows were darkly tinted.

"Anybody in the Buick?" I said.

Sedale shrugged.

"Been parked there since I came out," he said. "You in trouble?"

"Not yet," I said. I stepped off the porch and started across the street toward the Buick. There was someone in it, and as I approached, he drove away.

# Chapter 14

I went back in the hotel and called Farrell in Boston. Then I got directions from Sedale and walked on down toward Canterbury Farms. The racing stable was across town, but in Alton across town was not a voyage of discovery.

It had been early fall when I left Boston. But in Alton it was late summer and the thick leaves of the arching trees dappled the wide streets with sunlight. Traffic was sparse and what there was moved easily, knowing there was no hurry. The heat was gentle and closed around me quietly without the assaultive quality it always had in midsummer cities.

Beyond the Carolina Academy, I walked past a sinuous brick wall that stood higher than my head. There were no corners, no right angles. The wall curved regularly in and bellied regularly out. At the intersection of a dirt road, the wall turned cornerlessly and insinuated itself away from me. I went down the dirt road. It was soft red dirt, and my feet made a kind of chuffing sound as I walked. Here the trees didn't droop, they stood straight and very high, evergreens, pine I supposed, with no branches for the first thirty or forty feet, so that walking down the road was like walking through a columned corridor. There was no sound except for my feet, and a locust hum that was so persistent and permanent that it faded in and out of notice. Down the road I could see the training track open up and, in the center of the infield, a vast squat tree, framed by a column of pines.

The light at the end of the tunnel.

There were hoofprints in the soft earth, then the thick sound of hoof-beats. I reached the training track. Several horses were pelting around it in the soft red clay. The exercise riders were mostly girls in jeans and boots and hard hats, with their racing crops stuck in their belts in the back and sticking up along their spines. Hundred-pound girls controlling thousand-pound animals. As I got close I could hear the horses as they gulped air in through their flared nostrils, and exhaled it in big snorts. The breathing was as regular as the muffled thud of their hooves.

To the left, about a half mile up the track, was a portable starting gate. Three or four men were gathered around it looking at the horses as they ran. One of the men was mounted on a calm, sturdy brown horse. The other three were afoot. Beyond the starting gate was a parking lot with three or four vehicles in it, and beyond the lot, to the right, was a cluster of white buildings. I walked toward it.

As I got close the guy on horseback said, "Morning."

"I need to talk to somebody in charge," I said.

"That'd be Mr. Ferguson," the man on horseback said and nodded toward one of the other men standing gazing at the horses.

"Frank Ferguson," the other man said, and put out a hand.

I introduced myself.

"Come on over to the track office," Ferguson said. "Probably got some coffee left, though it might be kinda robust by now."

Ferguson was a short guy with bowlegs and a significant belly, which looked sort of hard. He had all his hair and it was gray and curly and worn long for a guy his age. He had on engineer's boots, and jeans, and a red plaid shirt and a beige corduroy jacket with leather elbow patches. He headed for the office at a quick step, and as he went he dug a curved meerschaum pipe out of his right-hand coat pocket and loaded it with tobacco from a zip leather pouch. By the time we got to the office he had the pipe in his mouth going, and the tobacco stashed back in his jacket pocket.

The office was in one end of the long stable where racehorses stood in separate stalls, looking out at the world, craning their necks, chewing hay, swaying, and, in at least one case, chewing on the edge of the stall. One horse, a tall chestnut colt, was being washed by a young girl with a hose. The young girl wore a maroon tee shirt that said *Canterbury Farms* on it, and her blonde hair was braided in a long pigtail that reached to her waist. She sluiced water over the horse and then soaped him and scrubbed him into a lather with a brush, and then sluiced off the suds. The horse stood quietly and gazed with his big brown eyes at the infield of the training track. Occasionally he would shift his feet a little.

The office itself was nothing much. There were pictures of horses and owners gathered in repetitive poses in the winners' circle. There seemed to be a lot of owners. Ferguson was in most of the pictures. There was a gray metal desk in the room, and a gray metal table with some file folders on it, and a coffee machine with a half-full pot of coffee, sitting on the warming plate and smelling bad, the way coffee does that has sat for half a day on warm.

Ferguson nodded at the coffee. I shook my head. He sat at the desk, I took a straight chair and turned it around and straddled it and rested my arms on the back.

"I'm a detective," I said. "And I'm looking into the background of a woman, used to work here, woman named Olivia Nelson. Be twenty-five years ago, maybe twenty-seven, twenty-eight. You here then?"

Ferguson nodded and poured himself a virulent-smelling cup of coffee. He put in two tablespoons of sugar and two more of Cremora and stirred it while he was listening to me.

"Yes, certainly. Been in this business forty years, forty-one come next spring. Right here. Helped open the damn training track in Alton. Everybody thought they had to be in Kentucky. But they didn't and I showed 'em they didn't."

He stirred his coffee some more.

"You remember Olivia Nelson?" I said.

"Jack Nelson's kid," Ferguson said. He shook his head. "Old Jumper Jack. He was a contrivance, by God, if I ever saw one."

"Jumper?" I said.

"Jack would jump anything that had no dick," Ferguson said.

"Nice to have a hobby," I said. "What can you tell me about Olivia?"

Ferguson shrugged.

"Long time ago," he said. "She was a nice enough kid, hot walker, exercise rider, just like the kids out there now, had a thing for horses. You know, young girls, like to control some big strong masculine thing between their legs."

"Nicely put," I said. "Anything unusual about her?"

"Nope, richer than most . . . why I took her on. Jack had a lot of money in my horses."

"Syndication?"

"Yessir. We got over to Keeneland, up to Saratoga to the Yearling Auctions. Buy some that look right and sell shares in them."

"Know anything about Olivia after she worked here?"

Again Ferguson shrugged and took in some pipe smoke. He was a good pipe smoker. He'd lit it with one match and kept it going without a lot of motion.

"Nope," he said. "Don't keep much track of the stable kids. I know she went off to college and her momma died . . ." He shook his head slowly. "Like to killed Jack when she died. You'd a thought he didn't care, tomcatting around the way he did, but he must of loved her in his way, a hell of a lot. He went into a real tailspin when she died. Took him couple years to get over it."

Ferguson drew on the pipe and without taking it from one corner of his mouth exhaled a small stream of smoke from the other. Then he grinned.

"Still wouldn't want to leave my daughter unattended around Jack."

I had a sensation in my solar plexus that felt like *whoops* sounds.

"What do you mean?" I said.

"Jack's nearly seventy, but if he can catch it he'll jump it," Ferguson said.

I was silent. Ferguson looked at me speculatively. He knew he'd said something. But he didn't know what it was. He waited.

"He's alive," I said.

"Was last week, anyway," Ferguson said. "Had a couple drinks with him. You got more recent information?"

I shook my head. "I'd heard he was dead."

"Well, he ain't," Ferguson said.

"I was misinformed," I said.

# Chapter 15

The seasons hadn't changed yet in South Carolina. The weather was still summer. But the earth's orbit was implacable and despite the temperature, the evening came on earlier than it used to. It was already beginning to darken into the cocktail hour when I left Ferguson in the track office and began to stroll toward the Alton Arms. As I came past the parking lot, I saw the blue Buick pull out of the lot and head out the paved road that ran from the stable area to the highway.

Along the dirt road, under the high pines, the evening had already arrived. The locust hum had vanished, and instead there was the sound of crickets, and occasionally the sound of night birds—which probably fed on the crickets. There was no other sound, except my footsteps in the soft earth. No one else was walking on the road. I could feel the weight of the gun on my hip. It felt nice.

Since Olivia Nelson's father wasn't dead, someone had lied to the cops. But there was no way to know whether it was Loudon Tripp; or Olivia who had lied to Loudon; or Jumper Jack himself who had deceived his daughter.

At the hotel, I went up to my room and called Farrell.

"You got anything on that license plate?" I said.

"You're going to love this," he said. "South Carolina DMV says the plate's classified. Information about ownership on a need-to-know basis only."

"You can't show a need to know?"

"Because it's following you, or you think it is? No. If it was in a hit and run and three witnesses saw it, that's need to know."

"It's part of a murder investigation," I said.

"You say so, South Carolina DMV doesn't say so. They say I can go fry my Yankee ass. Though they said it in a nice polite Southern way."

"Classified plate number is usually undercover cops," I said.

"Un huh."

"Okay," I said.

I listened to the faint hollow silence on the wire for a while.

"Okay," I said again. Farrell waited.

"I got something you're going to love too," I said.

"Yeah?"

"Olivia Nelson's father is alive."

"Yeah?"

"Control yourself," I said.

"Tripp said her parents were dead," Farrell said.

"Right," I said.

"Why would he lie?"

"Maybe he didn't lie," I said. "Maybe she told him they were."

"Why would she lie?"

"Maybe she thought they were dead," I said.

"Will you fucking stop it," Farrell said. "If her father's alive and we were told he died, somebody lied."

"Yowsah," I said. Through the window of my hotel room I could see the blue Buick, motionless under the heavy trees, across the street from the hotel.

"You going to see him?"

"Yowsah."

"You going to stop talking like the fucking end man in a minstrel show?"

"Sho 'nuff, Mr. Bones," I said. "Soon's ah do sumpin 'bout this guy that's tailing me."

"Why don't you just ignore him?" Farrell said.

"Well, for one thing, it's an open tail. Unless he's the worst cop in the old Confederacy, he means me to see him."

"Which means he's trying to scare you?" Farrell said.

"Yeah. I want to know why. And who."

"You find out, let me know," Farrell said.

"Sure," I said. " 'Less of course it's classified."

# Chapter 16

My rental Ford was parked in the lot at the rear right corner of the hotel. I went out the front door and headed for it. The guy in the Buick could see me. And he had positioned himself so that if I drove off he could follow. Tailing somebody is much easier if you don't mind them knowing.

As I started up the Ford, I could see a little puff of heat come from the tailpipe of the Buick. I pulled out of the driveway of the hotel parking lot, swung around the corner, and parked directly behind the Buick with my engine idling. Nothing happened. I couldn't see the interior of the Buick because of the darkly tinted glass. I sat. Across the street the Bluetick hound mooched around the corner of the hotel and sat on the top step of the veranda with his forefeet on the next step down. Sedale came out after a while and gave the dog something to eat. It kept its position, its jaw working on the scrap. Sedale picked up a broom and began to sweep the veranda. The place looked clean, but I suspected it was something Sedale did when things were slow, to keep from hanging in the lobby and chatting with the desk clerk.

The Buick sat. There was a slight tremor to its back end and a faint hint of heat shimmering from its tailpipe. I thought about whether Brooks Robinson or Mike Schmidt should be third baseman on Spenser's all-time all-star team. I was leaning toward Schmidt. Of course Billy Cox could pick it with anybody, but Schmidt had the power numbers. On the other hand, so did Eddie Matthews. In front of me the Buick slid into gear and pulled away from the curb. I followed. The Buick turned left at the end of the short street, then a sharp right, slowed at a green light, and then floored it as the light turned. I ran the red light behind him, and stayed with him as he went down an alley behind a Kroger's supermarket, and kept him in sight as he exceeded the speed limit heading out the County Road.

When we hit Route 20, he headed east, toward Columbia, going around eighty-five. The rental Ford bucked a little, but it hung with him. After ten miles of this, the Buick U-turned in an *Official Vehicles Only* turnaround, and headed back west, toward Augusta. I did the same. We slowed after a few minutes at a long upgrade. There was a ten-wheeler in the right-hand lane, and a white Cadillac in the left lane, traveling at the same speed as the tractor. They stayed in tandem, at about forty miles an hour. We were stuck behind them. We chased along at that rate for maybe five minutes. The Buick kept honking its horn, but the Cadillac never budged. There was no sign, in the Caddy, of the driver's head above the front seat. This is not usually a good omen.

At the next exit the Buick turned off, roared down the ramp, turned right toward Eureka. I followed and almost rolled past him. He had pulled in off the highway onto a gravel service road. I actually passed it before I got a flash of blue through a screen of scrubby pine trees. I stopped, backed up, and pulled in behind him. Again we sat.

There was a blue jay flying around from scrub pine to scrub pine, looking at us, and looking, also, at everything else. He would sit for a moment, his head moving, looking in all directions, then, precipitously, for no reason that I could see, he would fly to another tree, or sometimes merely flutter to another branch, and look in all directions again. *Semper paratus*.

Ahead of us the gravel road wound up toward some power lines that ran at right angles to the highway through a cut in the woods. Behind us, and above, the highway traffic swooshed by, unaware that a little ways ahead was a slow-moving roadblock.

Shortstop on my all-time team had to be Ozzie Smith. I'd seen Marty Marion, but he didn't hit like Ozzie. Pee Wee Reese, on the other hand, was one of the greatest clutch players I'd ever seen. That was the qualifying rule. This was an all-seen, all-time, all-star team. And Ozzie did things I'd never seen anyone do on a ball field. It had to be Ozzie.

The driver of the Buick came to a decision. The door opened and he got out and started back toward me. He had on a light beige suit and a maroon blouse with a bow at the neck, and medium high heels. He carried a black shoulder bag and he was female. Maybe forty, well built, with a firm jaw and a wide mouth. Her eyes were oval and set wide apart. Her eye makeup emphasized both the ovalness and the spacing in ways I didn't fully understand. I rolled down my window. Her heels crunched forcefully into the gravel as she walked toward me. She seemed angry.

As she came alongside the car I said, "You ever see Ozzie Smith play?"

"Okay, pal," she said, "what's your problem?"

"Well, I'm trying to decide between Ozzie Smith and Pee Wee Reese for my all-time, all-seen team . . ."

"Never mind the bullshit," she said. "I asked you a question, I want an answer."

I smiled at her. She saw the smile, and ignored it. She did not disrobe.

"You wouldn't want to go dancing or anything, would you?" I said.

She frowned, reached in her pocket, and pulled out a leather folder. She flipped it open.

"Police officer," she said.

The shield was blue and gold and had *Alton County Sheriff* on it, around the outside.

"That probably means no dancing, huh?"

She shook her head angrily.

"Look, Buster," she said. "I am not going to fuck around with you. You answer my questions right now, or we go in."

"For what, following an officer?"

"Why you following me?"

"Because you were following me. And your license plate was classified. And I figured that if I stuck behind you, either you'd have to confront me, or I'd follow you home."

She stared at me. It was a standard cop hard look.

"You decided to confront me," I said. "Now I know you're with the Sheriff's Department. Who put you on me?"

"I'll ask the questions, Bud."

"No you won't. You don't know what to ask."

"Whether I do or not," she said, "I can tell you something. I can tell you that you are in over your head, and you'd be smart to go home and find another case before this thing gets pulled up over your ears."

"You were showing me an open tail," I said. "Somebody tossed my room, and let me know it. I figured that I was being scared off. What I want to know is, why? Who wants to discourage me? What can you tell me about Olivia Nelson? Who does your hair?" I smiled at her again.

She gave me her hard cop look again, which was surprisingly effective, considering that she looked sort of like Audrey Hepburn. Then she shook her head once, sharply. And her eyes glinted oddly.

"Rosetta's," she said, "in Batesburg."

Then she turned on her medium high heels and walked back to her car, got in, U-turned, and drove past me out onto the Eureka Road.

# Chapter 17

I was in my room at the Alton Arms, lying on the bed with my shoes off and three pillows propped, talking to Susan on the phone. There was a bottle of scotch and some soda and a bucket of ice on the bureau. My shirt was hung in the closet on a hanger, which had been covered with pink quilted padding. My gun was on the bedside table, barrel pointed away for good range safety. I was sipping a drink from one of the squat glasses they had sent up with the scotch. It had a crest engraved on the side with an *A* worked into it. Padded coat hangers and monogrammed glasses. First class.

"How's the baby?" I said.

"She's fine," Susan said. "I took her for a walk after work and got her a new bone and she's on the bed now, looking at me and chewing it. And getting bone juice on the spread."

"How adorable," I said. "Does she miss me?"

"Do you miss Daddy, Pearl?" Susan said off the phone.

I waited.

"No," Susan said into the phone, "apparently not. Maybe after her bone is gone."

"How much crueler than the adder's sting," I said.

"I miss you," Susan said.

"That helps," I said. "But it's not the same."

"Why not?"

"You might just be driven by lust."

"Whereas Pearl's love is the stuff of Provençal poetry," Susan said.

"Exactly," I said.

She laughed. I always loved the sound of her laughter. And to have caused it was worth the west side of heaven.

"Are you having any fun down there?" Susan said.

"No. The local Sheriff's Department is attempting to frighten me to death."

"Really?"

"Yeah. I had a recent confrontation with a tough Sheriff's detective who gets her hair done at Rosetta's in Batesburg."

"Tell me," Susan said.

I did, starting with the part about the room being searched, including my conversation with Ferguson.

"So why would the Sheriff's police do that?" Susan said.

"Someone asked them to, I would guess. I can't see why the Alton County, South Carolina, Sheriff's Department would otherwise know I existed."

"Hard to imagine," Susan said. "But probably true. So who might ask them to?"

"Somebody who doesn't want me looking into Olivia Nelson's past," I said.

"I sort of figured that out myself," Susan said. "The real question is who doesn't want you to and why not."

"Yes," I said.

"And to that question you have no answer."

"None," I said.

"Another approach might be to think who has the clout to get the Sheriff's office to do it," Susan said.

"Good thought, Della," I said.

"Della?"

"Della Street . . . Perry Mason? I guess I'm too subtle for you."

"Subtlety is not usually the difficulty," Susan said.

"Anyway," I said, "there's too much I don't know to do too much guessing. The only name that's come up, that might have the clout, is Senator Stratton."

"Why would he want to discourage you?"

"Maybe he doesn't," I said. "He knows Tripp. I met him when Tripp and I had lunch at the Harvard Club. He's inquired about me to the cops in Boston. But that may be, probably is, just a routine constituent service to a big campaign contributor, real or potential."

"But he's the only one you can think of."

"Right."

"I would think that a liberal Senator from Massachusetts wouldn't have much clout in rural South Carolina," Susan said.

"Politics make strange bedfellows," I said.

"Maybe Olivia's father who isn't dead might have had something to do with it," Susan said.

I drank some more of my scotch and soda.

"Possibly," I said.

"What are you going to do next?"

"I'm going to have a couple or three drinks," I said, "order up some sandwiches, go to bed, and sleep on it all. In the morning I'm going to the track kitchen for breakfast. Sedale, the bellhop, who is my closest personal South Carolina friend, says it's a don't-miss place where everyone eats. Authentic Southern cooking, he says."

"And I'm missing it," Susan said. "What happens after breakfast?"

"I'm going to go out and see if I can talk with Jumper Jack Nelson," I said.

"That might be interesting," Susan said.

"Not as interesting as you are," I said.

"Of course not," Susan said. "But maybe you'll find out why the police were led to believe he was dead."

"I wish you were going to be dining with me at the track kitchen tomorrow," I said. "A cup of coffee, a plate of grits, some redeye gravy, and thou."

"Assuming I could restrain my carnality," she said.

"Assuming you couldn't, we'd never be welcome at the track kitchen again."

"Take care of yourself," Susan said.

"Yes," I said. "I love you."

"I love you too," she said, "and the baby probably misses you more than she knows."

We hung up. I lay on the bed with my drink for a while looking at the little square-toothed dentil molding that went all the way around the ceiling of the room. Then I got up to freshen my drink and looked out the window. Alton was dark and silent under a dark sky. There was no moon. And no stars were visible. The wind moved the trees some, and made enough of a sound for me to hear it through the closed window. Across the street, in the yellow glare of the street lamp, there was merely an empty stretch of grass-spattered gravel. No sign of the blue Buick. No car at all. Maybe they'd given up trying to scare me. Maybe they'd just decided on a different approach. I drank my drink thoughtfully, and shrugged the bunchy muscles in my back and shoulders, and looked at the Browning lying on the nightstand.

I raised my glass slightly toward the gun.

"Here's looking at you, kid," I said.

Then I picked up the room service menu and began to consider my choices.

# Chapter 18

The track kitchen was off maybe a quarter of a mile from the Alton training track, a low, sort of white, cinder-block building with a badly defined gravel parking area in front, where there were three pickup trucks and a green Jaguar sedan. An old metal Coca-Cola sign hung over the screen door. The door hung less square than rhomboidal. The cinder block had shifted a little and everything was slightly out of plumb. Long cracks, following the right-angled joinings of the cinder block, jagged across the building front. The rich smell of lard undulated from the open windows.

I went in. The building was divided front to back into two rooms. One of the rooms contained two pool tables and a jukebox. There were three or four exercise riders, in T-shirts and jeans, shooting pool and drinking Coca-Cola, and listening to Waylon Jennings. On my side of the archway, the dining area was filled with long plastic laminate tables. Across the back was the kitchen. A well-dressed man and woman were eating ham and eggs, grits, and toast at one of the tables. Three ample women in large hats and frilly dresses were at the table next to theirs. I walked back to the kitchen where two women were cooking. One of them was black and gray-haired and overweight. The other was white and gray-haired and overweight. Both had sweat beaded on their foreheads. The white woman wore blue jeans more commodious than Delaware. The black woman had on a flowered dress. Both wore aprons. Without looking up from the grill, where she was scrambling some eggs, the black woman said, "Whatchu want?"

I ordered grits, toast, and coffee.

"That it?" she said.

"That's all I dare," I said, "The smell is already clogging my arteries."

Still without looking up, she tossed her head toward the formica tables. The white woman placed a large white china mug on the counter in front of me and nodded at the coffee in its warming pot.

"Have a seat," the black woman said. "We'll bring it."

I poured myself coffee, added cream and sugar, and took it with me to an empty seat. The white woman came around the counter with a startling number of plates and put them down in front of the ample women. I could see how they got ample.

I sipped some coffee. It was too hot. I swallowed the small sip with difficulty and blew on the cup for a while. Around the room there were pictures pasted up on the cinder-block wall, most of them horse racing pictures, jockeys and owners in winning circles with horses. The horses were always the least excited. They were old pictures, black-and-white blowups that had faded, the corners bent and torn from being repeatedly Scotch-taped to the uncooperative cinder block. The only thing recent was a big calendar for the current year, decorated with pictures of dogs playing poker. There was a picture, not recent, of Olivia Nelson, a cheap head shot in color that looked like the kind of school picture they take every year and send home in a cardboard frame and the parents buy it and put it on the mantel. I got up and went to the wall and looked more closely. Clearly it was Olivia Nelson. She looked like her yearbook picture, and she looked not too different from the picture of her at forty-two that I'd seen in her living room on Beacon Hill. My coffee had cooled a little and I drank some while I looked at her picture. The white woman came out of the kitchen and lumbered toward me with breakfast.

"Where you sitting?" she said.

I nodded at the table and she went ahead of me and set the tray down.

"Excuse me," I said. "May I ask you why you have a picture of Olivia Nelson on the wall."

The woman's gray hair was badly done up and had unraveled over her forehead like a frayed sock. She tightened her chin and her lower lip pushed out a little.

"Got no pictures of Olivia Nelson."

"Then who is this young woman?" I said, pointing to the girl in the school photo.

Her jaw got tighter and her lower lip came out a little further.

"That's Cheryl Anne Rankin," the woman said.

"She looks remarkably like Olivia Nelson, you sure it's not?"

"Guess I ought to know my own daughter," she said. Her voice was barely audible and she spoke straight down as if she were talking to her feet.

"Your daughter? Cheryl Anne Rankin, who looks just like Olivia Nelson, is your daughter?"

"She don't look like Olivia Nelson," the woman said to her feet.

I nodded and smiled engagingly. It was hard to be charming to someone who was staring at the ground.

"Do you know Olivia Nelson?"

"Used to."

"Could you tell me about her?"

"No."

"Where is your daughter now?" I said.

She shook her head doggedly, staring down.

"Got to work. Can't stand here talking the damned day away," she said.

She turned and lumbered back into the kitchen and began to break eggs into a bowl. The black woman looked at her and then glared at me. I thought about it and decided that she was reluctant to discuss it further, that her associate thought I was worse than roach turd, and that if they came at me together, I might get badly trampled.

I went back to my table and ate my grits and toast and finished my coffee and looked at the picture of Cheryl Anne Rankin, who looked just like Olivia Nelson.

I was confused.

# Chapter 19

Jumper Jack Nelson's house was beyond the training track, on a hill with a lawn that rolled down maybe half a mile to the roadway. The drive was crushed oyster shells, and it curved in a white arc slowly up through the putting green lawn to a porte cochere, supported on gleaming white pillars. The house too was white and looked as if it had been built before the Civil War and kept up. It was three stories, vaguely like a European country house, buoyed by foundation plantings of shrubs and flowers I didn't recognize, so that, stark white, it seemed to float atop its hill on a wave of color. The house was silent. The windows were blank, the mid-morning sun reflecting off them without meaning. At the edges of the property, on either side, tall southern pines stood, their branchless trunks like palisades containing the estate. In their branches birds fluttered. I could hear them singing. As I got closer to the house, I could see the bees hovering over the foundation plantings, moving from flower to flower. My feet seemed intrusive as I crunched up the oyster shell drive.

When I rang the bell, it chimed deep inside the house. A number of dogs barked at the sound, though not as if they meant much. I waited. The dogs continued to bark without enthusiasm, as if they were merely doing their job, and didn't really care if the doorbell rang.

A small breeze moved across the tops of the taller flowers along the front of the house and made them sway gently. The bees swayed with them, unconcerned with the breeze, focused on the nectar.

I didn't hear footsteps. The door simply opened. Slowly. A huge hallway beyond the door was dark. A slow old Southern male black voice said slowly, "Yessir."

"My name is Spenser," I said and handed a card into the darkness. "I'm here to see Mr. Nelson." I smiled into the dark hallway. Friendly as a guy selling sewing machines. A black hand, nearly invisible in the dark hallway, took my card.

"Step in," the old voice said.

Inside the hallway, my eyes began to adjust. There was an odd fresh smell in the house. It was a smell I knew, but I couldn't place it. I felt something brush against my leg and looked down at an old hunting dog that was leaning against my knee. It was too dark to see him clearly, but the way he held his head, and the way his back swayed, was enough to know he was old. I reached down and let him smell the back of my hand. As my pupils continued to dilate I could see that there were three or four other dogs standing around, none of them hostile. They were all hunting dogs.

The black man said, "You wait here, sir. I'll see Mr. Nelson, can he see you."

His voice was soft, and he was very old. As tall as I was, but narrow; and stooped as if he were embarrassed to be tall and wanted to conceal it. He had on a worn black suit of some kind and a white shirt with one collar point bent upward, and a narrow ratty black bow tie, like a movie gambler, tied with the ends hanging long. The hand that held my card was surprisingly thick, with strong fingers. His hands were graceful, like he might play the harp, or deal cards.

"Sure," I said.

"Don't pay the dogs no mind, sir," he said. "They won't harm you."

"I know," I said. "I like dogs."

"Yessir," he said and moved away, his feet a whisper on the dark oak floor. He was wearing slippers.

The room was entirely dark oak, panels on the walls, panels and beams on the ceiling. There were no windows in the hall. The stairwell curved up toward the back half of the entry hall, and must have been windowed, because some light wafted dimly down from beyond the turn.

The fresh smell I'd noticed when I came in had lessened when the black man left, and as I heard his soft, whispering shuffle coming back from somewhere under the stairs it got strong again. I realized what I was sniffing. The house smelled of booze, and the black man smelled of it more so. No wonder it was familiar.

"Mr. Nelson say why you want to see him, sir?"

"It's about his daughter," I said.

"Yessir."

He shuffled away, and this time he was gone awhile. I scratched the old hound behind his ear and he leaned his head a little harder against me. The other dogs sat, respectfully, nearby, in a semicircle that probably had some dog order to it. The old one was obviously in charge. I could see well enough now to see how gray the dog's muzzle was. And around his eyes, sort of like a raccoon. His front paws turned in slightly, the way they did on a bear, and he moved stiffly.

Around the entry hall there were gilt-framed paintings of racehorses, most, apparently, from the nineteenth century, when they were painted with long bodies and small heads. On the other hand, maybe in the nineteenth century they did have long bodies and small heads.

The dog nudged my knee with his head, and I reached down to pat him some more. The other dogs watched. Under the fresh booze smell was a more enduring smell of dog. I liked both smells, though there were people who liked neither.

There was no sound in the house, not even the sounds that houses make: air-conditioning, or furnace, or the stairwell creaking, or the refrigerator cycling on; nothing but a silence that seemed to have been thickening since Appomattox.

"You guys have much fun?" I said. The dogs made no reply. One of them, I didn't see which one, thumped his tail once when I spoke.

The black man scuffed quietly back into the huge entry.

"Mr. Nelson say to come this way, sir."

We went to the end of the entry hall and under the stairs and through a door into a bright gallery along the back of the house that was full of sunlight through the long bank of French windows. At the end of the gallery we turned right into a huge octagonal conservatory with a glass roof shaped like a minaret. Sitting in a wicker chaise on a dark green rug in the middle of the bluestone floor, with the sun streaming in on him, was an old man in a white suit who looked like Mark Twain gone to hell. He had long white hair and a big white moustache. He probably weighed three hundred pounds, most of it in his belly. There was some in his jowls, and plenty in the folds of his neck that spilled out over his wilted collar. But there were hints, still, as he sat there, of strength that had once existed. And in the red sagging face, the vestiges of the same profile his daughter showed in her portrait.

On the wicker table beside him was a blue pattern china bowl of melting ice, a bottle of Jack Daniel's, partly gone, and a pitcher of water. He had a thick lowball glass in his hand. A blackthorn walking stick leaned on the arm of the chaise. Across the room was a wicker chair. Next to it a wicker side table held a big color television set. On the screen stock cars, gaudily painted, buzzed endlessly around a track. There was no other furniture. The room had the feel of an empty gym.

There were three or four more dogs in here, all hunters, long-eared, black-and-white, or blueticked, looking somewhat like Pearl the wonder dog. Except their tails were long. And the color. And they were bigger. And calmer. One of them thumped a tail on the floor when she saw me. The others watched me but did nothing. Sprawled on the floor, they moved only their eyes to look at me. Air-conditioning buzzed unseen somewhere above us. Despite the sunlight the room was cold.

The old black man gestured me to the other seat with one gnarled, still graceful hand. I sat. Jumper Jack stared at the car race. Sweat beaded on his forehead.

"Care for some whiskey and branch water, sir?" the black man said.

I thought about it. It might keep my teeth from chattering. On the other hand, it was ten-thirty in the morning. I shook my head. The black man nodded and shuffled a little ways off, near the door, and stood. Nelson continued to gaze at the stock car race.

I waited.

Nobody did anything. It was as if immobility were the natural order of things here, and movement was aberrant.

Jumper Jack drank some more whiskey.

The race announcer was frantic with excitement as the cars went round and round. The excitement seemed contrived in this room where time was suspended and movement was an oddity. The huge television set itself was inappropriate, a blatting, contemporary intrusion into this motionless antebellum room full of dogs, and old men, and me.

I sat. The black man stood. The dogs sprawled. And Jumper Jack stared at the race and drank whiskey. I waited. I had nowhere to go.

Finally someone won the car race. Jumper Jack picked up the remote from the table beside him and pressed the mute button. The television went silent. He turned and looked at me, and when he spoke his clotted voice rumbled up out of his belly like the effortful grumble of a whale.

"Got no daughter," he said.

"None?"

"No daughter," he said and finished his whiskey and fumbled at the fixings to make another one. The old black man was there. He made the drink with no wasted movement and handed it to Nelson and returned to his motionless post near the door.

"You know a woman named Olivia Nelson?"

He shook his head, heavily, as if there were hornets around it.

"No," he said.

"Did you ever?" I said.

"No more."

"But you did once."

He looked at me for the first time, raising his head slowly from his chest and staring at me with his rheumy, unfocused gaze.

"Yes."

I waited again. Nelson drank. One of the dogs got up suddenly and walked over and put his head on Nelson's lap. Nelson automatically patted the dog's head with a thick, clumsy hand. There were liver spots on his hands and the fingernails were ragged, as if he chewed them.

"Married a African nigger," he said. "I . . ." He seemed overcome, as much by forgetfulness as by memory. He lost track of what he'd begun to say, and dropped his head and buried his nose in the lowball glass and drank.

"And?" I said.

He looked up as if he were surprised to see me there.

"And?"

"And what happened after she married?" I said.

Again his head dropped.

"Jefferson tell you," he rumbled.

I looked at the black man. He nodded.

"Jefferson," Nelson said, "you tell."

He drank again and turned the sound back on, and faced back into the car races, as if I'd vanished. His chin sank to his chest. Jefferson came over and took the whiskey glass from his hand and put it on the table. From an inside pocket he produced a big red bandanna and wiped Nelson's forehead with it. Nelson started to snore. The dog withdrew his head from Nelson's lap and went back and lay down with a sigh in the bright sun splash on the bluestone floor.

"Mr. Nelson will sleep now, sir," Jefferson said. "You and I can talk in the kitchen."

I followed Jefferson out of the cold room where Nelson lay sweating in his sleep, with his dogs, in front of the aimless car race. Despite what Ferguson said, Jumper Jack no longer seemed a danger to virgins.

# Chapter 20

It was a servant's kitchen, below stairs, with a yellowed linoleum floor and a big gas stove on legs, and a soapstone sink. The room was dim, and bore the lingering scent of kerosene, though I couldn't find any source for it. A mild patina of dust covered every surface. The old Bluetick hound I'd met in the front hall followed us down to the kitchen and settled heavily onto the floor near the stove. Jefferson indicated a white metal table with folding extenders on either end, and we sat on opposite sides of it.

"Mr. Nelson has got old," Jefferson said.

"Lot of that going around," I said.

Jefferson smiled.

"Yessir," he said, "there is."

He gazed absently at the old hound lying by the stove.

"He something to see, when he younger," Jefferson said. "Ride a horse. Shoot. Handle dogs. Not afraid of any man. People step aside when he come."

Jefferson smiled softly.

"He like the ladies all right," he said.

I waited. It was a skill I was perfecting down here.

"Always took care of family," Jefferson said.

The old refrigerator in the far corner lumbered noisily into life. Nobody paid it any mind.

"Been with him all my life," Jefferson said. "He always took care of me too."

"Now you take care of him."

"All there is," Jefferson said. "Mrs. Nelson gone. Miss Olivia gone."

"Tell me about Olivia," I said.

His voice was barely more than a whisper. His eyes were remote, his hands inert on the table looked sadly frail.

"She broke his heart," he said.

"Married a black man?"

Jefferson nodded.

"She shouldn't have done that," he said. "Broke his heart."

"Doesn't break everyone's heart," I said.

"He couldn't change, he too old, he too . . ." Jefferson thought a minute. "He too much Mr. Jack. Wasn't even one of our Nigras. Peace Corps. She marry an African Nigra."

"Did you ever meet him?" I said.

"No, sir. They never come here. Mr. Jack say he never want to see her again. Say she dead, so far as he concerned."

"And now she is," I said.

Jefferson raised his head and stared at me.

"No, sir," he said.

"Yeah. I'm sorry, Jefferson. That's why I'm looking into her past. I'll let you decide how to tell him, or if."

"When she die, sir?"

I counted in my head for a moment.

"Ten weeks ago," I said. "In Boston."

Jefferson stared at me.

"No, sir," he said.

"Sorry," I said.

"I always kept in touch with her," Jefferson said. "Mr. Jack pretends she's dead, but she writes me letter and I write her. In Nairobi—that's in Africa where she live."

I nodded. The Bluetick hound stretched, all four legs taut for a long moment on the floor, and then lapped his muzzle once and relaxed back into sleep.

"I got a letter from her yesterday," Jefferson said.

His voice was still as ashes.

"She wrote it last week," he said. "She ain't dead, Mr. Spenser."

Nothing moved. Anywhere. It was so still I could hear the old dog breathing gently as he slept.

"You have that letter?" I said.

"Yessir."

Jefferson got up and went into a pantry and came back in a moment with a letter. It was written on that thin blue airmail stationery that folds into its own envelope and has to be slit the right way or you can't keep track of the pages.

"May I read it?" I said.

"Yessir."

The letter, addressed to *Jefferson, Dear,* was a compendium of recent activities at the medical clinic, which I gathered she and her husband operated in a Nairobi slum. AIDS was the leading killer of both men and women, she said. There were several references to Jefferson's last letter. It was dated five days previous, and signed *Love as always, Livvie.* There was no reason to doubt it.

"You'd recognize her handwriting," I said.

"Yessir. When she a little girl I help her with her homework. When she go away to college she write me every week. She been writing me every week ever since. More than twenty-five years. I know her handwriting, sir."

I nodded.

"I'm glad it wasn't her, Jefferson."

"Yessir."

"But it was somebody."

"Yessir."

I had a copy of the portrait I'd found in the victim's living room. I took it out of my inside pocket and showed it to Jefferson.

"Sure look like Miss Livvie," Jefferson said.

"This woman said she was Olivia Nelson. She was married to a prominent Boston white man, lived on Beacon Hill, and had two college-age children."

"Can't be Miss Livvie," Jefferson said. His voice was matter-of-fact, the way you'd remark that the world was round.

"Do you know a woman named Cheryl Anne Rankin?" I said.

"No, sir," Jefferson said.

He was lying. He said it too quickly and with too much resolve.

"Her picture's on the wall at the track kitchen," I said. "Woman there says she's her daughter."

"Don't know nothing about that, sir."

I nodded again.

"Be all right with you, sir, you don't tell Mr. Jack I writing to Miss Livvie?"

"No need to, Jefferson," I said. "But I bet he knows anyway."

"Sure he do, sir. But he wouldn't want me to know he knows."

"You sure you don't know anything about Cheryl Anne Rankin?"

"Don't know nothing about that, sir. Nothing at all."

Jefferson stood and I stood, and we went upstairs to the front door. I put out my hand. Jefferson took it. His hand was slender and strong and dry as dust.

"Nelson is lucky to know you, Jefferson," I said.

Jefferson smiled.

"Yessir," he said.

# Chapter 21

The phone in my room at the Alton Arms had a long cord on it. You could stroll around the room as you talked. I was looking out my window while I told Quirk about Jefferson's story.

"You got an address for her in Nairobi?" Quirk said.

"Yeah, took it off the envelope," I said and gave it to him.

"We'll give her a call," Quirk said. "If she's actually there, we'll maybe get somebody from the American Embassy to go over and interview her."

"Farrell going to come down here?" I said.

"Somebody will," Quirk said. "Say the stuff about Cheryl Anne Rankin again."

"All I got is her picture in the track kitchen. Looks just like Olivia Nelson did in her high school graduation picture. Looks like she'd grow into that portrait in the living room in twenty-five years."

"You think they're old pictures?"

"Yeah. And the woman who says she's Cheryl Anne's mother is probably around seventy."

It was bright and hot outside the hotel window. The trees across the street seemed to hang lower than usual, and their leaves were motionless. The blue Buick pulled up as I was looking at the trees, and swung in and parked in front of the hotel. A cruiser pulled up behind it and then another one. The shield on the side said *Alton County Sheriff*. Uniformed deputies began to unload. They spread out around the hotel, trying to be inconspicuous. A couple headed around back in case I made a dash through the kitchen.

"You thinking she could be the victim?" Quirk said.

"She looks too much like the victim to ignore," I said. "But right now I got another problem."

"Yeah?"

"I think I'm going to get busted by the Alton County Sheriff's Department," I said, and described the arrivals. There was a knock on the door.

"Here they are," I said. "Tell whoever comes down to see if I'm in jail."

"I'll come down," Quirk said.

I hung up and took my gun out of my holster and laid it down on the bedside table with the muzzle facing away from the door. Then I opened the door and smiled at the cop who had her hair done in Batesburg.

# Chapter 22

They didn't book me. They just took my belongings, including my gun, and stuck me in a cell by myself, in the Alton County Courthouse. Nobody said anything much. But the deputies hovered close and looked as alert as they were able to, until I was locked up. Then everybody departed and I was alone in a cell about 8 by 10 feet in the cellar of the courthouse. There were no windows and only a single light in the ceiling of my cell, and one in the corridor outside. There was a toilet in the corner of the room, and a concrete bunk built out from the wall. On the bunk was a thin, bare mattress, a pillow, and a wool blanket that looked like it might once have been worn by a plow mule.

I lay on the bunk and propped the pillow under my head and looked at the ceiling for a while. There was no noise in the cell block. Either Alton County was a low-crime zone or the other prisoners were somewhere else. The arrest wasn't legal. I hadn't been charged with anything, I hadn't appeared before any magistrate, I'd not been given access to counsel. I hadn't been read my rights, probably because at the moment I didn't have any. They probably hoped that when they came, I'd resist, which would give them a charge. But I didn't. I went without a word. There was no point in asking. They wouldn't tell me. It was quite possible they didn't know. But I'd done something to motivate somebody to something, and maybe it was something stupid.

I ran over my all-time, all-seen team again: Koufax, Campanella, Musial, Robinson, Smith, Schmidt, Williams, DiMaggio, Mays. No one was out of position except Mays, and certainly Willie could play right field. And I'd have Red Barber broadcast the game. And Red Smith write about it.

The lights went out silently. The darkness was absolute. No trickle of light from anywhere until, eventually, as my eyes adjusted, I could see the hint of light from under the door to the cell block at the end of the corridor.

My basketball team was easy for the first four: Bird, Russell, Magic Johnson, and Jordan. But who'd be the other forward? Should I choose Wilt and play Russell at power forward? It seemed a cop-out. Maybe Bob Pettit. Or DeBusschere, or make Bird the power forward and play Elgin Baylor. How about Julius?

I wondered if anyone was going to give me supper, and decided that they weren't. They wanted me to be isolated and hungry and in the dark down here while my resolve atrophied. I groped to the sink next to the toilet and ran the water. There was only a cold-water faucet. I drank some from my cupped hand and began to walk back and forth in the cell, feeling for the bars and wall at first, and then, coming to know the size, keeping a hand slightly out, but walking and stopping and turning at the right time by the floor plan in my head.

I remembered the first woman I'd slept with. Her name was Lily, and I remembered her naked body in detail as explicit as if I had seen her yesterday. That was sort of interesting, so I began to remember the other women I'd slept with and found I could remember all of them exactly: how they looked, how they acted, what they said, what they liked, what they wore, and how they undressed. Some had liked me a lot, some were lost in a private fantasy and I was a vehicle for its expression, some had just liked lovemaking, all of them had been fun.

I thought about Susan. She was the most fun.

I thought about football, and whether Joe Montana would finally replace Unitas. Jim Brown was eternal, and certainly Jim Parker. Sarah could sing, and Mel Torme, and Dave McKenna was the piano player, and The

Four Seasons, in New York, for that one meal, and Sokol Blosser Pinot Noir, and Catamount beer, and German Shorthaired Pointers, and Ali maybe was the best heavyweight, though Ray Robinson was, of course, the best ever, any weight, and Krug champagne, and Faulkner, and Vermeer, and Stan Kenton and Mike Royko, and fitful sleep.

# Chapter 23

I heard them coming and was sitting on the bunk when the lights went on and six of them came into my cell. Four of them were big Alton County Deputies with nightsticks, two of them were in suits. My friend with the hairdo and the almond-shaped eyes was not with them. All six were men.

A guy in a three-piece, blue pinstripe suit said, "On your feet, asshole."

Bust in suddenly, after hours of isolation, while I'm still asleep, scare me witless, and ask me questions. It was not a brand-new approach. I sat on the edge of my bunk with my hands relaxed in my lap and looked at him. His vest gapped at the waist, leaving two inches of badly tucked-in shirt showing over the belt line.

"On your fucking feet," he said.

"You want to wear a three-piece suit," I said, "you gotta get good tailoring. Otherwise the vest gaps."

Vest jerked his head and two deputies yanked me to my feet. I grinned at him.

"Or not," I said.

"Sit down," Vest said and shoved me with both hands. I didn't sit. I rocked back a little and kept my feet. Vest jerked his head and the same two deputies who yanked me up put a hand on each shoulder and pushed me down. I didn't go. Vest balled a fist and drove it into my stomach. He was slow. I had time to tighten my stomach and keep it from doing full damage. But it staggered me enough so that the deputies could push me down. I sat.

"Who's your trainer?" I said. "Mary Baker Eddy?"

He didn't know who Mary Baker Eddy was, but he tried not to let it show. His partner, wearing a seersucker suit and a straw snap brim with a colorful band, stood against the far wall with his arms crossed. Neither one showed a badge.

"We don't care," the partner said, "if you're a smart ass, or not. We'll take that out of you. Sooner or later, don't matter none to us. But we'll take it out of you, and you know that we can." He had a soft, almost un-inflected voice, with no sign of a regional accent.

He was right. They could, and I knew it. Anybody can be softened up; it's all a matter of time and technique, and if you have the time, the technique will eventually surface. Didn't mean it had to be soon, though.

"We'd like to know," the partner said, "what it is you're doing around here, and what you've found out about Olivia Nelson."

"You guys got any badges or anything?" I said.

In a perfectly flat and humorless voice, the partner said, "Badges, we need no stinking badges. What have you found out about Olivia Nelson?"

"She went to Carolina Academy. She liked horses," I said.

There were no other sounds here under the courthouse in the window-less room, only the sounds of our voices and the breathing of the deputies. The overhead light, unshaded and harsh, glared down at us.

"And what else?" the partner said.

He remained perfectly motionless against the wall, in a pose he'd prob-ably practiced a thousand times. Arms folded, hat tilted over his eyes, so that the overhead light put his face in shadow.

"That's all," I said.

The room was silent.

The partner eased himself languidly off the wall and slouched over to-ward me. Vest gave way and moved back and replaced him on the wall. The chorus line of deputies stood motionless, while the *pas de deux* took place. The partner put a hand out toward the nearest deputy and the deputy slapped a nightstick in his hand like a scrub nurse.

"You are in so deep over your head, asshole," the partner said, "you're about to drown."

He was a tall man with high, square shoulders and a wide, slack mouth.

"You don't seem like you'd be an Alton County Deputy Sheriff," I said.

The partner laughed.

"No shit," he said. And whacked me on the side of the left knee with the nightstick. The pain ran up and down the length of my leg.

"I'll help you think," he said. "Maybe you heard something, ah, government-related."

"Like what?" I said and he whacked my knee again and I felt the inside of my head get red, and, from a seated position, I punched him in the groin, which was about eye-level for me. He gasped and doubled over and staggered back. The nightstick clattered on the concrete floor. The deputies grabbed me. Vest lurched off the wall in a shooter's crouch with a small handgun. The partner stayed doubled over. I knew what he was doing; he was fighting off the nausea that came in waves.

"Cuff him," Vest said. His voice was raspy. "Cuff him to the bars."

The deputies hesitated. Vest stowed his gun, bent over and picked up the nightstick his partner had dropped.

"This ain't our deal," one of the deputies said. He was a beefy guy with sandy hair and freckled arms and a big, untrimmed moustache.

"Do what I tell you," Vest said. "This is a fucking federal matter."

"You say so," the deputy said. "But I ain't seen shit to prove it."

"You never hung nobody on a cell door before?" Vest said.

"Sure, but Sheriff don't much like us rousting white people 'less we have to."

"Fuck the Sheriff," Vest said.

"Sheriff don't too much like people saying fuck him, either."

"Okay," Vest said. "Okay. But this is important. National security. We have to find out what he knows. And we have to find out fast."

The partner had made it to the wall, and was leaning his forehead against it, trying to breathe deeply.

"You got the Sheriff's call, didn't you?" he said, wedging the words in between deep inhales. "It's on him, and us."

The deputy nodded, and looked at the other deputies, and shrugged. He put his nightstick under his left arm and took a pair of cuffs off the back of his belt.

"We got to do it," he said to me. "Hard or easy, up to you."

I said, "Hard, I think."

The deputy shrugged again, took the nightstick out from under his arm, and Martin Quirk walked into the cell. Everybody stopped in mid-motion and stared at him. He was as immaculate as always. Blue blazer, white Oxford button-down, maroon-and-navy striped tie, maroon show hankie, and gray covert slacks. He had his badge in his left hand. And he held it out so people could see it.

The partner had gotten himself upright, still breathing heavily, and turned so he was leaning his back on the wall.

"Who the fuck are you?" he said.

"Detective Lieutenant Martin Quirk, Commander, Homicide Division, Boston, Massachusetts, Police Department."

"We're in the middle of an investigation, Lieutenant," the partner said. "And, you know, this isn't Boston."

He had his breathing under control again, but he still leaned on the wall. And when he moved he did so stiffly. Quirk looked at him. There was something in Quirk's eyes. The way there was something in Hawk's. It wasn't just dangerous. I'd seen that look in a lot of eyes. It was more than that. It was a contemptuous certainty that if there was any reason to he'd kill you, and you had no part in the decision. Under all the tight control and the neat tailoring, and the pictures of his family on his desk, Quirk had a craziness in him that was terrifying when it peeked out. Here in the cellar of the Alton County Courthouse it not only peeked, it peered out, and steadily.

"I don't care what you shit kickers are doing," Quirk said, and what you saw in his look you could hear in his voice. "I want this guy, and I've come to get him."

Vest, who hadn't caught the look, and was too stupid to hear the sound in Quirk's voice, spoke while still looking at me.

"Hey, Lieutenant," he said. "Tough shit, huh? He's our prisoner and we are in the middle of interrogation. Whyn't you wait outside? Huh? Or maybe wait in Bahston."

Quirk stepped in front of Vest and put his face about an inch away from Vest's.

"You want to fuck around with me, dick breath?" Quirk said softly.

Vest stepped back as if something had pushed him. Quirk glanced around the cell.

"Before I came down here to this hog wallow, I talked with the U.S. Attorney in Boston, who put me in touch with the U.S. Attorney in Columbia. They both know I'm here."

He looked at me, and jerked his head.

"Let's go," he said.

"Certainly," I said.

And we walked unhurriedly out of the cell and down the corridor under the ugly ceiling lights and up some stairs and into the Alton County Sheriff's substation. Quirk demanded, and got, my personal stuff, including my gun, and we walked unhurriedly out onto the courthouse steps, where the sun was shining through the arching trees and the patterns of the heavy leaves were myriad and restless on the dusty street.

# Chapter 24

Quirk had parked his car in the fenced-in county lot back of the courthouse. We got in, and he pulled the car out the only exit, and parked on a hydrant across the street. He let the engine idle.

"How'd you get in there?" I said.

"Bullied the desk clerk," Quirk said.

"You're a scary bastard," I said.

"Lucky for you," Quirk said.

We were quiet.

"This a rental?" I said.

Quirk shook his head. "Federal guys in Columbia lent it to me."

"So why are we sitting here in it?"

"I thought we ought to see if we could get a read on the two suits in there," Quirk said. "I'd like to know who sent them."

From where we parked, we could see the front door of the courthouse and the parking lot entrance on the side street.

"We going to follow them?"

"Yeah."

"And they spot us?"

"They won't spot us," Quirk said. "I'm a professional policeman."

"Sure," I said.

Quirk grinned.

"And if they do," he said, "fuck 'em."

Some cars came and went from the parking lot, but none of them contained Vest or the Partner. People went in and out of the courthouse, but they weren't ours.

"Why didn't you send Farrell?" I said.

"He's got some time off," Quirk said. "Trouble at home."

"What kind of trouble?"

"Guy he lives with has AIDS," Quirk said.

"Jesus," I said.

Quirk nodded, looking at the courthouse.

"How about him?" I said.

"He's okay," Quirk said.

"So you came because Farrell couldn't?"

"Right, and Belson's tracking down the other Olivia Nelson, or the real Olivia Nelson, or whoever the fuck that is in Nairobi, and the case is getting to be sort of a heavy issue . . . and I figure I better come down and save your ass, so Susan wouldn't be mad."

"Thanks," I said.

"You're welcome," Quirk said. "I called Hawk and he said he'd keep track of Susan until this thing shook down a little."

"You think someone might run at her to get to me?"

Quirk shrugged.

"Being careful does no harm," he said.

The two suits walked down the steps of the courthouse, came down the side street and into the parking lot. In a minute they exited the lot in a green Dodge, and passed us, and headed out Main Street. Quirk let his car into gear and followed them easily, letting several cars in between. Quirk was too far back to stay with them if the suits were trying to shake a tail. But they weren't. They had no reason to think they'd be followed. Quirk and I should be lickety-split for home. In ten minutes, they pulled into the parking lot of a Holiday Inn, out near the little airport, where Cessnas and Piper Cubs came and went several times a day, carrying Alton's heavy hitters to and from important events. Quirk and I dawdled in the parking lot of the Piggly Wiggly across the street, while the suits got out and went into the motel. Then we pulled over to the motel and parked. Quirk adjusted his gun onto the front of his belt so that it showed as he let his coat fall open. Then we went into the lobby and walked briskly to the desk clerk. Quirk flashed his badge, and put it away. It could have said *Baker Street Irregulars* on it, for all the clerk had a chance to read it.

"Lieutenant Quirk," he snapped, "Homicide. I need the room number of the two men who just came in here."

The desk clerk was a middle-aged woman with a lot of very blonde hair. She looked blank.

"Come on, Sis," Quirk said, "this is police business, I don't have a lot of time."

"The two gentlemen who just passed through here?"

Quirk looked at me.

"Is she a smart one?" he said. "Is this one a quick learner?"

He looked back at her.

"That's it, Sis. The two guys just passed through here. Room number and make it pretty quick."

He drummed on the counter softly with his fingertips.

"Yes, sir," the clerk said. "That would be Mr. O'Dell and Mr. Grimes. Room 211."

"Okay, we're going up." Quirk said. "If you do anything at all, except mind your own business, I'll close this dump down so tight it'll squeeze your fanny."

"Yes, sir," the clerk said. "Stairs at the end of the corridor, sir. Second floor."

"No shit," Quirk said, and turned and hustled down the corridor toward the stairs with me behind him.

"So tight," I said, "it'll squeeze your fanny?"

We were going up the stairs.

"Cops are supposed to talk like that," Quirk said.

"I liked 'The Killers' bit from Hemingway."

" 'Is she a smart one?' Yeah, I use that a lot."

We were on the second floor and stopped in front of room 211. Quirk put his ear to the door. He nodded to himself. Then he knocked on the door. There was a moment of silence, then the door half opened and Vest looked out. Quirk hit the door with his shoulder and Vest stumbled back. The door banged open wide.

The Partner was sitting on one of the twin beds with his back to the door, talking on the phone. He half turned as we came in and I kicked the door shut behind us.

He said, "What the fuck?"

Quirk walked over and broke the phone connection.

"Exactly," Quirk said.

A small holstered gun lay on top of the television set. Vest made a grab at it and yanked it from the holster. Quirk barely glanced at him while he chopped the gun out of Vest's hand and kicked it under the bed. Vest threw a punch at Quirk's head. Quirk slapped it aside and stepped away. He looked at me.

"You want this?" he said. "Even up the business in the jail?"

"Thank you very much," I said, and Quirk stepped behind me.

"All yours," he said, and I snapped a straight left out onto Vest's nose and drew blood. He put both hands to his face and took them away and stared for a moment at the blood on them. Noses bleed a lot. His partner moved toward me, in a low crouch, swaying gently, his hands up and close together. I turned slightly and drove my right foot in against his kneecap. His leg went out from under him and he fell over. Vest lunged toward the door and as he went past me, I hit him on the back of the head with my clubbed left forearm and he sprawled forward and banged his head on the door and slid to the ground. His partner was on his hands and knees now, scrambling toward the bed. I caught him and dragged him to his feet and turned my hip as he tried to knee me in the groin and took it on my thigh. I banged his nose with my forehead, and pushed him away and hit him left cross straight right, and he fell over on the bed and stayed there holding his nose, which had started to bleed as well. Vest was not unconscious on the floor, but he stayed there on his stomach with his face cradled in his arms.

"You guys are in trouble," Quirk said, "at several levels."

I glanced around the room. There was a wallet and a set of car keys on the night table between the twin beds.

"First of all, when you had enough help you were banging on a guy, with a billy."

I walked over to the night table and picked up the wallet. Nobody moved.

"Now you are alone, without backup, in a hotel room with the same guy, and look what happens."

I opened the wallet and looked at the driver's license. It was a Washington, D.C., license, issued to Reilly O'Dell. The Partner's picture was there, unsmiling. And a Georgetown address.

"That's one level," Quirk said. He ticked it off on his thumb. His voice was quiet, without anger, a little pedagogical, as if he were discussing evidence evaluation at the police academy, but tinged with sadness at the plight these men were in.

"Then there's the fact that this asshole"—he nodded at Vest on the floor—"told me to butt out and go back to Boston, and he made fun of my accent, by pronouncing it Bahston."

Quirk ticked that one off on his forefinger.

"I am, of course, en-fucking-raged," Quirk said. "Which is not good either, because I also can whup you to a frazzle."

Quirk smiled briefly and without humor at both of them, and held up a third finger. In Reilly O'Dell's wallet I found some business cards, with his name on them, and the name of his company, Stealth Security Consultants. I passed the license and one of the business cards to Quirk. Still holding his third finger up, in mid-count, he read them. And put them in his pocket.

"Third," he said. "You guys were participating in the illegal arrest and interrogation of a man whose constitutional rights you have violated worse than Sherman violated Atlanta. Fortunately, I happened by, and seeing an illegal injustice in progress, made a citizen's intervention. And now"—Quirk held up a fourth finger—"I discover that Mr. O'Dell, here, appears not even to be a police officer."

I bent over Vest and took the wallet from Vest's left hip pocket. I opened it and learned that his name was Edgar Grimes and that he too lived in Washington. And he too worked for Stealth Security Consultants. I gave his driver's license and one of his business cards to Quirk.

"Dandy," Quirk said. "Now, what the fuck is going on?"

Grimes had turned over on his back and sat on the floor, his back against the wall. His head was in his hands and he was rubbing his temples. The blood continued to run between his fingers and soak his shirt. O'Dell sat up stiffly on his bed not looking at anything. There was very little color in his face, and I could see his Adam's apple move as he swallowed. His nose seeped only a trickle of blood.

I went to the bathroom, put cold water on a facecloth, wrung it out, and handed it to Grimes on the floor. He held it against his nose.

"You can't stonewall," Quirk said. "You're down here representing somebody with enough clout to get the cooperation of the local Sheriff. Since you're from DeeCee, it's probably somebody in government. You've participated in a kidnapping. You've been caught by a policeman. We get the U.S. Attorney down here from Columbia with one phone call. We get the press down here with one other phone call. You people have fucked the duck, and your only chance to step out of it is to talk to me, frankly"—Quirk flashed the humorless smile again—"and openly."

I could hear both breathing, and then O'Dell sighed.

"You got a good argument," he said.

We waited.

The late morning sun beamed in through the east-facing bedroom window, and highlighted the dust motes, which drifted in and out of sight as they passed though the sunlight. The motel room was generic. Combination desk, dresser with a television set. A straight chair, two twin beds separated by a table. A phone on the table, a lamp on the wall above it. The walls were beige, the rug was tan, there was an inexpensively framed print on the wall of some Anjou pears in a rose medallion bowl. The closet was behind a louvered door, the bath was past it. There was a brown Naugahyde armchair by the window. On top of the television set was a cardboard stand-up, which described the fun to be had in their lounge.

Grimes continued to hold the cloth against his nose. O'Dell sat up straight. His face was pale and scared; his wide, loose mouth seemed hard to manage.

"You used to work for the government," Quirk said. "Twenty years in, you took your pension and your contacts and set up in business for yourself."

"Yes," O'Dell said.

"And when you were a Fed," Quirk said, "you mostly spent your time subpoenaing records."

O'Dell started to protest and stopped and shrugged his high shoulders and nodded.

"You're in with tough guys, now," Quirk said.

O'Dell nodded. His hands were folded down at his paralleled thumbs, and he studied them, as if to make sure they were perfectly aligned.

"Your original question," O'Dell said.

Quirk nodded. Grimes's nose appeared to have stopped bleeding. But he continued to sit on the floor with his head in his hands.

"The thing is, we don't know what the fuck is going on."

"Tell me what you can," Quirk said. His voice was quiet.

Grimes's pale blond hair was thinning on top. With his head down, it showed the care with which he had combed his hair to hide that fact. The interchange with me had badly disarranged it, and, stiff with hair spray, the hair stood at random angles.

"We were told to come down here and try to get what he had found out about Olivia Nelson," O'Dell said.

Quirk smiled.

He said, "Un huh?"

"That's why we were kinda rough in the cell there," O'Dell said. "We didn't really know what to ask."

Quirk smiled understandingly.

"And you had four guys to help you," Quirk said.

O'Dell shrugged.

"Who asked you to find this out?" Quirk said.

"Mal Chapin."

"Short for Malcolm?" Quirk said.

"I guess."

"And who is Mal Chapin?" Quirk said.

O'Dell looked surprised. In his circles, Mal Chapin was probably an important name.

"Senator Stratton's office."

"He hired you?"

"Well, yeah. We're, like, ah, friends of the office, you know?"

"And the office steers business your way," Quirk said.

"Sure. That's how DeeCee works."

"Who arranged the deal with the Alton County Sheriff?"

"I don't know. I assume it was Mal. He's got a lot of clout with Party people around the country."

"And when you found out what Spenser knew," Quirk said, "what then?"

"We see if we can scare him off," O'Dell said.

"That'll be the day," I said.

I sounded exactly like John Wayne. No one seemed to notice. Quirk looked at O'Dell for a long, silent moment. Then he took one of the business cards out of his pocket and went to the phone. He read the dialing instructions, and dialed.

"This is Lieutenant Martin Quirk," he said. "Is Reilly O'Dell there? . . . How about Edgar Grimes? . . . I'm the Homicide Commander, Boston Police Department. Please describe O'Dell for me."

He waited. Then he nodded.

"How about Grimes?" he said.

He waited some more.

Then he said, "No, Miss, that's fine. Just routine police business. What is your name, Miss? Thank you. No, they are not involved in a homicide."

He hung up.

"Your secretary is worried about you," he said.

Neither of them said anything.

"What is your secretary's first name?" Quirk said to O'Dell.

"Molly," O'Dell said.

"What's her last name?" Quirk said to Grimes.

"Burgin," Grimes said. He continued to hold his head in his hands and stare at the floor between his feet.

Quirk looked at me.

"Got any questions?" he said.

I shook my head.

"Okay," Quirk said.

We went to the door. Quirk paused and turned back to O'Dell and Grimes. A bruise was beginning to form on Grimes's forearm where Quirk had hacked the gun free.

"Have a nice day," Quirk said.

And we turned and left the room. Nobody said good-bye.

# Chapter 25

When Susan and I made love at her house, we had to shut Pearl the wonder dog out of the bedroom, because if we didn't, Pearl would attempt tirelessly to insinuate herself between us. Neither of us much wanted to leap up afterwards and let her in.

It was Sunday morning. We lay under one of Susan's linen sheets with Susan's head on my chest in the dead quiet house, listening to the sound of our breathing. I had my arm around her, and under the sheet she was resting the flat of her open hand lightly on my stomach.

"Hard abs," Susan said, "for a man of your years."

"Only one of many virtues," I said.

There was a big old windup Seth Thomas clock on Susan's bureau. It ticked solidly in the quiet.

"One of us has to get up and let the baby in," Susan said.

"Yes."

The sun was shining off and on through the treetops outside Susan's bedroom window and the shadows it cast made small patterns on the far wall. They were inconstant patterns, disappearing when a cloud passed and reappearing with the sun.

"Hawk came by and took me to dinner while you were gone," Susan said.

"Un huh."

"Fact, he came by several times," Susan said.

"He likes you," I said.

"And I swear I saw him outside my office a couple of times when I would walk a patient to the door."

"Okay, Quirk asked him to keep an eye on you when I got busted in South Carolina. He knew something was up and he didn't know what. Still doesn't."

"And Martin thought I'd be in danger?"

"He didn't know. He was being careful."

"So Hawk was there every day?"

"Or somebody, during the night too."

"Somebody?"

"Maybe Vinnie Morris, maybe Henry, maybe somebody I don't know."

"Maybe someone should have told me."

"Someone should have, but I'm the only one who knows how tough you are. They didn't want to scare you."

"And you think it's all right now?"

"Yeah. With Quirk involved, and the Federal Attorneys in Boston and Columbia. The cat's out of the bag, whatever cat it is. No point in trying to chase me away."

"So I don't need a guard?"

"No."

"Wasn't Vinnie Morris with Joe Broz?" Susan said.

"Yeah, but he quit him a while back, after Pearl and I were in the woods."

Susan nodded. We were quiet for another while. Susan moved the flat of her hand in small circles on my stomach.

"One of us has to get up and let the baby in," Susan said.

"Yes."

The mutable patterns on the far wall disappeared again, and I could hear a rhythmic spatter of rain against the window glass.

Susan said, "I'd do it, but I'm stark naked."

"I am too," I said.

"No, you're just naked," Susan said. "Men are used to walking around naked."

"Do you think stark naked is nakeder than naked?" I said.

"Absolutely," Susan said.

She tossed the sheet off of her.

"See?" she said.

I gazed at her stark nakedness for a while.

"Of course," I said and got up and opened the bedroom door.

Pearl rose in one movement from the rug outside the door and was on the bed in my place, with her head on my pillow, by the time I had closed the door and gotten back to the bed. I nudged her over a little with my hip and got in and wrestled my share of the sheet over me, and the three of us lay there with Pearl between us, on her stomach, her head on the pillow, her tail thumping, attempting to look at both of us simultaneously.

"Postcoital languor," I said.

"First," Susan said, "you tell me about South Carolina, and then we'll go out and have a nice brunch."

So I told her.

"And the woman in Nairobi really is Olivia Nelson?" Susan said.

"Yeah, guy from the American Embassy went over and talked with her. She's the real thing. Fingerprints all the way back to her time in the Peace Corps, passport, marriage certificate, all of that."

"Does she have any idea who the woman was that was killed?"

"Says no."

Pearl squirmed around between us until she got herself head down under the covers, and curled into an irregular ball, taking up much more than a third of the bed.

"What are you going to do now?" Susan said.

She had her hand stretched out above the bulge Pearl made in the sheet, and she was holding my hand, similarly stretched. The rain spattered sporadically on the windowpane, but didn't settle into a nice, steady rhythm.

"Talk to Farrell, report to Tripp, see what Quirk finds out."

"He's still in South Carolina?"

"Yeah, and Belson's going to go down. They'll talk with Jumper Jack, and with Jefferson, and they'll try to get a handle on Cheryl Anne Rankin."

"I'm glad you came back."

"Quirk and Belson will get further, they're official," I said.

"There was a time," Susan said, "when you'd have felt obliged to stay there and have a stare-down with the Sheriff's Department."

"I'm too mature for that," I said.

"It's nice to see," Susan said.

"But I will go back if I need to."

"Of course," Susan said. "Too much growth too soon would not be healthy."

"It's not just to prove I'm tough. The case may require it. I can't do what I do if I can be chased out of a place by someone."

Susan said, "A man who knows about such things once told me, in effect, 'Anyone can be chased out of anyplace.' "

"Was this guy also a miracle worker in the sack?" I said.

"No," she said.

# Chapter 26

Farrell and I were in my office having some scotch from the office bottle. It was late afternoon, on Monday. Tripp was out of town. Senator Stratton's office had not returned my call.

"What do you know about Stratton?" I said. "Anything I don't?"

Farrell looked tired. He shook his head.

"Just what I read in the papers, and if you've ever been involved in something the papers wrote up, you know better than to trust them."

I nodded and dragged my phone closer and called Wayne Cosgrove at the *Globe*. He was in the office more now since they'd made him some sort of editor and he had a political column, with his picture at the top, that ran three days a week. When he answered, I punched up the speakerphone.

"You're on speakerphone, Wayne, and there's a cop with me named Lee Farrell but all of this is unofficial and won't go any further."

"You speaking for Farrell too?" Cosgrove said. He had a Southern accent you could cut with a cotton hoe, although he'd left Mississippi at least thirty years ago, to come to Harvard on scholarship. I always assumed he kept the accent on purpose.

I looked at Farrell. He nodded. His eyes were red and seemed heavy, and his movements were slow.

"Yeah," I said. "Farrell too."

"Okay, pal, what do you need?"

"Talk to me about Senator Bob Stratton," I said.

"Ahh, yes," Cosgrove said. "Bobby Stratton. First off he's a pretty good Senator. Good staff, good preparation, comes down pretty much on the right side of most issues—which is to say I agree with his politics. Got a lot of clout, especially inside the Beltway."

"How about second off?" I said.

"Aside from being a pretty good Senator, he's a fucking creep."

"I hate it when the press is evasive," I said.

"Yeah. He drinks too much. He'd fuck a snake if you'd hold it for him. I don't think he steals, and I'm not even sure he's mean. But he's got too much power, and he has no sense of, ah, of limitation. He can do whatever he wants because he wants to and it's okay to do because he does it. He's the kind of guy who gooses waitresses. You understand?"

"Money?" I said.

"Yeah, sure. They all got money. How they get elected."

"Married?"

"To the girl on the wedding cake, two perfect children, a cocker spaniel, you know?"

"And a womanizer."

"You bet," Cosgrove said. "Far as I know, it's trophy hunting. I don't think he actually likes women at all."

"You know of any connection between him and Olivia Nelson, the woman who got killed couple of months back in Louisburg Square?"

"Loudon Tripp's wife," Cosgrove said.

"Un huh."

"I don't know any connection with her, but she's female—and Bobby is Bobby. Her husband probably knows Stratton."

"Why?"

"Because he's got money and contributes it to politicians."

"Democratic politicians?" I said.

"Politics makes strange bedfellows," Cosgrove said.

"I'd heard that," I said.

"Trust me, I'm a columnist," he said. "Why are you interested in Stratton?"

"Some people working for him tried to chase me off the Olivia Nelson case."

"Probably fucking her, and afraid it'll get out."

"Doesn't sound like the Olivia Nelson I've been sold, but say it was, and he was," I said. "Is it that big a secret?"

"He's probably going to be in the presidential primaries," Cosgrove said. "Remember Gary Hart?"

"Ah ha," I said.

"Ah ha?"

"You can say *strange bedfellows,* I can say *ah ha.*"

"I thought the cops washed that case off," Cosgrove said. "Deranged slayer, random victim."

"You been punching the file up," I said, "while you're talking to me."

"Sure," Cosgrove said. "I haven't always been a fucking columnist. How come you're investigating?"

"Her husband wouldn't accept it. He hired me."

"You got a theory?"

"No."

"You make any progress?"

"No."

"Off the record?"

"No."

"So I tell you everything I know and you tell me shit," Cosgrove said.

"Yes."

We hung up.

Farrell and I looked at each other.

"You suppose she was sleeping with Stratton?" Farrell said.

I shrugged.

"I don't even know who she is," I said.

Farrell was silent. He nipped a little of the scotch. It was good scotch, Glenfiddich, single malt. We were drinking it in small measures from a couple of water glasses, which was all I had in the office. I was not fond of straight booze, but Glenfiddich was very tolerable.

"How is it at home?" I said.

"Home?"

"Quirk told me your lover is dying."

Farrell nodded.

"How soon?" I said.

"Sooner the better," Farrell said. "Final stages. Weighs about eighty pounds."

"He at home?"

Farrell shook his head.

"Hospice," he said.

His words were effortful. As if there weren't many left.

"How are you?" I said.

"I feel like shit," Farrell said.

I nodded. We both drank some scotch.

"You drinking much?" I said.

"Some."

"Any help?"

"Not much."

"Hard," I said.

Farrell looked up at me and his voice was flat.

"You got no fucking idea," he said.

"Probably not," I said.

"You got a girlfriend," he said. "Right?"

"Susan," I said.

"If she were dying people would feel bad for you."

"More than they would, probably, if she were a guy."

"You got that right," Farrell said.

"I know," I said. "Makes it harder. What's his name?"

"Brian. Why?"

"He ought to have a name," I said.

Farrell finished his scotch and leaned forward and took the bottle off the desk and poured another splash into the water glass.

"You can tell almost right away if people have a problem with it or not," he said. "You don't. You don't really care if I'm straight or gay, do you?"

"Got nothing to do with me," I said.

"Got nothing to do with lots of people, but they seem to think it does," Farrell said.

"Probably makes them feel important," I said. "You been tested?"

"Yeah. So far, I'm all right—we were pretty careful."

"Feel like a betrayal?" I said. "That you're not dying too?"

Farrell stared at the whiskey in the bottom of the glass. He swished it around a little, then took it all in a swallow.

"Yes," he said.

He poured some more scotch. I held out my glass and he poured a little in mine too. We sat quietly in the darkening room and sipped the whiskey.

"Can you work?" I said.

"Not much," he said.

"I don't blame you."

# Chapter 27

Hawk was skipping rope in the little boxing room that Henry Cimoli kept in the otherwise updated chrome and spandex palace that had begun some years back as the Harbor Health Club. It was a gesture to me and to Hawk, but mostly it was a gesture to the days when Henry had boxed people like Sandy Saddler and Willie Pep.

Now Henry had a Marketing Director, and a Fitness Director, and a Membership Coordinator, and an Accountant, and a Personal Manager, and the club looked sort of like Zsa Zsa Gabor's hair salon; but Henry still looked like a clenched fist, and he still kept the boxing room where only he and I and Hawk ever worked out.

"Every move a picture," I said.

Hawk did some variations, changed speeds a couple of times.

"Never seen an Irish guy could do this," he said.

"Racism," I said. "We never got the chance to dance for pennies."

Hawk grinned. He was working out in boxing shorts and high-top shoes. He was shirtless and his upper body and shaved head gleamed with sweat like polished onyx.

"Susan need watching anymore?"

"I don't think so," I said. "Who'd you use?"

"Me, mostly. Henry sat in once in a while, and Belson did one shift."

"Belson?"

Hawk nodded. From the rhythm of the rope, I knew that "Sweet Georgia Brown" was playing in the back of Hawk's head.

"She caught on," I said.

"Never thought she wasn't smart," Hawk said. "But I wasn't trying hard as I could."

"Know anything about the case?" I said.

"Nope, Quirk just called and said Susan needed minding."

I nodded and went to work on the heavy bag, circled it, keeping my head bobbing, punching in flurries—different combinations. It wasn't like the real thing. But it helped to groove the movements so that when you did the real thing, muscle memory took over. Hawk played various shuffle rhythms on the speed bag, and occasionally we would switch. Neither of us spoke, but when we switched, we did it in sync so that the patter of the speed bag never paused and the body bag combinations kept their pattern. We kept it up as long as we could and then sat in the steam room and took a shower and went to Henry's office where there was beer in a refrigerator.

Henry was stocking Catamount Gold these days and I had a cap off a bottle, and my feet up. Hawk sat beside me, and I talked a little about the Olivia Nelson case. Through Henry's window, the surface of the harbor was slick, and the waves had a dark, glossy look to them. The ferry plowed through the waves from Rowe's Wharf, heading for Logan Airport.

"You know anything about Robert Stratton, the Senator?" I said.

"Nope."

Hawk was wearing jeans and cowboy boots and a white silk shirt. He had the big .44 magnum that he used tucked under his left arm in what appeared to be a snakeskin shoulder holster.

"Know anything about a woman named Olivia Nelson?" I said.

"Nope."

"Me either," I said.

"I was you," Hawk said, "and I had to go back down there to South Carolina, I'd talk to some of our black brothers and sisters. They work in the houses of a lotta white folks, see things, hear things, 'cause the white folks think they don't count."

"If they'll talk to me," I said.

"Just tell them you a white liberal from Boston. They be grateful for the chance," Hawk said.

"And, also, I'm a great Michael Jackson fan," I said.

Hawk looked at me for a long time.

He said, "Best keep that to yourself."

Then we both sat quietly, and drank beer, and looked at the evening settle in over the water.

# Chapter 28

The call was from Senator Stratton himself. It was ten-twenty in the morning, and the fall sun was warm on my back as it shone down Berkeley Street and slanted in through the window behind my desk.

"Bob Stratton," he said when I answered. "I think I've got some explaining to do to you, and I'd like to do it over lunch today if you're free."

"Sure," I said.

"Excellent. How about Grill 23, twelve-thirty. I'll book a table."

"Sure," I said.

"Just the two of us," Stratton said. "You and me, straight up, check?"

"Sure," I said.

"I'll have my driver pick you up," Stratton said.

"My office is two blocks from the restaurant," I said.

"My driver will stop by for you," Stratton said.

I said, "Sure."

"Looking forward to it," Stratton said.

We hung up. I dialed Quirk and didn't get him. I dialed Belson.

"Quirk back yet?" I said.

"Nope."

"You talk to him?"

"Yeah. The old black guy, Jefferson, doesn't say anything he didn't say to you. The old man doesn't say anything at all. Quirk agrees with you that Jefferson's lying about Cheryl Anne Rankin, but he can't shake him. The old lady at the track kitchen seems not to work there anymore. Nobody knows where she is. Nobody ever heard of Cheryl Anne Rankin. If he can't find the old lady from the track kitchen today, he's coming home. Travel money gives Command Staff hemorrhoids."

"Thanks," I said and hung up and sat and thought. Stratton had called me himself. That meant a couple of things. One, he wanted to impress me. Two, he didn't want other people to know that he had called or that we were lunching. So what did that mean? Why had Cheryl Anne's mother disappeared? Why would Jefferson, who was so forthcoming about everything else, lie about knowing Cheryl Rankin? Since Jumper Jack seemed to be his life's purpose, Jefferson probably was lying for him. Which meant that Jumper had something to do with Cheryl Anne.

I finished thinking because Stratton's driver was knocking on my door. I didn't know anything I hadn't known before, but at least I didn't know less.

The driver was a polite guy with blow-dried hair, wearing a gray gabardine suit, and a pink silk tie.

"The Senator asked me to make sure you're not wearing a wire," he said. He seemed sorry about this, but duty-driven.

I stood and held my arms away from my sides. The driver went over me as if he'd done it before.

"May I look at the gun?" he said.

I held my jacket open so he could make sure it wasn't a recorder disguised as a 9mm Browning.

"Thanks," he said.

We went out to the Lincoln Town Car, which he had parked under a tow-zone sign. He held the back door open for me and I got in. Berkeley Street is one way the other way, so we had to go via Boylston, Arlington, Columbus, and back down Berkeley. I could have walked it in about a quarter of the time, but I wouldn't have been certified wire free.

Grill 23 is high-ceilinged and hard-floored. It is the noisiest restaurant in Boston, which is probably why Stratton chose it. It is hard to eavesdrop in Grill 23. The maitre d' managed to show me to Stratton's table without losing his poise. Stratton had a dark, half-drunk scotch and soda in front of him. He stood as I arrived, and put out a hand, made hard by a million handshakes. It was a politician's handshake, the kind where he grabs your hand with his fingers, no thumb, and spares himself squeezing. It was also damp.

"Bob Stratton," he said. "Nice to see you, nice to see you."

We sat. I ordered a beer. Stratton nodded toward his drink, which, from the color, was a double. Around us the room rattled with cutlery and china, and pulsed with conversation, none of which I could make out. For lunch the crowd was nearly all men. There was an occasional sleek female, normally lunching with three men, and one couple who were probably on vacation from St. Paul. But mostly it was men in conservative suits and loud ties.

"Well, how's the case going?" Stratton said. "Loudon Tripp is a fine man, and it was a real tragedy for him. You making any progress on running the son of a bitch to ground?"

It was a bright room, well lit, full of marble and polished brass and mahogany. Through Stratton's carefully combed and sprayed and blow-dried hairstyle, I could see the pale gleam of his scalp. His color was high. His movements were very quick, and he talked fast, so fast that, particularly in the noisy dining room, it took focus to understand him. I didn't answer.

The waiter returned with my beer and Stratton's scotch. It was a double, soda on the side. Stratton picked up the soda and splashed a little in on top of the whiskey.

"Gotta do this careful," he said, and smiled at me with at least fifty teeth, "don't want to bruise the scotch."

I nodded and took a sip of beer.

The waiter said, "Care for menus, gentlemen?"

Stratton waved him away.

"Little later," he said. "Stay on top of the drinks."

The waiter said, "Certainly, sir," and moved off.

Stratton took a long pull on his drink. There was a hint of sweat on his forehead. He looked at me over the rim of the glass like a man buying an overcoat.

"I've had my people check you out," Stratton said. "They tell me you're pretty good."

"Golly," I said.

"Tell me you are a very hard case, that you've got a lot of experience, and that you're smart."

"And a hell of a pistol shot," I said.

Stratton smiled because he knew I'd said something that called for it. I was pretty sure he didn't know what.

"Ever think of relocating?" he said.

"It's often suggested to me," I said.

"That a fact?" Stratton said. "I was thinking that there would be some real challenges for a man like you in Washington."

"Really?" I said.

"Absolutely," Stratton said. He drank most of the rest of his dark scotch, and his eyes began to look for the waiter. "Absolutely."

"That'd be great," I said. "I love those Puget Sound oysters."

The waiter spotted Stratton and came over, Stratton nodded toward the almost-empty glass. The waiter looked at me, I shook my head.

"What was that about oysters?" Stratton said.

"Nothing," I said. "I was amusing myself."

"You bet," Stratton said. "Anyway, I think I could help you to a pretty nice setup in Washington. You could be on staff, and still freelance."

"Gee," I said.

The waiter returned with Stratton's double scotch—soda on the side. The open bottles of club soda were starting to pile up. Stratton paused long enough to splash in very little soda, from the newest bottle.

"So whaddya think?" he said.

I took a swallow of beer. It had gotten warm sitting there while Stratton inhaled his wine-dark scotch.

"I think you have your ass in a crack," I said.

Stratton laughed professionally. But his eyes seemed very small and cold and flat, like the eyes of some small predator. He put his scotch down carefully.

"You got to be kidding, my friend. You have got to be kidding. I have been in some tight places before, and I know a tight place when I see one. I mean, I've been a United States Senator for twenty-three years, and let me tell you something, I have faced down some hard moments."

"You sicked the Alton County Sheriff on me," I said.

Stratton started to speak and then stopped and sat back in his chair and stared at me.

"And a couple of ex-federal shooflys," I said. "And one of them hit me on the knee with a stick, and it's still sore. And you either tell me what your interest in the Olivia Nelson case is, or I am going to raise a great ruckus."

Stratton didn't move. I waited. A broad, charming smile spread across Stratton's face. He let it rest there for a while for full effect.

"Well, by God, I guess my ass is in a crack, isn't it?" he said. "They were right about you; you are a guy doesn't miss a trick. Not a damned trick."

He laughed and shook his head. The waiter came over and asked if we'd care yet to order. Without looking at him, Stratton said, "Shrimp cocktail, steak rare, fries, a salad, house dressing."

"Very good, sir," the waiter said.

He turned to me. I ordered a chicken sandwich and a fresh beer.

"Would you care for another drink, Senator?" the waiter asked Stratton. Stratton shook his head and made a dismissive gesture with his hand. The waiter departed.

Stratton folded his hands and rested them on the edge of the table. He examined them for a moment after the waiter left. Then he raised his eyes and looked steadily at me, his face a mask of sincerity.

"Okay," he said. "Here's the deal. I was, ah . . ." He looked back at his knuckles. "I was . . ." He grinned at me, still sincere, but now a little roguish too. "I was fucking Olivia Nelson."

"How nice for her," I said.

"This is off the record, of course," Stratton said.

"Of course," I said.

"I got to know her at a few fund-raisers. Her husband's one of those Beacon Hill old money liberals, and one thing led to another, and we were in the sack."

Stratton winked at me.

"You know how those things go," he said.

"No," I said. "How?"

"Well, tell you the truth, it wasn't even my idea, I mean, Livvie was a hot item," Stratton said.

He leaned across the table toward me now, a couple of good old boys talking about conquests.

"You know there was the official version—great wife, perfect mother, charity, teaching, patron of the arts, all that public consumption bullshit. And Loudon, the poor, dumb bastard, probably believed it. He was one of those my-wife-this, my-wife-that guys, you know. Didn't have a clue, the dumb bastard. And every time there'd be a party or something, she'd pick out some guest and . . ." Stratton shrugged and spread his hands slightly.

"She was promiscuous," I said.

"The queen of the star fuckers," Stratton said. "You haven't had Livvie Nelson's pants off, you simply aren't important in this town."

"Always stars?" I said.

"Sure, it was like belonging to an exclusive club; you fucked Livvie Nelson, you knew you'd made it," Stratton said.

"Was it a long affair?"

"Not really an affair. It was great for a guy like me, just wham bam, thank you, ma'am. Usually she'd come to my office, when I was here in town. Very discreet. Nothing in public."

Stratton grinned at me again.

"I'm a married man," he said.

"I could tell," I said.

He shrugged and grinned at me further.

"And you were afraid," I said, "that my investigation would turn up this connection?"

"Exactly, my friend. Exactly right. At first, we thought you'd just go through the motions and take Loudon's money—he's got plenty. But then you went down there and we realized you were serious. And we figured maybe we lean on you down there, away from me, so there'd be no way to connect me to it, and off your home turf, you know, so you'd be a little more vulnerable? And we have a good friend in South Carolina, and he's holding some markers on the Alton County Sheriff . . ." He spread his hands again. "It's how things work."

"Who's the *we*?" I said.

"We? Oh, myself and my staff."

"So you went to all that trouble to keep me from finding out about you and Olivia Nelson."

"Yes. I told you, we had you checked out. We didn't like what we heard. You seemed to us like trouble and we wanted to get it under control right now."

"So your wife wouldn't know," I said.

"Well, Laura and I have a kind of understanding. But . . . we're planning for the presidential nomination, next time, maybe," Stratton said. "It could have hurt us."

"Still could," I said.

"Hey, this is off the record."

"What record?" I said. "You think this is an interview? I'm a detective. You could have killed her."

"Me?"

"You and your staff," I said.

"Don't be absurd," Stratton said. "I'm a United States Senator."

"I rest my case," I said.


# Chapter 29 ⎯⎯⎯⎯⎯⎯⎯⎯⎯⎯⎯⎯⎯⎯⎯⎯⎯⎯⎯⎯

Tripp's office was as peaceful as ever. Ann Summers was there at her desk, in a simple black dress today. She remembered me and was glad to see me, a combination I don't always get. On the other hand, given the activity level in the office, she was probably glad to see anyone.

"He's back," I said.

"Yes, he's just down the hall."

"Do you handle his checkbook?" I said.

"Mr. Tripp's? Not really, why do you ask?"

"His check bounced," I said and took the bank notice out of my pocket and showed it to her.

"Mr. Tripp's?"

"Un huh."

"Oh dear," she said.

"Probably a mistake," I said.

"Oh, I'm sure it is."

I waved it off and she showed me into Tripp's big office and sat me in the leather chair by his desk. The office was done in green. The walls and woodwork were green. The rug was a green Oriental, the furniture was cherry, the high-backed swivel chair behind Tripp's desk was cherry with green leather upholstery. The long desk had a red leather top, with a gold leaf design around the edges of it. There was a wet bar at the far end of the office, and a fireplace on the wall behind Tripp's desk. It was faced in a sort of plum-colored tile with a vine pattern running through the tiles, and it was framed on each side by big cherry bookcases. The books looked neat and mostly unread. A lot of them were leather-bound to match the room. In two of the four corners there were cherry corner cabinets with ornate tops, and gold leaf dentil molding highlighting them. The corner cupboards were filled with designer knickknacks, and in the middle shelf on one of them was a picture of Olivia Nelson, or whoever the hell she had been, as a younger woman. Tripp's desktop was empty except for the onyx pen set, a telephone, and a big three-check checkbook. The checkbook was set square in the center of the desk as if to demand reconciling as soon as you sat down. I picked it up and opened the ledger pages, and ran back through them looking for my check. As I read, I noticed that there was no running balance. Each check was carefully entered, numbered and dated, but there was no way, looking at the checkbook, to know how much you had. I found my check, right below a check to Dr. Mildred Cockburn. I read back further. There were checks every month to Dr. Cockburn. All the entries were in the same thin hand. I'd seen it on my check. Most of the other checks were obvious. Telephone, electricity, insurance, cleaners, credit card payments. The only recurring one that was not obvious was Dr. Cockburn. Many of the check entries had *Returned* written across the original entry, in red ink, in the same hand, including several of Dr. Cockburn's. I looked a little harder. There seemed to be no checks rewritten to make good the ones that bounced. Something else was off in the check register. I didn't get it for a minute. I went back through more pages. And then I saw it. There were no deposits. In the whole ledger, there was no deposit entry. I put the checkbook back, and sat, and thought about that, and in a while, Tripp came into his office carrying a folded copy of the *Wall Street Journal*.

"Spenser," he said. "Good of you to come."

We shook hands, and he went around his desk and got into his padded leather swivel. He put the paper on the desk next to the checkbook, which he straightened automatically so that it was exactly square with the desk.

"Do you have a report for me?"

"Not exactly," I said. "Maybe a couple of more questions."

"Oh, certainly. But I am disappointed. I was hoping you'd have something."

I had something all right. But what the hell was it?

"Have you ever met any of your wife's family?" I said.

"No. She had none. That is, of course, she had one once, but they all died before I met her. She was quite alone, except for me."

"Ever been to Alton?" I said.

Tripp smiled sadly.

"No. There was never any reason."

I nodded. We were both silent for a moment.

"Sometimes," Tripp said, "I think I ought to go down there, walk around, look at the places where she walked, went to class, had friends."

He gazed past me, up toward the ceiling. Far below us, where State Street met Congress, there was traffic, and tourists looking at the marker for the Boston Massacre, and meter maids, and cabbies. Up here there was no hint of it. In Tripp's office you could just as well be in the high Himalayas for all the sound there was.

Tripp shook his head suddenly.

"But what would be the point?" he said.

There was something surrealistic about his grief. It was like a balloon untethered and wafted, aimless and disconnected, above the felt surface of life.

"How well do you know Senator Stratton?" I said.

"Bob's a dear friend. I've supported him for years. He was a good friend to Livvie as well, helped her get her teaching appointment, I'm sure. Though he never said a word about it."

"And you and your wife were on good terms?" I said.

Tripp stared at me as if I had offered to sell him a French postcard.

"You ask me that? You have been investigating her death for days and you could ask me that? We were closer than two people have ever been. I was she. She was I, we were the same thing. How could you . . . ?" Tripp shook his head. "I hope I've not been mistaken in you."

I plowed ahead.

"And you were intimate?"

Tripp stared at me some more. Then he got up suddenly, and walked to the window of his office, and looked down at the street. He didn't speak. I looked at his back for a while. Maybe I should investigate other career opportunities. Selling aluminum siding, say. Or being a television preacher. Or child molesting. Or running for public office.

"Look, Mr. Tripp," I said. My voice sounded hoarse. "The thing is that stuff makes no sense. I know you're sad. But I've got to find things out. I've got to ask."

He didn't move.

"There's pretty good evidence, Mr. Tripp, that your wife's name is not, in fact, Olivia Nelson."

Nothing.

"That she was sleeping with Senator Stratton, and maybe with others."

Still nothing. Except his shoulders hunched slightly and his head began to shake slowly, back and forth, in metronomic denial.

"I've seen pictures of two different people, both of whom look like your wife."

His head went back and forth. No. No. No.

"Have you ever heard of anyone named Cheryl Anne Rankin?"

No. No. No.

"Your retainer check bounced," I said.

The silence was so thick it seemed hard to breathe. Tripp's stillness had become implacable. I waited. Tripp stood, his head still negating. Back and forth, denying everything.

I got up and left.

# Chapter 30

Quirk and Farrell and Belson and I were in Quirk's office. Quirk told us that while he was in Alton he had learned exactly nothing.

"Everybody agrees that Olivia Nelson is married to a Kenyan citizen named Mano Kuanda and living in Nairobi. Embassy guy talked with her, took her fingerprints. We've compared them to her Peace Corps prints. She hasn't been in the United States since 1982. Never been in Boston. Has no idea who the victim is."

"She know anything about Cheryl Anne Rankin?" I said.

"No."

"Never heard the name?"

"No," Quirk said. "You talk to Stratton?"

"Yeah."

"And?"

"He says he was sleeping with Tripp's wife regularly, and that he wasn't the only one."

Quirk raised his eyebrows.

"Our Bobby?" he said.

"Shocking," Belson said. "And him a Senator and all."

"That's why he tried to chase you off?"

"So he says. Says he was afraid I'd find out about them and it would spoil his chances for the nomination next year."

"For President?" Quirk said.

"Yeah."

"Jesus," Belson said. "President Stratton."

"How about Tripp?"

"I talked to him."

"And?"

"He says everything was perfect."

"You got anything, Lee?" Quirk said.

Farrell jerked a little, as if he'd not been paying close attention.

"No, Lieutenant, no, I don't."

"Why should you be different?" Quirk said. He kept his eyes on Farrell for a long moment.

"One thing," I said. "I don't know why you would have, but has anyone run a credit check on Tripp?"

"Worried about your fee?" Belson said.

It was two-thirty in the afternoon and his thin face already sported a five o'clock shadow. He was one of those guys who looked cleanshaven for about an hour in the morning.

"In fact, his check bounced. But I think there's something goofy about his finances."

I told them about the checkbook.

"Might be something," I said.

"Lee?" Quirk said.

Farrell nodded.

"I'll find out," he said.

"Anything else?"

"The name Dr. Mildred Cockburn shows up in his checkbook a lot."

"Written like that?" Belson said.

I nodded.

"Probably not a medical doctor," Belson said.

"Yeah," I said, "then the check would be to Mildred Cockburn, DMD, or Mildred Cockburn, MD."

"Maybe she's a shrink," Belson said.

"Or a chiropractor, or a doctor of podiatry," I said.

"Hope for a shrink," Quirk said.

# Chapter 31

Susan and I had dinner at Michela's in Cambridge with Dennis and Nancy Upper. Susan knew Dennis from them both being shrinks. Nancy turned out to be an ex-dancer, so I was able to dazzle her with the knowledge of dance I had gained from Paul Giacomin, while Susan and Dennis talked about patients they had known.

I asked if either of them had heard of Dr. Mildred Cockburn. Neither of them had. Still, there was risotto with crab meat and a pistachio pesto. The room was elegant, and the bartender made the best martinis I'd ever drunk.

"I've got to find out how he does that," I said to Susan on the ride home.

"Well, you're a detective."

"And how complicated a recipe can it be?" I said.

"Vodka and vermouth?"

"Yeah."

"Sounds complicated to me," Susan said.

"Recipes are not the best thing you do," I said.

We were on Memorial Drive. Across the river the Boston skyline looked like a contrivance. The State House stood on its low hill, the downtown skyscrapers loomed behind it. And strung out along the flatness of the Back Bay, with the insurance towers in the background, the apartment houses were soft with the glow of lighted living rooms. It was Friday night. I was going to stay with Susan.

"Why do you want to know about Mildred Cockburn?" Susan said.

"Saw her name in Loudon Tripp's checkbook, 'Dr. Mildred Cockburn,' every month, checks for five hundred dollars. So I looked her up in the phone book. She's listed as a therapist with an office on Hilliard Street in Cambridge."

"Odd," Susan said.

"You'd expect to know her?"

"Yes."

"When I talk with her, what is it reasonable to expect her to tell me?" I said.

"Ethically?" Susan said.

"Yes."

"I can't say in the abstract," Susan said. "She should be guided by the best interests of her patient."

On our left, the surface of the river had a quicksilver gloss in the moonlight. A small cabin cruiser with its running lights on moved silently upstream, passing under the barrel-arched bridges, its wake a glassy furrow in the surface. Susan's street was silent, the buildings dark, the trees, half unleaved, made spectral by the street lamps shining through them.

Susan lived in an ornate Victorian house. On the first floor her office was on one side of the front hall, and her big waiting room was on the other. We went up the curving staircase to the second floor where she lived. When we opened the door, Pearl dashed at us, and jumped up, and tore Susan's hose, and lapped our faces, and ran to the couch and got a pillow and shook it violently until it was dead, and came back to show us.

"Cute," Susan said.

We took Pearl down and let her out into the fenced-in backyard. It was shadowy in the moonlight, but not dark, and we could watch her as she hurried about the yard, looking for the proper spot.

Later we lay in bed, the three of us, and talked, looking up at the ceiling in the moon-bright darkness. Pearl had little to say, but she compensated by taking up the most room in the bed.

"Is this Olivia Nelson thing making you crazy?" Susan said. We were holding hands under the covers, across Pearl's back.

"Nothing is turning out to be the way it appeared to be," I said.

"Things do that," Susan said.

"Wow," I said.

"I'm a graduate of Harvard University," Susan said.

# Chapter 32

Dr. Mildred Cockburn had office space in a tired-looking, brown-shingled house on Hilliard Street, down from the American Repertory Theater. There was a low wrought-iron fence with some rust spots around the yard. The fence had shifted over the years as the ground froze each winter and melted each spring, and it was now canted out toward the sidewalk. There was some grass in the yard, and a lot of hard-packed dirt. The front walk was brick, which had heaved with the fence. The bricks were skewed and weeds had grown up among them. Many of the brown shingles had cracked, and a couple had split on through, and the front door had been inadequately scraped before being painted over. Cambridge was not a hotbed of pretentious neatness.

A sign said *Enter,* which I did, and took a seat in a narrow foyer with doors leading out of it through each wall. I had an eleven o'clock appointment, and it was five of. The walls of the foyer were cream colored, though once they might have been white. There were a couple of travel posters on the walls, and an inexpensive print of one of Monet's paintings of his garden. There was also the insistent odor of cat. The low deal table beside the one straight chair had two recent copies of *Psychology Today,* and a copy of the *Chronicle of Higher Education* from last May.

At 11:06, the office door opened and a pale woman with a thin face, and her gray-streaked hair in a bun, came out of the office. She did not look at me. She took a long tweed coat from the coatrack, and put it on, and buttoned it carefully, and went out the door, maneuvering in the mailbox-sized foyer without ever acknowledging another presence.

There was a three- or four-minute wait thereafter, and then the office door opened again and Dr. Cockburn said, "Mr. Spenser?"

She wore a black turban and a large flowing black garment which I couldn't quite identify, something between a housecoat and an open parachute. She was obviously heavy, though the extent of her garment left the exact heaviness in doubt. Her skin was pale. She wore a lot of eye makeup and no lipstick.

I stood, and she ushered me past her into the office. The office was draped in maroon fabric. The window had louvered blinds, opened over the top half, closed on the bottom. There was a Victorian sofa, upholstered in dark green velvet, against the wall to the right of the door, and a high-backed mahogany chair with ugly wooden arms, facing a wing chair upholstered in the same green. She sat across from me in the wing chair. She made a barely visible affirmative movement with her head, and then waited, her hands folded in her lap.

"This is not a therapeutic visit," I said. "I'm a private detective, and I've been employed by Loudon Tripp to investigate the murder of his wife, Olivia Nelson."

Again the barely visible nod.

"In the course of investigating, I came across your name."

Nod.

"I'm wondering if you could tell me anything about either of them," I said.

"That is unlikely," she said. She had a deep voice and she knew it. She liked having a deep voice.

"I realize," I said, "that there are questions of confidentiality here, but your patient's best interest might well be served by helping me find his wife's killer."

"Loudon Tripp is not my patient," she said.

Nothing moved when she spoke, except her lips. In her dark clothes and her deep stillness, she seemed theatrically inaccessible.

"Olivia Nelson," I said.

She remained motionless. I glanced around the room.

"You are a psychotherapist," I said.

Nod.

"Are you an M.D.?" I said.

She made the tiniest head shake.

"Ph.D.?"

Again, the tiny head shake.

"What?" I said.

"I am a Doctor of Human Arts."

"Of course," I said. "And the conferring institution?"

"University of the Southern Pacific."

"In L.A., I bet."

Nod.

"They give academic credit for life experience."

"That's quite enough, Mr. Spenser."

I nodded and smiled at her.

"Sure it is," I said. "So tell me about Olivia Nelson."

She paused for a long time. We both knew she was a fraud. And we both knew that if I were motivated, I could cause her a lot of aggravation with the state licensing board. And we both knew it. She shook her head ponderously.

"Troubled," she said, "terribly troubled."

I did a barely visible nod.

"And like a lot of women, terribly victimized," she said.

Her deep voice was slow. Her manner was ponderous. When she wasn't speaking, she remained entirely still. She knew I knew, but she wasn't letting down. She was going to stay in character.

I nodded.

"At the heart of things was the fact that her father rejected her."

"Original," I said.

"And so she sought him symbolically over and over in other men."

"She was promiscuous," I said.

"That is a masculine word. It is the product of masculine culture, judgmental and pejorative."

"Of course," I said.

"When she came to me for help, she had already tried the route of Freudian, which is to say, masculine, psychotherapy. The failure was predictable. I was able to offer her a feminist perspective. And understanding herself, for the first time, in that perspective, she began finally to get in touch with her stifled self, the woman-child within."

"And she slept around," I said.

"She gave herself permission to discover her sexuality. And to do so for its own sake, rather than in the service of a thwarted father love."

"Do you know the names of any other men she gave herself permission to discover her sexuality with?"

"Really, Mr. Spenser. That is privileged communication between patient and therapist."

"And one of them might have killed her," I said.

She chewed on that for a little bit.

"I would think it would be in her best interest for you to name them," I said. "I'll bet that in your studies at USP you learned that your patients' best interest was the ethical rule of thumb in difficult circumstances."

She chewed on that a little bit more.

"I don't make notes," she said finally. "I believe it inhibits the life force spontaneity necessary to a successful therapy."

"Of course," I said.

She allowed me to watch her think.

"And she never used names. She referred to the men in her life in various ways—the news anchor, for instance, and the judge, the broker, that sort of thing. There was an important clergyman, I know. But I don't know who he was."

"Denomination?" I said.

She shook her head. "Not even that," she said. "She always referred to him as the Holy Man. I think it pleased her to experience a man of the cloth."

I pressed her a little, but there was no more. I moved on.

"Did she tell you her real name?" I said.

"I was not aware that she had another," Cockburn said.

"What was her father's name?"

"I don't know. I had assumed it was Nelson."

"She ever mention the name Rankin?"

"No."

"Cheryl Anne?"

"No."

We were quiet. Dr. Cockburn maintained her ponderous certitude even in silence. The way she sat bespoke rectitude.

"She did say that she used another identity to get into graduate school, someone else's records and such," Cockburn said finally. "She herself had not finished high school. She left home at seventeen and went to Atlanta, and made a living as best she could, she said, including prostitution. At some point she came to Boston, motivated, I think, by some childhood impression of gentility, became a graduate student, made a point of frequenting the Harvard-MIT social events and met her current husband."

"She didn't say whose identity she used."

"No, but if in fact she is not Olivia Nelson, as you imply, then one might assume she used that one."

"One might," I said. "How did her father's rejection manifest itself?" I said.

"He failed entirely to acknowledge her."

"Tell me about that," I said. "How does that work? Did he pretend she wasn't there? Did he refuse to talk to her when she came home?"

Dr. Cockburn gazed ponderously at me. She let the silence linger, as if to underline her seriousness. Finally she spoke.

"He was not married to her mother. The lack of acknowledgement was literal."

I sat in the heavily draped room feeling like Newton must have when the apple hit him on the head. Dr. Cockburn looked at me with heavy satisfaction.

"Goddamn," I said.


**"Was that all?"** Susan asked later.

"Everything essential," I said. "I used my full fifty minutes, but the rest of it was just her doing Orson Welles."

We were having a drink at the Charles Hotel, which was an easy walk from Susan's home. Susan had developed a passion for warm peppered vodka, olives on the side. In an evening she would often polish off nearly half a glass.

"She did say that Olivia was obsessed with money, and that apparently the family business was slipping."

"That would support the bounced check and the checkbook with no running balance," Susan said.

"Yeah. Cockburn said she had some sort of desperate plan, but Olivia wouldn't tell her what it was."

"Plan to get money?"

"Apparently. Cockburn doesn't know, or won't say."

"Dr. Cockburn has, in effect, waived her patient-therapist privilege already. I assume she'd have no reason to withhold that."

"Agreed," I said. "What do you think?"

"Dr. Cockburn's theory about Olivia Nelson is probably accurate. It doesn't require a great deal of psychological training to notice that many young people attempt to reclaim a parent's love by sleeping with surrogates. Often the objects of that claim are in some way authority figures."

"Like a U.S. Senator," I said.

"Sure," Susan said. "Sometimes it's apparent power like that, sometimes it's more indirect. Money maybe, or size and strength."

"Does this explain our relationship?" I said.

"No," Susan said. "Ours is based, I think, on undisguised lust."

"Only that?" I said.

"Yes," Susan said and guzzled half a gram of her peppered vodka. "I always wanted to boff a big goy."

"Anyone would," I said.

"Why," Susan said, "if she were sleeping with all these prominent men, would the police not discover it?"

"Partly because they were prominent," I said. "The affairs were adulterous, and prominent people don't wish to be implicated in adulterous affairs."

Susan was nodding her head.

"And because they were prominent," she said, "they had the wherewithal to keep the event covered up."

"She wasn't telling," I said, "and they weren't telling, and apparently they were discreet."

I shrugged, and spread my hands.

"What's a cop to do?" Susan said.

"Especially when the cop is being told by everyone involved that the victim was Little Mary Sunshine."

"So they weren't looking for infidelity," Susan said.

"Cops are simple people, and overworked. Most times the obvious answer is the right answer. Even, occasionally, when it's not the right answer, it's the easy one. Especially in a case like this where a lot of prominent people seem to be pushing you toward the easy answer."

"Even Martin?" Susan said.

"You can't push Quirk, but he's a career cop. It's his nationality—cop. If the chain of command limits him, he'll stay inside those limits."

"And not say so?"

"And not even think there are limits," I said.

"But he sent Loudon Tripp to you."

"There's that," I said.

"But could Tripp really have been so oblivious?" Susan said.

"And if he wasn't, why did he hire me?"

Susan sampled a bit of olive, and washed it down with a sip of peppered vodka. She seemed to like it.

"It is, as you know, one of the truisms of the shrink business that people are often several things at the same time. Yes, Tripp probably is as oblivious as it seems, and no, he wasn't. Part of him perhaps feared what the rest of him denied and he wanted to hire you to prove that she was what he needed to think she was.".

"So, in effect, he didn't really hire me to find out who killed her. He hired me to prove she was perfect."

"Perhaps," Susan said.

"Perhaps?" I said. "Don't you shrinks ever say anything absolutely?"

"Certainly not," Susan said.

"So maybe the murder was the excuse, so to speak, for him to finally put his fears to rest, even if retrospectively."

Susan nodded.

"He would have a more pressing need, in fact, once she was dead," she said. "Because there was no chance to fix it, now. What it was, was all that he had left."

The bar was almost empty on a mid-week night. The waitress came by and took my empty glass and looked at me. I shook my head and she went away. The other couple in the bar got up. The man helped the woman on with her coat, and they went out. In the courtyard outside the hotel, a college-age couple went by holding hands, with their heads ducked into the wind.

"He doesn't want the truth," I said.

"Probably not," Susan said. "He has probably hired you to support his denial."

"Maybe he should get the truth anyway."

"Maybe," Susan said.

"Or maybe not?" I said.

"Hard to say in the abstract."

Susan smiled at me. There was compassion and intelligence in the smile, and sadness.

"On the other hand, you have to do what you do, which may not be what he wants you to do."

I stared out at the courtyard some more. It was empty now, with a few dead leaves being tumbled along by the wind.

"Swell," I said.

# Chapter 33

Farrell came into my office in the late afternoon, after his shift.

"You got a drink?" he said.

I rinsed the glasses in the sink and got out the bottle and poured each of us a shot. I didn't really want one, but he looked like he needed someone to drink with. It was a small sacrifice.

"First we went back over Cheryl Anne Rankin again." Farrell said.

He held his whiskey in both hands, without drinking any.

"And we found nothing. No birth record, no public school record, no nothing. The woman who worked in the track kitchen is gone, all we got is that her name was Bertha. Nobody knows anything about her daughter. There's no picture there like you describe, just one picture of Olivia Nelson with a horse, and nobody remembers another one."

"Anyone talk to the black woman that worked there?"

"Yeah. Quirk talked with her while he was there. She doesn't know anything at all. She probably knows less than that talking to a white Northern cop."

"Who's doing the rest of the investigating?"

"Alton County Sheriff's Department," Farrell said.

"You can count on them," I said.

Farrell shrugged.

"Per diem's scarce," he said.

He was still holding the whiskey in both hands. He had yet to drink any.

"You hit one out, though, on Tripp," he said. "He's in hock. First time around we weren't looking for it, and nobody volunteered. As far as we can find out this time, he has no cash, and his only assets are his home and automobile. He's got no more credit. He's a semester behind in tuition payments for each kid. His secretary hasn't been paid in three months. She stays because she's afraid to leave him alone."

"What happened?" I said.

"We don't know yet how he lost it, only that he did."

"How about the family business?"

"He's the family business. He managed the family stock portfolio. Apparently that's all he did. It took him maybe a couple hours, and he'd stay there all day, pretending like he's a regular businessman."

"Secretary sure kept that to herself," I said.

"She was protecting him. When we showed her we knew anyway, she was easy. Hell, it was like a relief for her; she couldn't go on the rest of her life taking care of him for nothing."

"What's he say about this?"

"Denies everything absolutely." Farrell said. "In the face of computer printouts and sworn statements. Says it's preposterous."

"He's been denying a lot, I think."

Farrell nodded and looked down at the whiskey still held undrunk in his two hands. He raised the glass with both hands and dropped his head and drank some, and when he looked up there were tears running down his face.

"Brian?" I said.

Farrell nodded.

"He died," I said.

Farrell nodded again. He was struggling with his breathing.

"I'm sorry," I said.

Farrell drank the rest of his drink and put the glass down on the edge of the desk and buried his face in his hands. I sat quietly with him and didn't say anything. There wasn't anything to say.

# Chapter 34

Leonard Beale had an office in Exchange Place, a huge black glass skyscraper that had been built behind the dwarfed façade of the old Boston Stock Exchange on State Street. Keeping the façade had been trumpeted by the developer as a concern for preservation. It resulted in a vast tax break for him.

"Loudon lost almost everything in October 1987, when the market took a header," Beale said. "I wouldn't, under normal circumstances, speak so frankly about a client's situation. But Loudon . . ." Beale shook his head.

"He's in trouble, isn't he?" I said.

"Bad," Beale said. "And it's not just money."

"I didn't know brokers said things like 'it's not just money.' "

Beale grinned.

"Being a good broker is taking care of the whole client," he said. "It's a service business."

Beale was square-built and shiny with a clean bald head, and a good suit. He looked like he probably played a lot of handball.

"He lost his money in '87?" I said.

"Yeah. In truth, I didn't help. I was one of a lot of people who couldn't read the spin right. I didn't think the market was going to dive. But mostly he lost it through inattention. He always insisted on managing the money himself. Gave him something to do, I suppose. Let him go to the office at nine in the morning, come home at five in the afternoon, have a cocktail, dine with the family. You know? Like Norman Rockwell. But he wasn't much of a manager, and when the bottom fell out he was mostly on margin."

"And had to come up with the cash," I said.

"Yes."

"Why was he on margin?" I said. "I thought the Tripp fortune was exhaustive."

Beale shrugged and gazed out the window, across the Back Bay, toward the river. The sky was bright blue and patchy with white clouds. In the middle distance I could see Fenway Park, idiosyncratic, empty, and green.

"Are the Rockefellers on margin?" I said. "Harvard University?"

Beale's gaze came slowly back to me.

"None of them was married to Olivia," he said.

"She spent that much?"

"Somebody did. More than the capital generated."

"So he began to erode the capital," I said.

Beale nodded.

"The first sure sign of disaster for rich people," he said. "Rich people don't earn money. Their capital earns money. If they start snacking on the capital, there's less income earned, and then, because they have less income, they take a bigger bite of capital, and there's even less income, and, like that."

"He tell you this?"

"No," Beale said. "He wouldn't say shit if he had a mouthful. As far as he was concerned, she was perfect. The kids were perfect. Christ, the son is an arrogant little thug, but Loudon acts like he's fucking Tom Sawyer. Buys the kid out of every consequence his behavior entails. Or did."

"And the daughter?"

"Don't know. No news is probably good news. Loudon never had much to say about her, so she probably didn't get in much trouble."

"And he's been economically strapped since 1987?"

"Broke," Beale said. "Getting broker."

"What are they living on?" I said. "They've got two kids in college, a mansion on the Hill, fancy office. How are they doing that?"

Beale shook his head.

"Margin," he said.

# Chapter 35

"It's simply not so," Loudon Tripp said.

"So why is everyone telling me otherwise?" I said.

"I can't imagine," Tripp said.

"Your secretary hasn't been paid her salary," I said.

"Of course she has."

He took his checkbook from its place on the left-hand corner of the desk and opened it up and showed me the neat entries for Ann Summers.

"And the check you gave me bounced," I said.

He turned immediately to the entry for my check.

"No," he said. "It's right here. Everything is quite in order."

"There's no running balance," I said.

"Everything is in order," Tripp said again.

"Do you know that your wife was unfaithful?" I said.

"By God, Spenser," he said, "that's enough."

His voice was full of sternness but empty of passion.

"I fear that I have made a mistake with you, and it is time to rectify it."

"Which means I'm fired," I said.

"I'm afraid so. I'm sorry. But you have brought it on yourself. You have made insupportable accusations. My wife may be dead, Mr. Spenser, but her memory is alive, and as long as I'm alive, no one will speak ill of her."

"Mr. Tripp," I said. "Your wife was not what she appeared to be, not even who she said she was. Your life is not what you say it is. There's something really wrong here."

"Good day, Mr. Spenser. Please send me a bill for your services through"—he looked at his watch—"through today," he said.

"And you'll pay it with a rubber check," I said. "And enter it carefully and not keep a balance so you won't have to know it's rubber."

"Good day, Mr. Spenser!"

I was at a loss. It was like talking to a section of the polar ice cap. I got up and went out, and closed the door behind me.

"He's crazy," I said to Ann Summers.

She shook her head sadly.

"Why didn't you tell me about him right off?"

"I don't know. He's, he's such a sweet man. And it seemed gradual, and he seemed so sure everything was all right, and . . ."

She spread her hands.

"Even when you weren't getting paid?" I said.

"I felt sorry, no, not that, quite, I felt . . . embarrassed for him. I didn't want anyone to know. I didn't want him to know that I knew."

"Anything else you haven't told me?" I said.

She shook her head. We were quiet for a while. Then she spoke.

"What are you going to do?" she said.

"I'm going to find out," I said. "I'm going to keep tugging at my end of it until I find out."

She looked at me for a long time. I didn't have anything to say. Neither did she. Finally she nodded slowly. In its solemnity, her face was quite beautiful.

"Yes," she said. "You will, won't you."

# Chapter 36

Williams College was located in Williamstown, in the far northwest corner of Massachusetts. The ride out was more than three hours whether you went on the Mass. Pike or Route 2. On the one hand, if you got behind some tourist in the two-lane stretches of Route 2, the trip became interminable. On the other hand, Route 2 was better-looking than the Mass. Pike and there was not a single Roy Rogers restaurant the whole way.

Susan and I had a reservation in Williamstown at a place called The Orchards where they served home-baked pie, and we could have a fire in the bedroom. While I talked with the Tripp children, Susan would visit the Clark Museum.

We drove out on Route 2. Susan had a new car, one of those Japanese things she favored that were shaped like a parsnip, and mostly engine. This one was green. She let me drive, which was good. When she drove, I tended to squeeze my eyes tight shut in terror, which would cause me to miss most of the scenery that we had taken Route 2 to see in the first place.

I met Chip and Meredith Tripp in the bar of a restaurant called the River House, which, in the middle of the day, was nearly empty. Chip and I each had a beer. Meredith had a diet Coke. Chip was cooler than kiwi sorbet, with his baggy pants, and purple Williams warm-up jacket, his hat on backwards, and his green sunglasses hanging around his neck. Meredith was in a plaid skirt and black turtleneck and cowboy boots. As before, she had on too much makeup.

"I need to talk with you about your mother," I said.

Chip glowered. Meredith looked carefully at the tabletop.

"What I will tell you can be confirmed in most of its particulars, by the police. So we shouldn't waste a lot of time arguing about whether what I say is true."

"So you say, Peeper."

*Peeper.* I took a deep breath and began.

"First of all, it is almost certain that your mother was not in fact Olivia Nelson."

Meredith's eyes refocused on the wall past my chair and got very wide. Her brother said, "You're full of shit."

"Did either of you ever meet any of your mother's family?"

"They're dead, asshole," Chip said. "How are we going to meet them?"

I inhaled again, slowly.

"I'll take that as no," I said and looked at Meredith. She nodded, her head down.

"Have you ever heard of anyone named Cheryl Anne Rankin?"

Chip just stared at me. Meredith shook her head.

"Do you know that your father is encountering financial difficulty?" I said.

"Like what?" Chip said.

"He's broke," I said.

"Bullshit," Chip said.

I nodded slowly for a minute, and inhaled carefully again.

"Did you know that your mother was promiscuous?" I said.

"You son of a bitch," Chip said.

He stood up.

"On your feet," he said.

I didn't move.

"Hard to hear," I said. "I don't blame you. But it has to be contemplated."

"Are you gonna stand up, you yellow bastard, or am I going to have to drag you out of your chair?"

"Don't touch me," I said.

And Chip heard something in my voice. It made him hesitate.

I tried to keep my voice steady.

"I am going to find out how your mother died, and the only way I can is to keep going around and asking people questions. Often they don't like it. I'm used to that. I do it anyway. Sometimes they get mad and want to fight me, like you."

I paused and kept my eyes on his.

"That's a mistake," I said.

"You think so," he said.

"You're an amateur wrestler," I said. "I'm a professional thug."

Meredith put her hand on Chip's arm, without looking at him.

"Come on, Chip," she said. There was almost no affect in her voice.

"I'm not going to sit around and let him talk about her that way."

"Please, Chip. Let him . . ." Her voice trailed away.

I waited. He glared at me for a moment, then slammed his chair in against the table.

"Fuck you," he said to me and turned and left.

Meredith and I were quiet. She made an embarrassed laugh, though there was nothing funny.

"Chippy's so bogus, sometimes," she said.

I waited. She laughed again, an extraneous laugh, something to punctuate the silence.

"You know about your mother?" I said.

"Dr. Faye says we all do and won't admit it. Not about her being somebody else, but the other . . ."

I nodded.

"Daddy would be up in his room with the TV on," Meredith said in her small flat voice. "Chip was at college. And she would come home; I could tell she'd been drinking. Her lipstick would be a little bit smeared, maybe, and her mouth would have that sort of red chapped look around it, the way it gets after people have been kissing. And I would say, 'You're having an affair.' "

"And?"

"And she would say, 'Don't ask me that.'

"And I would say, 'Don't lie to me.' "

I leaned forward a little trying to hear her. She had her hands folded tightly in front of her on the tabletop and her eyes were fastened on them.

"And her eyes would get teary and she would shake her head. And she'd say, 'Oh, Mere, you're so young.' And she would shake her head and cry without, you know, boo-hooing, just talking with the tears running down her face, and she'd say something about 'life is probably a lie,' and then she'd put her arms around me and hug me and pat my hair and cry some more."

"Hard on you."

"When I came to school," she said, "I was having trouble, you know, adjusting. And I talked with Jane Burgess, my advisor, and she got me an appointment with Dr. Faye."

"He's a psychiatrist?"

"Yes." The word was almost nonexistent, squeezed out in the smallest of voices. Her Barbie doll face, devoid of character lines, showed no sign of the adult struggle she was waging. It remained placid, hidden behind the affectless makeup.

"Know anything about money?" I said.

"Sometimes they'd fight. She said if he couldn't get money, she would. She knew where to get some."

"What did he say?"

"Nothing. He'd just go upstairs and turn on the television."

"What would she say?"

"She'd go out."

"You don't know what her plan was? For money?"

"She always just said she knew where to get it."

"How long did you live like this?"

"I don't know. All the time, I guess. Dr. Faye says I didn't buy the family myth."

I put a hand out and patted her folded fists. She got very rigid when I did that, but she didn't pull away.

"Stick with Dr. Faye," I said. "I'll work on the other stuff."

Susan and I were in the dining room at The Orchards, Susan wearing tight black pants and a plaid jacket, her eyes clear, her makeup perfect.

"There's a beard burn on your chin," I said.

"Perhaps if you were to shave more carefully," Susan said.

"You didn't give me time," I said. "Besides, there are many people who would consider it a badge of honor."

"Name two," Susan said.

"Don't be so literal," I said.

There were fresh rolls in the bread basket, and the waitress had promised to find me a piece of pie for breakfast. We were at a window by the terrace and the sun washed in across our linen tablecloth. I drank some coffee.

"It is a lot better," I said, "to be you and me than to be most people."

Susan smiled.

"Yes, it is," she said. "Especially better than being one of the Tripps."

"What I don't get is the girl, Meredith. How did she escape it? She's very odd. She's obviously in trouble. Most of the time she's barely there at all. But she's the one that will look at it, that doesn't buy the family myth."

"There's too much you don't know," Susan said.

"I may have that printed on my business cards," I said.

The waitress appeared with a wedge of blackberry pie, and a piece of cheddar cheese beside it.

"My father used to have mince pie for breakfast," the waitress said, "almost every Sunday morning."

"And sired beautiful daughters," I said.

The waitress smiled and poured me some more coffee, and gave Susan a new pot of hot water, and went off. Susan watched me eat the pie. She was having All Bran for breakfast, and a cup of hot water with lemon.

"What will you do," Susan said, "now that you're fired?"

"I'll probably go back down to Alton," I said. "And ask around some more."

"Will it be dangerous?"

"Probably not," I said. "Most of the cat is out of the bag, by now. There's not much reason to try and run me off."

"You think Alton is where you'll find out?"

"I don't know," I said. "I don't know where else to look."

# Chapter 37 ————————————————————

I was in the detectives' room at the Alton County Sheriff's Department talking with the pretty good-looking female cop who'd harassed me before. Her name was Felicia Boudreau, and she was a detective second grade.

"I didn't much like that deal," she said. "But you've been a cop. Do a lot of stuff you don't much like."

"Why I'm no longer a cop," I said.

She shrugged.

"You know who put us on you in the first place?"

I nodded.

"Senator Robert Stratton," I said.

"From Massachusetts?"

"That's the one," I said. "At least I never voted for him."

"What was his problem?" she said.

"I'm investigating a murder," I said. "Stratton was sleeping with the victim."

"Afraid you'd turn up his name?"

"Yeah."

"So what," she said. "That's mostly what they do in the Senate, isn't it? They get laid?"

"He wants to be President," I said.

"Sure," she said. "Give him a fancier place to get laid in."

"Who put the tail on me?" I said.

She shook her head. She was sitting with her feet on the desk, crossed at the ankle. It showed a long, smooth thigh line. She had on light-gray slacks over black boots, and a flowered blouse with big sleeves. Her bolstered gun, some sort of 9mm, lay on the desk beside her purse. Everybody had nines now.

"You grow up here in Alton?" I said.

"Yes."

"You know Olivia Nelson?"

"Jumper Jack's girl," Felicia said.

"Yes. Tell me about her."

"What's to tell. Rich kid, about ten years older than me. Father's a town legend, hell, maybe a county legend. Big house, racehorses, good schools, servants, hunting dogs, bourbon, and branch water."

"What happened to her?"

Felicia grinned.

"Town scandal," she said. "Went in the Peace Corps. Married some African prince with tribal scars on his face. Jumper never got over it."

"How about her mother?" I said.

"Her mother?"

"Yeah, everyone talks about Jumper Jack. I never hear anything about her mother."

"She had one," Felicia said.

"Good to know," I said.

"Sort of genteel, I guess you'd say. Sort of elegant woman who didn't like the muddy dogs in her house, and hated it that a lot of the time her husband would have horse shit on his boots at supper."

"That's genteel," I said.

"Yeah, it's hard to describe. But she was always like someone who thought she should have been living in Paris, reading whoever they read in Paris."

"Proust," I said.

"Sure."

"What happened to her?" I said.

"Committed suicide."

"When?"

"I investigated it. Lemme see, nineteen . . . and eighty-seven, late in the year. Almost Christmas. I remember we were working overtime on the sucker just before the holidays."

"1987," I said.

"Yeah. That mean something to you?"

"Year the market crashed," I said. "October 1987."

"You think she killed herself 'cause the stock market crashed?"

I shook my head.

"Doesn't sound the type," I said. "Know why she did it?"

"No. Went in her room, took enough sleeping pills to do the trick, and drank white wine until they worked. Didn't leave a note, but there was no reason to think that it wasn't what it looked like."

She got up and got two cups of coffee from the automatic maker on the file cabinet. She added some Cremora and sugar, asked me what I took, and put some of the same in mine. Then she brought the cups back to her desk and handed me one. The gray slacks fit very smoothly when she walked.

"How about Cheryl Anne Rankin?" I said.

"Your Lieutenant, what's his name?"

"Quirk."

"Yeah, your Lieutenant Quirk asked around about her. I don't remember her."

"He talk with you?"

"Nope. Sheriff said we was to stay away from him. Nobody would much talk with him."

"How come you're talking to me?"

"Sheriff didn't say nothing about you. Probably didn't think you'd have the balls to come back."

"There was a picture on the wall of the track kitchen," I said. "Looked like Olivia Nelson. Woman who worked there said it was Cheryl Anne Rankin, and she was her mother. Now the picture's gone, and the woman's gone."

"Don't know much about that," Felicia said. "People work at the track kitchen come and go. They get paid by the hour, no real job record, nobody keeps track. If you can fry stuff in grease, you're hired."

"If you were trying to find out things in this town, who would you go to?"

"About this Cheryl Anne?"

"About anything, Cheryl Anne, Olivia, Jack, his wife, Bob Stratton, anything. The only thing I know for sure down here is that you get your hair done in Batesburg."

"And it looks great," she said.

"And it looks great."

We both drank a little of the coffee, which was brutally bad.

"Friend of mine said I might talk to the household help," I said. "They're in all the houses, all the offices. They're cleaning up just outside of all the doors, and they tell each other."

Felicia took another drink of the wretched coffee and made a face.

"I've tried," she said. "No point to it, they wouldn't tell me anything, just like they won't tell you. They'll listen politely and say 'yassah' and nod and smile and tell you nothing."

"I'm used to it," I said. "All races, creeds, and colors refuse to tell me stuff."

"And when they do, it's a lie," she said.

"That especially," I said.


# Chapter 38

There was no picture of Cheryl Anne Rankin in the track kitchen. The white woman who'd claimed her wasn't there either, though the black woman I'd seen before was still there. She didn't know where the white woman was. Nawsir, she didn't know her name. Never did know it. She didn't know nothing about no picture. Yessir. Sorry, sir. Take a walk, sir.

I went back to the Alton Arms and sat on the front steps. The Bluetick hound that I'd seen on my last visit was stretched out in the sun on the front walk. He rolled his eyes back toward me, and looked at me silently as I sat down. I nodded at him. His tail stirred briefly.

"Contain yourself," I said.

Across the street a couple of jays were darting about in the branches of one of the old trees. While I watched them, I put my closed fist down toward the Bluetick hound. Without raising his head, he sniffed thoughtfully. Then he stood up suddenly and put his head on my leg. I scratched his ear. He wagged his tail slowly. Behind me the door of the hotel opened and a fat gray-haired couple came out. Sedale came behind them with four pieces of matched luggage. He stored the luggage in the trunk of a silver Mercedes sedan, accepted some change from the husband, and held the door while his wife hove herself into the passenger seat.

"Y'all have a nice day now, y'hear?" he said.

Then he closed the door and smiled at them. As they drove away, he tucked the change into his vest pocket.

"High rollers," I said.

The Bluetick kept his head on my leg, and I continued to scratch his ear. Sedale smiled at me.

"How're you today, sir?" he said.

"You got a minute to sit here on the steps and talk to me?" I said.

"Don't like me to sit on the steps," Sedale said. "But I can stand here while you sit."

"They don't mind if I sit on the steps?" I said.

"You a guest, sir," Sedale said.

The dog left me and went to Sedale. He put his hand down absently, the way owners do, and the dog lapped it.

"I'm a detective," I said.

"I know that, sir."

"Be hard to prove given what I've detected so far," I said.

"Probably a very difficult case, sir."

The dog returned to me for more ear scratching.

"What do you know about me?" I said.

"Know you a private detective, down from Boston, looking into a murder. Mr. Jack Nelson's daughter."

"Un huh."

" 'Cept she ain't Mr. Nelson's daughter."

"You know Jefferson?" I said. "Works for Mr. Nelson."

Sedale smiled.

I stopped scratching the dog's ear as I talked and he tossed his head against my hand.

"Sorry," I said to the dog and scratched some more. "I saw a picture on the wall of the track kitchen of a young woman who looked just like Olivia Nelson had looked at that age. The woman at the track kitchen said her name was Cheryl Anne Rankin and that she was the woman's daughter. Now the picture's gone, and the woman's gone."

Sedale smiled encouragingly.

"You know anything about Cheryl Anne Rankin?" I said.

"Nawsir."

I nodded.

"The thing is, Sedale, that it is too big a coincidence that there should be two people look like Olivia Nelson in town, and then find twenty years later that one of them has disappeared and someone is impersonating the other."

"Yessir."

"And since we know that the real Olivia Nelson is alive in Africa, it seems to me that the dead woman has to be Cheryl Anne Rankin."

Sedale's face was inert. He showed no sign of impatience or discomfort. I had no sense that he wanted to leave. He had simply gone inside; placid, agreeable, and entirely unavailable to a white guy asking questions about a white matter. He nodded.

"I want to find out who killed her."

Sedale nodded again.

"Tell me about Cheryl Anne Rankin," I said.

"Don't know nothing 'bout that, sir," he said.

"The hell you don't." I said. "Jefferson knows something about her, so do you. But you duck into blackface the minute I ask you. Until five minutes ago, you were an actual person. Then I started to ask about Cheryl Anne Rankin, and you turned into Stepin Fetchit. Your accent even got thicker."

"Yessir," Sedale said and grinned.

We were both silent. I continued to scratch the dog's ear. The dog continued to wag his tail. Sedale continued to rest his hips on the railing of the veranda. Then he reached into his vest pocket with two fingers and brought out a quarter and three dimes. He held them in the palm of his hand and showed them to me.

"See what those fatso tourists gave me for a tip?" he said.

"Let the good times roll," I said.

Sedale grinned suddenly.

"You ain't as fucking stupid as most honkies," he said.

"And your dog likes me," I said.

"For a fact," Sedale said.

He looked at his watch.

"I get off in an hour. You buy me couple of drinks at the Hunt Grill on Elm Street, I'll tell you 'bout Cheryl Anne Rankin."

# Chapter 39

I was the only white person in the Hunt Grill. No one appeared to care much about that fact, couple of heads turned and at least one guy nudged another, but mostly people were interested in their drinks and watching *Jeopardy!* The room was done in pine paneling. There were pictures of athletes on the walls, and sports pennants, and schedules of televised games. There were two very big-screen television sets, and a big sign advertising Happy Hour, which, according to the sign, I was in.

The bartender nodded at me when I squeezed onto a bar stool. I ordered a beer and got it. His dark eyes were without expression. His face held neither hostility nor welcome. He put a bowl of peanuts on the bar in front of me and moved away. I picked up a peanut and ate it carefully. No need for a whole handful. One at a time was just as succulent. I sipped a little of the beer. I picked up two peanuts. Everyone on *Jeopardy!* was having a hell of a time. Just like me. I drank a little more beer. I took a handful of peanuts and munched them vigorously.

Sedale came in and walked toward me. The Bluetick hound was with him. The bar was nearly full, but there was an empty stool on either side of me. Sedale sat on one. The hound sat on the floor near his feet.

"Seven and seven," he said to the bartender.

"Do you like that?" I said. "Or do you just order it because you like the way it sounds?"

The bartender put the drink in front of him and Sedale drank half of it.

"You know the difference between a toilet seat and a hotel worker?" Sedale said.

"No, I don't."

"Toilet seat only services one asshole at a time."

He drank the rest of his drink and gestured another at the bartender.

"His tab," Sedale said and jerked his head at me. The bartender looked at me. I nodded.

Sedale took a handful of peanuts and ate some and gave a couple to the dog. The bartender brought him his drink.

"My aunt Hester, my momma's oldest sister, she a midwife. Been a midwife fifty-something years. She a lot older than my momma," Sedale said.

He paused and sipped his second drink.

"Woman named Bertha Voss come to my aunt Hester 'bout forty years ago, little longer, and ask could she do an abortion for her."

The dog sitting on the floor had his nose trained on the peanuts. I took a couple, and held them down in the palm of my open hand, and he scarfed them off.

"Bertha was a no-account cracker. But she was white. Those days black people get lynched for things like that. My aunt Hester say, 'No, you got to find somebody else, or you got to have the baby.'"

Sedale sipped again. He took in his second drink quite delicately, holding the glass in his fingertips. The first one had been need. The second appeared to be pleasure. I finished my beer. The bartender looked over and I pointed at my glass. He brought a fresh beer and another bowl of peanuts. The first bowl had somehow emptied. Must have fed the dog too many.

"Well, Bertha couldn't find nobody, I guess, 'cause she married another no-account cracker name Hilly Rankin, and she had the baby. And she tell everybody it's his."

"Cheryl Anne?" I said.

"Yes, sir," Sedale said and there was a gleam of mockery in his eyes.

"Rankin believe he's the father?"

"Seemed to. Hilly ain't very smart."

"And do we know who the proud poppa was?"

"Sho 'nuff do," he said, "Care to guess?"

Sedale grinned at me like he was the host of *Jeopardy!* He let the pregnant pause hang between us.

"Jack Nelson," I said.

Sedale's grin widened.

"You a by-God real live detective, ain't you," he said. "Bertha told my aunt Hester that it was Jumper Jack knocked her up."

The Bluetick hound nudged his head under my hand and stared at the bowl of peanuts. I gave him some. On the big-screen television, *Jeopardy!* had ended and the local news was on. It looked and sounded exacly like local news everywhere: a serious-looking anchor; an attractive, though not frivolous, anchorette; a twit to do the weather; and a brash guy that talked fast to do sports.

"You know where Bertha Rankin is now?" I said.

"Sure."

Our voices sounded hollow to me. As if they weren't connected to humans.

"Where?"

"She and Hilly got a dump out on the Batesburg Road 'bout five miles. Right past the gravel pit, dirt road goes down on the right. They at the end of it."

"You know Cheryl Anne?" I said.

"Nope. She musta gone to school in Batesburg."

"They kept it a secret," I said. "All this time."

"Sure," Sedale said. "Only the niggers knew."

"And now she's dead," I said.

It was one of those things you know for a long time before you know it. The dead woman in Boston was Cheryl Anne Rankin.

# Chapter 40

The weather in Alton was still warm and it didn't seem like fall. But at quarter to seven in the evening it was dark on the Batesburg Road. And empty, as if no one wanted to go to Batesburg, even to have their hair done. On the other hand, maybe no one wanted to leave Batesburg and go to Alton. I would have preferred neither.

I passed the gravel pit and turned right onto the dirt road and bumped slowly down to the end of it. My headlights hit on a cinder-block shack with a corrugated metal roof that looked like it might once have been used to house tractors. Someone had filled in the big garage-type doors with odd pieces of unpainted plywood; and cut a person-sized door in the middle of one of them. The door hung on badly nailed galvanized strap hinges, and opened with a rope pull. There was the rusted hulk of what might have once been a 1959 Plymouth in the yard, and several old tires. A dirty white sow lying behind one of the tires raised her head and stared into my headlights. I got out and knocked on the front door and the woman from the track kitchen opened it. She peered at me, trying to see into the darkness.

"My name is Spenser," I said. "We met once at the track kitchen."

She flinched back as if I had pushed her and glanced over her shoulder.

"I don't know you," she said.

"Yeah, you do. And I know you. You're Bertha Rankin, formerly Bertha Voss. You have a daughter Cheryl. Where's your husband?"

"He's asleep," she said, and glanced back into the room again.

I could smell bacon grease and kerosene and a strong reek of whiskey.

"We need to talk about Jack Nelson," I said. "If you'd like to step outside."

She hesitated, and then stepped out of the house and pulled the makeshift door closed behind her. She was wearing some sort of shapeless dress, over some sort of shapeless body. Her gray hair was down and lank, and her face was red. There was sweat on her forehead and I could smell whiskey on her too.

"What you want?"

"I know that Jack Nelson is the father of your daughter, Cheryl Anne Rankin. I have no need to tell other people about that, right now. But I need to talk with you about it."

"How you know that?" she said.

"Doesn't matter. Tell me when Cheryl Anne was born."

"1948."

"Same year as Olivia Nelson," I said.

Bertha Rankin didn't speak.

"Did she look like Olivia Nelson?"

Bertha Rankin nodded.

"Where did she go to school?" I said.

"Batesburg."

"Her father know about her?"

"Yes."

"He give you money?"

We were standing in my headlights. As if on stage. She looked at me and then back at the house and then at the ground.

"Just you and me," I said. "Did Jack Nelson give you money?"

"He give me a hundred dollars every month."

"And told you to shut up," I said.

"Didn't have to. Hilly knew, it'd kill him. Hilly drinks some, but he loves me. I been faithful to him forty-three years. I wouldn't never want him to know."

There were tears now in her squinty eyes. Her face was puffy with booze and fat and age and tiredness.

"Did Cheryl Anne know who her father was?" I said.

The tears blossomed, and ran down her face. Her heavy shoulders sagged, and her breath began to come hard. She lowered her face suddenly and stared at the ground.

"She did, didn't she?" I said.

Bertha nodded.

"Be hard not to tell her," I said.

"I told her when she a seventeen-year-old girl," Bertha said. "I wanted her to be proud of where she come from. To know that she wasn't just like us."

"And a little after that," I said, "she left town."

"Yes."

"And you didn't hear from her anymore."

Bertha was crying full out now, her head down, her arms at her sides. She shook her head. I didn't have it in me to tell her that her daughter was dead. She'd have to know sometime. But it didn't have to be me who told her.

I put my hand out and patted her shoulder. She pulled away.

"I'm sorry," I said. And turned and got back in my car and drove away.

When I thought about it, on the dark road back to Alton, I figured that she probably sort of knew that her daughter was dead. Which didn't make me feel any better.

# Chapter 41

It was eight-thirty at night and starting to rain when Jefferson let me into the big white house on the rise where Jack Nelson lived. As I stepped into the dim front hall, there was the quiet movement of dogs about me, and the old alpha dog put his nose against the back of my hand.

"Evening, Mr. Spenser," Jefferson said.

"I need to talk to Mr. Nelson," I said. "He in?"

I could hear the smile in Jefferson's voice although the hallway was too dim to see it.

"Mr. Jack always in, sir. What is it you need to see him about?"

"Cheryl Anne Rankin," I said.

We stood silent in the dim, dog-smelling hallway. Jefferson still had a hand on the open door. The old alpha dog sat next to me waiting for me to pat him. I patted him. The silence dragged on. Then Jefferson closed the door softly behind me.

"This way, Mr. Spenser," he said and we went back through the house the same way we had gone last time into the vast glass room where Jack Nelson kept his whiskey.

The last time I'd come, the room had been flooded with light. Now it was dark except for the eccentric glow of the television set. The raindrops flattened against the glass roof, and ran together, and ran off in convoluted streaks. The sound of the rain hitting was a kind of steady rattle in the dark.

Nelson was propped in his chair by the television. The water and the bourbon were at hand. The silent dogs were there. The air-conditioning was still turned up and the chilled room felt like a meat locker.

Nelson looked at me without reaction as I walked toward him. Jefferson held back a little, among the dogs, silent at the periphery.

I said, "Mr. Nelson, remember me?"

Nelson stared at me and shook his head. He seemed to have become more inert since I'd seen him last. Three hundred nearly motionless pounds of booze and suet. The sound was low on the television, where two guys were pretending to wrestle. Nelson's breath wheezed in the quiet room.

"My name is Spenser. I'm a detective from Boston, Mass. I came a while back and talked with you about your daughter."

"No daughter," he rasped.

"I'm sorry, Mr. Nelson, but that's not true. In fact, there's two daughters."

At the dark rim of the glass room Jefferson made a sound like a sigh.

"Nigger lover," Nelson said. He drank some bourbon. His eyes went back to rest on the television set.

"Your daughter Olivia married an African," I said. "Your daughter Cheryl Anne married a rich guy from Boston."

Nelson's eyes never moved from the television. He seemed to settle more deeply into his own mass. The rain streamed off the black glass of the conservatory roof.

"She was murdered a little while ago," I said. "In Boston. I'm trying to find out why."

Nelson drank some more bourbon, and fumbled for the bottle and poured another drink and muddled water into it from the pitcher. While he did this he never took his eyes from the television tube. He spilled some of the bourbon and some of the water. He didn't bother with ice. I stepped in front of the television set.

"You have an illegitimate daughter named Cheryl Anne Rankin," I said.

Nelson bent his head to the side trying to see past me to the screen. I seemed to have no meaning to him. He seemed to know only that I was an object between him and the picture.

"He ain't going to talk, Mr. Spenser," Jefferson said. "He don't talk much anymore."

"Then you'll have to talk, Jefferson," I said. "One way or another, I'm going to find out about Cheryl Anne Rankin. And if that includes getting an extradition warrant on Jumper Jack, then I'll do it."

Jefferson turned a switch somewhere and indirect lighting brightened the room somewhat. Nelson seemed oblivious of it. Jefferson nodded at a couch against the inner wall of the conservatory. We went and sat on it, he at one end, me at the other. Across the room Nelson sat and watched the wrestling match and drank whiskey among his dogs.

"Been with Mr. Jack more than sixty years," Jefferson said. "Fourteen years old, graduate eighth grade, going to be a carpenter."

Jefferson stood suddenly and walked over to the table by Nelson's chair and made himself a drink and one for me and brought them back. He handed me mine and remained standing, holding his in both of his still-strong hands, looking out at the dark rain beyond the conservatory glass.

"Always like tools," he said. "Like to make a miter fit snug. Like things square."

He looked around the conservatory slowly.

"Started working for Mr. Jack's father on this room. Apprentice. But I was good at it, even then, and Mr. Jack's father he say, 'Boy, you a hard worker. Need a boy to work 'round here.' He say, 'You want to work for me?' and I say, 'Sure enough, Mr. Nelson.' And I worked here ever since."

He was looking at the darkness again, and through it probably, back down the corridor of his past.

"Cheryl Anne," I said softly.

"Sure, you right. She Mr. Jack's daughter. Mr. Jack, he a hand with the ladies. And maybe Miss Abby knew it, and maybe she didn't, but nothing come of it, 'cause Mr. Jack, he don't never embarrass her, you understand? He maybe have a fling with a lady, but it always a lady of breeding and position, nobody gonna embarrass Miss Abby."

"Miss Abby was Jack's wife?"

"Yessir."

Jefferson shook his head. Across the room Nelson fumbled together another drink for himself.

"Bertha come here to work in the kitchen. Not a cook, just to peel vegetables, and wash up, that sort of thing. She from Batesburg. She come over on the bus every morning, go home on it every night."

One of the dogs wandered across the room as we talked and jumped up on the couch and turned around three times and lay down between us. Jefferson patted her head absently.

"She don't look like much no more, but she look like something then all right. And she had that thing, you know, Mr. Spenser. She . . . she had a wiggle. She . . . hot, you know?"

"Yeah, I know."

"And Mr. Jack, he can't keep his hands off her."

"It wasn't his hands got him in trouble," I said.

"Yessir. And when she have the baby, Mr. Jack was ashamed. He felt real bad about it and he didn't want Miss Abby to know, and he don't want anyone else to know either. So he give her some money, and he say it is a secret, and long as it stayed a secret, he'd keep giving her the money."

"Hundred bucks a month," I said.

Jefferson shrugged.

"Those times that a lot of money to somebody like Bertha Voss," he said. "And she gets married to Hilly Rankin and she lets him think it's his kid. So it worked out that it stayed secret."

"Except she told her daughter," I said. "And she told her to be proud of who her father was and she told her how rich her father was and the daughter always remembered that, and always hated that he wouldn't acknowledge her, and for reasons that probably have to do with her being crazy, she took the legitimate daughter's name and history."

"Yessir."

"And when she was forty-three years old and broke, she remembered about how rich he was, and she came to him for money."

"Yessir."

The hokum noise of the wrestling match on the television made the silence in the rest of the vast atrium seem somehow more intense. Jefferson went and got two more drinks and brought them back and gave me one. Jumper Jack never stirred. His gaze remained fixed on the television screen.

"Did he pay her?" I said.

"Don't even know who she is," Jefferson said. "Or he says he don't. Hard to say what Mr. Jack know and don't know anymore."

"You pay her?" I said.

"Did for a while. Then no more."

"Why'd you stop?"

Jefferson shook his head softly.

"Ain't no money," he said.

"Jack too?" I said.

"Mr. Jack never had as much as everybody think," Jefferson said. "And he spend what he got."

Jefferson smiled thoughtfully, thinking back over the spending.

"Bought cars and horses, and whiskey and food and presents for Miss Abby and Miss Livvie, and he spent a lot on women. Mr. Jack always say he didn't waste none. He say he didn't get cheated. Horse players die broke, he say."

"So he's broke?"

"Yessir. This house free and clear, 'bout all."

"What's he use for cash?" I said.

"Don't need much. Feed the dogs, buy whiskey. 'Bout all."

"You get a salary?"

"I still do a little carpentry work, part-time, when Mr. Jack sleeping. My grandson come in, watch him for me. Put in some cabinets for people, do some finish work, that sort of thing. Can't do too much heavy stuff anymore, but I still got the touch for finish."

"You support him," I said.

Jefferson took in some of his drink. I sipped mine. Bourbon wasn't my favorite, but one made do.

"Yessir," Jefferson said.

"And you told Cheryl Anne that there wasn't money to give her."

Jefferson nodded. He was looking out again past the dark fields beyond the atrium. He raised his glass and drank slowly. From the look of the drink it was mostly bourbon, but he drank as if it were milk. The rain washed down along the glass walls of the room.

"And she was unable to hide her disappointment," I said.

"Say she don't believe me," Jefferson said. "Call me a thieving nigger. And she scream at Mr. Jack. He ain't right anymore. You can see that. Anybody see that. Say he her father and he owe her the money. Say he got one week to get her some money. It upset him, her screaming at him like that."

I sipped a little more bourbon. Jefferson finished his and looked at mine. I shook my head. Jefferson went for another and made one too for Jumper Jack. I scratched the hound's ear that lay curled next to me on the couch. I looked at the rain that slid along the curving glass. I looked at Jefferson. He returned the look and we were silent. We both knew. It seemed as if I had known for a long time.

Seeing me scratch the hound's ear, another dog got up and came over and put his head on the edge of the couch. The rest of the dogs noticed this change of position and stood and moved silently around the room, as if ordered by an unseen trainer, and settled back down in realigned order.

"And she left," I said.

Jefferson nodded.

"And went back to Boston."

Nod.

"And you took a framing hammer, with a long handle for leverage, because you're not as strong as you used to be, and you went up there too."

"On the bus," Jefferson said, looking straight at me with no expression I could see. "Three days on the bus."

"And found her address and waited until it was dark and when she walked by you beat her to death."

"Yessir."

Across the room Jumper Jack sat staring at his television, with three dogs in various positions of sleep on the floor around him. He drank half a glass of whiskey as I watched him and dribbled some down his chin and wiped it away with the back of his hand. It was the most active I'd seen him. He never glanced at us. It was as if he were alone in the room with his dogs and his whiskey, except that as I watched, tears rolled slowly down his face.

I put my drink down and rubbed my temples with both hands. The dog whose ear I'd been scratching looked up at me. I scratched his ear again, and he put his head back down on the couch.

"Jefferson," I said, "I'll get back to you."

# Chapter 42

I stood at my stove pouring a thin stream of cornmeal into simmering milk. As it went in, I stirred with a whisk.

"Cornmeal mush?" Susan said.

"We gourmets prefer to call it polenta," I said.

I put the whisk down and picked up a wooden spoon and stirred the cornmeal more slowly as it thickened.

"What are those crumby things on the platter?" Susan said.

She was sitting at my counter going through a glass of Gewürztraminer at the speed of erosion. She was wearing a pair of fitted tan slacks, a lemon sweater, and a matching tan coat that was part of the outfit and reached to her knees. She looked like Hollywood's vision of the successful female executive.

"Those are chicken breasts pounded flat and coated with cornbread crumbs," I said. "And flavored with rosemary."

"Will you fry them in lard?" Susan said.

"I will coat a fry pan with corn oil and then pour it out, leaving a thin film in the pan, then I will gently sauté the breast cutlets until golden brown," I said.

"Exactly," Susan said.

"And for dessert," I said, "there's sour cherry pie."

She poured a teaspoon more wine into her glass. Pearl reared up beside her and put her front paws on the counter and made a try for the chicken cutlets. She missed and I picked up a scrap from the cutting board and gave it to her.

"You are rewarding inappropriate behavior," Susan said.

"Yes."

Pearl dashed into the bedroom to eat the chicken scrap. I kept stirring the polenta waiting for it to be right.

"You haven't said a word about things in Alton," Susan said.

"I know. I need to think about it," I said.

"Before you talk to me?" Susan said.

"Yes."

Susan raised her eyebrows and widened her eyes.

"You know," I said, "since I saw you in that guidance office in Smithfield in 1974, I have never looked at you without feeling a small thrill of electricity in my solar plexus."

The polenta was done. I took it off the stove and let it rest on a trivet on the counter.

"Even first thing in the morning when I don't have my face on and I have my hair up?" Susan said.

"Even then," I said. "Although in those circumstances I'm probably reacting to potential."

Susan leaned forward over the counter and kissed me. I kissed her back and felt the residual darkness of that atrium room begin to recede. She pressed her mouth against mine harder as if she could feel my need and put her hands gently on each side of my face and opened her mouth. I put my hands under her arms and lifted her out of the chair and over the counter. It knocked her wineglass over and it broke on the floor. Neither of us paid it any attention. The feel of her against me was rejuvenating, like air long needed, like thirst quenched. We stood for a long time, fiercely together. We never made it to the bedroom. We did well to make the couch.

Afterwards we lay quietly with each other, and Pearl, who had managed to find room on the couch where I would have said there was none.

"In front of the baby," Susan said. Her voice had that quality it always had after lovemaking. As if she were on her way back from somewhere far that she'd been.

"Maybe she showed a little class," I said, "and looked away."

"I seem to recall her barking at a very critical juncture."

"For heaven's sake," I said. "I thought that was you."

Susan giggled into my shoulder where she was resting her head.

"You yanked me right over the counter," she said.

"I didn't yank," I said. "I swept."

"And spilled the wine and broke the wineglass."

"Seemed worth it at the time," I said.

"Usually I like to undress and hang my clothes up neatly."

"So why didn't you resist?" I said.

"And miss all the fun?"

"Of course not."

"When do you think you'll talk about Alton?"

"Pretty soon," I said. "I just have to give it a little time."

Susan nodded and kissed me lightly on the mouth.

"Let's leap up," she said. "And guzzle some polenta."

"Guzzle?"

"Sure."

"We gourmets usually say *savor*," I said.

Susan nodded and got off the couch and got her clothes rearranged. Then she looked at me and smiled and shook her head.

"Right over the goddamned counter," she said.


# Chapter 43 ———————————————

The rain had come up the coast behind me. It had traveled more slowly than I had and arrived in Boston only this morning, when Susan and I, with still the taste of polenta and chicken and Alsatian wine, went to a memorial service for Farrell's lover, whose name had been Brian, in a white Unitarian church in Cambridge. Farrell was there, looking sleepless. And the dead man's parents were there. The mother, stiff with tranquilizers and pale with grief, leaned heavily on her husband, a burly man with a large gray moustache. He looked puzzled, as much as anything, as he held his wife up.

Susan and I sat near the back of the small plain church, while the minister blathered. It was probably not his fault that he blathered. Ministers are expected to speak as if death were not the final emperor. But it came out, as it usually did, blather. Farrell sat with a guy that looked like him, and a woman and two small children. Brian's mother and father sat across the aisle.

There were maybe eight other people in the church. I didn't recognize any of them except Quirk, who stood in the back, his hands folded calmly in front of him, his face without expression. The church doors stood open and the gray rain came bleakly down on the black street. Susan held my hand.

After the service, Farrell came out of the church and introduced us to the guy that looked like him. It was his brother. The woman was his brother's wife, and the kids were Farrell's nephews.

"My mother and father wouldn't come," he said.

"How too bad for them," Susan said.

Quirk came to stand beside us.

"Thank you for coming, Lieutenant," Farrell said.

"Sure," Quirk said.

Farrell moved on with his brother on one side and his sister-in-law on the other. His nephews, small and quiet, frightened by death, probably, each held a parental hand.

"Tough," Quirk said. "You back from another visit to South Carolina?"

We were standing under an overhang out of the cold rain, which came grimly down.

"Yeah."

"You got anything?"

"I don't know yet."

Quirk frowned.

"What the hell does that mean?" he said.

"Means I don't know yet."

Quirk looked at Susan. She smiled like Mona Lisa.

"Christ," Quirk said to her. "You get better every time I see you."

"Thank you, Martin," she said.

He looked back at me.

"Call me when you know," he said, and turned his raincoat collar up and went down the steps to an unmarked police car and drove away. I turned up my collar too, and took Susan's hand, and walked down the steps and away from the church in the rain, which was cold and hard and without respite.

# Chapter 44

The morning was overcast, and hard-looking. I was in my office, thinking about Jefferson, and feeling like Hamlet, but older, when Farrell came in carrying two coffees in a white paper bag. He took them out, handed me one, and sat down.

"It bother you that Stratton was so interested in this case?" he said.

"He wants to be President," I said.

"And all he was trying to cover up was adultery?"

I shrugged.

"The cover-up was more dangerous to him than what he was trying to cover up," Farrell said.

"Guys like Stratton don't think that way. They think about fixing, about putting a new spin on it, about reorganizing it so it comes out their way."

"He stole most of the Tripps' money," Farrell said.

I sat back in my chair.

"Why do you know that and I don't?" I said.

Farrell was carefully prying the plastic cap off his paper coffee cup, holding it away from him so it wouldn't spill on him. He got the cover off and blew on the coffee gently for a moment, and then took a swallow. His face was still tight with grief, but there was also a hint of self-satisfaction.

"You been thinking about who killed the woman," Farrell said. "I been thinking about other stuff—like Stratton, like what the hell happened to all that money. Everybody says Mrs. Tripp spent it all, but on what? It's hard to go through that kind of money at Bloomingdale's."

"So you chased Tripp's expenditures," I said.

"Yeah. Checks written by him, or her. They had a joint account. His didn't show us anything unusual. He kept writing them even when there was no money. But you already knew that."

"Mine bounced," I said.

"There's a clue," Farrell said. He drank some more coffee. "Her checks were more interesting."

"I didn't see any of hers when I looked at his checkbook," I said. "But she'd been dead awhile, probably hadn't written any."

"Good point," Farrell said. "I went back about five years."

"Tripp didn't object?"

Farrell shook his head. "Didn't talk to him," he said. "I went through the bank's records. She wrote regular, like monthly, large checks to an organization called The Better Government Coalition, which is located in a post office box in Cambridge, and headed by a guy named Windsor Freedman. We're having a little trouble locating Windsor. He lists his address as University Green on Mt. Auburn Street. It's a condo complex, and nobody there ever heard of him. But the Mass. Secretary of State's office lists The Better Government Coalition as a subsidiary of The American Democratic Imperative in D.C. And the president of that operation is a guy named Mal Chapin."

Farrell paused to drink coffee. He looked at me while he swallowed.

"I know that name," I said.

"So did Quirk," Farrell said. "You remember where you heard it?"

"Motel room in Alton, South Carolina," I said. "Mal Chapin is in Stratton's office."

"Pretty good," Farrell said. "Of course I mentioned that Quirk knew it too; that was a clue."

"Yeah," I said. "I'm excited. Usually when I get a clue, I trip over it, and skin my knee."

"Quirk's talking with somebody in the FBI, see about getting one of their accountants to check out The Democratic Imperative, see what they do with their money."

"You figure it supports Stratton."

"Sure," Farrell said. "A charity with no offices, wholly owned by another charity, with no offices, headed by a guy works for Stratton. What do you think we'll find out?"

"That it supports Stratton," I said.

"That's what we'll find out," Farrell said. "Maybe there's a motive in it. Maybe Olivia Nelson knew what was going on and they had a lover's quarrel and she was going to blow the whistle on him."

"And he got a hammer and beat her brains out one night?"

"Maybe he had it done."

"By somebody that would use a hammer?"

"Possible."

"Sure," I said. "But likely?"

Farrell shook his head slowly.

"Not likely."

"Stratton know you've been investigating him?"

"Shouldn't," Farrell said.

"I'd like to bring them all together and confront him with it."

"All of who?"

"Tripp, his kids, Stratton, see what comes out of it."

Farrell stared at me for a couple of long moments. Then he shook his head slowly.

"You're still trying to fix that family," Farrell said. "You just want to shake the old man out of his trance if you can."

I shrugged, drank some coffee.

"You could just stick to finding out who killed the woman?"

"Might make sense to bring them together," I said. "Something might pop out. No harm to it."

"No harm to you," he said. "Might be some harm to a detective second grade who accuses a U.S. Senator of a felony without all his evidence in yet."

I nodded.

"Be stupid to do that," Farrell said. "Especially if being a gay detective second grade made command staff ill at ease anyway, so to speak."

I nodded again.

"Unless, of course, you made the charge," Farrell said.

"Without saying how I knew it," I said. "And you simply called us together to give the Senator a chance to respond privately, before any formal inquiry began."

"A chance to lay these baseless charges to rest," Farrell said.

"Sure," I said.

"Want to meet here?"

"I'm the guy making the baseless charges," I said.

"Okay," Farrell said.

There was silence while we both drank the rest of our coffee. Then Farrell put his cup in my wastebasket and stood.

"I'll be in touch," he said.

"I know you are going out a little ways on a limb," I said. "Thanks."

"Nice of you to come to the funeral," Farrell said.

# Chapter 45

They came. Nobody seemed very pleased about it, but Farrell got them there. The three Tripps came together, and Stratton came with two guys in London Fog raincoats who waited in the corridor outside my office, and looked intrepid.

Stratton looked at neither Farrell, nor at me. He shook hands with Loudon Tripp and put a hand on his shoulder while he did it. Unspoken condolence. Then Stratton shook Chip's hand and they gave each other a manly hug and clap on the back.

"Great to see you, Bob," Chip said. He wasn't very old and you could tell he liked calling a U.S. Senator by his first name.

We got arranged. Stratton and Loudon Tripp in the two client chairs. Farrell leaning on the wall to my left. The two Tripp children to my right, a little back from the group. Chip looking aggressive, ready to slap a half nelson on someone, Meredith looking passively at the floor.

"Okay, gentlemen," Stratton said. He smiled at Meredith, who made no eye contact. "And lady. Let's get to it. You called us together, Officer. What have you got?"

Stratton looked tanned and healthy. His hair was perfectly trimmed and trying its best to look plentiful. His pinstripe suit was well cut. His white shirt crisp and new. He still wore his trench coat, unbuttoned, the belt tucked into the pockets. All in all he was direct, competent, square dealing, straight shooting, judicious, and nice.

Farrell looked edgy and tired.

"Spenser here came to me with some allegations which I thought we'd best confront privately, Senator."

Stratton's glance shifted to me. The pale blue eyes as hard as chrome.
"Allegations?"

"Involving the Tripps," Farrell said.

Stratton continued to stare at me.

"You are becoming something of a pain in the butt," he said. "Maybe I should have put you out of business a while ago."

"Being a pain in the butt is my profession," I said. "What's the first word that comes to mind when I say The Better Government Coalition?"

Stratton's eyes became more opaque.

"The American Democratic Imperative?" I said.

Stratton didn't speak.

"Mal Chapin?"

Stratton stood up.

"That is just about enough of that," he said. "I am not going to sit here and listen to some cheap private eye trolling for some way to make a name for himself at my expense."

"I'm cheaper than you think," I said. "The only check I got for this job bounced."

Stratton turned toward the door. Farrell went and leaned against it.

"Why not hear him out, Senator, in front of witnesses. Maybe he'll do something actionable."

"You get out of my way," Stratton said.

Farrell's voice was soft. He was standing face-to-face with Stratton.

"Sit down," he said.

"Who in hell do you think . . . ?" Stratton started.

"Now."

Stratton stepped back from the force of the single word.

"I'm sick of you, Stratton," Farrell said. "I'm sick of the phony macho. I'm sick of the self-importance. I'm sick of the way you comb your hair over your goddamned bald spot. Sit and listen or I'll bust your stupid senatorial ass."

"What charge?" Stratton said. But it was weak. The game was over the moment Stratton stepped back.

"Violation of no-dork zoning regulations," Farrell said. "Sit down."

Stratton sat.

"What's the first word that comes to mind," I said, "when I say The Better Government Coalition? The American Democratic Imperative? Mal Chapin?"

"Mal works for me," Stratton said. His voice shook a little. "In my office. I don't know those other things."

"Mal work for you full-time?" I said.

"Yes. He's my chief of staff."

"Hard job?"

"Hard." Stratton began to make a comeback. He was on familiar ground. "And thankless. We are involved in very many crucial national and international issues. Mal works ten, fifteen hours a day."

"Not much time for another job," I said.

Stratton realized he'd been led down the path. He tried to backtrack.

"Certainly he works hard, but what he does in his off-hours . . ." Stratton shrugged and spread his hands.

"He's listed as the President of The American Democratic Imperative," I said. "A charitable organization based in Washington."

Stratton shook his head in silence.

"Before her death, Olivia Nelson regularly made large contributions to The Better Government Coalition, in Cambridge. The Better Government Coalition is listed as a subsidiary of The American Democratic Imperative, which is headed by your chief of staff."

Stratton stared straight ahead.

"And you have told me directly that you were intimate with Olivia Nelson," I said.

The words hung in the room, drifting like the dust of ruination.

Then Loudon Tripp said, "Enough. I'll hear no more, Spenser. I'm responsible for all of this. I hired you. I brought you and your dirty mind and your gutter morals into all of this. And now you contrive to dirty my dead wife and my friend with one lie."

"He's not your friend, Mr. Tripp," I said, "He slept with your wife. He stole your money."

"No," Tripp said. "I'll hear no more."

He stood up. Chip stepped in beside him.

"You can't stop me," he said to Farrell. "Come on, kids."

"Last chance," I said to Tripp. "For all of you. You've got to look at this. You've got to stop pretending."

"Get out of my way," Tripp said again. His voice sounded strangled. "Not my wife, not with my friend."

He moved past Farrell toward the door. Chip went with him, knotted with excitement, frantic to explode. Meredith stared at him with her mouth half open, motionless.

"Come along, Meredith," Tripp said. Except that his voice was strangled, he spoke to her as if she were dawdling by a toy store.

"He's . . . not . . . your . . . friend," Meredith said.

"Meredith," Tripp said. The squeezed-out voice was parental—exasperated, long-suffering—but not unloving.

"For crissake, Mere," Chip said.

"He . . . *was* . . . fucking her," Meredith said.

Tripp flinched. Chip's face reddened.

"He was fucking me," she said in a rush. "Since I was fourteen and he came in my room at one of those big parties."

The silence in the room was stifling. No one moved. Meredith was rigid, her hands at her sides, a look of shock on her face.

"Jesus," Chip said. "Mere, why didn't you . . . ?"

"Dr. Faye says I was getting even with Mommy, and I wanted Daddy to . . ." She put both her hands suddenly over her mouth and pressed them, palm open, hard against her face, and slowly slid her back down the wall until she was sitting on the floor, her legs splayed in front of her. Chip looked at his father, who seemed frozen in time, then he went suddenly to his knees beside his sister and put his arms around her and pressed her head against his chest. She let him hold her there.

Loudon Tripp stared for a moment at both of them, and then, without looking at anyone else, he walked across my office and out the door and down the corridor past the two guys in their London Fogs. They looked in the office uncertainly. Farrell shook his head at them and they stepped away from the door. Stratton continued to sit in his chair with his head down, staring at the floor, contemplating his ruin.

Human voices wake us, and we drown.

# Chapter 46

On a bright Sunday morning, Susan and I took Pearl over to Harvard Stadium to let her run. We sat in the first row of the stands while Pearl coursed the football field alert for game birds, or Twinkie wrappers. Her nose was down, her tail was up, and her whole self seemed attenuated, as she raced back and forth over the field where generations of young Harvard men had so fiercely fought.

"Your name was in the paper this morning," Susan said. She was wearing a black-and-lavender warm-up suit, and her dark hair shone in the sunshine.

"Did you cut it out and put it up on the refrigerator with a little magnet?"

"Most of the story was the Senator Stratton indictment. Detective Farrell is quoted extensively."

Pearl spotted a covey of pigeons near the thirty-yard line and went into her low stalk. The closer she got, the slower she went, until finally the pigeons flew up and Pearl dashed to where they had been and wagged her tail.

"He did the work," I said. "And he did it even though he wasn't feeling too swell."

"How are you feeling?" Susan said. "You did some work too."

"Not enough," I said.

"You're worrying about the Tripps," Susan said.

"Wouldn't you?" I said.

"Up to a point," Susan said. "You didn't get them into this dysfunctional mess. You have done something to start getting them out of it."

"By pulling the lid off," I said.

Susan nodded. "By pulling the lid off. Someone had to. If it could have happened more gently, and more gradually, that would have been better. But you didn't control that."

I nodded.

Pearl finished hunting the stadium, and came up into the stands, and sat in front of us with her mouth open and her tongue hanging out.

"Dr. Faye is a well-respected and experienced therapist," Susan said.

I nodded again. We were near the open end of the stadium. Across Soldiers Field Road, the river moved its oblivious way toward Boston Harbor.

Susan put her cheek against my shoulder.

"And," she said, "you're kind of cute."

"There's consolation in that," I said.

I put Pearl's leash on, and we stood and started out of the stands. Susan took my hand and we strolled back through the Harvard Athletic Complex toward the Larz Anderson Bridge. There was a red light at the pedestrian crossing. We stopped.

"What are you going to do about the murder?" Susan said.

"When Jefferson told me the truth that night," I said, "there were six or eight dogs sleeping in the atrium."

The light changed and we started across.

"I think I'll let them lie."